MEANING THE WHILE

A grotesque

By DAVID MORRIS

First published in the United Kingdom in 2025 by

The Cloister House Press

ISBN 978-1-913460-91-4

MEANING THE WHILE
A grotesque

For *Lynn*, as always, even if she hates it
And In Memoriam to *Jim* and *Mac*, both great
chucklers and
Peter, who would have said,
'What you could have written dad'

Chapter 1

I t was more than a scream, worse than a shriek.
Let's settle for an amalgam of the two in its penetrating
intensity. It issued from Muriel Rasher's bedroom.

Barry Rasher, her husband, though no longer admitted to
his wife's bedroom, felt his toes curl and knew at once what the
dreadful sound foretold. There had been an inbreak of 'cess'
into Muriel's Holy of Holies, into her inner sanctum.

Cess: as in cesspit, not as in success or as in incessant,
even though the cess was presumably a result of the incessant
rain. Words, they can be lethal. Can be and were becoming
ever more so.

Muttering incoherent platitudes Barry hurried upstairs
and humbled himself at the threshold; the door was ajar and
there she stood, gaunt and vehement, pointing to the dreaded
inbreak. From the top corner of her bedroom there hung a
brown, pullulating blob, threatening to drop at any moment
onto her dressing table.

Muriel's dressing table: something needs to be said here
and now about her dressing table. It had belonged to her
grandmother and was venerated beyond words. Placed in
the left-hand corner it presented itself as a triptych of bevel
edged mirrors, the outer pair could be adjusted, the angle of
reflection from zero to almost but not quite ninety degrees.
As a child Muriel had been told that one day that dressing
table and all its tranklements would be hers. It was to be
her inheritance, so to speak. Its cabinet body was of French
polished walnut veneer. Flames could be imagined within
its deep surface sheen. There were three sliding drawers

on each side. All the tranklements were neatly displayed in order on its top surface. Silver backed brushes, hair and clothes, silver backed, octagonal hand held mirror, cut class containers with lids, also of cut glass, precisely placed on lace doilies. Everything reflectively precious, all one day to be hers. Some old friend of her mother's, Fanny Fenshaw, a name that somehow remembered itself, had explained to her the great value it represented, all the time gently rubbing the back of her hand with her long fingers. Fanny's hand was speckled with large freckles and Muriel, distracted from the message by those large freckles hoped that she wouldn't ever grow old. Perhaps the dressing table and its mirrors would … preserve her … And then, a year or so later, she had played at being a Mrs Muriel, she would brush her hair with the long, silver backed brush and hold the octagonal silver backed mirror to her face and then in elate aggrandisement she sat back on the stool, admiring her reflection as a belle to be, a trophy for some future beau. When she got bored, she would fiddle, trying to negotiate the side mirrors to face each other, so that she could peer at herself in a tunnel of ever repeated reflection. It did not happen and to force the issue would be to damage the hinges and that would of course never do. There were other treasures, a cut glass casket with a silver lid that contained a necklace of cut glass beads, a necklace of pearls and a precious stone pendant: all providing futures to be imagined, to be realised.

But to the point; all was now threatened by this bulbous dollop of cess, glistening with amber scintillations, seemingly having a life of its own and ready, at any moment, to fall and splatter all over the dressing table and engulf those precious tranklements.

Cess; it had become an increasingly common feature of life, at least since 'the rains' had started. Barry knew that it was inevitable that they would one day 'get a packet', as the saying went, but he had expected that it would be like what had happened at his Uncle Harold's, merely a quivering blob on the flat garage roof, which had been prodded to the floor with a broom from the top of a step ladder and shovelled into a black plastic bag. With a bit of luck the council would take it.

But no, oh dear no, this was of a different order of intrusion altogether.

'Look at it! Look at it!' Muriel hissed, holding her arm out and pointing while looking away from the pendulous horror. Briefly in stance and demeanour she was the very essence of a tragic muse, though that signification was quite lost on Barry.

'Yes love I can see.' And he sucked his teeth. She could have sliced his head from its trunk in frustration at this habit of his. She waited till he stopped and then said, with such an acid tone, 'Well!!' (there needs no question mark here, it was no question).

'It's due to all this rain we've been having.'

She shuddered at the sheer inanity of the observation. She couldn't give a damn for any theory of origin; she wanted action, its immediate removal.

'They do say as it's happening all over, everywhere, dollops of cess on folk's walls and drives …'

'Barry, I'll say this just once, GET RID!!'

* * *

The rains, they had been ceaselessly happening now for what must have been nine months, well, at least the best part of, as the saying goes. Ceaselessly? Yes, but with varying intensity, everything from a drifting drizzle to a hammering downpour. It was all very lowering and tempers could get frayed, but then that is the way of things. What is more the conditions could be extremely local, for instance one side of the street could be splashed about by a steady precipitation while just across the road the gable ends were being slammed with gales of water, beneath which it was difficult to even breathe. Your only remedy was to cross the road, bent backed and crawling like a crab to take deep breaths once you got there. So it was and it was no use complaining because nobody could do anything

3

about it. Naturally some did surmise about the reasons for the state they were in. And it wasn't just rain, not by a long chalk as the saying used to be. Not when a thirty hour hammering of a torrential downpour could be the reason for the first barbed flush of Thorn spreading across a redbrick gable. Could be, but only could be, nothing was certain, as yet. Whatever, more of Thorn later. The main point was, as most agreed, there was no point thinking about it because there was no remedy and when did thinking change anything when all is said and done, you've just got to get on with it. All you could do was to keep your drains raddled, that did seem to stop the flooding somewhat.

'Put the light on!' she now instructed.

'Why?'

Her look transcended mere words. He put the light on and the cess shimmered all the more. 'Blimey', he muttered

'For god's sake get something to scrape it off, into a black plastic bag. I'm not having all that gunk dropping onto my dressing table and then onto the carpet. Now Barry, do it NOW!'

Snuffling downstairs in his slippers he made himself busy following her instructions. The best way to dislodge the stuff from the ceiling would be a garden hoe. But, he didn't want to go out to the shed in his slippers, however, the sound of deep shuddering from above persuaded him. 'Needs must when the devil drives' he thought-muttered to himself. Ignoring the cold pang of wetness to his soles, he crossed the yard, grabbed the hoe and yes, a green plastic bag, better option, it being stronger than the council supplied black bags-not that they bothered to supply them anymore- another sign of the times. But no time for that now, he bounded upstairs, attempting a cheerful hum and began.

'Barry!' she complained, as he shouldered her aside.

'Sorry loveliest' There was nothing he liked better than being given a positive, clearly defined job to do. Murmur-humming tunelessly (he was so like his uncle Harold in this) he began deftly hoeing the ceiling. It had to be admitted that he showed some dexterity, slithers of cess were separated from the greater mass, scraped free from the ceiling and caught in the posed gape of the plastic bag. 'Slumppf ! Gotcher,yer blighter'.

Aghast and against the door, Muriel shuddered, pointed at the stain on the ceiling once all had been despatched into the bag and complained, 'It's oozing!'

'It's slime, that's what slime does' and without so much as a by your leave he stood on the dressing table stool, just about managing to reach the ceiling, and using a paint scraper, he meticulously removed the ooze, wiping it into the neck of the plastic bag. 'There you go love, job done.'

'There's still a stain.'

'You'll have to live with that, at least till it dries out, then I'll see what I can do with some sugar-soap.'

And that was that, he jumped down, full of himself, grabbed the bag, one thing about cess was that there was no weight to it, and hurried back downstairs, out onto the yard, dropping the slobber into the bin and chuntering a risible merriment all the time.

Job done, man of the house and when all was said and done Muriel would have to admit that at times like this he was, well, let's face it, indispensable. Imagine having to have a man in to do the job and all the palaver that would create, not to mention the intrusion of a working male, in boots and almost certainly with a fag stuck in the corner of his mouth clumbering about in her bedroom! No, Barry had proved to Muriel that he still had utility values.

* * *

The following night brought yet more distress. Muriel's sleep was torn into turmoil by fractured dreams. She gulped and shouted, scrabbling into a consciousness that was little better than a psychic rictus. Hearing much of this distress, Barry, cuddled on the camp bed in the next room, made a brave decision. He carefully entered her bedroom, mute whisperings gathering in his mouth and in doing so trod on, or rather into, another blob of cess. Suppressing an involuntary hiss he was surprised to discover it provided a not unpleasant sensation; a cool, clinging smoothness. No matter it had to be dealt with swiftly, before Muriel was properly awake, she seemed to be still in a quiver quake of her dream state. This was easier, it being on the carpet, and in no time he had wrapped it up in an old copy of The Daily Mail, an old copy because like all other services, deliveries of the papers had ceased to occur. Snuggling it under his arm, he went downstairs, onto the yard and dolloped it into the bin. Apart from soggy pyjamas, all was as if it had not happened and for Muriel it hadn't.

Over a solitary slice of bread and jam, Muriel not yet up, he decided that he would go and visit his uncle Harold. It had been a week or so since his last visit and he liked to keep in touch. He could have gone by car, the roads were still passable, no question about that, but you did have to swerve all over the place to avoid shimmering drifts of cess that hardened quickly when they were outside; still squishy inside but with a hard carapace that could cut sharp on fingers or tyres; it was resilient stuff alright. In any case he fancied that the walk would do him some good; fresh air and all that. He shouted up his intention to Muriel but got no reply, she had obviously gone back to sleep

The distance was just over half a mile, a kilometre, Harold insisted, but Barry, in spite of his much younger age stuck to miles, hundredweights and acres, better that way. Of course Harold having been a draughtsman years back was at home with all manner of mensuration. Well, that was the nature of folk, what concerned Barry now was his feet and he was glad he had had the forethought to put on a sensible pair of shoes; he was confident that he would get there with dry feet.

Since Alice had died Harold was on his own, so Barry's regular visits were tolerated by Muriel, who given a choice, would not willingly be in the same room as Harold; he irritated her so, particularly with the constant clacking of his false teeth when he spoke. Families can be funny that way; no two ways about it.

As soon as he got there he knocked the door and let himself in, shouting, 'Hello, it's me, Barry.'

'In here Barry'.

He went straight in to the dimly lit lounge; a standard lamp threw a solitary light onto the lounge table. A large table with both of its flaps up and littered with sheets of an A to Z map of the local district, all Sellotaped together. Harold did have a workspace in the garage but since Alice's demise he did all of his work in the lounge. In any case this was paper, not fretwork, and he lifted the spread of the Sellotaped sheets gently off the table. The image should have suggested a tent but in the instant of its display, Barry thought, for some reason, of an armadillo.

'Come on in Barry. Muriel alright?'

The question was a formality. Barry chirpily confided that Muriel was fine, considering …

'Considering what?'

'You know, this and that. These days, they're not the easiest of times Harold. Not for anyone as a matter of fact.'

Harold pursed his lips and gave a sagacious nod.

Barry was happy to let the matter drop. He gestured towards the kitchen, Harold nodded and a few minutes later Barry emerged with a tray, bearing two mugs and a biscuit barrel. Coffee, teabags were kept on the carpet by Harold's feet.

It's the rain, it's beginning to get her down, well isn't it everyone if the truth be told.

Harold murmured, opened the biscuit barrel and offered it to Barry, his eyebrows raised. He took a couple, looked at them and said, 'I don't know how you do it?'

'Do what?'

'Keep 'em dry.'

Harold enthused and spittled, 'It's a damn good biscuit barrel is that, had it for … well let's just say it was part of Alice's bottom drawer. You wouldn't get one as good today in a month of Sundays. These days … .

Eager to steer Harold away from the subject of his deceased wife, because, given half a chance Harold could maunder on about her for hours, Barry inserted with alacrity, 'I can't stand a pappy biscuit. Never could.'

'Each to his own, as they say, but I take your point Barry lad. Now, getting back to Muriel, so long as she's not off her legs, she'll be alright, I'm guessing, but you might need to think about getting her some elastic stockings, while you can, if you get my drift.'

Barry snorted and in almost a triumphant mood added, 'Not Muriel, she wears proper stockings, and suspenders. Always has and still does.'

'Well', mused Harold, 'glad to see you've still got it in you. Of course, elastic stockings were a great help to Alice, right to the very end.' He paused, snapped at his biscuit then mused, 'And suspenders you say?'

'Yes'

'Mind you she always was a comely wench, she could always turn a man's head when she put her mind to it. Could and I dare say did. But of course you know that Barry, though that's not to say … .'

He let the conversation trail away as he watched Barry dunk his biscuit, a ginger nut. It was always a test of practice as to how long a ginger nut could be dunked before it became sloppy and broke, dropping back into the tea; drink ruined. It varied, naturally from biscuit type to biscuit type but ginger nuts were particularly difficult to ascertain. He was pleased to see his nephew had got it down to a fine art. Harold always admired dexterity, no matter what form it took.

'It's just this rain that's getting her down, well truth to tell it's getting most people down.'

'More fool them,' snorted Harold, 'and you should tell Muriel in no uncertain terms to snap out of it. Folks are only too happy to find an excuse to moan. And this lot,' a nod here through the window at the weather, 'just gives them the excuse to slobber about all day on their sofas. Exert yourself Barry, 'cos your not that way inclined. Get her up and about, old son.'

Harold broke off here because in spite of his age the thought of Muriel slobbering about on a sofa, in suspenders and stocking gave him a pause for breath. He gestured to the biscuit barrel. 'Another one?'

'I won't say no.'

'You never do yer varmint.'

Eventually Barry announced that he was on his way to the supermarket, adding that when he had tried to do so a few days previously he hadn't been able to get in. 'It was absolutely rammed'.

'Tell me about it.'

'Do you know uncle, there was folks sitting on the floor, scrabbling about and scratting and wailing. It was a real carry on and no mistake.'

'It doesn't surprise me one bit. What did you do?'

'I didn't go in and I didn't ask. Woman on the till was trying to shove them into a huddle but they were having none of it, at least they didn't seem to. I said to myself, Barry, this is not for you, come back another day, when things have quietened down. And this is it.'

'What?'

'The other day.'

'Got you. But I'll warn you Barry, it'll be mostly empty shelves. It seems the only thing you can be certain of getting is dog biscuits. Apparently the demand for them as fallen well off the scale. Odd isn't it, the way of folks and things. Sheila did say as folks just come to stare at the empty shelves, as if they they're in a trance.' He rattled his teeth and added, 'Cos they've got nothing better to do, I said, and let the matter rest.'

Not knowing who Sheila was, her name had never come up before, Barry concentrated on his biscuit, simply murmuring that it was all the fault of the rain and it's not showing any sign of stopping. Slowing now and again but not stopping.

* * *

Supermarkets ... The cathedrals of our age. In the nineteenth century Hardy had proclaimed that the large railway termini were the cathedrals of his age ... not now

… there has become a fervid indifference to their activity, trains like electric eels sliding inconspicuously in and out of smoke free termini, no longer the stated manifesto of serious intent from steam locomotives, billowing and clattering away to distant parts. No, nowadays it was the pale, serene interiors with tiled aisles of the supermarkets that induced the availability of desire. The Holy Trinity of commodity, cash and consumption, and just to linger the aisles was to be devotional.

Referring to the weather, Harold growled, 'We've had worse before.'

'I don't think so.'

'Before you were born.'

'What, in the times of Noah?'

'Now lad, less of your cheek. What you've got to do is to find yourself a project, take yer mind off things.'

'A project?'

He gestured towards the table with its armadillo of sellotaped A to Z sheets. I admit it's a bit of a mess at the moment but do you know what it is?'

'No, not really. I mean it's a map of sorts, but what of … ?'

Harold threw his arms wide and beamed at his chubby, round-faced nephew. 'My map!' he exclaimed, 'of what used to count in this area. You can forget all this worrying about the weather when you've got a scheme like this underway. Come and take a closer gander and I'll explain.' The armadillo was shuffled across the table and a chair was beckoned.

'Eh Barry, what about that? Get the picture?'

It was, on close scrutiny, now it was held up, albeit as a sagging, tessellated display, a map of the local area, town centre and environs but with discreet areas marked up in coloured paint, neatly coloured in, although Barry would have expected nothing less from his uncle Harold.

'It looks a bit of a mess at the moment, being all loose but do you know what it is?'

'Well, it's obviously local but what are the marked in areas?'

Harold laid the map back on the table. His arms were aching and its spread well beyond the span of his hands. On the table it draped over all sides, the unsellotaped gaps pouting like toothless mouths.

There was a silence, into which Barry pitched, 'We've got it Harold.'

'Got what?'

'That slime stuff ... cess. It was in Muriel's bedroom, directly above her dressing table.'

Harold sniffed and largely preoccupied himself with attempting to smooth down the pouting map on the table. It was a measure of their friendship that he could countenance Barry's digression in silence.

'It was awful. I got it down and cleaned up but there was another dollop this morning.'

'Tell me about it. I had a dollop on the garage roof, but you know all about that.'

'But this was inside Harold, in her bedroom, and that's pretty sacrosanct, as you know. A garage roof is one thing ...'

'D'you know what I reckon, it's that the more you moither about it, the more it comes. Don't think about it. I mean look at me, since I got this project underway, I've seen neither sight nor sound of it again. Garage roof's as clean as a whistle. Now do you want to know what this project is about or not?'

'Yes, but I'm worried for Muriel's sake. I mean another dollop on the bedroom carpet, and a bedroom is not a garage roof, you've got to admit it Harold.'

'What did Muriel say?'

'Nothing.'

'Nothing?'

'Not a word.'

'That's not like Muriel.'

'She was still asleep but as I was just finishing, after I'd dropped it in the bin and was wiping her bedroom carpet, just in case, she suddenly sat bolt upright and made a strange gulping sound.'

'Gulping?'

'Well gasping then, but funny gasping. No, come to think of it, it was definitely gulping.'

'Gulping, like she was drinking?'

'I suppose so, sort of.'

'That's shock, Barry, that's what that is. Shock and no mistake about it. So, what did you do?'

'Well, I'd already done it, cleared up, as I said, and there was no stain on the carpet, not that you would notice, not unless you went down on all fours, on a bright sunny day, and we don't get any of them any-more.'

'What you need is a blow torch.'

'In the bedroom? On the carpet? In any case I have heard as a blow torch won't touch it.'

'I don't know who told you that nonsense because there isn't much as a blow torch won't shift, if you hold it on long enough.'

'I'd end up setting the house on fire.'

'Well acid then. Sulphuric, there's not much that can resist that. I think I've still got a canister in the garage, you're welcome to some, I could let you have a bottle if you wish.'

'I'm not sure, I mean … well, it's strong stuff …'

'Colourless though and by God, it does a job, does sulphuric. There are those who swear by Hydrochloric, but I say, give me Sulphuric, every time.'

'I'm not so sure uncle …'

'Think about it. The offer still stands if you've a mind to try it. As I always say, nothing ventured, nothing gained. Right, now, this map …'

Barry nodded thoughtfully. 'I had to get my own breakfast.'

'Well, there you go. Blowtorch and or acid, get yourself some brownie points. Who knows you could soon be sharing a bed again and she'd have got over …'

With closed eyes, as if in pain, Barry snorted, 'Your map Uncle Harold, you were going to explain it.'

Harold's map. It was the realisation of a long cherished plan to mark in all the old factories that had once worked in the area. No easy task because the site of many had been obliterated, gouged out, built over, so it was difficult to mark them in precisely. But with determination and a fastidious memory he had all but accomplished the task. Factories, workshops, forge, foundry, fabricating shops, a welter of once busy and fuming industry all now lost, but not to Harold's record. Places where metal had been melted, cast, stamped, twisted, extruded; fashioned into a multitude of practical uses, sold and despatched all over the world; everyone clearly delineated. The boundary *edges* carefully marked in with a hard leaded pencil, 3H, recovering on the map from what had been obliterated by the sites of contemporary stuff: car parks, housing estates, municipal gardens even. On Harold's map, with the neat outlines carefully coloured the past had obliterated the present. And the coloured in areas, marked with different colours for different trades. It was an immaculate work. Barry recognised as much, and even though being much younger he didn't remember all the factory sites, he recognised enough to be fascinated.

Harold was almost delirious with delight. 'Hey, who'd have thought it, when it's set out like this. And what's more who remembers it now, like this, in its entirety? Our history, our heritage, and but for this,' he tapped the sag of the map, 'submerged, forgotten under car parks and cul-de-sacs. Heritage, and I'll tell you one thing, once you've lost that, you've lost everything. You're nothing. And you tell me we've got to worry about cess. This is what counts lad, this … !' And he chortled as Barry scrutinised the map.

'Blimey Harold, you've fashioned something of a masterpiece here.'

Harold clacked his teeth and enthused. 'What is more, there will be two side pieces in white card and from every site marked on the map there will be a length of white cotton, to the card, where the name of the factory will be printed, an index so to speak, giving also the nature of that factory's products and the date of its demise.'

'It'll be epic Harold.'

'It will.'

'But …'

'But what?'

'You're going to need a tidy piece of card to fix the whole thing to.'

'D'you think I haven't thought about that?'

'But …'

'But nothing. Not card but ply, the whole thing, glued onto card will then be stapled onto a sheet of ply.

'Two sheets of ply, at an angle so the whole thing will be free standing.'

'That means there would be a crease in the middle, and I don't want that. Creases are the bane of maps at the best of times. No, I'll make a couple of free standing legs with feet and a couple of back braces to hold it in position.'

'I can see you're going to town on this, so to speak.'

'Indeed I am. No half measures …'

Barry continuing to admire the map, albeit as yet still in shambolic armadillo mode, gave a little sniff and advanced a notion. 'What you could do …'

'What?', somewhat of a terse tone because the project was both firmly fixed and was intended to be warmly received by all, at least in Harold's mind.

'Well … ?'

'Go on.' Terse again, possibly even terser.

'Well, and I'm only saying, that's all Uncle, but what you could do is colour in the canals, seeing in particular …'

Harold grabbed Barry by the elbows.

'Because', the younger man persisted, 'Most of them factories were on or very close to a canal.'

'Barry, Barry, why didn't I think of that before? It's obvious, you're right. What is more it'll link everything together. Prussian Blue, I'll paint the canals in Prussian Blue.

'And there's also the river, for what it's worth, seeing as the main canal followed the river valley.'

'Why not my boy, why not, but a different shade of blue.'

'Of course, there's logic in that and no mistake.'

There was a pause, one of mutual satisfaction: nothing admonitory about that pause as Harold slurped the last of his drink and Barry asked his uncle what he proposed to do with the thing once it was finished.

Harold rubbed his thumbs against the side of his forefingers, a typical gesture, and announced, 'D'you know what? I'm going to take it down to the library and get them to put it up in the entrance foyer. Folks will be fascinated. I mean you could even bring Muriel along to see it, she'll remember quite a few of these old places, from back when she was a kiddy.'

Barry demurred somewhat. 'She's not much into old factories, or any sort of factories if the truth be told.'

'Don't you underestimate Muriel. Who knows what floats her boat. When she see's this all coloured up, I bet you a pound to a pinch of salt, she'll be delighted.'

'You may be right.'

Harold made a curious but generally affirmative noise deep in his throat while Barry had his mind cast back to a disastrous canal holiday: a projected week of cruising that ended in two days of bouncing in and out of dreary locks. But he had to say something that was at least smeared with affirmation. 'I'll give it a go once it's installed.'

'Do that, get her out of the house, stop her moithering, It'll do her good, you mark my words.' Harold was slightly ecstatic and Barry smiled, well given the nature of the circumstances he thought it was all he could do.

Returning home, and it may have been pertinent and it may not have, he could not but help noticing the increasing trespass that the vari sized and vari shaped dollops of Cess were having. There was almost no traffic, and at that time of day' mid-morning. It wasn't just Cess, motorists knew by now that you couldn't just plough through it. A few wild souls had tried that and look where it always got them-clogged up suspension and front wheels skewed off. But no, in addition to the irregularly scattered isles of Cess, all glimmering or even shimmering, the road surfaces were buckling and cracking open. Seemingly some ruthless root system was extending and thickening beneath the surface. Probably the roots of Thorn that fierce brown entanglement of spikes, stiff and sharp growing out of a ribbed stem that had first been witnessed on gable ends of houses and said to be all but indestructible. Barry noticed that there were now more cases of it growing up against garden walls certainly but gable walls in particular. The more it grew the more it bushed up. But it did not seem to do any damage, at least, not yet but he thought that, yes, the council would face an almighty bill when it became time to clean up. Word was that Thorn made Pyracantha seem like watercress, neither secateurs or even bolt cutters could sever its trunk.

Even so there was something to be gained from the way things were: less traffic, buses it seemed were non existent and very few trucks out and about. Obviously the perpetual steering from one side to the other that had to be done escape any contact with the treacherous Cess got boring, resulting in far fewer cars. All to the good, all things considered.

He turned into the Crescent where he and Muriel had lived since their marriage. The Crescent, and its adjacent streets were the product of a nineteen thirties speculative housing development. All detached houses, each secure within its own generous plot of land; significant front garden, ample curving drives, large back lawns with border shrubs, each offering a languid confection of domestic harmony. The gardens all sloped upward, ending at the edge of a sharply defined ridge. But that ridge and what it defined. Suffice to say that the ridge then dropped precipitously down to a sprawling council estate in which dwelt a very different class of person altogether. Before its building there would have doubtless been a vista of field and copse, nourished and spangled under the sun by the thin, persistent brook, that emerged from a spring amidst a clump of trees, two thirds of the way down the cliff. The Dingley Dell was the name of the brook and its precipitous valley. The upper part still survived, though cluttered by rubbish tipped by the habitués of the housing estate, such being their nature. And further, when its trembling fall levelled out, it disappeared into cast iron pipes. Who knows what went on down in the spread reaches of the council estate? Who wanted to know? Suffice to say Barry and Muriel's back garden, and those of their neighbours, culminated in a high privet hedge. Some had the additional protection of a fence; some had a hawthorn hedge, some had all three.

Returning and removing his coat, it was sodden, for the last ten minutes he had scuttled through a downpour, Barry hurried straight to the kitchen, rubbing his hands together.

'Do I smell cooking, he chimed optimistically. But he couldn't. Muriel was there, standing over the table with a tin of baked beans in her hand. She stared at her husband, Barry stared back, wary rather than hopeful because he deduced by his wife's manner, her stance and demeanour, that for some reason the beans weren't going to be cooked. Not just not by Muriel but by anyone.

Gawping inanely at the table, he offered in his meek voice, 'No toast love?'

'Toast!'

'Yes, beans on toast.'

'Bread, is it?'

'Well if you're going to make toast.'

'There'll be no more bread. It gets covered in mould in a couple of days. Vegetables the same, fruit likewise. It's spores from that filth that was upstairs.'

'Spores?'

Barry could be excruciatingly exasperating but Muriel had long known that it was a futile defence mechanism and she was having none of it, not any more.

'Spores, germs, slime, sludge, whatever, words make no difference.' Then with a shudder of disdain she reached into the kitchen cabinet and brought out a tin of corned beef and slammed it on the table. 'Have that with your beans if you wish but be warned, once you open a tin, of whatever, beans or corned beef, both if you wish, but whatever you open you finish, in one sitting, because within an hour it'll be covered in mould.'

'Not if you put it in the fridge though.'

'Particularly if it's put in the fridge.' And she swung open the pale, toothless gape of the fridge, to reveal an interior already muffled with brown drifts of mould.

'Blimey.' He stooped to sniff inside the fridge then rose and made a loose gesture with his hands.

Muriel then slammed a bottle of tomato ketchup on the table.

'You don't have tomato ketchup with beans, they are already in tomato sauce, you know that Muriel.'

Muriel, with a venomous hiss, then slammed a bottle of brown sauce on the table. Same stands, once they are opened, they go. Now, open your beans and eat.'

'But not in one go, Muriel love, alright, a tin of beans, at a push, because it is approaching lunch time, but not with a whole bottle of brown sauce, I mean ...'

'Then no brown sauce. It's a simple as that. What is more there will be only one can, bottle or jar opened a day. So, make your mind up 'cos you've got to get used to it.'

Barry murmured incoherently, and then, as was his wont, changed the subject. 'That fridge cost a pretty penny and we haven't had it for a year yet.'

'And now it's useless. So, when you've finished your beans, you can get it out, onto the drive. I hate any clutter on that drive, as well you know, but needs must ...' Muriel's tone and stance spoke volumes, her eyes hard, lips set firm, even her voluptuous lower lip was pursed.

'Council won't take it, not nowadays and you can't book a slot at the tip, not any more. Anyway there's no saying that the tip is still open, here's betting as it's not. And anyway I'd need help getting it in the boot because what with the size of it, it won't fit, no doubt about that and it's illegal to drive around with the boot not properly shut, and that's the last thing we want is a fine, on top of all the rest of what's going on.'

Muriel maintained her stare and Barry said nothing further, just ran his index finger round the rim of the tin of beans.

Several minutes later, scraping the remains of the beans from the tin with a spoon, he was struck with a constructive idea. He beamed. Without a fridge there would be a sizeable gap on the kitchen wall. So space, for shelves, several shelves in fact. If everything was to be tins, bottles and jars, the whole wall needed to be covered with substantial shelves, because they would have carry a considerable weight. Size ten screws. And the shelves themselves, three quarter ply but with a nice bevel beading to edge them and of course the corners cut at 45 degrees, chamfered, didn't want anyone catching themselves on a sharp corner, particularly as one of the shelves would be at eyelevel. Constructive images, verging on the rapturous plundered his mind. He had not noticed that Muriel had left the room, gone back to her bedroom, no doubt, so pushing the empty tin aside, he shouted up the staircase, 'If it's to be nothing but tins and suchlike, we're going to need good sturdy shelves. Floor to ceiling shelves. I'll start measuring up straight away, and then I'll pop down to the D I Y store and get what's needed.'

'Move the fridge first.' Came the terse reply.

He gave a little chuckle, of course he would move the fridge first, he would have to move the fridge first, he couldn't measure through it. It was quite delightful the way Muriel didn't understand the procedures of the job, the job that was now well and truly in hand. A set of shelves, what better project?!

'I'm on it straight away.'

He was but given the bulk of the fridge freezer, its weight was on him. Not just strength but also dexterity was required. He shimmied first this corner then that till he got to the door. It would go through, but the shimmying was now by smaller amounts and of course with no room for the bulk of his body, also in the aperture, he lost control and the damned thing tippled over and crashed to the floor. He hurried back to the stair well and listened. No response. So in a blather of sweat he squeezed himself onto the drive and dragged the thing to the boundary wall. How it screeched and scraped with every tug. It fair set his nerves on edge. Even so, once he had got it upright against the wall he realised that it was visible from the kitchen window and he had gumption enough to realise that that would just not do, not if Muriel was to see it every time she looked out of the kitchen window.

A dilemma, did he scrape it back up the drive to the side gate that led to the garden? But that would mean it was all the farther to drag it down to the pavement when some means of its further removal was found. On the other hand if he dragged the thing down to the gatepost, then it could be seen by all and as Muriel would surely argue, a fridge freezer left by the gate post lowered the tone.

No matter, no point standing there in the rain, he would risk Muriel's wrath and drag it to the pavement, the downward slope was much easier and the scraping not so piercing.

Mission accomplished, he returned to the kitchen, dried his hands and began measuring. 'Happy days are here again'. The tinkle tune from nineteen thirty tripped through his mind. Granny rasher used to sing that over his cot. There was little that, given the present circumstances, could have enticed him more than erecting a well constructed set of shelves. So yes he chuckle muttered the tune happily as he measured and the tape obediently rasped the lengths.

Chapter 2

H arold had been up all night, colouring in canals and
rivers, and now the night had gone and he didn't know
what to do next.

Since Alice's demise he had slept on the sofa, she wouldn't
have approved, but then, seeing as she was no longer here it
didn't matter. Well it did in an acute corner of his conscience,
but the devilment in him could let that ride.

What did very much matter was the way the assembled
map was to be mounted. On ply, chip or conti? The size
needed, well that was a simple calculation, no problem there,
but the assembled weight? Now that did have to be taken
into consideration. He concluded that a trip to the D.I.Y.
store would be in order. The same conclusion that Barry had
reached, vis a vis his shelving requirements. And Harold had
a van, Barry didn't, Muriel would never have allowed it … on
the drive, a van, lowering the tone. Hence it was with a chortle
of surprise that Harold heard Barry's chiming tone as he let
himself in, his sunbeam face fresh with expectation.

Explanations were congruent: the van, the shelving
timber, the display boards … their schemes coincided and
so, each busy with thoughts about his own project, they set
out in Harold's rickety van for the D.I.Y. store.

The store was busy, shelves were being plundered by men
with frantic faces and women cumbered with all manner of
tools, their faces distraught as they waited their turn at the
cash tills. Harold was able to grab a trolley and with dexterity
they loaded it with their requirements then, likewise, patiently
waited in the queue.

And then a calamitous situation that immediately commanded everybody's fearful attention. A tall, skinny young man, his face avid with mean intent, was jumping from checkout to checkout, jeering and screaming as he raked out the trays full of cash- till offers and all the time turning with balletic skill to avoid the bulbous security guards, who themselves were bellowing commands over the spew of terrified customers, some shouting, some screaming in distress. A climax was reached when one of the guards caught the miscreant by an ankle and brought him crashing down onto a cashtill. Somebody cheered, many gasped, but the youth swivelled free, gave a snarl of triumph, kicked out at the cash till with such force that it snapped off its pod and fell clattering to the floor. Further disturbances accrued and much more shouting, the benefit of which gave the youth a brief opportunity to leap forward and down to the floor, to dart through the closing gap of the sliding door out onto the concrete apron and away.

A couple of security guards gave chase, but their cause was forlorn and they returned hot and expostulating into their intercoms. Once all had subsided a suited manager appeared made brusque apologies before giving his attention to the young woman cashier whose cash till it was that had been snapped off its pod. He ushered her to his office, promising a cup of tea.

To Barry's surprise Harold had watched the incident with a bemused smile. Nudging his nephew, who nervously clutched their trolley, he almost purred with satisfaction. Barry, disconcerted by this reaction, he did not take to violence in any form, was somewhat perplexed when his Uncle said with a sly smile, 'You know who that was don't you?'

'Him ... who?'

'Skirker. He lives on the estate below the back of you.'

'Never heard of him, or seen him before.'

'You probably will, get to know him, I mean. Best to be on the right side of Skirker. And what do you think that performance was all about?'

'Sheer bloody hooliganism, now I've said it. No excuse for that sort of behaviour.'

'Excuse, no, but reason, yes. You see on other side of the store his mate Lez will have been loading armsfull of stuff into a trolley and then hurrying it out to their van. No guards about, thanks to Skirker's diversion.

'You think that's what it was?'

'As sure as God made little apples.'

'Blimey. And he'd got tattoos all over his face!'

'His brow, not his face, just his brow.'

Skirker had the words, FUK IT, tattooed across the narrow band of his brow and Barry pointing this fact out to Harold complained, 'I mean what can you say, except it hardly does much for his job opportunities.'

'Skirker has never had a job, never needed one and won't ever. His mate Lez is speechless. By that I mean he doesn't ever say a word. Well, not now. He did once, but things happened. But he got into Skirker's good books when he put Skirkers brass eagle into the back of his van, just when they looked like getting into trouble with a demented preacher. They've been the best of mates ever since and the fact of Lez's not talking suits Skirker, because he never was much of a one for words.'

Barry regarded his uncle with a new curiosity. 'You seem to know a lot about him.'

'I'll tell you. I needed a skip once. And it was a Sunday morning when he happened to pass the drive just as I was looking at all the rubble that had got to be cleared. He saw me looking, said I needn't bother with a skip, that he would get all the rubble cleared at half the price. I said to him there was probably well over a ton of rubble. He said no problems, fifty pounds cash.'

'And you gave him fifty pounds?'

'It was a bargain.'

'Even so, you had no guarantee that..'

'I trusted him, something about his manner.'

'And?'

23

'Well he got rid alright, he came in the middle of the night with a barrow, I knew that because it had a squeaky wheel, and yes Barry, he took the lot, must have been, ooh, forty barrow loads. I lost count, fell asleep. Well it was best to leave well alone. But come the morning the drive was clear, he'd even swept the block paving, and it was Autumn too, plenty of leaves lying about in drifts. I was best pleased, believe you me. Next time I saw him I tipped him another tenner. Well you know me Barry, I likes a job well done and this was exemplary, no mistake.'

'Where did he take it?'

'Where did he put it more like.'

'O K, where did he put it then?'

'On some chaps lawn a couple of streets down. It seems he had offered to cut the lawn, the bloke whose lawn it was had just started and Skirker didn't think as he looked up to the job. Well the bloke gave him a mouthful, told him to skedaddle in no uncertain terms, and of course, need I say anything further … ?'

'Blimey, Harold, you do get around.'

'A word of advice Barry, don't you ever get on the wrong side of young Skirker, there's those that have and wished they hadn't.'

'And you're on his right side.'

'A couple of weeks ago I asked him if he could get me some of my tablets for my water works; I need them to pee properly and not be getting up five times a night. It used to drive Alice spare. They're a boon. And fact of the matter is, that you can't ask Skirker for the wrong thing. Always a step ahead, he'd been raiding chemists' shops for a week or so, all manner of stuff. And sure enough he turns up at mine with a casefull of 'em, enough to keep me till the end of.'

'Where's he put all this stuff as he nicks?'

'He's got a lean-to the side of his house, well it's his Aunt Carol's house really but he sometimes lives there and it's a workshop of sorts, but he keeps the stuff in there until he trades it on.'

All this while they were loading ply for shelves and for Harold's display into the back of his van. It took up more space than they had bargained for and the backdoors wouldn't quite shut, they had to be secured with a piece of string Harold kept for the purpose. Barry did wonder how often Harold had to overload the van that he needed such a device at the ready. Tangentially this brought him back to that no-good ruffian, Skirker. 'Well I noticed that some of the cans that had been bundled into his trolley were cans of car wax and tins of Brasso. Who wants those these days?!

'You need to get about more, Barry. Haven't you noticed the lack of vehicular traffic on these roads?'

'Well as you have said yourself, the roads are becoming evermore cluttered with Cess and ...'

Harold sniffed. 'Hasn't it struck you that you don't see any cars parked by the kerbside, almost none on drives?'

'Well, now you mention it ... but I suppose that ... .'

'Suppose nothing. Word was put about that this rain is acidic. Only slightly so, but seeing as it doesn't stop, there are those car owners who will do anything to protect their cars. Cars mean more to them and their kith and kin.'

Barry regarded his Uncle Harold with a raised eyebrow.

'Oh yes Barry. Auto-umbilicals, I call them. Now it's rumoured that every covered multi-storied car park is choc-a-bloc full, even the aisles and ramps that are covered. And they are all of a ferment, what with the owners wax polishing them, day in, day out, to ensure they don't begin to rust. Here, have a look at this ... .' Harold, growling with effort, made a sudden turn, heaving at the wheel as they turned off the road and onto a main road.

'Where are we going, Uncle?'

'The shops.'

'What for? We've got what we need.'

'Just have a gander out of the window as I drive past and you'll see what I'm on about. See the Auto-umbilicals and what they'm doing.'

Barry did and was surprised. All the shops were empty, they had been broken into by four-wheel drives reversing into the shop interiors. There was a diamond canopy of shattered nuggets of plate-glass all-over pavement and road. What is more, the varied contents of the shops retail commodities had obviously been slung onto the pavement, to accommodate the slugs, several of which protruded with shiny waxed bonnets Sometimes just one bulbous slug had been accommodated, sometime two or three, and over each bonnet an Auto-umbilical (to continue with Harold's terminology) was polishing away with demented energy, his face all a quiver, his brow laced with sweat.

'Don't they ever stop?'

'They won't till the rain stops and then they will parade about the streets in their gleaming steeds.'

Barry detected a joyous disdain in Harold's composure. 'And this has been going on …?'

'Since the rains became prolonged and cess started appearing everywhere. And look at those who are not polishing. What do you think they are about … ?'

Barry scrutinised more closely as Harold continued to drive past. Shop after shop, store after store had all been ransacked by backed up cars, mostly by four-wheel drives, though there was the occasional sports saloon. But those not polishing were, clearly loitering with intent and yes, Barry gasped, those not polishing had hammers or wrecking bars in their hands. Weapons?!

'I see what you mean Uncle … if we were to stop …'

'They would come over with malicious intent. Unless, of course …'

'Unless what?'

'We were bartering tins of car wax polish. See what I mean, about Skirker?'

'What's he get in return?'

'Who's to say but it will be something he'll be needing, that's for sure. C'mon, let's get out of here. We've work of our own to get done.'

Harold turned up a side street just as a burly man in overalls made to approach them, with a lump hammer, held aloft and ready for assault. 'Shift yer arse out of it!' he bellowed, waving the hammer. Barry noticed that his hands were scabbed and cleft, fissured by the unending contact with wax polish, his face distorted with rage. And yes, the few slug's bonnets they had seen, glimmered under the unending splatter of the rains.

'They'm demented varmints all right and there's few who drive down the high street nowadays, so consider yourself lucky to have seen them.'

'Lucky.' murmured Barry, whose mind had become distraught. Organisation ... yes ... he could applaud that. His whole essence was wedded to systems, it was his training, had become his life's intention, its essence ... but ... method had to serve a purpose of organisation. And such threats of violence, merely for looking at a gleam polished bonnet ... well it beggared belief.

Such were the run of his thoughts as they motored gently back.

They had regained their original route when the van suddenly skidded on a slime of Cess and shimmied into the kerb. Negotiating the roads was obviously becoming an ever increasing problem and time would soon be when most roads would be all but impassable for the general run of vehicle: you'd need a dumper to be safe. With much scraping and frowning, they regained a safe, albeit wavy length, and continued back. To Barry's first, to unload the shelving. Muriel was either somewhere about or else incommunicado, there was no response to Barry's excited hailing.

They jointly unloaded the shelving into the hall and then both went back to Harold's, he could not unload those sheets of ply on his own, it wasn't fair to expect him to.

It was on the way to Harold's that Barry suddenly gave out a shout of alarm.

'What!?' Harold was startled and stopped the van.

'That house, the one with the big bay!'

They both stared through the windscreen, the view obscured by scuttling ribbons of rain.

'What about it?'

27

'What about it!? Look.'

'What am I supposed to be looking at Barry?' a querulous tone here and then, 'Sludge, cess or whatever?'

'It damned well is, it's from inside and it bust its way through the bay window.'

'Then they should have bloody well done something about it before it got to that state.'

'And next door, look at next door, that man … just staring and his mouth wide open.'

'A Gawper.'

'A what?!'

'They calls 'em Gawpers, you not seen any of 'em yet, there's two or three around these parts. They just stand and stare, mouth wide open.'

'How long for?'

'What do you mean?'

'How long do they stand there, without moving?'

'As long as it takes, I reckon.'

'As long as what takes, Harold?'

'I don't know. There's a woman as lives in one of the bungalows just down the street from me, she's been 'gawping' for days.'

'And she doesn't move?

' Doesn't seem to. There's neither rhyme nor reason to it, but then there's neither rhyme nor reason to this lot keeping on, day after day.' A nod at the mottled windscreen here. 'Come on, there's no time to lose, let's get back and unload this stuff. There's a display to be mounted.'

As they drove off Harold commented only that he was surprised Barry had not come across any 'Gawpers' before.

Barry said nothing but screwed his neck to catch a last glimpse of his first sighting of a Gawper. It troubled him, the silent gape of the mouth, the fixed stare, the utter immobility. Was the man in the bay still alive? If not, what kept him upright?

'Leave it alone Barry, there's nothing to be gained by wondering. They'm there and that's all there is to it. They don't trouble us so we won't trouble them. At the end of the day, it's each to his own. Live and let live, I always say.'

Somewhat consoled, Barry nevertheless mumbled, 'Even so, uncle, even so, I've never seen a mouth gaped so wide.'

Harold said nothing but winced as he crunched the gears.

'I mean, standing there, immobile, I reckon as you could throw a brick at him and he wouldn't have shifted.'

'Well, we'll leave that kind of behaviour to the likes of Skirker, shall we.'

'I thought that you said Skirker was a one off.'

'Well, you get my drift, but yes, you're right, Skirker definitely is a 'one off' as you put it.'

Already Harold was thinking ahead. Mounting his map would not be a great problem, neither the fabrication of a stable display board, but what would be a problem would be getting it dry and intact to the library because it was obvious that with the way things were turning out, driving the van to the library would be impractical, if not impossible.

What Harold had not disclosed was that, Miss Eversholt, in the bungalow opposite and just a few doors down had been stiff and gawping, immobile, for several days. It was best not to dwell on such things, after all, what difference did it make, when all was said and done? Barry would do best to leave well alone, stay concentrated on building his shelves for Muriel. Muriel ... and to think she still wore stockings and suspenders, black stockings at that, he'd no doubt. Well, the way things are there's no point in trying to reason and as far as Muriel was concerned, there never had been. And what is more, perhaps it was best that the less Barry knew about the nature of things, the better. He'd got enough on his plate with those shelves, and after they were completed, well, he would have to inveigle his nephew into giving him a hand with getting his display to the library. It wouldn't be easy but Barry being Barry would certainly lend a hand.

Chapter 3

S kirker had long been recognised as a 'bad lot', even down in the remoter regions of the council estate. There had once been, rather surprisingly, ministrations of a Christian persuasion to try and model him otherwise. Even from the age of six or seven his anarchic nature was becoming noticeable. And yet it has been said that there was some kind of obscure, Christian connection, back in the days of his toddler hood. Whatever, that was all in the past and obviously nothing had come of such missions. Except to say that his obsession with that brass eagle … a lectern … may have had its origin in those early days. Possible but whose to say? Of course the tattoo on his brow now denied any attempt at social amelioration and the young man, with his ferocious energy, became, at least in the upper reaches above the sandstone cliff, with their assumptions of superiority of bearing and breeding, 'the worst of a bad lot'.

Now, everywhere is local but everywhere doesn't have locality and there is no divide so deep as that between working class and lower middle class. Muriel was very much an avatar of the middle class, she would disdain the adjective 'lower', living in a steeply roofed detached house whose garden, as already indicated formed a terminal boundary along the top of the cliff with a hedge, privet spiked with hawthorn. Beyond was an indecent descent, both geologically and sociologically, to the sprawl of the estate. That the two areas shared the same postcode, Muriel took to be a deliberate act of spite by the council.

Many of the council houses were now privately owned but that mattered not one jot. And if some even effected glassfibre

Romano-Greek porticos and-or appliqué Tudor it made not the slightest difference. The classical porticos could be scoffed at while the appliqué Tudor was just that, laid on' not like the substantial beams in Muriel's, which had a structural value; proper Tudor, so to speak; albeit of nineteen thirties lineage.

But there was so much more in the way of cultural habits to delineate the difference. Radios blared when they worked on or under their cars. It always seemed to be that the vehicle was supported on a pile of bricks with the front wheels off and, in a strange way, Muriel always thought that there was something indecent in the sight of a car with its wheels off, the naked brake discs gleaming. In warm weather scuffed sofas were dragged onto clumpy, unkempt front lawns and sprawled upon. And what sights were afforded, slumped figures, fat bellies exposed and a fringe of lager cans about their feet. Fag in hand they barked ferocious commands to their scattered children, which were competently ignored. Once, one such, a man in a vest, fag on the go, can in hand, had bellowed at Muriel as she passed, 'Alright Missus?!' She had ignored him obviously and hurried on, inwardly contorted in a spasm of hatred. It was an exceptional reason that had forced her to such an excursion but the less said of that the better, suffice to say Barry knew nothing of what he didn't need to know. In any case it was to be her last time down there.

Barry ... Oh dear ... 'Live and let live', he had once opined concerning the folks off the council estate, and immediately knew never to dare venture such a view again. But that was his way, Muriel had long recognised that he was given to such benign utterances and she just had to live with them: it ran in his family.

Barry had always retained something of his teenage Methodism, Muriel, definitely less so. And why had she ever married Barry Rasher in the first place? She had never really liked him-and such a ridiculous name ... Rasher! She had been Muriel Wentworth, a name that carried some clout, not only in the chapel but also in the town. Her father, Samuel, was the Sunday School Superintendent for the whole area and their chapel, easily the largest in the district, which in its architectural style and size approximated to a church, but with a Roman portal. Oh yes, there was certainly importance and influence there. But that was not all. Muriel was the pretty, curly haired niece of Alderman Wentworth who with his dark suit and well polished shoes was an exemplar of municipal authority. He chaired several committees, all of which strove to do 'the right thing in the right way'.

So, how had it happened? She, Muriel, no more than thirteen at the time, was encouraged to be in awe of her uncle, whose reputation, like his belly, and as sizeable, went before him. To this must be added the undeniable fact that his mode and manner exuded a confidence to be shared, he was someone she could talk to, he seemed to understand the complexities of behaviour and belief that a lively, thirteen year old girl, who could be taken for sixteen, endured. He had suggested that he could tutor Muriel, whose schoolwork did not live up to her supposed intelligence. Most Thursday evenings he would call at seven and spend a couple of hours with her, ensuring she understood and could manipulate sums of simple and compound interest. He taught her the significance of ratios and led her into the arcane world of profit margins. His confidential manner and the consoling whispering, his breath on her cheek, when she had failed to fully grasp the principles he so gently instilled into her understanding, established a dangerous intimacy of trust. This tutoring, so thankfully received by her parents, took place in the infrequently used 'front parlour' with, it being winter, the gas fire hoarsely burning and making its strange ticking noise as its casing expanded. He had such a comforting style, with words that went beyond arithmetic, to begin to explain the ways and necessities of the wider world beyond home and chapel, a world of potential she could realise … a world of suggestive powers. Intimacies that encouraged peculiar confidences were shared, so too oblique, personal admissions. His lack of faith was bluntly expressed but how it led to a teaching that the realm of 'chapeldom' could be used to serve a secular polity, fascinated her. Power, she came to understand was all. Nothing could be achieved without it and she could be cuddle tutored into an understanding as to how it could be achieved. That she sometimes blushed at his so very tentative advances was no matter. He would briefly cuddle and console in a way that put her effervescent self at ease. What she came to understand, in these later tutorial sessions, was that percentages and ratios were for manipulation by lesser beings, but to produce relevant figures lay in the domain of those who made decisions. No decision was required to work out a percentage, but to create those figures, that others fiddled with, that was the prerogative of those who wielded power. Of course the intimacies and cuddles became, well, more confident, more cherished, and something unspoken was soon shared between them. Her soft cheek against his waistcoat as he stroked her arm induced in Muriel a sense of a stirring potential. She never suffered more than a slug of saliva on the arm of her blouse and a broken syllabled murmur of inarticulate delight indicated only the potential of her power over him. His mature authority exuded power but it was a power over which, as she delightfully realised, she had a growing control. And what a delicious quality for a girl to possess, control over power!

Alderman Wentworth, as already explained, managed his authority and influence without the encumbrance of faith and that for the adolescent Muriel was also something in itself to be admired. Faith was both a hindrance and a limitation and how much more pleasurable it was to override these limitations. The world was not as the Sunday School painted it, it was as Alderman Wentworth lived it, a world of serious authority that could be fractured by an intimate indulgence … and their secret relationship was becoming intoxicating, for the both of them. Dare one say it: authority became reciprocal.

In spite of the difference in their age and status, it was the young Muriel who learned the most, who gained the most. In any balance of blame, the Alderman would be deemed totally culpable, but in the understanding and use of sexual power, it was Muriel who was soon in control. She learned that she could captivate, entice and reduce him, a man of standing and reputation, to an incoherent slaver of indecipherable utterances: the grovelling guilt of the Alderman, which, when he came to admit it, embarrassed everyone. She wanted none of his guilt, his confession, his apologies; they aggravated beyond reason. The awe in which she had held him dissolved into palpable disdain. Those blubbered confessions had been issued because one evening when her mother had entered the front parlour peremptorily with a cup of tea; the clumsy shuffle out of the cuddle had not been quick enough. But did he destroy her innocence? In a court of law, undeniably yes. But much else had happened; she was vouchsafed in the knowledge that men had could be manipulated. Better say no more: the cloisters of the mind are forever secret even in the blare of incompetent daylight.

It was a few years later when Barry, who had flourished at Sunday school, first met Muriel. Bumbling and embarrassed, he could never believe, when introduced to her by her father, the Sunday School Superintendent, that there could be any sort of dalliance between them. But, invited back for Sunday tea and then allowed to escort her to Evensong at six-o-clock, some kind of relationship was established. There was also the Friday evening youth club, when he called for her and walked her back home at half past nine. In all of their burgeoning relationship she seemed only to tolerate him, but that was only natural, given her beauty and popularity. It was a proclivity that had deepened over the many years since and to the present day he felt that he could never give Muriel sufficient reward for having bestowed her regard upon him. He well knew at the time that he could not be regarded as a catch and had spent hours in his room contemplating his reflection in the mirror, hoping the image, which he manipulated in stance and gesture, would give some suggestion of prowess. It never did.

Muriel's manner deepened as she came to realise that Barry Rasher was now all that life had to offer her. The only reason they lived in such a substantial property was that it had been her parents' house; they had moved in after the chapel marriage, attended by the Alderman with an inscrutable expression on his face, it was almost as if he felt betrayed. And there they stayed, in her parents' house, until, in the fullness of time, both parents died in short order, as the phrase goes. And, there were one or two who intimated that it was Muriel and her reputed 'misdemeanours' who had much to do with their early deaths. They had both seemed to wither away with worry. Matters were kept close but of course, close is never close enough. This day and age things are different but they weren't then. But one thing was certain, they would never move out of that house, if only for financial reasons; Barry's production controller's wages would never have managed the expense of a move to a bigger, or better, property. So they stayed put and, in diverse ways, it suited them both.

And what of Barry Rasher? Never the sharpest chisel in the tool box, he had managed bravely in comprehending the Sunday school lessons, but at school not so. He was methodical, no teacher could ever criticise his exercise books, notwithstanding the fact that there were as many crosses as ticks on the neatly written pages. And yes, he did have an ability at arithmetic, that indeed he carried through in his night school studies where he gained a certificate of sorts in Production Engineering and there, academically, things stopped. Of course there were no children to clutter the interior tidiness of a house that was more than roomy for the two of them and visitors were rare and isolate. Barry was a Production Controller at a local factory and the rest was stasis: other than to say his role came to be designated as 'Senior Production Controller' in the course of time, which was a mystery, seeing as he was still the one and only Production Controller.

Production Control, such a calling probably no longer exists, what with computers and other advances. The essence of a production control job was to ensure that the machines on the factory floor always had sufficient components to process so that production was never halted. This meant a liason between the factory stores, the purchasing office, and the lines of machines in the assembly shop. A failure of communication between any of these could result in a machine, or even a whole line of machines, coming to a halt. The disruption this entailed could range from the short term stoppage of a particular machine to, in extremis, a whole line of machines standing silent. One had to be nimbly numerate as well as having a detailed knowledge of sub-assemblies. Such were the vagaries of light industrial manufacture, that even the best Production Controller may cause a slip up. Works Managers would be annoyed, machine operators on piece work would call you a 'cunt', behind your back, usually, and matters could be taut, to say the least till things were remedied.

Barry, it must be said, being punctilious, and having a head for elementary arithmetic: proportions, percentages and the divisions of large numbers, that sort of thing, and being able to use a slide rule and calculators, was generally admitted to be an ace production controller. It was rare that he was ever called a 'cunt' and never to his face. And yes, it has to be admitted that his round, boyish face, his pleasant attitude, his ease with the human race in general, all helped him here. That and Muriel.

So often it was muttered of Barry, 'Have you seen his missus?' If the answer was no, there would be a facial gesture accompanied by a sound in the throat. And the response to that would be, 'really?' or, 'you're having me on'. Such was the obvious mismatch between Barry and Muriel. It was widely agreed that she was a 'corker' and other less salubrious notions were entertained.

And no children!

Barry had his own office, a pressed metal and glass box above the main assembly shop, with a metal filing cabinet, a desk and a phone: he had his own extension. If all this seems dated, it was and it wasn't, so to speak. The factory had been built during the Second World War with government money to produce aircraft instrumentation. So in its time it was state of the art systems and equipment that had been installed. However, since the demise of Adolf Hitler and the Japanese surrender, nothing equipment wise, had moved on and, it has to be said, not that much staff wise. The senior management team were still rigidly in place, as were their attitudes to both workforce and production techniques.

Barry was of course staff. He ate in the staff canteen and could take up to three days absence without a doctor's note. Perks! On Barry's desk there was no clutter, everything neat and tidy, no surprise there. Close to the phone was a coloured photograph of Muriel, no surprise there either, but in spite of Muriel's being a 'corker', no photograph of children, neither as toddlers nor as a graduand with gown and mortar board. No children and Barry had had to learn to live without them. Such were the transparent nature of things, at least at surface level. Subsurface, well that was a different matter and once again, the less said the better.

The name of the factory, was M.C.L.Myers & Repetitions, and no, it did not appear on his Uncle Harold's map. Outside the town (once) and now part of the city spread, it had been built on a Greenfield site, to avoid the bombing, that as a matter of fact, never happened.

So, comfortably ensconced and happily deployed, Barry was a fixture and nothing would persuade him to seek more advanced employment elsewhere.

In any case, given the recent situation regarding the rains, work at the moment at M.C.L.Myers &Repetitions (no apostrophe by the way) was out of the question, so it was fortunate that he could bring his organisational skills to the kitchen shelving project without interruption. All was well and he worked unhindered but at the back of his mind was Skirker, Not the name but the appearance, the action. He seemed to remember that a youth, that could have fitted Skirker's description, yes, surely it must have been him, who, according to Muriel's outraged account, had dropped his trousers at her. She had told him of an altercation with a particularly disreputable youth she had had, oh, a couple or more years ago now. According to her account at least, she had happened to glance out of the front window and seen a 'scabby faced youth' halfway up their neighbour's drive with one of their garden gnomes in his hand. So, clutching the yard broom, she had advanced on the culprit, bellowing. Both in appearance and manner she had surprised him, so much so that he had dropped the gnome on the drive which, being nothing but plaster, had split apart, the head rolling free. It was all credit to Muriel's fierce manner that he had not stood his ground and argued the toss. Instead he skipped over the garden wall and across the road to a van, its motor running and with a grinning confederate waiting at the wheel. It was at this point-such ignominy- he dropped his trousers and mooned at her, until she made for the van, waving the broom and shouting like a deranged Valkyrie, at which he jumped in the van, blowing her a kiss as they drove off, the van's exhaust laying a carpet of blue smoke along the road. She was stranded, mid road and mid rage, and yes there were onlookers, alerted no doubt by the noise, hers and Skirker's. She returned to her house and stood in the hall cursing and fuming, retching with hatred and hissing repeatedly, 'That such people …'

And now it had become lodged in Barry's mind that it could well have been Skirker who had been the miscreant: mode and manner fitted the bill. All of this now caused him to chortle, particularly as at the same time his drill bit was sinking easily into the wall. He did not hear the soft galumphing sound as great dollops of cess dropped from the back roof onto the garden and what is more, to tell the truth, he wouldn't have been too bothered if he had. The new kitchen shelves were all: there was a whole world of possibilities in shelving.

And to the point, yes, tinned and bottled food now had to be the rule and no sooner than the shelves were erected, the edges sanded and beaded, than he would make repeated forays to shops and supermarkets to stack up on suitable provisions. A few items at a time, that would be his strategy, a quite opposite one to that of Skirker.

In this decision he was sagacious. People had to at least attempt to carry on as normally as possible. What else was there to do? Factories, some of them, for the time being at least, continued processing stuff, haulage trucks still splattered their way over broken roads, sliding this way and that through flaccid pools of Cess; their drivers, wanted wages. The system was slowly choking, but it was still a system that engaged people, provided dividends, even if those rewards were much reduced. The system had a purpose: profit, and though increasingly frustrated, nothing or no one had the means to change that purpose. Yes, all was sclerotic but not seized up, not quite yet. So after the engagement of constructing his shelves, Barry set about several clandestine excursions to get tins, etc., to stock those shelves.

There was a sadness, a sense of despair even about rows of all but deserted, unstocked aisles, their own plasti-coated metal shelving for the most part empty. Metal shelving had its potential but no purpose in a domestic setting, there wood had to be the rule.

The conditions within and about the shops were chaotic but nothing that a steadily cautious procedure couldn't successfully manage. A clutter of bodies, some bundled on the floor, others in what seemed to be a permanent slobbery leaning against the shelves hindered progress. They were moaning and regressing, the loss of the normal clearly having adverse effects on them. They seemed to have lost all purpose, store assistants would try to shoo, or even shove them off the premises, with some success, though it had to be a continuous process, because they mostly came back in through the door and immediately struck up similar attitudes. They seemed to coagulate in groups and their monotonous moaning, usually mumbled names of dearly loved products, sadly echoed from the farthest reaches of the store. Almost a choir, because at a particularly favourite intonation, tinned peas, or tomato soup, for instance, the volume rose, as did the pitch. A weird wailing and then at other times a surly denunciation, as if the product being chanted was now forever gone, almost lost to memory; toilet cleaners seemed to fit into this category. So, all clumped against each other and the shelves in forlorn bunches, they seemingly found a sad comfort in owning their joint loss.

And it was the same but different in the other stores he visited. In one, a woman, clearly demented was attempting to scrub the tiled floor with a block of butter, she obviously thought it was a scouring agent in her hands. She worked feverishly, moaning all the time. A store assistant hauled her to her feet and she blabbered incoherently while a fellow store assistant sprinkled the buttered patch with ground coffee shaken from a jar; such a waste, but it did save other customers from sliding and falling and hurting themselves and making complaints, so, in extremis, it was perfectly logical. Why not give the woman a scouring agent? That would have saved everything but he said nothing, best not interfere, in any case he had those pristine shelves of his own to load up.

And to be fair, there was not a Gawper in sight, and that was something: not a single Gawper blocking the aisles with outstretched arms and a void gob-hole echoing your stare.

Of course Barry was not inclined to bunch and wail. And there were others like him, intent about their own purpose, who carried a basket, moving a trolley was not possible, and took what of the stock that was left that they could sensibly use. Sense and sensibility, in some at least, was maintained. During the course of the next few days he made several rewarding forays, not always getting the commodities he wished, but always with foodstuffs they could manage to eat. For instance Muriel couldn't abide gherkins, so although there were quite a few jars of them available after a recent delivery, he only rescued one jar, which of course was for himself. In doing so he muttered to himself, but loud enough to be heard, 'And gherkins for you Barry' at which some of those lying on the floor repeated the name of the commodity in a groaning tone of voice. It was unnerving and he was glad to get away from the shop. Another thing, the staff were so busy shoving the stupidly distraught custom, moaning, leaning and crawling about the place, they could not staff the tills, everything was free. That was certainly a consideration.

He didn't count the days, but eventually with the new shelves completely loaded, and how wise he had been to make them so strong, fixed to the wall with size ten screws, and the kitchen floor itself piled high, he decided that enough was enough, at least for the time being. Skirker would not have proceeded in such a piecemeal fashion, he was all for a vanload at a time, achieved by variants of the accomplished raid on the D I Y store. That could never be Barry's way but then again a hurled tin of pineapple slices would be a lethal weapon in Skirker's hands, not so in Barry's. Unlike Skirker, he had to be discrete if he was to survive until things changed back to as they were. Be methodical and always show a fastidious discernment, that was his manner throughout.

This raiding of shops and supermarkets could not continue, the deliveries were getting scarcer, with ever fewer loads and the artics, in spite of their size and weight, were facing increasing difficulty in getting through, the wallowing drifts of Cess, ever more voluminous, obliterating most of the surface area. What is more those roots of Thorn were breaking through the surface everywhere. It was due to such worsening conditions that Skirker, ever the entrepreneur, came up with an ace idea. He had noticed, because he kept his eyes open more than most, that there were evermore Gawpers, their rictus faces distorted in a silent scream, staring out of their front windows. Did they only ever stare out of their front windows? Well maybe no, although he thought probably yes, and in each of those houses there would be a kitchen, or larder, whatever, still with a supply of food of some sort. So simple, break into those houses and raid the larders. He didn't think there would be much in the way of resistance, and if there was, he would be able to deal with it. Food, it was the only necessity now; folks had long since given up on scrapers, wire-wool and chemicals to try and get rid of Cess, that battle had been well and truly lost. Meanwhile it was gangs with JCB's that took over the supermarket raids. So yes, small scale but repeated, he could build up his own stock, and store it in the long lean-to workshop Funky had erected years ago against the side of Carol's house. Carol, by the way, was Skirker's aunt and he lived there, mostly, and she wouldn't complain. She never did, she was the easiest person to get on with, unlike her friend Irene who lived across the road. Irene could be gobby and always enjoyed a good moan, but that was just her way and in the end she was no obstruction to anything very much. Irene was also his aunt, not in the same way as Carol though and he didn't stay with Irene, not even occasionally.

The new scheme was put into place immediately. There were several gangs competing with each other for the shops, and he didn't want to get entangled with them because in a ruckus Les was a distinct liability, no doubt about that. The first raid was a bit nerve wracking. Les sat in the van, smiling and keeping watch while Skirker went up to the front door and knocked. Best to be polite, at least to start with. As he was invariably to find there was no response, however long he knocked, so it was a case of going round the back and breaking in, which had never proved to be much of an impediment to Skirker. Inside he shouted out a name, any name, but 'Roger' usually, to give him an excuse if one were needed, should there should be a response. But there never was, most Gawpers, it seemed, lived alone. So yes, it was always decidedly creepy. The house empty, apart from the front room Gawper, the large rooms forlorn and silent. He would go to the front room first, where the Gawper would be standing, frozen in attitude amidst plush chairs and bountiful sofas, the thick carpets crinkled up under accumulating drifts of domestic Cess. Then, not even bothering to prod the Gawper, he returned to the kitchen to find that he was correct in his thinking, there was varied but considerable stock of food stuffs. It was simplicity itself to take what he wanted and carry it down the drive to Les in the van. They could minister to several houses every day.

Within a few days he had got hold of a trolley and tipped the contents into the back of the van, Les didn't even have to get out, all he had to do was to keep the engine running and keep watch. They were the first to this game but soon there would be others; it had always been the way of things in this life of ours.

They spent long days, working all hours, up and down, to and fro. And all the time the lean-to workshop was filling up to the rafters. No matter, in spite of Carol's uncertainty, he wasn't going to stop, even if the stuff was to be stored in her front bedroom. It was a case of striking while the iron was hot. And in all the houses with a Gawper in the front window, often with its arms stretched wide, there was never another, living occupant. Soon they were forgetting which houses they had 'done' and it was Lez who came up with a convenient solution; paper hats. In one of their last and least successful raids, on a post office, Lez had carried out a box of paper hats. Skirker had remonstrated with him over the box but denied Lez's gestured offer to take it back. Getting away from the scene as quickly as possible had been their sole priority, so they were left with them and now they came in handy, because every Gawper whose home had been pillaged, had a paper hat placed on his or her head. Trouble was they would soon run out of hats and they were not an easy commodity to replace these days. But no matter for now. In the end Skirker adopted the practice of marking the front window with a simple calligraphic design made with a stick of lipstick he had found lying about. All worked well to full capacity and say what you like about Lez, he was always up for another foray in the van. But every time Skirker entered a fresh house, he now began to get a distinctly, creepy feeling. It wasn't just the stillness, though that was disconcerting, it was an abiding sense of a strange otherness and the fact that, not to put too fine a point on it, the Gawpers didn't seem to rot! Were they dead or not? What did it matter, given the scheme of things? Skirker was the last person you'd expect to dwell on anything to do with the nature of existence but even so, he found the matter irksome.

But he had made the right decision, they worked unimpeded and Carol said that Billy Bateman, who lived at the far end of the estate, had been caught by a gang when he was on a shop raid on his own and they had banged his head against a wall several times and that was a week or more ago and he wasn't right yet. He'd got back home blubbering and with nothing more than a handful of envelopes, and what use were they this day and age? Skirker took note and upped the number of 'Gawperised' house raids, even though you couldn't even get a tin of peas into the workshop and Carol wasn't having her front bedroom stacked to the ceiling with tins of food. She said the floor would collapse and she clearly had a point. Skirker acknowledged the circumstance with a scowl but already was beginning to develop an idea, an idea whose realisation was considerably advanced when Irene, the very next day, came "a bloody great 'perler'", falling over her step, that caused her no end of pother and pain but as things worked out, made Skirker's new plan an absolute necessity.

Chapter 4

The long, high and in its uppermost part, very steep, sandstone cliff has already been mentioned, but a little more of its provenance needs to be explored. The sandstone is of the Triassic age, a time when saurian monsters strode about seeking lesser of their type to rip apart and eat. Such specimens no longer exist, at least in body, though they certainly do in mind. This will be the way of things, until evolution adopts a stratagem that promotes a species that eliminates the human type. Not a slow, continuous evolution, as is the accepted mode of evolutionary development, but a sudden, world transformative saltus ... a sudden jump. The wiseacres of evolutionary science tell us such things simply do not happen. Well, that is their dogma, but all dogma is a spiritual rictus, itself something of a fossil.

The top ledge of the cliff, crusted with high hedge or fence screened the two worlds from each other, worlds that of between working class and lower middle class represents a deeper divide than that between the Jurassic and Us. From the bottom not even a chimney pot of Muriel's house could be discerned. The aforementioned, Dingle Brook, obscured by scruff vegetation, descended into metal pipes. Here were swathes of plastic waste, the occasional mattress, and other domestic goods that were deemed to be no longer fit for purpose. The estate dwellers vehemently swore that it was the 'snooty fuckers' from the top of the cliff that tossed the waste down, while those from above swore otherwise. Whatever, the Dingle Brook babbled haphazardly through its camouflage of vegetation and litter, through the pipes and to a far beyond, till it was to be found creeping around a distinctive hillock that, for some reason or other, persisted under the name of, 'The Old Chronicle'. Where do such names come from? What is more, why do they persist? Verbal lassitude is, in its blunt way, a distinctive force besetting human communication. Though there were those who insisted they had the answer, it was generally felt that such answers couldn't be trusted. Funny the way some things work out, one way or another.

Suffice to say, the Dingle Brook bubbled alongside Irene's house, on the upper avenue of the estate, then under the road to re-emerge the other side, by the side of Carol's house, continuing its precipitous descent into the beyond. Irene's front door, was reached by four steps from the pavement and these, as she repeatedly affirmed were treacherous when wet and, and well, when wasn't wet these days. And of course, given the way of things, before this present season of rains and cess, the Dingle Brook, often flooded; a few days of winter rain, a sudden summer storm, that's all it took and the brook swilled fast and deep across the road. It had taken several complaints to the council before a remedy had been commenced. However, given the onset of persistent rains, that remedy was probably going to be ineffectual. Yes, work had started but it was merely at a halfway stage. A couple of men in high viz jackets with spades, cutting undergrowth back: what good was that going to do? Probably only making matters worse further down the Dell. But then a large tank, painted green, was installed, right next to Carol's house, and surrounded with high fencing and a double locked gate. A siphon tank, one of the workmen explained, a sort of mini reservoir, not that there seemed to be much of the mini about it. Irene was pleased about the development until she realised it was the wrong side of the road- Carol's side, so it wouldn't stop any flooding her side. Bloody council, as always getting arse before face. Carol did point out that Irene's house, perched above the four, steep steps never got flooded itself, whereas it was Carol's side that received the swill that swept to do untold damage below. However, as things turned out, it was to Irene's benefit that some workmen were still messing about with a valve of some sort when she, stepping out for Carol's, let out a shriek as she fell, like a sack of potatoes, slap down on the top step. Carol heard it from in her kitchen, the slap and the shriek, and hurried out to take a look. The workman who had described the tank as a 'mini reservoir' was also nearby. He had seemed to be in charge, given that he had never been seen with shovel or spade but was always taking notes. Whatever, he came across and up the steps to Irene's immediate aid. Carol joined them, hands a quiver, face rippled with concern. It seemed obvious that Irene had done herself no little damage; her face was the colour of a mug and she hissed 'Jesus Christ' as she attempted to roll over onto her side. It was not that she was religious but it is odd and has to be admitted that even the most irreligious of people will invoke the name of a disbelieved in deity at a time of stress.

Anyway the workman took charge. 'Don't try to move' he instructed and Carol noted that he did have authority in his tone and manner.

'Wriggle your toes' he ordered, slipping her slippers from her feet. Such authority that …

'She should never have stepped out in her slippers' Carol commented, adding, 'You was asking for trouble, Irene love.'

This was unheeded. The workman, he must have been a foreman, he had a name tag fixed to the chest of his high viz, Dr. Stone: Apex Hydraulics it read. He was not satisfied that Irene could wiggle her tones, even though he said 'Good' when she did so. He then told her to follow his finger as he slowly waved it to and fro in across her face. Irene did so and at this Dr.Stone nodded again.

What's a bloody doctor doing with drains and siphon tanks? thought Carol, well she did have time to wonder, especially as she just had to stand there gawping. Circumstances and situations, well they can make you think.

Whatever, this Dr. Stone seemed well pleased, he announced in a level tone that 'she' had done no serious damage and that it was safe to try and get her on her feet.

'I'll give you a hand.' Carol offered.

'No need madam, I'm used to lifting.'

Madam indeed! But yes he did, manage, got her to her feet, steadied her, and then eased her back through the front door and into the lounge. She hissed and waved her free arm about, her other being grasped at the elbow and allowed herself to be lowered into the soft vacancy of her sofa. That new sofa, it half filled the room but its comfort was luxurious, not that she had paid for it yet. Such were the adjacent but futile thoughts that flashed through Carol's mind, as she smiled seeing Irene settled and nodding as she took in this Dr Stone's advice.

'You're lucky young lady that you haven't broken anything.'

'She'd have been a bloody sight luckier if she hadn't come a 'perler' in the first place.'

Dr Stone looked at her. 'A perler?'

'She means a 'Cogwinder' whispered Irene, hissing through pain as she shifted her leg on the sofa.

'You're going to need some strong painkillers for a few days, and if your friend here can help you get to the bathroom, a long soak in a hot bath will help.'

The manner with him, so assured, thought Carol. One thing for certain though, he was no foreman, he was obviously a gaffer of some sort. And a Doctor to boot, but well, what sort of doctor was it that dithered around with drainage?

The two ladies thanked him, he declined the offer of a cup of tea, even of a glass of sherry and made his exit. Before any discussion could take place, and discussion there would be a plenty, concerning this strange Dr Stone, Irene, grasping the bottle of sherry yelped for Carol to pass over a couple of cups and make herself comfy, not on the sofa though, of course.

Chapter 5

Horror, albeit in a minor key. Muriel had insisted they eat whatever she took from the shelves, one container only. He had ventured to complain that half of tin of soup, for instance, didn't keep him going for the whole day. They ate in the morning and then nothing else at all; Muriel taking to her bedroom straight after the 'meal' and remaining there for the rest of the day, fuming. But in response to his complaint, he had made one on a couple of occasions, she did relent and open two tins. But, oh dear, one a tin of oxtail soup complemented by a small tin of condensed milk. She then emptied both into a bowl and stirred vigorously until the white flecks of condensed milk were subsumed evenly in the brown swamp of the oxtail soup and commanded him to eat, 'and not to slurp!' Then she slapped the bowl down before him and watched, standing over the table as head bent and without even a murmur of complaint, he began to sip nicely, Muriel could not abide noisy eating, until he had emptied the bowl, at least he thought he had, but no, she snapped for him to lick up the faint smears, which he did, till the bowl was spotless.

'You've got to learn Barry, if we're going to come through this we are going to have to be utterly ruthless, and those who aren't will pay dearly, now get on with what you were planning to do.' And with that she went back to her bedroom with the toasting fork in her hand.

He told himself that things were coming to a pretty pass, wincing as the bedroom door was slammed shut but acknowledged there was nothing he could do about it. Once the rains stopped yes, but they hadn't yet and until then, well

… . But, well, yes he did have a plan, he would walk round to Harold's the next morning, see how he was progressing with the stand for his map, give him a hand even, that would brighten him up. He would have to be tactful though, offer to do too much and Harold would be thinking his nephew was trying to muscle in on his project and would take umbrage.

He retired early himself. Not now sleeping in what had undeniably become 'Muriel's room', he had long had to make do with the smallest bedroom, situated over the 'reception hall', its little window looking down on the drive. He slept on a camp-bed, a relict from a disastrous camping holiday years ago. But though long enough, it was too narrow and its metal framework dug into his body, whichever way he turned. And this night he had turned incessantly. Remedy, and it always worked, was to grab the eiderdown, made for a double bed, much too large for that camp bed, wrap it about himself, like a bulbous shawl, like a bishop's cope, and thus ensconced go and stare out of the narrow window.

The eiderdown was a family heirloom, his family's heirloom. It had, so he was told, belonged to a grand Great Aunt and was stuffed with real eider feathers. It would, his mother had assured him, keep them warm on even the coldest nights and their house, perched up on the top of the knoll would undoubtedly be cold on a winter's night.

Muriel hated it, its faded floral pattern, its diagonal pattern of quilting and even the plain purple colouring of its underside. So it went with him to the 'storage room' to encumber the camp-bed. Keep him warm if that's what he so much wanted.

At the narrow window, staring out into the night, with it draped over his shoulders, listening to its soft hush as it scraped across the bare boards as he strode to the window, he felt confident and relished what he would see. The house was high, the narrow window higher, it easily overlooked the roofs of the facing bungalows, and at night betrayed what could not be directly seen in the daytime. He could see the spill of the traffic lights in the trees, a couple of streets down. Not only that but the genial orange spill of the lights of the nearby pedestrian crossing. 'Belisha beacons' Harold always insisting on calling those lights, though heaven knows why, though it was a word once heard was likely to stick. Again the contrary way with words is difficult to ignore. But to the essence of the matter, clad and coped in his eiderdown, Barry could count the seconds between each change of light, could match that interval with the shorter, more insistent rhythm of the 'Belisha Beacons'. They formed the essence of a productive process, to his mind at least, when viewed in tandem. It was such a solace: a system working, silent and efficiently: uniquely satisfying. Whatever was happening in this newly drenched world of incessant deluge, things could still be ordered.

But then, and to be fair, it gripped him like a nervous spasm, like a crick in the neck, the knowledge that the sequence had ... failed. He had witnessed it, not just a flickering like a failing bulb, that would have been understandable given the enduring wetness, no, he saw red and green at the same time! blatantly showing for over a minute, then the amber, flashing, twitching as if in sympathy with the 'Belisha Beacons' at a pathetically insistent rhythm that immediately suggested a malfunction and then they too abruptly went out ... were extinguished ... failed. The system ... extinct! It was then that, perhaps for the first time, Barry grasped something of the enormity that was overwhelming them, super seeding (sic) all life as they knew it. One thing he guessed was that, for certain, those lights would never again be seen in a correct sequence, probably never be seen again at all. As a systems man he felt himself overcome with an immense sorrow. He could have wept, stained his feverish face with cold tears that yet scolded his twitching cheek. He turned abruptly, only half making it back to his camp-bed, before he heaved up the soup and condensed milk onto the bare wooden boards, splattering his cold, upturned toes in its hot torrent. He did have the notion, as he heaved again and again, bringing everything up, that perhaps what he had seen with the lights had been a product of his nausea. But no, shivering now, he knew that had not been the case. He scrambled onto the camp-bed, his face now wet with tears from the heaving, consoling himself with the renegade thought that it wasn't just him, but Harold and indeed Muriel were both in the same boat, destined henceforth to live in a society with no reliable traffic lights. He slipped into a slumber with the resolution that there would still be order and he would work to find and indeed, manipulate that order.

The ensuing morning he woke up determined. Determined didn't cut it … oh no … he would find a mission, a means to instill, somewhere, somehow, a new regime of order. So besotted with this thought he ignored the stale splash of vomit, it would harden and could be scooped up later: a dustpan and brush job … menial work for later. But for now …

Struggling into his mackintosh, he called up, 'Goodbye love', and set out, head lowered, into the rain. He had worn his mack the previous day when moving the fridge freezer to a more suitable place on the drive, wondering if there was any way he could get in touch with that 'Skirker' fellow, pay him to get rid of the damn thing. In doing so he had got sodden, with the result that today his mack was damp through and as stiff as a bone. Distinctly unpleasant. Still, as with the condensed milk and oxtail soup, Muriel was right, he had to knuckle down and get on with it … be ruthless with himself … that is what he assumed she meant.

It was bleak though, roads all but impassable and Thorn encroaching ever wider and higher upon the houses it attacked, in some cases even reaching to the chimney pots, which it toppled down to the ground. It did seem that having reached the topmost of the building it attacked, it then proceeded to thicken out, into an impenetrable bush, except that, for some reason, it never seemed to cover the windows, never excised the Gawpers, and there seemed to be ever more of them, some he noticed, wearing silly party hats. Strange times: strange people. Still there would be work a plenty to do when it did stop raining, no doubt about that.

Harold was in the best of moods when he arrived, he had seen Barry picking his way down his drive, which now had its own first globules of Cess breaking through. He bellowed for his nephew to come on in and all but hugged him when he did so. And, yes, there it was, taking up most of the length of the lounge and almost all its ceiling height, a stable, self supporting wooden frame on which was displayed, flat and neat, the factory and canal map. Splendid, he had to admit, and a considerable achievement, no doubt about it. Barry shook Harold by the hand, 'Well done, Uncle, it looks splendid; a complete history of a by-gone age. And there, displayed, soon for all to see.'

'Test me!' Harold exclaimed, rattling his teeth about in his mouth; they gave out an enthusiastic clatter.

'But …'

'No Barry, but me no buts, as the Bard said. Buts and bickies come later, for now, test me, challenge me, shout out the name of any one, or all, of those old manufactories and see if one has been omitted. Go on, don't hold back and I think you won't be disappointed.'

What else could Barry do? He held his uncle gently by the shoulders, but in a kindly manner, and waited for the rictus of enthusiasm to pass. Even so his brow was bathed in sweat. Barry, ever diligent, rifling his own memory of the forgotten factories, called out some of the familiar names: Jones and Attwood's, Josiah Hingley's, Enoch Smith's Hollowware, and so on, the older the factory the more biblical the name. He went through quite a list and to every name Harold pointed to a spot on the map with a white cotton cord to its listed name. They egged each other on, voices rising in anticipation and both blustering with joyful accomplishment … until … well it began to go wrong. Barry expressed a certain sadness that 'his' factory'" M.C.L. Myers & Repetitions was not listed.

'But it's not a closed factory, it's still there, and these are all long gone.'

'I know uncle, I appreciate that, but it may not be there for much longer, there was already talk before this lot happened about a falling off of orders. Light assemblies are certainly not what they were. So, if it did close, then … .'

'But it was only built in the last war, it's not Victorian, in fact many of these..' a finger tapped on the map to emphasise his point, 'are Georgian, Barry, Georgian! No, it can't be admitted, your Myers and Repetitions, I'm afraid.

Barry knew there would be no shifting Harold, his opinion was set. And to be fair Barry recognised both this and the reason for it, because, when closed, if it was to be, it would still be modern. Harold was right, but it jarred that his place of employment, as a production controller would be voided from the map. Was there a mischievous undertow that led him to exclaim, 'But uncle why haven't you shown any of the old glassworks!?'

Harold's face became stern. 'Works, he hissed, you said it yourself, works, glass works!!'

'Yes, but they were factories and they were old.'

'Have you ever heard anyone call them, 'Glass Factories'?' Barry sniffed, he sensed he was on 'Okifinokee' ie, trembling ground-an Indian word from a film he had watched as a child, a swamp that put a foot wrong, it would suck you down to your death. He had never forgotten the word, but then that's the way some words are memorable, no matter how difficult to spell, like Popacatapetl for instance. No matter, uneasily standing on Okifinokee, on trembling ground, he realised that, as far as his uncle was concerned, he had most decidedly put a foot well and truly wrong.

There was a moment's silence, for them both to recuperate.

Harold first. 'As I said, glassworks, not factories, and stop a minute and ask yourself, what did these factories here,' a tap of the map with his knuckle, 'produce, eh? I'll tell you: iron works: iron tools, spades and shovels and pipes, cast iron casings, forged bedplates, structural steelwork, cranes ... oh the list goes on and on, Plummer blocks, turnbuckle screws, face plates, manhole covers, on and ever on. Now, consider for a moment, what did the 'Glass works make?' Pretty little things, fruit bowls, vases and silly little cut glass containers for your woman's dressing table. Expensive fripperies, things that were brittle and got broke, things that no man, who called himself a man, would ever own to. No, Barry, the factories made the world, whereas the glass works ... well, 'nuff said.'

At this Harold was exhausted, he turned away to wipe the slaver from his lips with a folded handkerchief. Barry knew that to stay quiet was not enough so he quietly, but most definitely intoned. 'Now you come to say it, I can see you have a point Uncle Harold, I really do.'

It was not enough but it was a start at reconciliation and for the time being it would have to do because Barry's mind was being taken on a sideways excursion, vis-a-vis the mention of cut glass decorations on women's dressing tables. What was that all about and should he know the answer?

Such peregrinations were interrupted. Harold had swallowed his ire and offered, 'Let's have a biscuit or two, settle us down a bit. I'm afraid there's no Digestives left, nor Malted Milks come to that but there are some Lincolns, a much underrated biscuit if you ask me, seems to have fallen out of favour for one reason or another, only the larger supermarkets seem to stock them nowadays.' With that he went to the kitchen for the famed biscuit barrel, offered it to Barry and in no time they were both contentedly nibbling away. Or were they? Was there a thin vein of malice in Harold that now surfaced and he began relating a caustic tale?

'You've been a good companion to me Barry, especially since Alice died, definitely, oh yes, but there's something that needs to be said, something I need to tell you: family matters.'

He took a deep breath and Barry waited, curious but apprehensive.

'It's not ever been said, not out loud at least, but now it needs to be and in no uncertain terms, so brace yourself. It might hurt but in the long run it will perhaps help, at least I hope so.'

He paused and fixed his nephew with a level stare.

'Go on.'

Harold sniffed, rearranged his mouth and pronounced, 'Alderman Wentworth. D'you know about him?'

'I've heard of him, yes.' Indeed he had in snippets of chapel rumour, but if that was going to be the worst, after all Muriel had been young and exploited and whatever had taken place he didn't want to know. Water under the bridge-and he was about to say as much when Harold cut another sliver from his tale

'There's more, I'm afraid, and you should be told because it might end up affecting the course you're going to take. No, Barry, the fact of the matter is that Alderman Wentworth wasn't the last. His doings were all but nullified, after all the Alderman had deep pockets and he could reach beyond the realm of chapel, yes indeed, but no, there's another chapter to the chronicle, and worse, I'm afraid. Remember Reverend Lurgan? Oh what a barnstormer he was. Muriel's father, 'Sunday School Superintendent', as he was, said that the Reverend Lurgan brought new life to the chapel. Well he certainly did that, and it was whispered she wasn't the only lass in the congregation that he tupped.'

'She being … ?'

'Your Muriel: of course she was nigh on twenty by then but they were at it in the vestry, all hours, all manner. Miss Belper caught them going hell for leather. She snook away and if you ask me she would have said nix if she had had her turn, but that wasn't to be, so she blabbed it about. Now of course this was a different kettle of fish entirely and no one was going to say as Muriel was exploited as she was now older and obviously ready to fly her knickers in the wind with the buccaneering preacher. So no, no sympathy this time for Muriel but it still had to be hushed up, put beyond doubt, beyond rumour. And that Barry was where you came in. Muriel's mother couldn't cope, seemed as if she was going 'do- lally- tap' over the issue, at the very least a nervous breakdown was on the cards, but, the 'Superintendent' he took matters in hand, read the runes, so to speak and constructed a different chronicle. Muriel was to cosy up to you, the last character you would think of, if I may be blunt, because I mean, not to put too fine a point on it, Muriel, she was a luscious peach, was then and in the eyes of many still is, Barry. That raven dark hair, those full sensuous lips, that smile that taunted and of course, with a full bust and legs that went up to heaven … you can almost sympathise with the Reverend Lurgan. No it wasn't just a case of him leading her astray, it was also her driving him to perdition, at least that's the way as I see it. When Miss Belper's reports were circulated, he was finished, hounded out, persona non grata everywhere, his career destroyed. Because … well, we'll leave the 'becauses' beside for now. Anyway … Where was I.. Muriel, well her father took matters in hand, and you were that matter, Barry. You were quiet, studious at night school, full of faith, well at least so it could be contrived and then, well, shall we say, a steady though uninspiring chap, a sound fellow, a reliable young man, Barry you fitted the bill and you would destroy the rumour mill. I'm sorry lad but that's the way the tale was told. So, there you have it.'

Barry looked ashen. Yes it all fitted together and the doubts, little ancillary fracture thoughts that had persisted, were now explained. How she, Muriel had cosied up to him, but in a strange, distant sort of way, and then all those Sunday afternoon teas with peaches and single cream he had been invited to and her mother, every now and then giving out a harsh cackle, apropos of nothing, her face turned to the ceiling. Whatever she had thought of her daughter and her behaviour, Barry Rasher was a come down. She could have done so much better for herself, he had actually heard it whispered thus, and yes, he did detect the sour cream smiles at the wedding. A coldness from all, apart from her father, he seemed to have a forlorn sympathy for the groom, perhaps intuiting the nature of the life he would be leading in future, a life of ignorance and private ignominy.

And then only a few weeks after the marriage, and it was consummated, but by no more than a frigid moan as she lay, stiff, though unresisting, under his uncontrollable whimperings of delight, he was told she had to be whisked off to some aunt in Stoke-on-Trent, whom he had never heard of before, but was now, apparently at death's door. But he didn't question. She was back a few weeks later, after the aunt had died, and their life together settled into an abrasive stasis from which it never emerged.

He looked at Uncle Harold but said not a word: he didn't need to. Harold, feeling somewhat cold within himself, broke the ice.

'What say we take the map and stand down to the library and get it set up in that entrance lobby?'

'Yes, why not uncle?' such a flat tone, bereft of the enthusiasm Harold would have wished for. Perhaps he should have kept his mouth shut, at least until later; but then, thoughts, they come into your mind uninvited, surely no one can be blamed for the thoughts they have. Even so, yes, even so. And he tried to light a little flame of enthusiasm.

' Tell you what, I've a big tube we can wrap the map in to it, then we'll put it in a black plastic sack, in two if necessary and once the stand is dismantled, and there's no great weight to it, we'll bundle and tie the pieces together and put them in a couple of sacks. How about that?'

'Now!?' … tone, not to be ignored …

'Right now, no time like the present, because if we wait for this rain to stop, we could be here for a month of Sundays, so to speak. So yes, best foot forward and I'll tell you one thing Barry, they'll be falling over themselves to have it up and showing in that large foyer with its terrazzo floor, no two ways about it. Strike while the iron's hot and we'll have some more bickys when we get back. Fair enough?'

'Why not uncle, good idea, let's get started.' But again the tone of voice suggested that his heart was not yet fully in it; suggested even a note of aggression. That was not like Barry at all.

But they did as Harold suggested and at least the careful packing of map and stand, once completed, seemed to indicate that all irritation between them was dissolved. Perhaps, Harold thought, he had been right after all to disclose what he had when he did. They exchanged safe smiles but remained silent as they set out for the library, neither of them having the slightest intimation as to what was in store for them.

Chapter 6

The library, described as being in the town centre, was a tidy stretch and Barry's mind was still adrift. Harold's account had plundered both thought and feeling to the extent that it was as if he was chewing mould. Fragments floated to the surface: you must be ruthless, last thing she had said, and yes, she certainly had been, and what else swilled up for sharp reflection: Rasher, silly surname ... Barry Bacon at school and still carried over by some. Rasher than whom? He could imagine her snort as she responded, 'rasher than none!". Placid formulations of his live and let live universe, of his ingrowing gospel of, 'there's good and bad in everyone' buckled, dissolved in the inner spasms of hurt and realisations that now beset him. Be ruthless to survive, but he couldn't, it was not in his nature, he ruthlessly denied he had any aptitude for ruthlessness. There was not even a snort at how ridiculous this conclusion was. Except ... except ... he could begin to feel a sharp hatred, not towards Harold in person but certainly towards his ineptitude. What had he said? ... 'There's something you need to know Barry'. Well why? How did it help things, it certainly didn't improve anything, and now, even as they were walking to the library, thoughts with the sharpness of paper cuts, thoughts that previously he would not have had the wit to even acknowledge, now caused previously unexposed areas of his imagination to bleed.

Yes, and yes again, that first night, which was well after the honeymoon and her trip to Stoke-on-Trent was done with, she had tolerated his bumbling attempt at intercourse, head turned aside, lips pursed; he gathered that much even in the curtained darkness, and wondered was it his lack of striving, or her delicacy concerning the brute details of sexual intercourse, that made the bedroom frigid. There had been other times, other excursions, aiming at variety and exultation but there had never … And here his present condition prevailed because he had to wait for Harold to catch up. He had been walking at a furious rate and his uncle left behind and wailing, spluttered a request that they slow down.

They did, though it was probably a small mercy that Harold, just at Barry's shoulder, could not see the fierce expression on his nephew's face, as his torturing thoughts still raced and gambled ahead.

Lovemaking, what a stupidly inarticulate term; having sex---he had never had sex, with Muriel, or anyone else of course, he had not plundered … plundered! … . he had only dabbled with an all but inarticulate penis, experiencing at best a remote entanglement of emotion and feeling that entailed, in the long run a curious sense of vacancy, a strange sense of loss. Compared to all this, and with his attitude to such things foundered like a keel cut upon rocks, is it any wonder that his career, and yes it was a career of sorts, as a production control engineer at M.C.L. Myers & Repetitions, gave him stability, purpose, resolution, a sense of achievement even: a basis on which to build a life worth living?

Of course not, he had told himself. But now these impossible to tolerate thoughts lacerated … the Reverend, yes, he recollected him now, beaming upon his flock; not of devout worshippers but of sexual whimperers, the young and not so young women of the congregation, who beamed back at the pulpit, slimy mouthed and secretly … some not so secretly … wanting … no waiting to be tupped. Up and at 'em Reverend Lurgan with your white hot gospel and semen spurtling throughout the parish.

Yes … he had spread Muriel's white thighs apart, serialised his lust into the wealth of her dark triangle, again and of course again and again, her sighing and groaning in such ecstasy as he bellowed supremacy.

Yes it would have been thus and so, now, in his mind it turned and turned, till he could have spat his venom in a torrent on the Cess covered pavement.

What was it Harold had said … ? 'something you need to know Barry'. Need to know, why need? Why now? It all suggested a purpose. A purpose for him, Barry, apropos of what had been divulged. Curious, intimations failed to connect, as he thought of Muriel's remonstrance … 'If you want to survive you've got to be ruthless?' That is what she had said, holding the toasting fork in her hands and in such a strangely menacing way. If you want to survive, in this new way of the world … if you want … it was advice, yes and yet more, an invitation, a request even, be ruthless Barry and I will be yours. A new world, one in which, even Barry could ascertain, would offer little scope for production controllers. But … perhaps no, it could even offer an increased scope for such men, men who could organise, control, manage and delegate. Muriel was offering something she had never offered, never even countenanced before. An opportunity, a chance … a …

His mental turmoil was abruptly severed at the root as Harold issued a strangulated moan; they had arrived at the library and it was closed; the doors locked and chained, dollops of Cess lining the steps.

And then, because the psychic flow of thoughts and ideas constantly intrude upon the block simplicity of facts, Barry suggested in an urgent tone … 'The city library! Why not Harold? You'll get more viewers there, in the city library, and let's face it, probably a more knowledgeable clientele. Folks as will understand the difference between factories and glass works and won't worrit about there being no gasworks either marked on your map. The city library will still be open after all.

Harold coughed, clutched the wrapped-up stand and supports closer to his chest and pondered nervously the abrasive tone of his nephew's suggestion. Except … the tone … it wasn't a suggestion, it was an exhortation … it was an order. 'It's …' he began but got no further, Barry swapped the parcels, he taking the supports and pushing the lighter and infinitely more delicate parcel of the map into his uncle's chest. 'Come on, Harold, this way.' And he set off up the hill, head bent against the drench towards the city centre. Harold sluiced juices in his throat, he wanted to but never would, of course, expectorate in the street. So he gobbled a sort of agreement and followed behind, endeavouring to keep up; something had got into his nephew alright.

Barry, always a few steps ahead was on a mission, urgent but undefined. Definition would come later.

The city, it was a good three mile step and uphill all the way, although the rate of steepness varied. Their destination, however, could be clearly seen, a cluster of high towers, all idiosyncratically the same, the same- same the world over, mostly purposed for office work. Corporate headquarters, regional centres and a hotel, all with windows that darkly gaped at each other. They competed in style and scope of their atriums, but for the rest were monotonously uniform. 'Centre-Citadel', that had been the name dreamt up by the developer of the last towerful encrustation of concrete and glass, which marginally out topped the others. And the name, just shortened to 'Citadel' had stuck and was taken to refer to the whole towerbristle of the city centre area.

The Central Library was different of course, a nineteenth century 'look at me facade' with redbrick frontage, gothic windows and truculent features in terra-cotta; its major dimension was its length. Seen from a distance the deciding features of a confidently placid design were, the spacing of the fenestration and the main entrance, which sported a portico that was an amalgam of the classical and the municipal: a steam hammer and cupids. Beneath were large doors with stained glass windows, the design of which exhibited portraits of cultural avatars, in large roundels, one to each door. The six steps up were shallow, even so there was a central brass handrail, supported by uprights of twisted iron that, to a child at least, suggested writhing serpents- indeed they still did to Barry. Large, curvaceous brass handles on each door and it was a municipal fact that every morning, without fail, excepting Christmas and Easter Holidays, and Sundays, the brass work was lavished with large dusters and polished to the gleam.

Thanks to contemporary developments, the library could not be viewed from a necessary distance any more. The towers had cooped up against it, the hotel in particular had a circular ramp leading to a car park which obscured the facade. And to the library itself, a new floor, a glass and steel skeleton, had been added, which destroyed the roofline, with its prominent central lantern. No doubting it was a bit of a mess and no mistake. But it also suffered the indiscretions of the now seemingly new age of rain and Cess and Thorn, only the towers, at least in their dark upper reaches seemed to be immune, as yet at least.

But, yes, it was open. Well, to be precise, one door, its brass handle pitted and tarnished, opened on the oh so spacious foyer, with a mahogany enquiry desk, with its familiar array of display shelves cluttered with shiny leaflets-though they were not shiny anymore, coagulated into clumps of drooping paper. There was no one about. Barry called out a loud 'Hello! In a confident tone as he pushed through a further door and into the library itself.

And, well, what a sight it was. Books, en masse, convey a certain atmosphere, no matter how drab and forbidding to those unaccustomed at turning pages and perusing. To the bibliophile the sight of an array of shelves of bookage, contrive to create a happy expectation of a delightful dalliance, flitting from title to title, each a legend of possibility. Harold and Barry fitted into neither category, for them a book was a useful text, explaining methodologies; books were textbooks, in the main, and if there had been diversions, e.g. crime fiction, they were slight, occasional and disposable, having no right to appear on library shelves. As it was, as they stood gawping at the shelving in dismay, they observed that all titles were obscured, mottled with green clusters of mould. Not Cess, curiously there seemed to be no trace of that in sight, as yet at least, just common or garden damp mould. They were caught staring open mouthed when all of a sudden, from somewhere deeper in the entrails of the library a musical instrument began playing a familiar tune.

'It's a trumpet.' said Barry and began humming the oh so familiar but unlocatable tune.

'It's a cornet!' snapped Harold, distinctly out of humour.

'Think of it like this, if the bloke playing that instrument is …'

'Cornet, it's a cornet, in spite of what the majority of folks say.'

'A cornet then, but if that bloke is the only bloke in the library, then when he leaves, if we set it up sharpish, he'll see your exhibition.

'You're assuming it's a bloke as is playing that cornet but this day and age …'

'Does it matter Harold? C'mon, let's to our purpose. We'll set it up, in the foyer and then explore the rest of the library, pointing out the exhibition to anyone we find.'

'Anyone and not everyone', thought Harold, and in a big library like this. But it was the purpose of their visit and so he snuffled his thoughts and shuffled back to the entrance lobby, leading the way because Barry seemed to be intent on peering down the glum aisles. And there was something in Harold's spirit that didn't welcome the notion of his masterwork being perused by an itinerant musician. Musicians never cared about anything but their music and if it was popular tunes they were puffing out, any interest they exhibited would be feigned. It was all nothing but notes with musicians; always had been, always would be.

Working in silence, in no time the display was all set up, tested for stability and admired.

No one coming in could ignore its wide spread, try as they may and that brought a mutual satisfaction. The cornet playing ceased, and yes, there was the sound of footsteps on the oak-block flooring but they didn't seem to be coming their way, not towards the exit. Indeterminate footsteps and an incoherent cough, from a decidedly deeper space within the entrails of the library were heard. Was it the cornet player's cough or were there others wandering the gloom?

They looked at each other, in different degrees of despondency. What to do now? Nothing more they could do, if anybody came or left, they would see the exhibition, no doubt about that, Harold just had to hope that there would be more coming and goings in the days ahead. Perhaps word would get around. In the meantime they both felt that they had to get out of the dank, clammy stillness of their surroundings; there was nothing to be gained by hanging about. Perhaps if they returned in a few days time. Such were the constrictions of their thoughts till suddenly Harold piped up, 'Hector! We could go and visit Hector's bookshop, it's only round the corner, you must remember Hector's, I've taken you there before. Hector will have a straight face on all this palaver, I bet his books aren't all modged up like those in the library. It's the council, they don't take enough care, and letting some nutter rampage about with a cornet, well, it beggars believe. C'mon Barry, lad, Hector will give us a better perspective on the lie of the land. This way now …'

Chapter 7

Out on the pavement, back in the drench, Harold whispered to himself, trying to decide the best way to go.

'I guess any way will do uncle seeing as you were saying it's not too far.

'Not too far at all, just a step, but there's an alleyway that halves the difference. Now let's see …'

They found the alleyway, eventually, although such were the false turns and repeated step-backs, Barry was doubtful of the point of finding it. But then he didn't know, neither did Harold, that by going down the alley, cramped but straight, they had avoided the main square, 'Citadel Place' and so avoided a sight that would certainly have discountenanced them beyond measure, that of a crumpled body, human but unrecognisable, the head having been splattered to a pulp.

Hector's shop, once located, proved to be a disappointment. Its frontage was boarded up, both display windows and the central door, nothing in fact to indicate it was, or ever had been, a bookshop. Harold was not to be further disgruntled, he banged on the chipboard covering the front door, bellowing Hector's name. It took two or three minutes to get any answer, but Harold assured Barry there would be a response, because Hector lived on the first floor of the premises and it would 'take him time to come down'.

Having got Hector's attention, a scraping and muttering from the other side of the door ascertained that communication had been made, it was a further couple of minutes before the door was scraped ajar. A wizened, world weary face scrutinised them as Harold pathetically whined,

'It's me Hector, Harold, and Barry, you remember Barry, my nephew from years back. I bought that book on Battle tanks of the Second World War from you, for his thirteenth birthday. Remember? Say hello to Hector, Barry. You going to let us in, though I see you are not open for business in the usual way, so to speak?'

Hector just gawped over their shoulders, each way, up and down the street and only then cautiously beckoned them in to a session of much dithering and moithering as he explained the danger they were facing.

Harold beamed back as Hector spluttered. 'Just look at him now, Hector, not a thirteen year old stripling. Barry here is the Senior Production Control Engineer at M.C.L.Myers & Repetitions. Would you believe it? Eh?

Even Barry recognised that his aggrandisement in this fashion was entirely apropos of the earlier business between them concerning Muriel and the opening of her legs. Hector snuffled. He had some sort of running sore on the side of his cheek and a pink plaster, intended to protect it, hung loose, as a pink strap over the ooze.

'And', continued Harold, still in an exulting vein, 'he still has that glossy paged volume on ...'

Hector snorted and turned away. 'Don't you know what's going on?!' he demanded.

'Well, of course, all manner of things, Hector, but then isn't that always as it was. The world's always been overburdened with stupidity: nothing new there.'

'They don't want books. It's dangerous even to have them. There's burly fellows banging on my door all the time ... threatening..'

'Threatening what?'

'Violence, destruction, to books and ...' He paused angrily to try and refix the loose strap of plaster to his cheek, hissing with pain as he did so. 'They did this, pinched my cheek and twisted, till the nail went in. I've got to be off and out before they come back. And where am I supposed to go? I live here.'

'I know. But look on the bright side Hector, it must be cramped in that flat upstairs. And, I can tell you, in the better class of suburbs there's all manner of decent houses becoming empty, well sort of. I mean have you heard of the Gawpers? Now there's a tale to be told and no mistake about it.' ...

Hector moaned in desperation. 'My life's in danger ... these books. As I've said they have got it in for books.'

'Nonsense Hector, everybody has to read something, at some time or other. Perhaps they think you've got the wrong sort of books. Take my advice and set up a good window display of Second World War books and that'll be the ticket, they'll all be gawping and leafing through them. Three things you can't go wrong with, when it comes to books, or even conversation, and they are, Hitler, Warfare and Railways ... steam locomotives, although there is still interest in trolley buses, and they had those in these very streets, years gone by, so there you are. Perk yerself up and try dabbing Iodine on that sore, and you'll be right as rain in no time at all.'

Exhausted by this diatribe, Harold, who had been trying to at least convince himself of the veracity of his strictures, sat on a trestle table, already overloaded with tottery piles of volumes.

Barry felt a growing disdain for his Uncle.

Hector still fiddled with the plaster and all stood rigidly alert as outside banging on the wooden sheets that blinded the windows reverberated within. Hoarse shouts, incoherent, yet managing to convey violent intentions echoed within.

* * *

No such indecision attended Muriel, who at almost the selfsame time made her way to 'Citadel'. Citadel was the way she prefigured it, no definite article, because it was to become a term that indicated a force, a forceful new organisation, a force for order.

She set out in a glossy raincoat, with high heels and black stockings, seams strictly straight. A defensible handbag at her side, also glossy, completed her outfit. She was protected from the downpour by a large umbrella, the ends of its spokes white with the run of droplets.

She took no heed of the of the dereliction she strode past: ruined shops, gaping frontages, often with jagged tooth glass panes and frequently trails of discarded produce, sodden and rotting, littering pedestrianised areas, even the grand plaza its stone tiled magnificence, stained with marks of dereliction. She tightened her lips at the thought that she would see an end to that sort of thing. Indeed. The new organisation she intended to bring about would soon get a rote of 'masstidyingup' in hand. Her strength of mission tightened. To achieve such works would require a new order of organisation, that much was obvious, but before that the collapsing old order had to be … she paused in her thinking but not in her resolute pacing and cherished the word that erupted into her mind … extirpated. 'Extirpated!' Yes, that was it. She would extirpate the old bureaucratic order; destroy the multifaceted council, its offices and officers, lay waste … good old Roman term, vasto..I lay waste … hence devastate … lay waste to the old order, eradicate conglomerate policies, it's 'nanny state' stipulations, and minority protections. Sweep them all away. Scrape the space clear … Citadel Force … a new order.

She paused, noted a human corpse, picked at its obliterated face with her umbrella and confirmed to herself with pressed lips that there would have to be killings, of course … but not random, not incidental, and certainly not left lying about as litter. Tidiness bespoke of a higher purpose. Oh yes, there was so much for her to do!

Such in sorts were her thoughts as she strode on, across the plaza to the Council Tower, not the vacated Town Hall, that was still cosseted in its twentieth century gothic behind the library, derelict and unloved. Council Tower: the brave new face of global municipality; here there was much activity taking place, the tall atrium windows, both inside and outside were being scraped clean by teams of black coated workers. Their bending, straightening and reaching made her think of the futile movements of insects trapped in a bottle, even so it was nevertheless to be commended, a degree of organisation that she could use as a base, something she would build upon, to effect a forceful re-ordering of the collapsing status quo.

And surprise, surprise, a man in a uniform, with braiding on his lapels and an officer style cap with a polished peak opened the door for her. She strode past, no acknowledgement, none needed, but she did notice the wasted expression in his eyes, a sense of … futility. Well that would soon change, purpose would be instilled and without hesitation she strode across the atrium floor and up the staircase that led to where her mission would be accomplished. On, she strode-stepped and into to the blundering busyness of the first floor.

With determined, resolute thighs, the cruel ferrule of her now folded umbrella pick-tapping the tiles, she already commanded the attention of some, who paused from their dilatory paperwork. One or two busy menials coughed or made exploratory gestures but they were comprehensively ignored as she strode on, through the crowded bustle of the first floor through sliding doors that were wedged permanently open with bulky document files.

Inside all was a complicated incoherence; a feverish coming and going of white shirted minions, but going where to or coming where from was decidedly uncertain. It was all a busy, purposeless blather. Through the swirling throng a large desk could be seen, a desk so large and elaborately carved its original purpose had been nothing to do with mundane work and everything to do with status. So be it, here would be the target of her purpose.

The room was so very large, occupying almost all of the floor space. And it was busy, thronged with scurrying, besuited men, clutching plastic folders to their chests, all nudging and pushing their way to that huge central desk. Programmes, projects, procedures, schemes of work were hurried past, each of which needed to be validated with a rubber stamp by the man occupying that desk. And more, all around that desk, slithering to the floor like dead fish from a trawler's net, discarded schemes and projects. The air was foetid, rancid with ingrowing despair, so very few of the projects gained the rubber stamp. When given, it was applied with such force that the monotonous, blunt thump sounded throughout, aggravating the demeanour of those still waiting, not in file but pressed against the edges of the desk. The thump echoed and they twitched, eyelids, cheeks or chins, but they fluttered in recognition, probably of something they no longer understood.

Watching all this was a frail, twisted young man, clad in a wretched suit. He seemed to be making mental notes, nodding at the proceedings, always at the shoulder of the large man sitting at the desk.

And there he was, the same but distorted, blubbered up and face creased somewhat, black suited, a striped tie, horn rimmed spectacles, flaccid cheese coloured complexion, fat belly, protruding through a gap in his white, ketchup stained shirt: a great panjandrum once. All of a bluster, sweat sparkling on his creased brow, as he distributed fat folders of designated procedures to his avid underlings. He bellowed orders and they were obeyed, so it would seem, as the designated juniors would then scuttle away with the proffered folders just as others arrived with fresh bundles of information. Process, perhaps, but purposeless process; this is what things had come to, this now their way of life in such dereliction. But she would retrain and enforce a new order. 'Citadelisation', perhaps.?. a new word, but not yet. She had work to do. But first a task, not pleasant but extremely necessary. An accomplishment that had to be seen to be done if it was to give her control.

She would demonstrate to him what she had learnt on his lap.

She pushed forward till she stood at the desk, forcing herself to the attention of this Great Administrative Bureaucrat, this blubbery grand administrator, this sweat pappy panjandrum. He stared awhile, blinking and then demanded, 'yes!?' Not the slightest recognition through the sweat glazed stare.

The essence of propitiating change is surprise, effortlessly inflicted. Such that the action is completed before there is time for response.

And so it was, without either a flicker of doubt or hesitation, without so much as a word, she levelled her umbrella, directed its ferrule straight at the right eye of the Municipal Panjandrum, flicked his glasses casually aside, they rattled onto the desk, and then with a severe pressure forced the point of the ferrule quickly through the eye and deep into the folded grey modge of his brain. A coup de theatre ... a trompe l'oeil, so to speak.

He gasped, then emitted a strangely muffled snorting choke, squirming in his chair, hands ineffectually clasping at the umbrella, as it's point slid to the other side of his skull, at which still in a snorting spasm, blood issuing down his nostrils, he quivered, croaked incoherent sounds and died, his fat tongue waggling obscenely as it had when ... well enough of that. She pulled the umbrella free and wiped the stuff off it with a nearby document.

Stage one of her mission accomplished.

What would be done now by the swarm of the blathering clerkdom?

Nothing. It had all been completed before any even realised that something was afoot. They just fell back aghast, and waited for her orders.

She poked the fat slump of the body and said simply, 'Get rid!', in the same tone as she had instructed Barry to, 'Just eat'.

And it worked, of course it did, the bulk of humanity wants purpose and little else. So, one way or another, they did ... 'get rid'. What she noted was not those who obeyed her clearly stated order but those who commanded others to do so. One in particular caught her attention, that painfully thin sliver of a man, in a dark blue suit but with a black waistcoat, all of which hung about his gawky frame in a twisted droop.

His brow was unlined but pimpled, he had bony wrists but nothing suggesting bodily strength and yet there was a ruthless purpose to his manner and a sullen smile as he repeated her order. Here, she thought was treasure trove, a lieutenant that would obey without question and at the same time be himself obeyed by faceless minions.

And, clear as a new daylight, she discovered that that name, bestowed upon her by marriage to Barry, a ridiculous joke of a name, now connoted a different meaning. Rasher ... would become Rasherfication ... the new process to create a higher order of disciplined society. Hearing the dull clonk-clonk of her victim's head against the stairs as his body was dragged away, she jerked her umbrella upwards and they cheered. Yes, they actually cheered.

Not the old order but a new 'dement-ion' was sliding into place.

Returning with certain sharp steps back down to the atrium, having gestured for the suit and waistcoat, skin and bones individual to follow and aware of the bushfire crackle of clapping that broke out behind her yet again, she was strangely reminded of her one and only visit, many years previously, to M.C.L. Myers & Repetitions.

Barry had been nervously effervescent at her presence, introducing her to his elite superior, smug and happy at that gentleman's response, and then waved her generously towards the busy assembly line. She studied the moving process, the clattering along of components to machines which with devious cleverness assembled them into intricate contraptions, purposed for further incorporation into a machine able to perform functions of who knew what. It didn't matter, what had creased a smile across her face was the realisation that what was significant was not the devilish cleverness of it all, but that it needed no human input. Process was all. Whatever gadgetry was purposed at the end was neither here nor there. She observed the few workmen attending the line, themselves mere devices, monitoring a process they neither understood nor cared for. That realisation, kept from Barry, as he gulped enthusiastically, hurriedly explaining the this and that of the process, now came to fruition. 'Rasherfication', she would ensure it would be so named. Rasherfication, whereby essence of being became process and nothing more.

She also realised that speed was of the essence. Thought must instantly become praxis. And other nomenclature needed to be installed. But no, not Citadel, it had all manner of diverse connotations, but … she paused for a moment on her traverse of the atrium, but.. 'Uniate'!, Yes, that would be the name of the new order. 'The Uniate, and what a convincing simplicity there was to it.

The thin, suited slovenliness at her side asked for instructions. Not what to do but how to do it, that was the issue. She pressed the ferrule against his chest; would she poke between his ribs with it? To his credit he did not flinch, he held her stare and said, slowly, a pause between each word, 'Just instruct me, Ma'am and I will obey.'

'We need a higher floor where things can be ordained to our purpose.'

He smiled, was it guile or subservience to be read in his face? No matter now, he simply responded, 'Then this way Ma'am', leading back up, past the room of her triumph to a higher floor, the fifth as she counted, empty, as yet, devoid of purpose but a space into which the new regime could come into being.

She was well pleased, except, with a tremor of annoyance, she noted that any further passage upward to yet higher floors was blocked by a tangled interlocked mass of metal framed chairs and tables. That would not do, she would open every floor, everywhere within the tower would become the province of The Uniate. Everywhere, and it was a spasm, a flick-flitch of answered desire, as she fingered the faux cane handles of her handbag and life felt good; an underground sun shone through dismal pavilions of spiritual despair. Rasherfication: the Uniate: Consumer as Commodity. The triad of the new realm!

Chapter 8

'Bloody Hell, Abdul, what you doing here?!' This, Skirker to a slight young man, sitting in the rain, in front of the lean to next to Carol's house.

Carol, alerted to Skirker's arrival, shouted from within, 'You leave him be Skirker, he's calculating.'

'Calculating what?'

'Never you mind, just leave him be to get on with it.'

'I would if I knew what I was leaving him be to get on with.'

'It's no concern of yours.'

'Who's to say as it's not?'

'I'm saying.'

'But it's only me as can say if it's a concern of mine or not.'

' He's calculating, that's what, now leave him be.'

'I'm not interfering, just asking.'

'Well, let's say as you'm asking too much and that's the interfering.'

'Well I haven't interfered then have I, because he hasn't answered.'

'Bloody hell, Skirker, you'm always the same. You won't ever be said.'

'I only fuckin' asked Carol and asking isn't sayin' as you put it.'

'Ignore him Abdul.'

'He is.'

'Good.'

'All the same.'

'All the same nothing!'

' Bloody hell, talk about not being welcome.'

'It's not as you'm not welcome but if you've come to prevaricate …'

'Prevaricate, me, I like that, you'm the one prevaricating Carol.'

'Ignore him Abdul.'

'He is.'

' 'cos he's busy reckoning, that's why, and there's no one else that can reckon like Abdul, not round here, and well you bloody well know it. Talk to that Doctor Stone about it, he knows Abdul and it's him as sets him the sums as he has to do.'

'So … ?'

'So bloody nothing Skirker.'

Such interlocution could well have carried on for several more minutes had Abdul not stood up and announced, 'Seven thousand, three hundred and forty, approximately.' His voice was somewhat muffled and he looked from Carol, now leaning against her door jamb, to Skirker who unloaded a rucksack full of provisions before her.

'That all you got?' The tone wasn't helpful in discharging the growing irritability between them. And that was unusual, Skirker and Carol normally got on softly, there being an uncharted easiness between them.

'Lez has got another bagful.'

'Where is he then?'

'Just down the road.'

'I've told you not to leave him on his own.'

'He's just down the cowin' road.'

'On his own'

'There's no doing with you Carol, look there he is, he's not been out of sight for a minute.

At this 'within a minute' Lez arrived. He nodded at Abdul and emptied his bag alongside Skirker's pile and stared, first at Carol and then at Skirker then back to Carol.

'It's not much.' Carol intoned, now a certain sadness to her tone that Skirker felt to be unfair.

'There's not much more to be had, Carol, truth to tell. We'm running out of new gawpers and all the shops are ravaged empty, not so much as a packet of biscuits left anywhere, so we'll just have make do, and that's an end to it.

'That's why Stone got Abdul calculating.'

'Calculating what?'

'I don't know, ask Abdul.'

Skirker gave a snort of disbelief. 'He's got Abdul calculating, you said so yourself, but you don't know what he's calculating. How the bloody hell does that work out ?'

' I know but Dr. Stone is hardly forthcoming, not to me at least. Irene's a different story.'

'Oh, and how's that come about?,

'Ask yerself and put two and two together, do yer own sums, it's simple enough even for the likes of you. All I know is that he barely said a word to Abdul, just something about the capacity of that tank, gives him a pencil and a scrap of paper and in no time at all Abdul's covering both sides with numbers. I ask you how can a few words lead to both sides of the piece of paper being covered with numbers … nothing but numbers, scrawled, but scrawled little. It don't make sense to me and it won't to you, so don't interfere and let Abdul just get on with it.'

Skirker winced. 'He has finished, look at him, he's not figuring now, now is he?'

They both stared at Abdul who simply stared back but with a smile.

Carol was irritated by something that had nothing to do with Abdul. No, it was Irene and her doings as were scratting about in her mind. Two and two making four: Irene was humping that fellow Stone. Well, they hadn't wasted any time, but then it's surprising what a couple of cups of sherry could do, particularly this day and age. Even so.

Skirker didn't take to Stone, not from the start. In his green weatherproof jacket with name tag and employer labels attached, with a yellow high viz waistcoat on top of the jacket he was all 'about what he was about' and the assumed authority he seemingly claimed over both his aunts. He didn't trust the fucker, had been given no cause to trust him and he had no right to be getting Abdul to do his sums.

What was he, too lazy to do his own figuring? Or couldn't do it, not up to the complication of it all? No, he wasn't going to kowtow to Doctor fuckin' Stone. As far as Skirker was concerned he was no more than a cracked cup of phlegm. He couldn't be doing with him, not that he was going to say any of this … the fellow obviously had some use. But he would find out the lie of the land, as far as his circumstances were concerned. Best way to be till you knew what was what. In any case it was bloody Wassif who should be getting Abdul to do things, not Doctor bloody Stone. Even so, Carol was right, Abdul, when it comes to numbers is all over the place in no time, it's this and that and I don't know what else, but even so.

Lez sniffed and Skirker gave Abdul a long, silent stare.

'Aunty Carol … .'

'I'm not yer aunty Abdul, I'm sorry.'

Skirker winked at Carol and then to Abdul, Carol is not your aunty. I calls her aunty from time to time because she is my aunty, family, but you can't be …' Then after giving Abdul a long stare, muttered, 'Fuckin' hell Abdul, how come you'm so bright with numbers but you can't understand families … .?'

Abdul, uncharacteristically sharp, snapped, 'I like to call Carol aunty. It does no harm to Carol.

Lez chuckled.

'No it does no harm' Skirker conceded, 'Even so …'

'Course it don't, so let's leave it be.' This from Carol who was now feeling not just irritated with Skirker but also a certain protectiveness towards Abdul, who looked quite dejected.

Emotions were difficult territory for Skirker, always had been, so he decided to move things on by reverting to his earlier question. So, what were you reckoning, Abdul?'

Before he could respond Carol interjected. 'Dr. Stone just asked him how many tins as we could store in that siphon tank of his.'

'It's not his fuckin' tank. It's the council's tank, and stop all this Doctor nonsense all the time. How can he be a doctor if he hasn't got a practice. Doctors don't work for the council.

It's all a load of baloney … .I ask you, fuckin' Doctor … Just call him Stone and be done with it'.

'For God's sake Skirker … !!'

Skirker said nothing further; things could get out of hand.

Abdul explained, 'He asked me how many units of food would fit in the tank, bearing in mind it's not just tins that are going in there. Bottles and jars and they of course have different volumes, so we need a ratio, a percentage, for tins and jars and bottles, to get a reasonably accurate figure and so …'

'See what I mean?! See what I mean?!' wailed Carol.

'I do but I also see what Abdul means.'

'No you bloody well don't Skirker, so don't pretend as you do.'

Lez looked from one to the other, this was new territory. Abdul just fingered a tin of peach slices in his hand.

'Yes I do Carol. Abdul's saying that what with bottles and whatever, everything's not the same size and …'

'I know that. D'you think as I'm that stupid as I don't know that?!

'No but …'

'But nothing. I tell you what Skirker, I've just about had enough of your prevaricating, because when it comes to it you don't know nothing.'

'Oh yes, and what do you know? I'll tell you what, you know nothing about nothing, at least not when it comes to sums.'

'Who does?' This from Irene who had sidled across on hearing the row. She was better enough now to sidle, although standing up and sitting down caused her to wince.

'Don't you get involved Irene.'

'She don't know enough to get involved' snapped Skirker.

'Who are you to say what I know and don't know? I know's a dam sight more than you realise. What you won't bloody well know is that I was a dab hand at sums when I was at school. Isn't that right Carol?'

'So you say, Irene, and I'll take your word for it.'

79

'You know bloody well as I was, all that squared paper, much better than lines. Yes ...'

It would all have trailed away, if Skirker had not interjected with, 'But what about rations, it's not just numbers Irene, it's rations and percentages, you got to reckon with those'.

Les raised his eyebrows and looked from one to the other.

'Ratios ... not rations ... you daft bugger!' murmured Carol.

'We did do those, It's just that I don't remember all the words. But yes, ratios, as you call them, we did those. But it's not the words but the numbers that count

'For Christ's sake Skirker, will you not be said!!' screamed Carol and that brought all matters to a grumpy, lumpy end.

Abdul, sullen and unhappy, he hated disturbances, made to leave but Carol grabbed him by the elbow and forced the tin of peaches in his hand. 'Have them Abdul', she insisted.

He seemed reluctant, at which Skirker grabbed hold of the tin and snapped, 'We'll all go in out of this pissing rain and share them.'

'One tin, between the five of us?' moaned Irene.

'Then I'll sort out another from the lean to. Yes? Get the ratio right ... One to one, eh Irene! Or should I say one upon one, which is the same whichever which way you do it.

Skirker, thought Carol, he was such a bloody chancer.

But Skirker had a point. At school his work had been dismal. Dismal in the sense you couldn't see through it, except perhaps by squinting. History, Geography, English even; he made marks on the paper, many marks but they didn't seem to add up to anything concise. Except that the general gist of what was written was ... dismal. He had come away with nothing, except fond wishes from relieved teachers at the end of it all. But it hadn't been the end of it all, because at the final assembly, everyone in his class got a small leaving prize, a book usually. But not Skirker. One after another his class mates went up onto the stage and got a free handshake and a book. But not Skirker. It had been an oversight, not a deliberate slight, a mistake surely but that only made it worse. He could have lived with the slight, championed it even, but to be forsaken by a mistake ... ! He would teach them all not to forget Skirker. He fumed, sitting, as all his class was, on the front row for the occasion, as Stryne, the head teacher, with his Punch (as in Punch and Judy) face, gave the ceremonial end of year speech. What a scrag-end morsel of aggravated humanity the man was with his waggled front tooth and parched eyes, his corrugated hands all a dither, giving the speech, wishing them 'all well in life's great adventure'. But he did have a voice that was varnished with authority, had to give him that. So too the rumoured reputation that he had once been in line to become a bishop, whatever that meant, other than prancing about in a fancy dress costume, but couldn't because he had threatened to kill his own cousin. Had he done so would have added greatly to his esteem in Skirker's eyes. As it was Stryne had to be satisfied with his wistful, yet powerful, voice and a name that somehow couldn't be used to conjure a suitable nickname. Stryne he was, always just Stryne.

Non of that registered at the moment with Skirker. Taut, his mouth set, his cheeks flexing with rage, he had concentrated on Stryne's hands, those long, thick dithery fingers clutching the brass eagle lectern, staining the polished brass with sweat. And then it came to him ... not to leave at the end of the day ... but to hide away until the caretaker had done his rounds, knocked out his pipe on the playground wall and left. Then, back into the hall, Skirker went, to give himself a prize beyond all ... the brass eagled lectern. It had no great weight but it was an encumbrance but what an unforgettable prize. It toppled into the two pieces that comprised it, the top part rolling in the gutter, making a distinctive clatter. But none in the street seemed to have cared to observe Skirker's demented errand. So, back to Carol's, where he had installed it, snuffled in sacking in the lean-to, behind the anvil and the piles of reinforcing bars that 'Fucking Funky' had been messing with until Skirker had driven him out, the both of them screaming with murderous intention and Funky, his scalp peeled off his skull, streaming blood.

But the brass eagle, that was a considerable prize, a vauntable trophy prize; trouble was it couldn't be triumphed. And what good is a triumph that cannot be proclaimed? And what is a more unfitting place for a brass eagled lectern than to be wrapped in sacking beneath a slither of reinforcing bars?

* * *

One thing that could be said with certainty about Abdul is that he was not in any way truculent which certainly could not be said for Skirker, Irene or even at times Carol. Abdul had been befriended by Skirker because he was vulnerable, Skirker could be generous in that way. It also has to be said, however, that Abdul was valuable. Vulnerable and valuable, an unbeatable combination and Abdul knew that if he ever was threatened with harm, he could always come to Skirker for help.

Abdul's vulnerability lay in the twin facts that he was a tall, thin, gawky youth with never much to say about himself but always wanting to oblige, and fact B, that he ran a small corner shop that sold bits of everything. He didn't own the shop, his uncle Wassif did, but it was Abdul who spent fifteen hours a day behind its wooden counter, peering and thinking, because there was only a spattering of regular trade. Wassif used the fact of small trade to justify the long opening hours, seven in the morning to ten at night. 'We have to make a living Abdul.' Wassif regularly insisted although he was rarely seen on the premises, usually only when he turned up in his rust scutted white van to summon Abdul to unload new stock. There was nothing regular about these deliveries, nor their content, but then that was the saving appeal of the shop, it sold bits of everything and it was rare that the occasional, enquiring customer would be turned away. The only skill that uncle Wassif had imparted to the young Abdul was that of engaging the customer, stimulating that customer's curiosity to such an extent that he, or she, eventually bought something. It might be out of curiosity, exhaustion or even desperation but Abdul very rarely failed to close a deal.

His success relied on the protean good nature of local folk from the nearby estate. 'Oh go on then, I'll try one, Abdul.' or, 'For fuck's sake Abdul, just one packet, and it had better work, or I'm bringing them back.' Wassif had taught his young nephew well, no denying that, but there was equally no denying that Abdul had a winning way and lovely eyes, even Irene would rapture on about his eyes and Carol often said she could give him a cuddle. Ironically it was only Skirker who would put his foot down and say 'no' as regards making a purchase. He could never really see the point of purchasing what could always, one way or another, be taken.

Abdul had been working the shop since he was fourteen, at least so Wassif said, though the fourteen was probably thirteen; he was a tall lad and could pass. Yes, of course there had been problems with the school; until he was fifteen his stints behind the counter had no regularity and as Wassif bellowed at the head teacher, at the governor's meeting, at the council's truant official, 'Abdul's never had a day off. He's a good lad and does his homework, always.' In this Wassif told a truth, the trouble was that he had so many part days off; if he completed two full days a week he was doing well. In the end, given the way of human nature, some sort of accommodation, vague and possibly illegal, was reached. Once a year Wassif would write a moderately generous cheque for the school sports fund; 'hush money' in a way, because the one area of education that Abdul completely avoided was sports, even uncle Wassif had no power in that department. On the one occasion when he had been pressed on to a football pitch he dramatically crashed to the floor if another player, of whatever team, came closer than a couple of feet.

At most other subjects his results were tolerable, even art, although his paintings seemed always to consist of a curiously complicated scribble. Well it was different and on more than one occasion a painting of his would be exhibited on the main corridor that ran alongside the assembly hall to the staffroom.

All in all, give or take, swings and roundabouts, so to speak, a tolerable arrangement had been agreed upon, although Wassif did curse and spit for a few days after writing the annual cheque. 'I shouldn't have to pay for your education Abdul, you know that, boy, it shouldn't have to happen.' Abdul said nothing.

And here is the curious fact, for the unwritten arrangement with the school, the turning of a blind eye to the gaps in his attendance, was due largely to that timetable being organised by Mr. Rockwell, his maths teacher.

Mr. Rockwell was in his last years at the school, he retired the year Abdul became sixteen. A pale stick of a man, his attire snuffed with chalk, he had an infinite patience with his students. If they could divide and multiply, that was an achievement. As for percentages, ratios, reciprocals, well they constituted an arcana of hieroglyphic absurdity for the most of them. Yes there was a maths class, even a higher maths class, but the proceedings and products were of a decidedly average nature. And it wasn't that Mr Rockwell was a bad teacher, he was not even a poor one, he tried various approaches to his subject, but they all failed. He was aged beyond endurance and his retirement at fifty five surprised no one; he could have passed for seventy five.

The one spark in the dense dreariness of his professional life-it was never known if he had a hobby- was Abdul. Here, at the end of his career, this sensible stalwart, who had by now been reduced to exclaiming formulae and their proofs repeatedly for rote learning, was treasure. What is more, treasure such as he had not witnessed in his entire career. Abdul was not just good at the subject, he excelled at it. He didn't just 'do' mathematics, he lived them.

Of course it was a forlorn hope, that Abdul would in any way realise his potential as a mathematician, they both understood this. As far as Mr Rockwell was concerned it was a waste, but in the nature of things, his own future had been blighted by the immediate need to earn a crust, after his first degree, teaching was to be his only option.

In the final year of his 'A' levels he been awarded a prize, a Cambridge University volume, with smart blue-black binding and gilt lettering on the spine, 'The Infinitesimal Calculus' and also in gilt, the university coat of arms. He had treasured the volume but hardly used it, the gilt covered guilt, he had not dared to mention that much of the material in the text book had already been covered in his Scholarship paper for the same university. Unused but treasured, much like the Shakespeare and Milton on his parents' sole bookshelf, it served only to denote an acquaintance with the right kind of learning. It was in good condition, its pages still crisp, and he passed it on to Abdul, who would never have the opportunity to study at 'A' level.

But Abdul ravished those thin pages, working through example after example in the long periods when he didn't have to rummage the shelves, or go hunting in the back, stockroom for whatever it was a customer wanted. He would mutter in a sing-song tone, 'I'm sure we have it', and usually he did, or something like it. Wassif's purchasing nous had to be admired and it was instilled in Abdul as securely as his experience of mathematics.

But the flittering of those thin, severe pages was almost complete within a couple of months of him leaving school for good. All the graded questions had been worked through, each arriving at the correct answer. So, when on an errand for his uncle, he bumped into Mr Rockwell, still in his same greyish green sports jacket, with leather patched elbows, pouting at the edges where the stitching had come undone, warm greetings were exchanged.

'Well, well, how are things with you Abdul?' he queried, though his tone was different, no longer that of the teacher, more that of a friend.

'I've finished the book you gave me, Mr Rockwell'

'Finished it …'

'Yes, Mr Rockwell, worked out all the examples.'

Rockwell was astounded, for every chapter there were dozens of problems, graded and the last few were really quite hard, even at university level. 'That's excellent Abdul, we must ...'

He was interrupted by Abdul, not meaning to be rude but effervescent with enthusiasm. 'I am setting myself some examples, very difficult mostly, at the moment I'm thinking of a solution of the integral of x to the x.'

Rockwell gulped, he had not come across this integral before, so simple but, a mere moment's reflection told him it would probably be absurdly difficult. Abdul's eyes blazed, sensing his former teacher's surprise and delight.

'And have you solved it?'

'Oh yes, nearly, I just have to ...'

'The explanation would have taken long and it was coming on to rain so Mr Rockwell promised he would call into the shop the following day and they would go through it together, tomorrow, because at the moment he was rather busy. This was true but he also wanted time to have a go at it himself, even though doubting he would make much of a fist at it ... the integral of x to the x. Indeed, that would be a puzzler.

They agreed and both looked forward to the promised session. But Mr Rockwell didn't call the next day, in fact the last Abdul saw of his befriending ex teacher, was him shouldering away from their chance encounter, alongside the wall, almost trotting as the rain began in earnest. A stroke stifled him the next day, a severe stroke because he got neither attention nor medical aid seeing as the stroke occurred while he was in the public library; he just sat slumped in a chair for several hours, until closing time in fact, and even then the ambulance took an age, as the saying goes.

Abdul did not know this, he was most upset that his teacher had not shown up, particularly as he had solved the simple but difficult integral sum. Strangely he didn't even think that perhaps he would turn up the next day, the next week even, surely that was possible. Not in Abdul's world. He carefully folded the three sheets of calculations and placed them in his wardrobe in his bedroom upstairs. Neither did he know that Mr Rockwell had died that next day. Never could he ever know that the reason Mr Rockwell was in the library was to borrow a couple of selected texts for Abdul's study: Matrix Algebra, Vector Analysis. He would teach Abdul new mathematics, there was more, far more than the curious intricacies of the Infinitesimal Calculus, far, far more. There was joy unbounded in his breast there was new … and then the slow slope of the face and the bubbling breathing as the stroke took its cruel course. Yes, there was a short article in the local paper, but Abdul didn't read papers, newspapers were one of the few common or garden commodities his shop did not sell.

Mr Rockwell, MA. Cantab had left behind two old but incredibly crumpled parents, who survived him for a few months and then went together, in short order. Their wedded life had never been quite reconciled to their academic son whose arrival as a squalling baby had inflicted a deep intrusion into their moderate life. Such is the way of things, though undoubtedly the Bard would have provided some finely tuned line to encapsulate the insanity of it all, but that line would be on a page in a book unopened on their bookshelf. Too late now anyway.

That day, when Mr Rockwell had hurried away with a promise to return, had been the day that the rains started, the unending rain, the rains that in an oblique way made Abdul's life easier. Wassif could not cope with the changing circumstances, his van loads of commodities and provisions became even more irregular, both quality and quantity diminishing. The last time, and it really was the last time, there were merely a dozen or so, sodden through boxes of children's sweets that had to be stacked in the entry, even though it ran with water. It was said that Wassif had taken to the mosque, forlorn in prayer, aching for faith. It never came, decades of plain and double dealing had expunged all faith from his being: no matter how much he craved, it wouldn't come. All in all it gave Abdul more time to work away at his mathematics. He set himself further problems, recognising that their complexity was a gift, it was as if he was been guided, led on, into some alternative but ultimate realm of existence … that of numbers. After all, what were they? Did they really exist? And if so, was it anywhere other than in the human brain? And why did they work to explain the physical universe? Surely numbers could not explain the nature of numbers … and if not … words, no that was impossible. What was needed was thoughts that had never been thought before … perhaps.

Chapter 9

'These, what are these Dublo!?' This was Madame Rasher, as she was for the time being to be addressed. She nodded at the cluttered barricade of metal framed chairs and tables, all interlocked together, preventing access above the fifth floor.

The thin, callow youth with pimples and a twisted suit, she had decided to name Dublo and he had accepted the appellation, but then, he had no choice. He wasn't going to argue with such a forceful personality.

Dublo because, well, Hornby Dublo, an electric model railway system that ran endlessly round in a futile circle: its appeal to boys and even to some men made such sense to her, given men's pathetic proclivities. Barry at least had not succumbed to the appeal of toy trains, not that she would have let him indulge had he so wished, but he didn't. And Dublo because without her ordering, his life would have been as equally senseless as the clickety-clackety toy train. Dublo was to be usefully purposed and he could wish for nothing more: they both knew it.

'They are chairs Madame.'

'And tables, all locked together. What for? And how far up the staircase do they go?'

'Council workmen put them there. I think they go up several flights, certainly to the eighth floor at least.'

'For god's sake why? How many floors are there?'

'Twenty,or thereabouts.

'Thereabouts?!'

'Well, it depends if you count the top floor as a floor, because it wasn't offices but a hospitality plaza-for the bigwigs, posh banquets, that sort of thing. Of course the chairs and tables would have been stuffed, all interlocked, right up to the top but we couldn't find sufficient to go that far, so, as I said, up to the 8th floor at least.

'But the purpose?!'

'To stop anyone coming down, they are a barrier and if anyone did try and come down, they'd have to disentangle that lot, it would be slow work and noisy, so we'd have plenty of warning.

She sniffed. Point one, if there was anybody 'up there' as you put it, they'd have come down as soon as you started erected the ...'

'Barricade, ma'am, we refer to it as a barricade.'

'Whatever, but who is it that would be up there wanting to come down?'

'Would that be your point two, Ma'am?'

For a fraction of a second she suspected him of sarcasm, but a hard stare and his reaction to the stare told her no, he may be functionally sound but when it came to purpose, he bordered on the imbecilic. It was a useful combination in a factotum.

'Answer my question, are we to suppose some marooned 'bigwigs' corpulent and sodden with drink would present an invasive threat?'

He gave an artless chuckle, then with a frown, added. 'You don't understand Ma'am'

Her look needed no words, so he did his best. 'Above the top floor, above the plaza suite is the roof and there is a staircase that leads up onto that roof. Now, I'm told that there was, well still is, for that matter, a helicopter pad on the roof. It has only been used once, when royalty came to officially open the council tower.'

She was interested but still perplexed, she stared hard into his shifting gaze, it did the trick and he explained further.

'The executive team thought that the billionaires would come from their mansions and attempt to seize control.'

'In helicopters, one at a time?!' Her incredulity was obvious. 'What for?'

'As I said, well as the 'Exec' said, to seize control of The Citadel'

There was no point in wasting more time listening to this blathering nonsense, she simply commanded him to get a team together to dismantle the barricade and to let her know when it was accomplished.

And he did; the willingness to obey gratified her. She would bring order but more than that was required. At first she watched the readily assembled team begin picking away at the interlocked tangle of chairs and tables, heard the scraping, saw the shaking of segments being prized free. Who were they, these attentive labourers? Workmen? Some perhaps but in the main they appeared to be white shirted office workers, eager possibly for some directed physical activity, freed from the push button slavery to their computers that were now quite useless. Who were they? What were they? these pale minions, so eager to collapse and dismantle a futile clutter of chairs and tables they had presumably entangled together in the first place? Clerkdom, that is how they would be specified. Clerkdom, the obeying force of Citadel. No, be careful … of Uniate.

She returned at intervals from her own labours, after all she was setting up a new order, to monitor the progress in dismantling the barricade of senseless clutter.. Progress was steady; as each new floor was cleared, together with a rather wistful Dublo, she strode along the dismal corridors, examining every empty room that led off those corridors, to happily discover … nothing! All had been emptied; the last orders of the municipality had obviously been carried out to the letter, even though the process was manifestly stupid. What had been gained? Nothing, there was not, nor ever going to be, a raiding party of billionaires' hit men, uniformed, masked, pointing guns, hurling stun grenades and barking orders, the clerks lined against the corridor walls hands held high, till at a single, syllabled order, they would be shot into quivering death throes in their sweat stained shirts.

Muriel paused this picture, her lips now tighter as she considered how easy it was to imagine how such a ridiculous scenario could become a belief. Ridiculous but how potent its working, for even now, as the teams, labouring around the clock to dismantle the futile assemblage, she witnessed their growing apprehension. Until finally there was an obvious fear in their faces, as the uppermost level was achieved and the blank doors to the banqueting suite were before them.

All stood back, it was not just their labours that caused the clerkdom workforce to back against the corridor walls, mouths gaping, panting but otherwise silent; it was fear.

She could admire the creative invention of some otherwise unknown managerial myrmidon who had invented this fable of helicoptered billionaires with armed henchmen, ready to slaughter all opposition. As a method of social control it was excellent. How easy the self validating imagery had flickered through her mind, imagery whose availability from once popular films constituted its power. Such similar devices for social control would probably be desperately needed, if the Uniate were to survive. For the nonce her power was all the greater for dismissing the myth. Good, but to hold power she would have to create her own myth: one that disentangling a clutter of tables and chairs couldn't destroy.

She ordered the doors to be opened. None moved. Fear ruled. She ordered again, not louder but sharper. Some quivered, a few moaned, some cried. If only a billionaire, with a military henchman had strode from behind those doors, they would all have fallen to the floor, grovelling and begging for a role to fulfil, something of rote, no matter how awful, that would give purpose to their doubt sullied minds. If such an apparition had stamped out of that banqueting suite and ordered them to kill her, they would have done so, at once. If an armed billionaire had ordered them to tear each other to pieces, till just one was left, bloodied and ravaged, but standing, ready to obey, it would have happened.

But nothing did happen. The still closed doors were blank pages before them. She said nothing but, looking at Dublo, clicked her fingers and pointed to the doors.

Dublo, now a quivering sliver, with fearful step, went to the door and ... knocked?! Nothing, he cast her a trembling look and then knocked again, louder but not with authoritarian conviction. Nothing happened, well of course not, there was nothing inside to happen. She waited a while longer, the ragged ranks of the workforce moved away from the walls, peering as she clicked her fingers again. This time Dublo gave a determined knock and stepped smartly back. Again nothing. Well of course. With sharp, even fierce motion and mien, she pushed the right hand door open, stepped inside and shut it after her.

Inside ... destitution ... raddled rubbish and ... could she believe it? a tottering ... carnival ... no, don't dwell on the insipid wasness of the gone municipality; to her purpose was how to create the new order. Uniate she had termed this new order, and if this top floor 'plaza' were to have a purpose, it would be one that she would designate.

Slowly ... languorously, she paced the littered floor. Inspiration would come. Her cruel heels crushed some slivers of glass, her potency was half glimpsed in fractured reflections in a ruined mirror. And yes, her head seemingly detached, her consciousness for the moment floating above the meaningless ruin of all things known, that name came to her again THE UNIATE !!!. It would have to be proclaimed, beyond the frail reach of question. And for that to succeed she would need confederates ... two, would do. With Dublo they would make three, equal but subservient, in complementary roles. They would rule, each in their own sphere, but she would reign ... reign over all, an ineffable presence, the source of ultimate authority: unquestionable. The numbers of survivors would diminish, that was unavoidable ... a new order can't be accomplished without slaughter, but slaughter to a purpose.

Afire with a bestowed authority, she returned to the landing corridor. There were gasps. She pointed her umbrella at them, its spike, unwavering at eye level, as she ranged it to and fro, until one, Dublo the factotum, dropped to his knees, slavering. The others, one or two at a time, but finally all of them, knelt, staring in supplication, awaiting the bestowing of her authority upon them.

'To you all here, who have cleared that formidable tangle of nonsense for me, who have allowed in me the transformation of meaning, have granted unto me control of the Uniate, I grant you citizenship. You are my disciples and through you, the Uniate, in its many ways shall protect and grant survival. Protect and survive in and through the sacred Uniate.

This last, her voice screeching, or was it screaming, was certainly ribbed with suppressed violence, cowed them all, Dublo included. Then, her arms held high, she turned went back through the awesome anonymity of those doors and slammed them after her. Dublo, in an effervescence of obedience, commanded them to, disperse but never despair. Which they did.

She did not have to wait for long before Dublo politely requested that she, 'consider a certain Inspector Stryne for elevation'

She regarded Dublo with a mixture of suspicion and satisfaction. She was as yet uneasy with his impertinent ability to assume he had the qualities necessary to discern who could be considered for high office in The Uniate He was just a factotum after all, his role being designed as one to carry out her instructions, to investigate and report back but only to ever implement her instructions. But here he was, requesting she give this Inspector Stryne an interview. What authority did Dublo have that he had the effrontery to even make such a suggestion?

As an answer to that inner question she thought about Barry. She had neither curiosity nor concern as to his whereabouts but she did recognise the dogged duty he had when it came maintaining a system. Presumably Barry's subservient quality was attached to the numerical systems of production control, it gave him his raison d'etre as a human being. But in Dublo's case, there was no obvious answer and that gave a twinge of concern. But why? He fawned at the feet of her manifest authority, at the mystery of its transcendental nature. Without her, he was nothing, just an item in the swill of human affairs. But yes, if things worked out as she intended, she could formalise his authority. He would be elevated to the rank of Secretary General, an official title that had a right sounding ring about it, a certain familiarity even. It suggested power and subservience in equal measure. By such oblique reasoning, she decided to take his advice and interview this Stryne fellow, whoever he was.

All this flickered through her mind even as she beckoned for this 'Inspector' Stryne to be brought before her. Inspector of what? Well she would decide that. He entered with a curious shambling gait, staring about with an indifferent gaze. What she saw did not inspire. He was a short, round shouldered figure, the very stutter of a man, unable, it seemed to even stand upright. There was a curvature of the spine and the narrow shoulders were rounded. He wore a uniform, of sorts, but it failed to impress, nothing was denoted by its shabby, ill fitting tunic. His face was concave, both laterally and vertically, which meant that he had a pointed chin and an upward tapering brow. Ensconced in such concavity were slitty eyes, of indeterminate colour, a sharp nose and a narrow mouth full of little teeth, one of which was prominent, over sized and discoloured. It protruded, that tooth, it indented his lower lip. His breathing was a constant sniffing. What on earth could he offer The Uniate, this little Punch puppet of a man?

'You need to explain …' she began, and the creature, for this was what she conceived him to be, approached a step or so towards her, scraping his one boot across the floor as he did so. For heaven's sake, snarled the thought, not only is he little more than a dwarf, he is a cripple!

He gave her an oration in measured tones.

' Existence, in and of itself is valued as nothing. Endurance is the quality that can give existence meaning, an overcoming. In these challenging times, it is endurance that must be chanelled to a purpose. It only needs a minority to survive, but that minority needs endurance to give it focus. Direction is needed, a direction that only the highest authority of a small but unified hierarchy can bestow. In other words, yourself, Madame Rasher. But the fact needs belief. No society has ever existed without religious belief of some sort to bind it together. But don't worry, no society has ever existed that follows that religious belief, not in the gross generality at least. But our present task will be task to convince the ranks that they are directed by a powerful hierarchy, one that is manifestly ordained in a spiritual purpose. To do that we need a new religion and I can provide just that. I will proclaim a religion for our new order. We will endure in life's long journey.'

There was deception even in his sincerity, deviancy in his authority. She recognised that, she could see through him, but knew that others would not. She realised his vision would be a stifling nullity, but he would make 'the ranks' believe in its reality to the point of devotion … abject, unthinking devotion. And that voice, it caressed authority. His tone somehow commanded attention. He would have them transfixed, mesmerised and frustrated, like a dog looking for a ball trapped under the sofa; wanting but unable to achieve its stated goal. Ideal. Yes, and all this from what she would describe as a 'diminutive cripple' with a reassuring scrape of a voice. Well why not? If he could come up with the goods, and she could well believe that he would … so yes; in a sour way, he fascinated.

He interrupted the pace of her thinking, thought tripping over notion, ideas intermingled with plans by shovelling his spread palms into the space before him and abruptly announcing, 'We need a religion, a religion of the new elect, a religion that bestows authority upon The Uniate itself, a religion of faith that bestows reward.'

Dublo interrupted this 'Inspector' Stryne with a pertinent question. 'And what is this church to be called?' and then added before anyone could catch their breath, 'Surely not a Christian church, that saviour as long dropped off his cross.'

Stryne took a deep breath, regarded them both, a knowing sneer slid across his concave face, 'Not Christian but Christophanic.'

Muriel smirked, the word was good, it had hints of both familiarity and difference. She liked it.

'Christophanic?' queried Dublo.

'The First Uniate Christophanic Kingdom!!' He snarled in such an insistent tone, his arms spread wide and high, as if he himself were a newly crucified martyr.

'Yes!'Madame Rasher intoned, that's it. First Uniate' … it had a certain familiarity … and there had been Methodist breakaways … 'New Connection' and 'Ebenezer', she had sort of been aware of them, on chapels in Wales. First Uniate … yes and Christophanic … an overall process … a dispensation. And Kingdom, hadn't there been a Kingdom Hall somewhere in town, signed up on a large tiled facade of a once cinema?

'But it spells …' Dublo began in a complaining tone.

'Shut up Dublo, it spells perfection of purpose' and she repeated the new appellation with wonder, 'First Uniate Christophanic Kingdom' so exactly right.

That was settled then and Stryne vowed he would make it his mission to immediately begin the construction of the church, although what this entailed was uncertain. Nevertheless he demanded and was given the keys to the cathedral: immediate and sole possession, in which to begin his work, his mission, his vision.

And then there was Stent: Colin Arthur Stent, to give him his full name. Known simply as 'Coll' to his few confederates, who loafed about the venues where he was invariably to be found, watching, sniffing and waiting. Stent was a huge oaf who felt himself, in some obscure way, to have become inferior to Clerkdom. They had a blind method that gave them purpose within the new order. And he craved purpose … designated purpose that is. But his particular aptitude for physical violence had not been rewarded, not even recognised. He despised them, the Clerkdom, for their enthusiastic servitude whereas he still had nothing but a vicious disgruntlement and no one to turn his violence upon. And now, this emerging elite that seemed to think it was in control of Citadel and of whom Dublo, who was becoming the foremost exemplar, had ignored him. He fantasised about taking Dublo into an empty room and beating him to a pulp.. How could such a slimy sliver of a man gain authority? How could anyone be wary of Dublo? But there were many who were, seeing as he was protected by his own appointed team of clerical over staff that he was busily selecting. And they jointly exercised an air of authority, issuing commands with the sharp expectation that those commands would be obeyed. And of course Clerkdom loved to obey. Whatever the staircase to authority, Stent had not as yet even put his boot on the bottommost step. He could not fawn, bow or scrape before power. So he had become an irrelevance, a 'loafing oaf'. All that could be said was that there none who would dare confront him in word or deed.

He was such a large man with wide shoulders and brutish hands that were not made for work unless destruction was the purpose of the work. But there was no destruction to be carried out in Citadel, it was all a question of salvaging and reconstruction. Anything that could not fit into that category was best left alone to dribble into oblivion but it wasn't being destroyed, not as a deliberate act, just left to waste away and that was so very wrong. And then consider, how many there were, such as the likes of Harold and Hector, each nothing but a bag of bones that ought to be crumpled up straight away. They could never serve anything. A cadre of street warriors would dispense with them up some back alley in a matter of minutes. And as for that litter down the Dingley Dell, they were, for the moment, too far from Citadel, ignorant of the growing power of The Uniate and so irrelevant … for the time being at least.

It was clear to Stent that violence had to be inflicted on identifiable targets that could be labelled as being destructive to the higher purpose of The Uniate. If it was to flourish … it had to crush. That much was obvious and he heaved the large spread of chest and shoulders in frustration. His narrow head, and it was very narrow indeed, was supported on a long, thick throat, that would suddenly flare bright pink when he was angered, as he was now, pacing the confined limits of a small yard. And the face surmounting that throat? Well it was small featured: tiny, darting eyes, snub, flat nose, frequently smeared with a quivering bulb of snot, and a glisten of fat pouting lips.

As to his uniform, well it wasn't exactly a uniform, not as such: combat fatigues that designated a notion of armed force, a khaki neck scarf and scuffed boots. He had worn the same for years, loitering about, shouting the odds, fag in his mouth, can of beer in his hand. He had a formidable local notoriety; few ever argued with him and those that did soon regretted it.

But it was one of those curious coincidences, with which life abounds, that Stent was rescued from his self destructive vortex by the very apex of his hatred, Dublo himself. He had occasioned upon Stent in the process of kicking another man to the floor, clearly intending worse, and had intervened. He'd been on his way back from Central Stores with a box of whistles. Mr Horncastle, who ran the department, had rustled up a few dozen for him: he was a treasure in that way. Dublo had discerned there would be an authoritarian purpose for them, in the right hands, to summon control; their tone was so harsh and shrill, it couldn't be ignored. And here was just such a situation, he took a whistle from the box and blew it long and loud. It had been many years since such had been heard in Citadel and all manner of pale faces now peered from several quarters. More to the point, Stent, having the piercing sound emitted close to the small crumple of his right ear, turned from his ruthlessly damaged victim and made for Dublo with dangerous intentions. Dublo made to blow the whistle again, but gasping with fear, the sound emitting from the instrument was not a fiercely high pitched shriek but a flutter of notes that surprisingly gave Stent a momentary pause. So Dublo, all of a tremble, seized the moment and gave Stent the whistle.

Stent was astounded, not too strong a word. He took it with a snarl but kept it tight in his hand. And from that moment it was a case of one thing leading to another.

There would need to be patrolling squads of a streetwise force to keep discipline. Citadel could not afford to dissipate its citizenry; the Uniate needed to be seen to be a functioning entity.

Handing the whistle over and explaining its purpose, Dublo received a snarling laugh. 'We'll need more than one.'

'We?'

'You're going to need a group of us, patrolling all the time.'

'A group?' This in a musing tone. And then, things fell into place. 'You mean a squad of you?'

'That'll be the size of it. Several squads, patrolling all over, all the time, a whole ruck of us. We've got to keep things tight.'

Dublo thought, gave this unwholesome brute a chuckle and told him to call at his office the next morning, promising to set up something along those lines. Stent said he would think about it but held on to the whistle. That was when Dublo knew he had him.

And that was when Stent knew he had a mission.

So was born that fearsome, street patrolling body that came to be known as 'The Stompi.'

Stryne naturally loathed Stent who let it be known that the feeling was reciprocated, but both had to recognise they needed each other, and that in fact it was only through the interaction of their two organisational bodies that The Uniate was stabilised. This was due to a singular circumstance, the discovery, or rather observation, by one of Stent's marauding patrols, that the Gawpers may well be dead to all intent and purpose, but the fact was they did not rot.

Stryne recognised the importance of this fact and organised his own patrols to cruise the suburbs, to 'harvest' the Gawpers and bring them to Citadel, to the cathedral. His own cadre of helpers, dedicated to the witness of the Christophanic Mission, men, soon to be referred to simply as 'The Christies' were protected by groups of the 'The Stompies'. Christies and Stompies between them ruled the streets and squares and outward domain of the Uniate. Meanwhile the ranks of Clerkdom always busy at their replicatory tasks, reviewing and storing documents, were kept safe. On occasion they would look out of their office windows and see Gawpers, bent neat, folded into wheel barrows being trundled to the cathedral, where they were unfolded and installed in the balconies and aisles, standing, and of course gawping, down the nave. A witnessing of the saints, as Stryne had once muttered.

Muriel, previously chapel, was having none of that nonsense about saints, 'The Resurected', she had purred, to which Stryne replied, 'The Resurectibles' and Muriel conceded, the term suggested process and process was all.

And so it was accomplished; Uniate was comprised of Stompi, Christie and Clerkdom … a triumvirate. Dublo controlled the pavilions of Clerkdom-offices and despatch bays and, most important of all, Central Stores, under the purview of the redoubtable, Mr Horncastle, who seemed to be able to provide whatever it was that the Uniate needed, in particular uniforms for both Christie and Stompi … boots and badges, belts and buckles and whatever other paraphernalia was required.

The Uniate as a Triumvirate? Not quite so because overall still reigned the sole fascinating persona of Muriel, except she was henceforth no longer to be known by that name, not even as Madame Rasher, all too … domestic. Stryne had suggested, in a reverential tone, that her appellation should be …. Astarte? No, not quite but, Astartobe, she had responded and such was her undisputed authority, so it was.

The annunciation, in a crowded cathedral, the nave thronged with kneeling Clerkdom, and rows of the uniformed forces of Christies and Stompis standing to attention, the balcony and aisles packed with ever still Gawpers, was a culminating success. Muriel-Astartobe dressed for the occasion in a wrap about glass bead curtain and little else, emphasised the ethereality of the occasion. She had found the glass bead curtain in amongst the detritus in the Plaza Suite, the senior managerial entertainment suite on the top floor of the building. She alone had dared to enter, fear of 'lurking billionaires' had kept the rest out. In reality it was a fear of what they did not know, but it took the form of avenging billionaires; fear has to have a face if hatred is to get to work. Hence that fear which she had been seen to have manifestly overcome' strengthened her growing authority. She now resided beyond those closed doors.

And behind them, well what a palaver of stuff there was in there, and amongst the detritus a glass bead curtain had lain in a glitterscratched pile which she easily fashioned into a wrap around glass bead robe. It was all glimmer and shimmer and tinkle as she moved. And so, entrancing to her following of simpering clerks, she gave, not a speech but rather an incantation, beginning low but soon rising to a sustained screech, in which she lavished hatred upon all and everything that was not Uniate. She imaged the Uniate as a transcendent mothering and played out the warning that there would be, beyond the realm of Citadel, forces that would seek to destroy Uniate. And these were to be expunged. Affirmative sighs from the Christies and guttural snarls from the Stompies at this point as the virulence of her hatred was communicated into them as a lascivious trembling, inciting all with a devout sense of mission. All culminated in bursts of hurrahs and applause as she hoisted her umbrella high, the virulence of the action parting the glamour-shimmer of her glass bead threads to reveal a cleaving acreage of white thigh and black topped stocking. And what else but that ever uncovered by the Venus of Willendorf of course, her black matted cunt. At the end of the fervour, watching as they all filed out, Stryne noted, that when she bent to gather up some of the glass beads that had fallen from her gown, she had the arse of an Artemis. No, of the Godess Pomona, goddess of Easter, with a curled knife in her hand. Oh, the toxic delight that raddled his loins.

Chapter 10

'Oh dear' Harold muttered, to himself, as he pootled past the turning into Barry and Muriel's avenue. He was making his way, unaided, to the path down into the Dingley Dell, hoping to find Skirker. He was hoping Skirker would be able to supply him with a fresh batch of his waterworks tablets. He hadn't run out of them yet but could clearly envisage a time when they wouldn't be available at all and then he'd be bent, in pain, wincing and cursing every time he thought he wanted a pee but couldn't, except in dribbles and him wincing for hours at a time.

Until the other day there was no way that he would not have called in on Barry en route. But now, well no: the blether was still rancid, his fault, he should never have told Barry the history of Muriel's misdemeanours, particularly the doings with Preacher Lurgan. He wished he had held his tongue, too late now, perhaps in a few days time, let things cool down a bit, hopefully things would heal. As it was, descending the steep, swollen path down into the Dell, now swimming with waters from the gushing torrent the little brook had become, was decidedly tricky. Keeping his balance while having to wade ankle deep through welts of mud was difficult, particularly as he was no longer fleet of foot. He muttered aloud some sort of stammered exculpation for what he had said to Barry and as he did so, his breath whistled through the rattle of his false teeth. No matter, press on, he was determined, decidedly determined, to complete the descent because … well because there was nothing else to do. His map- cum chart project was completed, mounted and displayed and until another project of comparable magnitude arose all he was left with was his contrition towards his nephew. How long could Barry take the hump? Well not more than a few days, surely.

At one point, about half way down, there was a shoulder of the bank that was still above the unaccustomed torrent and he sat down, soddening his trousers as he did so but calming his breath and easing the ache in his spindly legs. Scraping his heel in the earth, just like a child, he created a slippage of mud that eased itself into the torrent to reveal a fossil. He bent wincing and muttered aloud, 'Fancy that!' It was clearly the fossil of a dinosaur, Cretaceous not Jurassic, about the size of a turkey, with only slightly diminished front limbs and, as they all had, a great beakfull of teeth. Small but nasty if you came across it … not that a human ever could have done of course … but then imagination takes one to such places; it would probably have bundled about in the likes of these very bushes that now surrounded him, lurking, ready to snap the calves out of the legs of anything that happened to pass before scuttling away, waiting for the injured party to weaken before it closed in and began to eat into the softness of its prey's tender stomach. Life wasn't easy in those days but it had to be said, it wasn't that easy in these present times, when you couldn't just go to the doctor's and get a prescription. He was only too glad that Alice had not had to face the dilemmas and strictures of this rainy season: she would never have survived.

Fortified at last, he continued his descent. The most perilous part had been accomplished, the gradient now eased and within the quarter hour he could discern Carol's house, and then Carol herself, who was clearly having a set to with Skirker, who was waving some sort of metal contraption about in a long handled pair of metal pliers; the contraption was red hot. A row with Carol, surely not; but then folks on the estate did have the occasional, violent altercation, but then they did make up and forget. They did not let matters fester like nephew Barry may well do. And, yes, funny the circularity things can take, because as he approached closer, Harold heard Lurgan's name being bellowed. Funky Lurgan to give him his full name, at least down on the estate. Or just Funky to Carol, who did not seem to be in the least perturbed by the still red hot metal contraption being waved about in front of her face.

'Oh, aye up, we've got company.' This came from Irene, sitting on the garden bench on Carol's front lawn alongside Dr. Stone who just frowned.

Harold made a sort of beckoning noise and collapsed on Carol's garden wall.

'What do you want?!' demanded Skirker, lowering the metal contraption, it was losing its glow but still spitting in the rain.

'See what I mean … jumping to conclusions, there's no need to talk to him like that.' snapped Carol.

'I know you, you'm from up top aren't you.'

'Seeing as he's come down from there that seems bloody obvious Irene.' Carol's annoyance with Skirker was being transferred to her friend.

'Don't get mardy with me Carol, just because …'

'Because Skirker's got this mad notion about Funky.'

'Notion! It's no bloody notion, Irene, he's set on killing him. That's what!!

Irene harrumphed. 'Well we already knew that. Fat chance he's got of doing anything about it, seeing as Funky's not lived around these parts for some time now.'

Skirker cast the metal contraption aside and leant towards Irene, his brow so crinkled that it was illegible, to snort that he knew that Funky was back in the area. 'He's living amongst the Fenris people and he's got my Liz with him!'

'Fenris folk, don't make me laugh.' snorted Carol, What do you know about them, eh?'

'Enough. I keep my ears to the ground.'

'Enough is never enough though is it Skirker. You abide by Carol and let all this nonsense about Funky go. Fenris Folk! And you've never set eye on ne'er a one of them. It's all baloney if you ask me. Funky's well gone by now, there's nothing as would bring him back here; or her, come to that. He's got Liz under his control and we won't ask what he's doing with her, cos it probably doesn't bear thinking about, but that's the fact of the matter and you'll just have to live with it. We'm all blood, the lot of us and there's nothing you can even hope to do about that. So put that sodding hook down and let it cool off.'

'I have Irene, it's on the floor, hardening.'

'We'll see' grumped Irene.

'Yes we will. Now be said Skirker and have done with it.' So saying Carol went and sat on the wall beside Harold.

Irene, not quite willing to let things settle just yet, turned to Doctor Stone and asked if he had ever heard or even seen anything of these so called 'Fenris Folk'

'Nobody has!' snapped Carol.

'None of us have, no, but Doctor Stone may have, seeing as how he gets about with his construction work.'

'Have you?' ventured Carol.

'Never.' said Stone and that was that.

Skirker frowned, sighed and sat down beside Harold. 'I didn't mean no harm Harold, it's just that you caught us at a funny time.'

'Everything's a funny time with you these days, Skirker, and no messin'.'

'Yes, and you know why don't you Irene, because he's been workin' his arse off for all of us for weeks, getting supplies, so many bottles and tins as we don't know where to put 'em all and now that supply has run out, everything's barren: shops, stores, whatever. There's no more of anymore. He's cared for us but time goes on and the tins are limited, so, not to put too fine a point on it ... .'

'And that's why Dr Stone's here to help.'

'Help yes, but with storage, not supply.'

'Bloody hell Carol, look a gift horse why don't you!'

'I'm not looking a gift horse at all. And yes, thank you Dr Stone, but that tank is storage and just that. We are going to need more supply.'

'At times there's no doing with you Carol.'

'Look, as I said, thank you Dr Stone. I appreciate what

you've done, what you are doing, I really do, if it's only to get that lean-to cleared.'

'So Skirker can use Funky's old forge again.'

'He's already used it.'

'Not to make anything useful, I mean a claw to rip Funky's head off. I ask you. That's not going to help anyone.'

'And that's never going to happen, not even if Funky did show up here, which he won't.'

'You hope not.'

'Shall we just give it a rest, Irene ... Shall we?

Skirker spat and then chortled as Harold explained the purpose of his visit, in muffled tones and in a circumlocutory purpose, as he found the condition rather embarrassing to speak of in front of ladies.

'Don't you worry,' chortled Irene, 'most men have difficulty having a proper waz when they gets to your age.'

' I'll see what I can do, I'll have a look in a moment.'

They all stopped talking when Lez appeared on the scene, distinctive in bright yellow waterproofs and a souwester

'You'm wasting yer time with that clobber, you'll get soaked in that tank whatever you'm wearing.' Irene proclaimed.

'Not if we empty the tank first, which is the plan.' This from Dr Stone who winced his bulk to his feet and motioned for Lez to follow him to the tank.

'There you go Irene.' chuckled Skirker, 'empty the tank first' attempting to imitate Stone and then, muttering, 'As if you'd try and get into it when it was full of water.' Then he spat on his brutally forged claw to see if it was still hot. It was, it hissed and nobody said anything, they just sat and moped until they heard Stone and Lez returning, Lez carrying a plastic tray loaded with a variety of tins and jars, the heavy rain making a distinctive sound as it hammered against Lez's Sou'wester. Irene frowned but it was Carol who summoned them all together, saying that there was no point in trying to sit out the downpour on the garden wall and it would be better if they crammed into her lounge and had a bite to eat. Perhaps, she hoped, this would ease the cross currents of tension flowing between them.

'And you can bring that claw thing inside, if it's cooled off.'

'I'll bring it in anyway.' snarled Skirker.

'Not if it's going to make scorch marks on the carpet, you bloody well won't Skirker.'

Skirker sniffed adding, 'Of course it's cooled off, yer daft wammel.' and entered the house, the rest following. It was a bit of a squeeze, what with Irene and Dr Stone occupying most of the sofa, Harold had to squeeze himself in at the end because there was no way Skirker would sit next to Stone … he never used the honorific, he didn't take to him, didn't trust him and it annoyed him even further seeing as Irene was clearly going doo- lally tap over him, now they had 'got it together', as the saying goes. Only the other night when he was returning from one of his forays, he'd heard the sound of Irene whimpering as they were obviously hammering away at it. He recognised the sound and guessed that Irene would be on top of Stone, scratting at his head as she wimpered, her pillow- big knees quivering. Well best of luck to her but Stone was not a good choice. He wasn't to be trusted, not to Skirker's way of reckoning. He knew too much and said too little. And when he did speak, it was as if he was telling you something you should know but, as far as he was concerned, you clearly didn't.

But it was because of Stone that they were all assembled … it was because of Stone they had to do as he told them, well Lez and Skirker, certainly, because without his guidance, the huge siphon tank was useless.

The point was that it was not locked: any fucker could creep along at night and help himself. The point was that it could only be locked with a special spigot key. The point then was that the special spigot key could only be obtained from Mr Horncastle at Central Stores, which could only be accomplished if Lez and Skirker accompany Stone to Central Stores to countersign for the release of the key and the promise of its return later. Stone had the necessary authority but it needed other signatures for him to be able to take the spigot key to the tank, load it up and then take it back, once it had been used to close the siphon tank. But then what? What was the point if it was closed, how could they then get food out when they needed it?! Well, Skirker would see about that. He knew precisely what had to be done, hence his practice with the forge and the making of a scalp cleaving hook.

Carol handed him a tin of baked beans, Irene and Stone slithered sardines from a tin into each other's mouths and Harold, being a guest, so to speak, was given a choice and had feverishly taken a jar of Marmite. He muttered incoherent words of delight as he fingered it into his mouth; clearly he had never expected to dine on the stuff again.

With the mastications concluded, Stone got to his feet and said it was better they make tracks. Harold, with one cheek rimed with Marmite asked if he could come along but Stone, in no uncertain term said, no, because he would never manage the gravel.

'What gravel?' demanded Skirker.

'You'll see.' Was the terse reply. He stamped his boots, Irene gave his thigh a squeeze and Lez was already at the door. With a few murmured grunts they set off and it was Carol, Irene and Harold as were left to themselves.

The journey certainly took some time. Silently, because Lez never spoke and because Skirker was not of a mind to, they galumphed along some sort of track, each wrapped in his own thoughts.

And what thoughts they were; Skirker was becoming, not saddened but … well absented from the world this unfamiliar domain presented. Oh, he knew where they were alright, off Boundary Way and turning into Prospect Road … but there were few distinct markers to give the game away. Prospect Road! Well there was a prospect right enough but not that that the road namers in the last century had in mind. Then and until recently the prospect had been one of large factory sheds, strips of housing and haulage depots and garages laid back from the road. Now, well some of such was just about discernible, the factory sheds stood aloof certainly, but the rest was smothered in that evermore familiar amalgam of Cess and Thorn, mingled together, mutually supportive, into billowing clumps of spiked, brown entanglements dripping huge brown slobs. It was not just that they were obscuring almost everything but that they were clearly all but impassable. It was only by the narrowest of zig- zag ways they managed to slowly proceed, Skirker scowled all the more as he realised they were totally at Stone's mercy. Should he decide to leave them … . but then why would he do that? They needed the spigot key; it was the means, not just to their present condition but to their very survival.

As they tortuously progressed, Skirker realised that the morass of Cess and Thorn they were travelling beneath was beginning to dissolve any thought of purpose, any scheme of human intent … it was dissolving his very awareness of who he was and what he was about. He was even beginning to forget about Funky … well not forget but to lose his imaginative picture of his wicked father He didn't panic but narrowed his purpose to a sharp blade of unquestionable determination … one foot in front of another. Don't think, just know yourself to be. I am, he thought muttered to himself. Skirker am I called … .Skirker I am!

It must have been another hour or so before Stone stopped and announced, 'We're here and now the hard work begins.' And so it did because before them abruptly the cruel foliage stopped and they were confronted with a grey wall … of gravel.

'Up there?' snorted Skirker, although his tone suggested its own answer. Lez slapped his arms against his sou'wester but followed Stone, as did Skirker, there was nothing else for it.

With every step forward they slid more than half a step backwards. And they were thigh deep. Hands and arms were useless. Stone had a method, he had obviously done this before, he swung his thighs and shoulders with every step and every step was partly sideways, while all the time his hands were clutched at the back of his neck. It was clearly a method so both Les and Skirker silently adopted the same technique. Painful and exhausting as it was, it worked better; far better than mere plundering about in irregular steps. Even so it took more than hour to reach the shifting top, by which time they were all of a welter of sweat, ache and raw breathlessness.

Some uniformed guards approached at a trot. They had dustbin lids strapped to their feet and carried spades, which were not implements of aggression but tools, because here and there, beyond and about, could be heard the distinctive sound of gravel being shovelled. Such a clean sound, it came as a sort of relief to all three of them, still ragged with strenuous breathing. Had the spade bearing guards been intent on aggression, none of them could have offered any meaningful resistance.

Stone shouted some words and pointed to the insignia on his high viz. They stopped, waiting till all three of them had got to their level and stared, not aggressive but wary. Skirker was very uneasy, this was his first confrontation with Stompis, albeit a particular troop known as Shovel Stompis. His travels had not taken him into Citadel, although this place was not Citadel, it was related, it was adjacent, an adjunct sharing a mutual purpose. Clearly, because now he could see that there were several platoons, all about, furiously pushing wheelbarrows of gravel and emptying them at the top of the gravel cliff they had just climbed. Barry would have marvelled at the sight of it all: regular trips, those with shovels spreading out the load from the tipped up barrows, a continuous chain, skill and speed in action. But, Skirker wondered, where had all the gravel come from? And then he got his bearings, from way beyond the aloof factory sheds in the distance, over a dozen of them he could make out, lay the old gravel quarry, long left derelict (although could a quarry ever be other than derelict?) but now purposed back into use. Its gravel had been mined into piles that were loaded into lines of wheel barrows then wheeled to this periphery and tipped, suffocating the Cess and Thorn as it advanced and also providing an impregnable defence at the same time. Yes they had climbed up the gravel face but would have been at the mercy of those shovels had not Stone bellowed out some authority that they recognised. Even a weak guard detail could have dispatched them, paling them about the head with their shovels.

Walking, still unsteady and weary, they gained the firm security of a concrete apron that ran the length of a long shed that housed Central Stores. A fresh detail of Stompis cross questioned Stone, one of them fingering Lez's souwester with curiosity while a couple pointed to Skirker's lettered brow and muttered. He had no idea of course of its apparent significance to them but they did keep their distance. An officer, he certainly must have been such because there were coloured shoulder flashes on his uniform, escorted them into the shed, into the dim, echoing entrails of Central Stores and to its master Mr Hornchurch.

A long, zinc-sheeted bench ... behind an array of pigeonholes, behind them a dim recess of storage space organised, not littered, with dozens of various implements: pick axes, rakes, spades and such like, all tagged and tied in bundles.

After a while Mr Hornchurch arrived, a tall but awkward shape, he wore a cowgown and a peaked, flat cap. The peak was shiny with grime, the cowgown daubed with industrial filth, oil mostly, judging by the smell, but the most alarming feature of Mr Hornchurch, was his glasses; thick obscuring lenses, the frames held together with torn strips of black tape and sitting at an angle, clamped to his twisted nose and anchored to his enormous ears, forested with hairs, by elastic bands.. It was obvious he was all but blind because when he picked up some implement from the zinc plated bench, he scrutinised it by holding it up to his glass lenses, screwing his face severely, so much so that saliva drivelled down his chin, before handing it to an assistant, muttering some number. The assistant then took the implement and scuttled away to place it in its correct storage pigeon hole or bin..

'Mr Hornchurch ... Sir.' intoned Stone.

Mr Hornchurch frowned, screwed his face about and growled ... Dr. Stone?

'Indeed', Stone replied.

'And what is it this time?' He sniffed, judiciously, adding, 'It has been registered that your flood relief project has been finished.'

'Finished it is, complete though, it is yet to be, because, as regards the siphon tank we stand in need of a spigot key'

Skirker was perplexed, Stone's tone was confident enough but there was a note of subservience. Was this grubby old lubber with jam jar glasses of any significance? Hornchurch's response satisfied that query, at least in part.

'A spigot key!!!' he bellowed. The interior of the stores building echoed his volume and grey faced diminutive Clerklets peered down the aisle at the redoubtable Hornchurch, their master and teacher of the so many of the intricacies of store keeping and docket recording. Repeated echoes proclaimed both the volume of his ejaculative response and its tone, a blend of disbelief and outrage, declining to a distinct murmuration throughout the long depths behind them..

'We can't test the efficacy of the syphon tank without its spigot key.' Stone was reduced to explaining, 'To ensure that we can fill it, empty it, or adjust its levels.'

Hornchurch leant across the zinc plated counter, thumping it with his fist, as he hammered out, word by word, 'Dr Stone I do understand the functions of a spigot key, there is no need to explain its purpose, and yes we will have such an implement. It will be fetched for you but understand this, it will only be for a day. We only have one such item in Central stores, only one mind you, that making it, by my reckoning at least, unique. So you will return it by this time tomorrow and no later. Understood?!

'That goes without saying, Mr Hornchurch.' Dr Stone's attempt at jocularity betrayed a definite wariness. Skirker was perplexed.

'The Spigot Key!' he shouted defiantly and what one could possibly imagine to be a smile, betrayed by a puckered rupture of his mouth, adorned Hornchurch's face. He hummed and then while waiting, leaned across the counter and whispered hoarsely, 'And I would suggest that when you return the spigot key, tomorrow, you come via Citadel and the main entrance, so much the better if you do. So much better all round, if you see what I mean.'

'Indeed, Mr Hornchurch. We came this way in order to get the measure of your gravel barricade and very impressive it is sir. And as for the spigot key, I will probably test it later today and it will be back with you first thing tomorrow morning.

'No!', snapped Skirker. 'It will be tested at regular intervals, to ensure it will work at different levels. After all if there is only one spigot, we have to be certain … that it works under all pressures and conditions.'

Hornchurch buried his elbows into his sides, shook and growled. 'Point One, it is a Spigot Key … not just a spigot. Point Two, your junior's perspicacity does him justice Dr Stone, because we don't want somebody turning up at every verse end demanding the lease of The Spigot Key, now do we?!'

A junior Clerklet, face down, brow furrowed, appeared from within the array of storage shelves with an implement cradled in his arms. He had been trained in this fashion of portage, there being less likelihood of dropage thereby and although the spigot was metal, on the hard concrete store floor, a minor dent could well have been inflicted.

Stone reached out to take it but Hornchurch's arm intervened. 'Sign for it!'

This was effected by a thumb being pressed against a wetted pad and then transferred to a blank sheet of paper that had been ripped free from a memo pad, which was then impaled on a spike. Meanwhile the Clerklet stroked Les's Souwester, murmuring 'nice, nice' as he did so. Lez kept moving aside step at a time towards Skirker but Hornchurch snapped for his trainee storekeeper to desist and keep his distance.

All secured, they left the dismal far reaches of General stores and crossed the apron, this time with Skirker taking a closer look at what was displayed on the long reach of the concrete apron; he could see distant lines of factory machine tools and containers marked up as 'Bosh' and to the far side dimmer boards, stacked up leaning against each other. What use were all these?, he wondered.

A few of the Stompi Shovel Brigade watched as they began their descent. So different from the exhausting labour of the ascent, they plunged their thighs deep into the gravel and with each step they slid gently a pace or two down. What fun, what japes ... Lez was audibly grinning, even Skirker eased the frown from his brow ... he could remember doing this sort of thing coming down sand dunes with Liz ... long ago ... before ... his frown tightened back as they stepped out of the chattering spill of gravel at the bottom ... before Funky Lurgan appeared on the scene and took her away with him. Carol had said he had a right, considering. But he had no right. And to keep her in captivity, as he must be doing, because she had never come back ... Well, time would come when he would catch up with them and what he'd do to Funky didn't bear thinking about: except he never stopped thinking about it.

Such are the curious obliquities of mental processes that Stone, smarting from Hornchurch's way of speaking to him, focussed his annoyance on something purely imaginary. He could imagine that the aged clatter gob would, if told about the true purpose of their errand, be apoplectic, because he knew just what Skirker would do as soon as they got it back.

And he did. He left the spigot key in Skirker's hands as he nudged Irene to her feet and they made their exit. Probably to go-a-humping on Irene's sofa; what would they have done without the comfortable clumber of that recently part purchased sofa ... talk about a destiny that shapes our ends.

Good, thought Skirker, he now had work to do. Harold was still running his finger round the rim of the Marmite jar ... or had Carol found him a second one to empty? Whatever ... no matter, job to do. He went with Les to test the spigot key, it worked, they opened and closed the valve several times, and each time the water spilled out or stopped, according to the position of the valve. Skirker then instructed Lez to let the siphon tank empty completely and then to shut the valve tight, so it would stay empty. Then, and only then, Lez was to start filling the tank with tins and bottles and jars, all neatly stacked, repeating it all until Lez nodded in agreement. Then he pointed out the ladder to be used to get in and out of the tank. Lez would stack them tighter and neater than any of them could ever manage, he had an aptitude that way, and he would keep at it till the job was completed. This gave Skirker time to get his forge going again, heaving and pushing the tins and bottles to one side, allowing him more room to swing his hammer.

And swing it he did, till the sweat glazed his brow and his muscles rippled. He, 'Hey dah'ed and … Hey doh'ed. chanting, to mark the rhythm, until within a couple of hours of continuous hammering, bending and shaping of red-hot reinforcing bars, he had fashioned, by twisting and forging, an exact replica of the spigot key they had collected earlier.

'You and your "He dahs and Hedo's", snorted Carol when he had finished and wondering why he had poured most of a bottle of vinegar over the cooling but still hot new spigot key. She had had to rummage high and low for it in the clutter of bottles still stacked up against the wall of the lean to. That tank couldn't be filled soon enough as far as she was concerned. What was the point of a lean- to which you couldn't even swing a cat round in.

'Anyway, what do you want two of them keys for?' she demanded.

'I don't want two … I want one … and this', indicating the one they had brought back from Central Stores, 'has got to go back in the morning, but not until it's been made a bastard.' And with that he began hammering the original, the official, the supposed one and only spigot key out of true, sufficiently so to render it useless.

'You'm a crafty bugger Skirker, and now I've said it.' She mused and then stepped aside as Harold came to offer his view, not regarding the malfunctioning spigot key, but as to the what and why of everything that had been happening, not just to them but to the world in general and everyone in it. He had been thinking about the purpose of things and his chart in the narrowing scheme and had reached some sort of conclusion. But nobody was listening, not even interested. No matter he carried on to the end, finishing with, 'Well, that's what I think anyway and nobody as yet has proved me wrong.'

'Good', retorted Skirker, his whole naked torso now glistening with sweat, 'but the point is Harold, there's none that gives a monkey's, because all we can do about it is to survive, survive longer than the rest anyway. That not right Les?' This as Les, who'd not heard a word of Harold's exposition, came to join them. He snuffled and nodded.

'See, Lez knows, he don't ever say anything, but he knows what's up and what's down, don't yer Lez?'

Lez nodded, not to affirm but to point out Carol who came hurrying towards them on a mission of kind intent; it was always her way.

'I couldn't find another Marmite, but here's a Corned-beef Pie' and she handed Harold a plate sized tin.

'Bloody hell Carol!'

'We can afford it Skirker, and what else has he got to go home to, his wife's passed away, he's been telling me about it, his life and his nephew, Barry ... Barry Rasher, well I said as I knew him, from when I used to work at Myers. Barry Rasher controlled the lines and he was a real gentleman, because one Friday, when we were well behind in making the batch up and they could have kept us back for a couple of hours, Barry, Mr Rasher ... Bacon Barry as we called him, not to his face mind, well he shut the line down, so they had to let us go at four ... it was always at four of a Friday. He was a real gentleman ... and Harold here is his uncle. What do you think of that? Small world isn't it. So before you get settled, you go and help Harold up to the top of the ridge ... set him on his way ... because that path is getting really treacherous, and you're none too gain on your feet, are you Harold. So stop moaning Skirker, get off yer arse and help him up.'

'There's a dinosaur, well the remains of one, a fossil as you'd call it, washed out of the sandstone by the rains.' Harold offered, and set off, clutching his dinner plate tin tight to his chest.

'Go on Skirker, he can't manage on his own and he needs to get back before it's dark'.

'It's never light.' Growled Skirker. 'Come on Lez … !'

'You leave Lez alone, he's done enough for today, still got more to put in that tank tomorrow and it's not easy work, in and out, up and down, all the time, that right Lez?'

But of course Lez said nothing, he never did but he was distinctly relieved to see that Skirker had already set off, steadying ramshackle Harold by the elbow, urging him up the steeply, slithery path. He sat down on Carol's sofa, and though it wasn't a nightingale singing … it was close to a rapturous cooing that could be distinctly heard from Irene's house. Carol seemed to be embarrassed. They were at it again.

Chapter 11

D ays passed but that was all they did.

Though not quite, Barry now began to take control of what was in fact a new life, a life without Muriel, without any cognisance of her whereabouts or her well being. Truth to tell, he didn't care. Apropos of Harold's tale of her misdemeanours and falsities, he was becoming a new man, becoming case hardened, as it were; she was not missed. The few pieces of shelving planks left, he nailed across the entrance to her bedroom, long masonry nails that penetrated not just the plank and door jamb but bit deep into the brickwork beneath the wall plaster. It brought him out in a sweat, but simmering anger was for a time abated. If she came back and he was not there, well, she would know the score. He was having no more of kowtowing to her assumed control, things had changed. If she wanted to return, and he imagined her mute and doe eyed, she would have to cosy down on the sofa beside him and … yes, like it or not, she would have to share from the jar of pickled gherkins with him. She hated them, always saying that they served her up something rotten with indigestion, well so be it. She had been wrong when she said that whatever tin, jar or bottle that had been opened that day had to be finished the same day because pickled gherkins, if kept below the vinegar line and if the screw top lid was heated before being repositioned, were fine the following day and the day after that. He knew of what he spoke, and speak he did, muttering these facts aloud to her imagined presence.

Quite often he found himself mentally sharpened and in a sweat, but never in a dither, those days had long gone. And this was the state Harold found him in when he called, many days later, hoping the bad blood between them had … well whatever bad blood did … evaporate? He said nothing, standing in the kitchen doorway, surprised at his nephew's uncharacteristic demeanour, because Barry stared back with a brutal scowl.

'Barry', he murmured, in a congenial tone.

Barry narrowed his stare, thinking that if Harold wanted him to go to the city library to … well.. no, that was not going to happen, not today. Truth to tell he had a diminishing interest in the map, it was rapidly ceasing to have either consequence or circumstance as far as he was concerned. In spite of the logic, the non inclusion of Myers and Repetition still rankled..

Possibly intuiting something of this, Harold stood stock still in the kitchen doorway, gaping.

Barry smiled unpleasantly and his voice was edged when he said, 'This is what you need to see Harold, come on now …' and with that he clutched his uncle's elbow and led him into the hall and to the foot of the stairs, then, pushed him from behind, up the staircase and across the landing to the door of Muriel's bedroom, entrance barred by several pieces of planking, all at odd angles and nailed fast.

Harold was for the moment dumbfounded. He made a dry croaking sound, plucked at Barry's sleeve and eventually said, 'But..?' and then, staring into the fierce delineation of his nephew's face 'Is?' A further gasp, 'I mean …?

'Mean what!?'

He waggled his hands about, 'She isn't, is she?'

Barry eased, relaxed his expression, 'Do you mean?'

'Yes, you haven't, have you?'

'Haven't what uncle? Spell it out.'

Harold sniffed, he was about to become curmudgeonly.' You know full well what I mean.'

'Do I? I don't know as I do.'

'C'mon Barry.'

'If for one moment you think that I've barricaded Muriel in there you're wrong, you'd have known if I had, she would have been screaming and shouting, kicking the door down, don't you think?'

'Not if … Well'

'Not if what?!'

'Well, if …'

Barry's face loosened its mood, he chortled, the old familiar Barry, instantly putting his uncle at ease. He gently jabbed Harold in the chest. 'You were wanting to say, what if I had tied her up and gagged her. Hey, that's what you were thinking wasn't it.'

'Well, yes, and no, so to speak, I mean, in the light of what, well let's put it this way, in the light of what I told you, about her, you know what I mean, look, do I have to say it out Barry?'

'What if I have killed her? That's it isn't it, what you were wanting but couldn't bring yourself to say. Oh God above Harold, what sort of man do you think I am?!.

And with this, he chortled, but a very different kind of chortle, with more than a hint of menace, as he led the way downstairs, knocking a sharp rhythm on the balustrade. 'Dear, oh dear Harold, what kind of mind have you got.'

'I just thought Barry.'

'That I could what, murder Muriel, my own wife? Why would you think that? Is it in the light of what you told me about her that you're thinking such a thing?'

'No of course not, look Barry you know as I would never think you would, or could do something so awful as murder your wife, of course not.

'Why not? There's many as have done so for less, far less.'

'But not you, my boy, never you, you haven't got that kind of wickedness in you.'

It was those last few words that did it. How little his uncle knew of the transformation that was taking place within him? Of the irreversible and continuing case hardening that was taking place within his inner being. He snapped open the jar of gherkins and silently nodded for Harold to take one. Harold, not exactly enamoured of pickled gherkins, took one nevertheless. As an act of appeasement? Perhaps because he correctly sensed that had he refused, he would be bullied till he did take one. He nibbled away, Barry bit and swallowed his, then offered Harold another.

'Just a minute lad, I haven't finished this yet … .oh all right, just this other one because.'

Barry screwed the top back on and chortled but it wasn't a happy sound, not by any means.

'Well there's that I suppose.' Harold murmured meaninglessly and then, struck by a notion that would change the direction he had planned for the day, came out with, 'I don't suppose you'd care to help me Barry?'

'What with?'

'Well … I just thought that perhaps you would come with me …'

'Back to Central? No way, there's nothing for us there.

'My map.'

'It's in the library, it's doing its job … that is if anyone goes to the library. If not, well, nothing matters does it'.

'Things aren't as simple as that Barry. Let me explain.'

'Not now uncle, I've got a few more six inch nails to hammer in.'

'Six inches?'

'Six inches … through a piece of three quarter ply and into the wall.'

'Barry, tell me honestly lad … .you haven't … well?'

'I'm just making sure that when she comes back, if she comes back, that is, because I know as there's no reckoning on any certainty, but if she does, then she will know that she can't just swan her way back into her bedroom and take all those tranklements of hers away to wherever. She will bloody well have to ask me first, and then it'll be a case of who'd ever have thought it. Get my meaning?'

Harold sucked his teeth, pothered for a moment or two and the timidly announced, 'Tomorrow then?

'Yes, uncle, tomorrow will do.'

'First thing?'

'First thing it is.'

'And I'll explain ...'

'Tomorrow Harold.' And he ushered his uncle downstairs along the hall and out of the house without a further word.

* * *

Tomorrow came inevitably and just so with Harold, clattering on the front door knocker. There was a sound of some sort from inside and then a pause. Harold turned about and regarded Barry's front garden and block paved drive, or rather what was left of it. That was when, perhaps for the first time, that it came to Harold the awful enormity of the transformation that had taken place to the world. Barry's lawn, cut crisp, its curving edge trimmed sharp, the circular bed in the middle, again crisp and sharply delineated, with a collection of stems of 'Red Hot Pokers', he never knew the correct name for the plant, but so what? The point being that all was obliterated by quivering slobs of Cess, a sort of cumulus of the brown, glistening stuff. And as for the block paving, and the countless hours that Barry spent every summer scraping out the faintest filaments of weed, well, the less said the better. It was all Humpty Dumpty, with split blocks and knuckle intrusions of Thorn that would ... and he gulped apprehensively at the thought ... .eventually envelope ... well, everything.

This dire conclusion did not in any way distract his intention to go back to the central library and rescue his map. If anything it reinforced his intention, as he would explain to his nephew as soon as he bestirred himself to come and open the door. So exasperated he had become that when the door was opened and Barry's once ever genial, round face presented itself, he pursed his lips and stared uncomfortable, intoning Barry's name. Barry, no longer genial but clearly purposed, said not a word, merely opening the door wider and stepped aside. A silent entrance, not a word between them: the world was changing, irrevocably changing and they both knew it.

They sat at the kitchen table and slowly Harold presented the circular, plate sized tin of corned beef pie. A peace offering and something quite special, as he guessed there wouldn't be many of those knocking about these present times.

'For me?' murmured Barry, fingering the pie dish and, in some way, put out of sorts by the sudden familiarity of its shape and lettering. It was a sort of word spill, that forgotten familiarity of everyday things ... it sort of ... scratched the mind. Well of course ...

'For us.' Muttered Harold ... a peace offering, I thought we could ...'

'Thankyou, yes, Harold, but not now. I'm still working my way down that jar of gherkins and to tell you the truth ... well, no matter.'

'When we get back then?'

'From Citadel ... from the library?

'With the map.'

'But I thought that you wanted it to be installed there for anyone to see.'

'Times are changing Barry, changing fast ... and'

'Tell me something I don't know uncle.'

'But listen a moment, lad. I've come to a different way of thinking. On the one hand I've got a theory about what's behind all this mess with Thorn and Cess and ...'

'And the rain, don't forget the rain, because if you ask me it's the rain that is in some way responsible for Thorn and Cess.'

Harold tapped the side of his nose and whispered closely, 'There's more to it than that, much more.'

'Then tell me later, uncle.'

'That's it, later, when we've been to the Central Library and rescued my map.'

'And what will you do with it when you get it back home? After all isn't its purpose to be exhibited, for it to be seen, to inform?'

'That's what I thought but things are different, as you well know, getting more different all the time. Left in that library it will eventually ... and perhaps that eventually will be quicker than we thought ... whatever, but it will eventually be swallowed up in a swamp of cess, and it will do no good to anything or anybody. But I do have a plan.'

'Which is? Look sit down a minute, I'll just put this pie dish on one of the new shelves. Eh.' And he did just that, it fitted neatly, propped up vertically behind a jar of damson jam.

As he did so Harold crackled his knuckles and began. It should have been a short explanation but it didn't work out that way. He began ... 'I went down the Dingley Dell the other day.'

'What you want to go down there for Uncle?.

Harold held his hand up and closed his eyes. He wanted silence. Barry murmured an apology and Harold got his silence.

'Initially to see Skirker, for some more tablets for my water works. But he went off with some fellow from the water board, or such like. A Dr. Stone, no less. Heard of him?'

Barry silently shook his head.

'Well, whatever, he and Skirker and a fellow called Les went off to some gravel pit for a key ... a spigot key, no less. Can you imagine that?

'A spigot key?!'

'Yes, a spigot key. Anyway while they were gone, Skirker's aunt 'Rosy sorted me out a jar of Marmite. You'll know her, she mentioned your name. Used to work at Myers..said as you deliberately stopped the line one Friday, so they couldn't be kept in to make up the numbers..'

'I don't remember any Rosy, not at Myers, at least.'

'Rosy?! Did I say Rosy? I meant Carol. Carol, Skirker's Aunt Carol.'

'Still don't recall her.'

'Well you should. She's a very kind lady. A whole jar of Marmite she gave me and then that corned beef pie to be going away with. That's the sort of woman she is ... generous. But she's also a knower, about the old ways and she told me about some sort of place called The Old Chronicle. You won't have heard about it because it's about times long past ... Arthur ...'

' Now if you're going on about Arthur Raybould, because, yes I do remember him, he used to be in charge of the plating shop years back.'

'Not Arthur Raybould, yer numpty … Arthur, the real Arthur … King Arthur.'

Barry chuckled, 'Arthur Raybould is more real than any King Arthur, at least in my book he is.'

'In your book Barry?! But you don't have a book do you. Carol does though, well at least she knows about them, books that are full of the truth of things that happened way back, before pen and paper were common purchase. And, what is more, when I got to telling her about my map, and its heritage, its knowledge that shouldn't ever be lost, she said that the place for it was not in a drab library, but in the Old Chronicle, with all the other time told legends that live on for ever. So, bit of a surprise, eh? Something of a turn up for the book, eh?'

'And where is this, Old Chronicle, as it's called?'

Harold harrumphed, wagged a finger in Barry's face, and hissed … 'Secret Barry lad but she promised that if I got the map to her, she'd take it there for me.'

'How do you know she won't just … well … take it somewhere and leave to rot away/'

Harold clapped his hands. 'What an untrusting old turnbuckle you're becoming, oh nephew of mine!' Harold snorted. 'That's what will happen to it if it's just left to malinger on in that library. One thing we've all got to learn now is that you can't place trust in the municipality any more, and that's for sure.'

'So, you put your faith in old legends about King Tut and whatever?!!'

'You do, you precisely do just that, because, Barry, lad, the whole point about legends is that they don't die … .the live on and on and on.'

There was a moment's mutual silence, intense with the looking into each other's wondering eyes.

'So, Barry lad, get your skate's on and lets go and retrieve my map. Then we'll be back for a nice pie and I'll tell you my theory.'

'What theory's this Uncle?'

'About all what's happening, that's what. C'mon now.'

As they cluttered out the front door Harold felt so much the happier than when he had arrived ... he could have run all the way to the library, except his age and the growing dereliction of the built landscape rendered that type of activity quite impossible. Well so be it, he maundered on about this Old Chronicle palaver as they slowly navigated the ever growing intrusions of ever great galumphs of Cess many of which were now almost shoulder height, obscuring the way ahead and the space between them becoming narrow threads through which they often had to step sideways, this way and that. Not all that bad, not yet, but beginning to get that way.

All the time Harold rattled away, like a babbling brook, about this Old Chronicle he'd been told about ... 'and these old legends, or as Carol would have it, 'those' old legends ... well I have to admit, I've never had any truck with them because there's not a single statistic in any of them ... fables don't do numbers but ... and this is a big but Barry ... they don't fade away. In fact Carol reckons that not only do they live on and on but that their meanings change. Can you imagine that?'

Barry snorted, to clear his nose, not to express disapproval, though he did. 'But as I asked before, where is this Old Chronicle ... what is it?!'

'Ha, now there's the problem. Apparently some do say as it's a tree.'

'A tree!?'

'A tree as old and ancient as Old King Cole but others claim it's a place ... in a rock.'

'A cave?'

'Could be, yes, why not, a cave, you're certainly thinking along the right lines Barry ... but then some say it's an ancient inn run by an old man with a scooped out face ... mind you I find that rather difficult to believe but then again some have said that an old woman, someone skilled in the old herbs, as folks used to use before there was proper medicines like Paracetamol and that Tamsolusin, as I have to use ... but, and this is the biggest but of all, Carol reckons that my map shouldn't slime away to nothing in a library, perhaps never being read, but that I should take it to her and it could become a fablement and live as long as the memory of … .well everything and everyone. Now, what about that?!'

Barry muttered acknowledgements to Harold's continuous ranting, he had always been this way about things, but things that were objectively real … or had been … not this obscure obsession with … . 'Oh! Uncle Harold!'

Harold stopped his clatter and clutched his nephew with a stare 'Uncle and Harold, well it's always been either Harold or Uncle, never the two Barry, or should I say Barry Nephew?' And he chortled, a sound like gravel being rattled in a tin mug. He said nothing further but was elated; the bad feeling between them soured no more, the old ease had returned. And yes, they both now regarded the scene that confronted them, it produced a scintillation of awe. The last broad paved rise to Citadel proper was all but cleared of cess, even more so than when they last came this way; the floorscape correctly delineated, its neat paving up to the official buildings clear. They could stroll straight into Central Library without even having to step over dollops of cess, everywhere had been scraped clean and the scurrying spill of the present downpour, wavering white rills of water, flowed unimpeded. Here was method, here was progress: advancement of seriously maintained purpose. Harold's immediate reaction was to wonder if indeed he was doing the right thing by removing his map from the library because, he had to admit, it was now much more easily available for perusal or inspection.

As for Barry, well as a production controller, was there anything more to be said beyond the registering of an unfeigned delight?

They stepped it out; pedestrian ways in Citadel were now all but clear of cess, were clean emptiness across which purpose could be written. But what purpose? … Several purposes obviously because there were small squads of Stompis and Christies, the latter with silent Gawpers being trundled up to the cathedral in wheel barrows, or hurrying back with empty barrows to collect more. He could study their procurement procedures, see if the system couldn't be accelerated. Even though he didn't know the purpose of the rounding up and deposition of them in the cathedral, it didn't matter: efficiency was all and retrieval rates would be drawn up and achievement levels increased. He, Barry Rasher was going to put his skills at the service of this clearspace 'renewelmentation' of Citadel that was producing such amazing results.

Settling into a bemused admiration for what was being achieved, he barely nodded in agreement when Harold whispered at his shoulder that he would just trot across to the library, rescue his map and then take it to Hector's bookshop for storage. He offered to help, pointing out that Harold would never manage the whole contraption of boards and supports on his own. But Harold's eyes gleamed, perhaps his mood also had been burnished brighter by the tidying up that had been achieved all about them. He notified his nephew that he intended to dispense with the boarding. Barry looked surprised, startled even but Harold assured him that it was only the map that was needed, coiled carefully in its metal tube, it would be neither weight nor hindrance and be all the easier for Hector to accommodate, till it was time to take it to the Old Chronicle, once it had been ascertained where, precisely, that place was.

Barry murmured a sort of agreement and promised he would meet his uncle at Hector's 'Bookstop'. With that Harold trotted off and Barry was left to peruse the cleansed lineaments of Citadel as they spread out before him: cleanliness at his leisure: accomplishment, order, neatness, so much had been achieved. But it was from behind him that the danger came, a harsh kick on the back of his legs, a fierce downwards thump on his shoulders and he was on the floor and a couple of Stompis standing over him. He would have been rigid with fear had he not been so outraged.

They cajoled him with a nasty, raw edged mirth. One prodded him with the toe of his boot while another made a sort of ceremonial double stamp and yahoo'd, He tried to get to his feet but was pushed back to the floor and another two arrived on the scene, gawping and snarling.

There was no telling what might have happened had not an officer, he wore a smarter uniform and boots that reached to his knees, intervened. Barry noted he seemed to be more curious than antagonistic.

'What's your unit man?!' the officer demanded. Probably it was Barry's gabardine mack, belted and with copious sloping pockets, and not a single button missing, that made him curious. He struggled to his feet bellowing that he was a production control engineer, lately and perhaps still, in charge of production flow at M.C.L. Myers and Repetitions.

One of the two Stompis snarled a ripsaw laugh, possibly ignited by Barry's indignant tone as the other went to force him back down.

'Stop that!!' snapped the officer. 'Get him to his feet!'

They obeyed and then stepped away.

'Engineer you say?! And your name?!

Barry swept his hands down the sides of his mackintosh and said evenly, 'Rasher, Barry Rasher'

The officer looked startled and took a step back. The Stompis, registering something of his wariness, also stepped back.

'Did you say Rasher?' the officer demanded in a low voice.

'Yes, Barry Rasher, always have been and always will be.'

' Rasher?' the officer insisted in a low voice.

'As I said.' muttered Barry with a slight but mystified smile on his face.

Whatever malignant intention had been entertained by the Stompis had disappeared, they registered their officer's perplexity and simply gawped, slack jawed and staring at him.

'Then it would be best if you came this way sir.' The officer murmured, encouraging him by a slight tug at his elbow.

'Where are we going?'

'This way sir, I am going to have to pass you over to a higher authority, a much higher authority in fact.' And with that he led the way with a purposeful stride, the two Stompis coming up behind with a paradestep stamping.

* * *

Harold had no difficulty in the library. He called out an 'Halloo' several times, hoping against hope for a reply, desperate, one way or another, to cajole an opinion from somebody, anybody, as to the relevance and indeed efficacy of his 'once upon a time factory' map. But no one came, the only sign of human habitation being his own echo. No matter, it convinced him as to the rightness of his decision: The Old Chronicle it had to be, and let's face it' he told himself, if in a future age none understood the nature of the pattern of markings that his once factories meant, at least they would study and wonder, marvelling perhaps at the neatness of the abstract pattern before their eyes. Had there been any residual doubts, these were violently vanquished no sooner than he had stepped out of the library and made his way to Hector's bookshop.

Hector's 'once upon a time' bookshop it should be, because that emporium was now in the destructive process of becoming a ruin. Stompis were running riot both inside and out of the shop. Luckily they were so engrossed in their destructive work they did not see Harold, who clutching the precious cylinder of his map in its tube, stepped back into a doorway and observed, unobserved.

Inside, a determined squad of Stompis, threw piles of books out onto the cess cleared paving. They obviously had hammers and wrecking bars for the wrench and splintering of wood could be heard, the screeching of nails being ripped out and shelves scattered outside into a pile. As the handfuls of books came clatterspilling out, Stompis kicked them into a pile before setting them alight. Petrol was poured over the heap of splayed books and ignited. At first all flared into flame and burnt fiercely, but then, though some pages curled, browned to a crisp, the flames merely spluttered and went out.

It is enormously difficult to burn a book; especially one with glossy pages. Belatedly, the Stompis began ripping clutches of pages free from their binding and scattering them into the flames. Yet no great success was achieved. Harold noted that the large format pages, gleaming with clearly recognisable photographs of Nazi Nuremberg Parades and similar paraphernalia, blistered but did not burn, though the acrid smell of their scorching drifted throughout the nearby plaza. Driven to greater effort, the shattered remnants of the bookcases were littered on top of the gasping flames, but the fire was not hot enough for anything more than singeing and black smouldering, all hissing venomously in the rain.

In spite of his growing sense of outrage and indeed fear, Harold was reminded of the Nazis and their book burning, in the days gone by. Well they at least got a huge pile flaming before they tossed their books into the inferno. In any case they didn't try and do it in the rain. Did the Nazis do anything in the rain? In fact did it ever rain while the Nazis were in power? Certainly not if newsreel footage is to be believed.

But enough of such nonsense, the rain became heavier, not quite a downpour but certainly heading that way when Harold, almost choking on his teeth watched in horror as Hector was bundled out of the gutted shop and thrown to the floor. With whooping they surrounded the old man and began stamping and jumping on him, till his bones cracked, his head became a splodge and his body all but shapeless. Then, to complete the horror beyond reckoning, they shovelled the lump of him onto the fire, emptied more sheaves of torn pages and pouring the last of their petrol, set light to him.

Harold remained, frozen still in a rictus of horror, waited until they grew bored and wandered away chanting and whooping and indulging in a freelance form of dance stomping. He waited till their echo was lost and he swallowed.

What now?

Chapter 12

That 'much higher authority' the Stompi officer had referred to, would eventually reach the Triumvirate: no office or rank beneath that level was prepared to come to a firm decision as to what was to be done with this Barry Rasher. With that name could he be determined or even discerned as being of any particular rank?

It was agreed by the three of them, by Stryne, Stent and Dublo, that any discussion of the matter with Astartobe was best not considered, given the situation. That name though; who was he? Any relation? If so what relation? And more to the point was she prepared to be well disposed towards him, or even the knowledge of him? And then again, if there was no relationship, was he going to be of any use to them? Questions, questions, but Dublo, as always, diminutive, his suit swirled about him insisted that this unreconstituted Barry had to be taken on board, and given a chance. At the same time it would give them an opportunity to see what metal he was made of. But, certainly, at the same time they must jointly try and circumnavigate Madame Rasher's miasma of hatred towards anything that was not Uniate to try and discern what her attitude to this self proclaimed Barry Rasher would likely be if she were ever to be confronted with him.

Agreement yes but, each with different reservations, and then it was discussed what was to be done with him in the meantime. Was he to be kept a prisoner? And if so under what conditions? A prisoner was certainly a novelty in Citadel. One was either working living or dead. It was Stent who came up with the solution.

'I suggest he be put on an Unwording duties' stick him on a wodge patrol, just as an observer at first, see how he reacts. If he survives that, and most don't, we can think of alternative employment.

Surprised at Stent's logic, they agreed, though of course each had reservations. Stent on the one hand was pleased, that it was his practical idea that had been taken up and she, Astartobe, surely wouldn't find fault with that; would she? If so he would recommend some form of punitive action, a drastic failsafe option so that nothing had been lost by giving this Barry Rasher a trial. Practical, always be practical and keep it simple, be resolute, that had always been her way when she was known as just, Madame Rasher. So yes, he was pleased because he was sure that she would be pleased, and that, these days, her being pleased was what it was all about.

Stryne had his doubts but they were both, he and Dublo, also pleased, for the same reason but in a different way: it hadn't been their idea. What is more they both realised that they would each react to its success or failure differently, but for the time being they both felt safe in acknowledging Stent as the author of the dispensation, on his head be it, so to speak. So yes there was pleasing and the hopeful expectation of pleasing all round, though for pleasingly different reasons.

Barry was brought in. He was quite prepared to be polite, humble even, before such seniority They were all upper board members he was being confronted with; shareholders in the future of Citadel, and clearly there were fixed methods and iron procedures throughout the human structure of the place that healed all sense of loss of the old order and bound them tight to the prescriptive future. Clean plaza, determined work roles. This he could understand and admire. At the same time, and it wasn't arrogance but belief in his own ability as a Production Controller, he knew he could arrange fresh roles, speed up target achievement and enhance target cognisance. He had that ability.

And yet ... and yet ... at this most important meeting, when everything had to be succinct, if he was to survive and realise his potential, he found himself spitefully distracted by the buttons on Dublo's suit. The others wore authoritarian attires; Stent undeniably had a uniform and thin lipped, Stryne a black cassock … neck to ankle, with a thin black leather cord, or was it a thong, tied tight about his waist. Dublo was different, in his wretched dark suit, somehow twisted tight about his severely diminutive form, the jacket billowed up under his armpits, so much so that buttons and button holes seemed to be on the verge of being wrenched apart. The middle of the five buttons was merely hanging by a dangerously limp thread. At any moment it could snap and the button would drop to the floor.

Barry tried to concentrate on other features of Dublo, his alarmingly large, pointed Adam's apple, with a few long hairs attached, the swollen knuckles of his never still hands, patting his knees, tweaking his chin or lugging his ear as he spoke of need and commitment. But try as he may, Barry couldn't get those buttons out of his mind: they weren't right. They were hemispherical, nut brown, ridged buttons such as one only ever found on a sports jacket … .never on a suit … .a dark suit at that. Had the suit jacket been manufactured with those buttons? He seriously doubted it. In which case, sewn on by whom, and under what circumstances? Did he, Barry wondered, even know of the sartorial error? He had on the rail hanger in his bedroom, next to his camp bed, a couple of tweed jackets with just such shiny kernels of buttonry about them. Oh, yes indeed, it went without saying that Muriel would never have let him go to work in a sports jacket. He'd say that much for her. A suit, always a suit, and rightly so. But here, and at this level, sports jacket buttons … on a suit … heavens above!

And so it came to pass that being thus distracted, he missed much of Dublo's warning that the tasks he would be presented with would be dangerous … and there was much talk about Wodge and Wodge patrols … And, Stent interjected … warning about the danger of 'Garking'. Stryne just smiled, stared at the ceiling and murmured … 'Stampi Patrols.'

Stent, effervescing like a can of Vim, screwed every filament of aggression into twisting his mouth and snarled … 'Stompi … it's Stompi …'

'So sorry, of course, silly of me Commander Stent. Stompi it is.' And he gave a supercilious smile, his blackened, prominent tooth, biting deeper into the pink strand of his lip.

Did it matter? Not really. Barry's incontinent optimism was his safeguard. He felt it was his destiny to master these circumstances and to show Citadel in all its myriad inconsistencies, just what an able and resolute Production Controller could achieve for its betterment.

And so, without any more ado, Stent led him out. He was to accompany a Wodge patrol on a lowest level tour of inspection.

Dublo and Stryne stood as he left, joined by one thought, though relished by each in a different manner. That thought was that if this Barry, in his gabardine mackintosh, a garb which, let's face it, suggested some sort of authority, should succumb and himself be mindwasted by splurges of wordcess, then, well, so much the better, for all. No more worries about his name, vis- a- vis Astartobe.

Of course … but they didn't at this point entertain the ramifications of that, 'of course', except to say they both agreed, it was to be as Barry he would be known … Barry always and as for the Rasher … dispense with that at all times.

* * *

It was the most hazardous of Wodge Patrols he was assigned to, working the dark ramps and chambers that extended below the basement level. Any wordage happened upon down there would not be paper or plastic but metal and possibly hidden in the long, smooth welts of mud that had been slithered by drainage waters up against the raw concrete walls. Mudbanks several feet deep in many cases. Of course the inevitable lips of paper and plastic trash, mostly word stained, had long since been harvested, rendered and destroyed.

Why, it may be asked, seeing that no furtive groups of clerkdom ever penetrated to this level, did they have to search under slimy mud for any fixed signage? Why did they bother?

That was a question Barry quickly came to understood should never be asked. Wordage led to Wodge and Wodge was lethal.

He found the air clammy, the rank smell sickening, and as he unbelted and unbuttoned his mack the sweat was oozing out of him. There were six in the patrol; between them they carried an array of implements for attacking any signs as may be found: hammers, screwdrivers, wrecking bars, spades, shovels and such like. The platoon leader had a whistle on a cord, about his neck. Well, well, whistles as well.

At first progress was sharp, the blades of the spades scraped against the wall tiles. Methodically they moved along the drift, ensuring that nothing but clean tiles were left on view. Nothing could be simpler, a neat labour of practised dexterity, piling a sloppy mud ridge down the middle of the walkway. But the air' gradually misting slightly yellow as a result of their uninterrupted labour which released foul gases from beneath the mud, became painful to breathe. Ossy, that was the name of the platoon leader, the one with the whistle about his neck, counted random numbers out aloud.. (numbers, although words, were not properly deemed as such; they had no connotation) and counting them out served to instil some sort of confidence, urging them to maintain pace, to keep up the progress … to concentrate on blank tiles.

Barry was impressed, he could even have grabbed a shovel himself and joined in but that would not have been allowed, of course not … .method and means … So it was just the regular slip and slop of the mud being lifted and turned and the bland benediction of a blank wall that sustained their non stop progress, matched to clipped shouting of numbers.

And then, the unexpected, the unsuspected, the vehement evil that Wodge represented. Not a sign on the wall but a broken cast iron plate, a sign not fixed but lying detached in the mud and turned up by a spade. Split across its middle the words, 'Municipal Gas Works could be read. And they were read, it was the obviously random happenstance of the sign's uncovering that meant that the discovery was delayed, just for a few seconds, enough for the words to be recognised, to be involuntarily read. And here was the cruel happenstance of the occurrence, all signs did not mean the same to all men. Far from it, indeed some would have simply turned the cast iron fragment face down and smashed it beyond recognition, but not this particular platoon member, not with this sign. It triggered something unfathomable, and he fell, quaking violently, heaving and sound snorting. Quarking, or was it Gwarking they called it? No matter the sound was hideous and terminal. Worse it was infectious, others in the platoon began whinnying and tottering about in circles. The platoon leader, Ossy, immediately began blowing his whistle; the sound was piercing, it echoed back to them but with seemingly little effect. With a snort and his eyes closed, Ossie snatched up a hammer and rained blows down on the head of his quarking, fellow patrolman. The sound was sickening, but it brought its own silence; no more whimpering, no more whistle blowing and most important of all no more Quarking. They all stood backs to the wall, breathing heavily and Ossie grabbed a thick plastic sack, which until now had been neatly folded and tucked within his belt, gave it to Barry and said simply, 'Put him in there and all the bits of signage as well, gather them up, it has to be a clean sweep!'

There was a triumphalism in the tone of the order: this newcomer had to learn procedure; experience anger at the loss of a fellow Wodge patrol man and endure the realisation that they were never completely safe. Quarking ... or was it Gwarking? was contagious. If Ossie had not acted with all due diligence immediately, the whole patrol would have gone under, choking on a slew of disjointed syllables as their consciousness dissolved. Barry understood this, of course he did, but it was difficult to get the body in the sack, particularly as he was constantly having to wipe fronds of brain tissue from the sleeves of his gabardine. Keep your mind on method and execute that method with due promptitude; this he instinctively understood, as a production controller, and such was duly expedited. He stood up and looked at Ozzie, who, putting his whistle back into his breast pocket, simply gave an affirmative nod.

They waited a while, just staring at each other, not a word spoken until three officials of some sort arrived, wearing goggles (in this semi darkness!) and trailing grappling claws. Words were exchanged with Ozzy, who made a snorting affirmation and then attempted a stamp of his boots, although it was just a splodge, standing in a welt of mud as he was at the time. Everything that needed to be was negotiated and Ozzy led his patrol back to a street level region, where they were urged into a compartment with sodden plasterboard walls that had already crumbled away to a slop along the bottom edges.

'It can happen at any time' Ozzy protested in a wail of frustration, to a senior officer who seemed quite unprepared to accept this excuse.

'You should be more alert, always be in charge of events and ...'

He was interrupted by Stent's entry, followed by Dublo, who only just managed to squeeze into the space which, even without furniture was little more than a cubicle. The questioning officer crammed himself into a corner, worried at being before such eminences as two members of the Triumvirate. Stent demanded to know what had happened, then sniffed, causing the temporary retreat of the green ball of snot that trembled in his left nostril.

Ozzy related the events as they had occurred, even praising Barry who, in spite of his newness, had stood his ground and urged the body into the sack ready for collection by the Reclaim Unit.

Reclaim for what and to be taken to where? Barry wondered.

'It's happening all the time,' protested Ozzy, 'you know it is.'

He clearly felt that loss of status, such as it was, or even punishment would be his lot. Dublo seemed to be sympathetic, murmuring aloud that they would continue to lose Stompis until the last sign in Citadel had been destroyed.

'And it's my men that are being lost, that are being sacrificed in this futile campaign.' bellowed Stent.

'It is not futile Commander Stent … others, less hardened than your Stompis will occasion upon them, no matter how remotely they are located them and the result could be a multiple outbreak of mind cess and then …'

Stent sharply interrupted. 'When are clerical clones ever going to be working in those sub basement levels, eh? Tell me that?'

It was all getting heated until Barry interposed. 'It doesn't have to be like this, it's the methodology that's all wrong. Ossy lost one of his men because of the methodology. He comes across a sign …'

'Wodge.' insisted Dublo.

'Whatever, the point being is that the operative who discovers the wodge has to stare at it while he destroys it. And it's that staring at it that does the damage …'

'He's got to look at it to destroy it.' snapped Stent in a tone that suggested that Barry was a fool. 'Otherwise he'd be just hammering the wall.'

'How else can he do it?' queried Dublo, clearly perplexed.

'Simple,' Barry was now in his stride, 'Your men must always work in pairs, one with the implement of destruction … the hammer, the other with a can of spray paint, any colour, it doesn't matter. On a sign or fraction of a sign being uncovered, the other immediately begins to spray it with paint, thereby obliterating it while the first, the one who has uncovered the sign, smashes it. All he will see will be the paint …'

Dublo interrupted, though his tone was reasonable. 'But the one using the paint spray will see the sign … while he is spraying it …'

'Not so,' snapped Barry, hot with the expounding of his method, 'anyone who has ever done any painting knows that you see the spread of the paint, not the surface being painted. Both men will be safe.

Stent and Dublo looked at each other, Ossy looked at both them and then at Barry, who gleamed at what he could see was his obvious success. 'All you need is a supply of cans of spray paint. Do you have a supply?'

Dublo pursed his lips. 'If we do, Mr Hornchurch will know.'

Stent snarled and the globe of snot disappeared again. 'Best of luck there. He won't release anything he doesn't want to' Look at the way he is over the wheel barrows!'

'Then Barry must persuade him!'

And that was that, first thing the next morning they set out in a driving drizzle to test the munificence of Centralstores and the pliability of Mr Hornchurch.

Chapter 13

Morgendaemerung haeftichkeitgeschlaft!!!!
If there ever was such a word it would come some way to describing how Barry felt that grey, wind lashed morning, the slighting rain almost horizontal, as he strode effortlessly across the long extension of the concrete apron that stretched before the oh so long corrugated steel shed of Central Stores.

What munificence lay batched, racked and shelved inside … it was too exciting to contemplate. He wore goggles, that eased the predicament of the fiercest storm they had had for some time. Dublo also, who shuffled along at his side, breathless, struggling with the ruin of a plastic mack that the intensity of the storm was rapidly ripping into shreds. Not Barry's gabardine mackintosh, made to last, to endure all weathers. Even so, such was the power of the wrenching wind, that its lower flaps were blown upwards and apart to reveal its shotsilk lining.

No matter. Did anything matter when he could stride the ever extending length of the concrete apron, feeling the slight ribs in the concrete's surface through the soles of his shoes? The concrete had been poured in discrete slabs and there were long thin threads of black mastic at the joints. He would have counted these but his mind was still distracted by the extended enormity of the Centra Stores shed, with its cylindrical, fabricated sheet steel ventilators, squat and stern, equally spaced along the crown of its roof; they invoked work and intensity of purpose in the echoing space beneath them.

What possibilities lay within that shed for production control methodology, as regards the interaction of needs and supply between Citadel and Central Stores. His gaze took him beyond such unstructured wonderment as his attention was caught by Stompis, Shovel Stompis to be precise, that could be seen at the far end, where there was a termination of the apron At this point loaded barrows, most with wobbly and squeaky wheels, having come from some distant location, were upended and the gravel tipped down a steep slope.. But, and it was like a bit of something sharp caught in his eye, there was a wavery, thin trail of spilt gravel. For heaven's sake, he thought, was there no Shovel Stompi detailed to sweep it down over the edge? Or was it left as a task for the shift's end? Even so he had to admire the capacity of the undertaking, counting twenty three loaded barrows in line and as many empty barrows being trundled back … to where? … well to a quarry somewhere, he supposed. Yes, it would have to be a quarry.

Wibble … wobble … squeak … trundle bumble … It was, in its way, so impressive that such repetitious industry went on still, all about them, undeterred by the ferocity of the storm.

He eased his pace … probably much to Dublo's relief, whose breath was hoarsely raucous, and strode with a confident ease through what now seemed a blessing of rain, it kept that magnificent apron clean. And as he strode, the pace and indeed rhythm nudged a tune into his mind, the magnanimity of which almost ennobled his presence. The tune, yes, he turned the snap of it over in his mind, something from Tchaikovsky … he and Muriel did occasionally make a concert in the Town Hall, every now and again … and yes, the Fifth Symphony … that bit before … and, as he seemed to remember … after the last movement … the bit that went " dah de dah diddy dudah..dah dah dadedah" resplendent ceremonial music … a tune of serene accomplishment. He hummed it aloud and for a moment restored Muriel to his recollection. Her favourite was the 1812 Overture and on one occasion when the performance had been augmented by a fusillade of live canon by a regimental band, she had dug her nails into his arm. Yes, they had been Tchaikovsky people, through and through.

Whatever, his humming, his mood of resplendent paced power striding, was interrupted when Mr Horncastle clambered towards them, furious with a complaint. Dublo began to explain that they were on an errand to collect cans of spray paint and, would he oblige? He snorted, pushed Barry aside, in order to be able to swing his arm in an arc that traversed the length of the line of squeaky barrows. Not that he could see them through those spectacles but they could be certainly heard.

'Don't dare think as you can come here, without so much as a do you like it, from the fuckin' Uniate with more requests because you fuckin' well can not. If you do think that, then let me tell you, here and now, that you've got another think coming because I'm doing sod all demands till I get them barrows sorted. And what is it you say you want?. Spray paint? Eh? Spray-fuckin' paint. I ask you, who the fuck wants spray paint this day and age? Eh? Fuckin' tell me that. And what do you think all this is?' another sweep of his arm to encompass the black shed of his stores, 'a knacker's yard, eh? Of course I've got paint: gloss, emulsion, spray, indoor, outdoor, water repellent for kitchens and bathrooms, shed stains, in every shade from willow to pine, from ash to dark fucking oak but if you think for one moment that I'm going to take time out to get anything for you to take back to sodding Citadel, you've got another think coming. Look at, them sodding barrows, not a true wheel on any of them. Not one fucker is fit for purpose and can we get time to repair them, can we fuck. Christ on crutches, it shouldn't be that difficult and it cowin' well wouldn't be if every other bugger wasn't requisitioned by that cunt Stryne for carrying his stupid bloody bodies to and from the cowin, cathedral. So, in a nutshell, no, fuckin' definitely no, so you can piss off the two of you, toute, fuckin' suite. Got it,? Have I made myself clear!?'

Dublo gabbled, gargling saliva in his thin throat. Barry relaxed, it was good to hear a storekeeper ranting again, quite like the old days. Dublo began, his voice back to a splutter, trying to explain the niceties of the transportation of Gawpers and the ethereal niceties of their purposed destination but Hornchurch just snorted and went to stride away.

Barry shouted after him, 'Every barrow in Christendom, every last one will be yours in a couple of days!'

Hornchurch turned about, no doubt the clouded eyes behind those impenetrable glasses stared. His jaw fell slack. Was ever storekeeper in this nature won? What he was being promised was nothing other than 'barrow manna'. But suspicions remained.

'Oh yes, and how the fuck are you going to even try and manage that?'

'Not try', snapped Barry curtly, there'll be no trying about it. By the end of the week, you'll have barrows to spare. Promise.

Hornchurch scowled from one to the other silently.

'Who is he?!' he demanded of Dublo.

'New recruit, senior management ...'

'Fuckin' management!!' snarled Hornchurch and spat on the all but sacred concrete apron.

'I'm Barry Rasher, previously Senior Production Controller at M. C. L. Myers & Repetitions ... I'm sure you've heard of them.'

'Rasher? Did you say Rasher?' whispered Hornchurch, pulling the oil stained peak of his cap further down over his brow, his voice low. He repeated the question in an even lower tone, this time addressed at Dublo.

'No' whimpered Dublo, 'of course not ... it's Trasher, his name, Barrimore Trasher.' There was a moment's silence, filled of course by the winnowing rainfall and shrieking snatches of wind.

'I could have sworn ...' began Hornchurch, his own tone low and circumspect.

'Of course not.' insisted Dublo, 'never in a million years. Barrymore Trasher ... .Trasher.'

Hornchurch shifted uneasily from foot to foot but held his silence, then, almost gently and certainly hesitantly, he began with ... 'Because ...'

'Because nothing Mr Hornchurch, no 'becauses' today. Now I'll just go and show Barry here ... Barrymore, but we tend to shorten it for comfort of the tongue's sake, show him the great tipping procedure, and, then, we'll be back to your counter for …'

'Spray paint,' stabbed Barry, irritated, 'Any colour.'

'How many cans, Mr Trasher … ?' there was a tone of suspicion, of disbelief even.

Barry turned to Dublo. 'How many Stompi Wodge patrols are there?' The curt, precise tone impressed.

'About fifteen.'

Hornchurch snorted, 'We don't do abouts here Mr Dublo, we do exacts!, as well you should fuckin' well know by now.'

Barry interceded. 'Twenty, Mr Hornchurch, exactly twenty.'

Hornchurch muttered something that was better left incomprehensible and strode back to the zincplated bench of his stores.

They watched his departure until he was within the sombre cloak of the shed before Dublo, clearly uneasy with the nature of the transaction, urged Barry in the direction of the gravel bank, to its edge where the wheelbarrows were being discharged.

'What is this business about me not to be called Rasher?' he asked but Dublo, clearly irritated, simply snapped, 'Forget about it!' and led the way forward. Beyond the edge of the gigantic concrete slab they trod on gravel, their feet sinking ankle deep. Barry did notice that there were four lines of paving slabs, not laid as such but dropped in straight lines to provide an easy pathway for the barrows. The slabs went straight to the edge but they were naturally forbidden to step on these lest they in some way impair the impressively regular passage, to and fro, of the barrows, loaded or unloaded.

Standing at the very edge they looked down; looked because you can't peer down a gravel bank, its slope is too easy and never severe. Barry was impressed at its height, and for that matter its extent, not a straight edge but gently curving.

'This is to smother Cess and Thorn?' Barry queried, he could clearly see clumps of both being submerged by the spread of pinkish, grey gravel.

'In part.' Murmured Dublo, his words almost obscured by

the now voracious flapping of the torn remnants of his plastic mack. 'But only in part; there are other functions. The most important of which is to provide a defensive barrier, against invaders, they would easily be picked off as they struggled to climb the bank.'

'What if they came by night?'

'We have lantern patrols.'

'But if you were to be invaded and I can't think who these invaders could possibly be, well they would surely choose some other way into Citadel. I mean the way I came is … well just up a gently sloping street. In sufficient numbers, they could manage that without any difficulty.'

Dublo smiled, or was it a sneer, his bottom lip protruded, a voluptuous pink. 'If they come, and one day they will, then it'll be up this bank.'

'But why?'

'Look ahead, straight into the rain, you'll find your answer.'

Doing as he was told, squinting through the lashing curtain of rain, the wind now full in their faces, he could discern the bulky shape of another factory shed, not old enough to have figured on Harold's map, but morosely impressive in its promised immensity, all but dissolved to vision in the torrents of rain. His mind lost focus, it was snatched up in a false consciousness, such that he inwardly stammered to himself, 'agenbite of inwit', as the old saying used to be … he couldn't remember who had taught him that … .but … Oh damn these 'buts'. He should be focussing on the productive possibilities of that factory at the bottom of the gravel bank. Should be concentrating on how its inner productive potential could be harnessed to serve The Uniate, not be deluded by the morose tones of grey its forlorn immensity presented.

Claude … his mind snatch-snitched, like the shot silk of his mac's lining, now green, now brown. Claude, yes, probably him, now he came to think of it. He had said the term … 'agenbite of inwit'.

Claude had been a senior member of the youth club, crinkly hair and a bit of a nervous twitch in his right hand. No matter, Claude had been a dab hand at the cricket club, making sandwiches for the change of innings interval break. To watch Claude slice and place a tomato onto a buttered slice of bread, whisk a traipse of malt vinegar over it and then place another slice on top, neatly, edge matching edge, before the clean, dividing slice with a long knife, well it was a wonder to behold; the rapidity and exactitude; with cucumber sandwiches he was even quicker, and all the time that twitching right hand offered not the slightest impairment. Yes … Barry had been there because for a couple of seasons he was the scorer, kept the score book records. His joining up of the dots of a maiden over, he liked to think carried the same degree of neatness as had Claude's trimming up of his crusts. They had become friends for a while and, involuntarily, he wondered what had happened to him now; if he had to place a bet it would be on him having become a gawper … there had always been something a little bit ethereal about Claude.

'Well?!' demanded Dublo.

'A factory', responded Barry.

'You'll need to do better than that', murmured Dublo. That's a processing plant. A food processing plant. When the rain is not so intense you can read the lettering on the shed wall. Nobody can or wants to take them down.'

'Them?'

'The letters, because they are made of metal and they stand over six foot high. You see Barry the point is that those workers in those sheds can't see them but they know that we can, so they act as a gigantic wodge trap. What is more there are high fences all round that factory, razor wire scrawling along the top of them.

Barry scrutinised squint eyed through the rain. But who is in that factory?'

'You may well ask, Barry.'

'Well, yes, I am, asking.'

'Well the old workforce for one and …'

'And?!'

'Well, not to put too fine a point on it, security guards,

hundreds of them, in total, armed, trained in combat and vicious. One day, they will break out and invade, or try to invade Citadel. And they will be fit and strong because in that giant shed, there will be thousands upon thousands of tins of pet food. See what I mean?'

Barry nodded. 'And the purpose of the gravel bank is to ...'

'Keep them out ... or rather to keep them in those sheds.. until ... well.'

'I get it, keep them in until the gravel bank reaches the factory, then submerge everything under gravel.'

'Not that simple, if we did that we would be submerging all those thousands upon thousands of tins of food and let's face it, Citadel is going to need that food supply one day.'

Barry sniffed. 'Well I suppose that depends on the ratio of our survival rate and the food we have in store.'

'Forbidden figures, or even unknown figures. Nothing we can do about that. However, Commander Stent has drawn up a battle plan, and as soon as the gravel reaches the approach to that factory, then specially trained squads of Stompis will charge the gates, break them open, and raid the stores. Weapons are being prepared that should enable us to overcome the security guards, kill them and claim those thousands upon thousands of tins of petfood. The factory processes pet food. But this is all 'Hush-hush', so don't say as I ever said a word to you about it. But come the great day ...'

Barry turned away and began to walk back to the stores, thinking that what had not been factored in to this scheme, was how the thousands upon thousands of tins of pet food were going to be negotiated up that daunting gravel bank. He said nothing, that conundrum could be solved later. Perhaps sledges, trays hauled up the bank ... perhaps ...

They entered the store, stood a while at the zinc plated desk. No one was about. Mr Hornchurch's name was halloo'ed but no reply. Then Barry noted a neat batch of cans of black spray paint at the far end. They took them and made to leave when a warning voice, Mr Hornchurch's, bellowed after them,

'You'd better deliver on the promise of those wheelbarrows!' They turned, no one was about, so they hurried out and back to Citadel through the unremitting drench. Dublo's plastic mack was nothing but a fringe of shreds around his collar, the rest lost to the wind, and his suit, mangled into a twist, was distinctly sodden.

The walk back to Citadel was something of an anticlimax, its swept plaza offered no comparison with the vastness of the concrete apron before the long shed of Central Store. One day it would be Barry's domain. He didn't think it at the time, but later, in a mute moment or two of self appraisal, it came to him that he was displaying something of the strident ambition that Muriel had so wanted in him; an intimation of a ruthless conqueror.

The rain had eased to a slight veil of drizzle, no more ripping sounds of Dublo's mack being shredded but the wind turned cold. This was unusual, temperatures since the rains had been kept at the level of a foetid warmth. Now he experienced the slight suggestion of spears of dank coldness running up his back, it was disconcerting. The more so, or in tandem perhaps, as the exalted mood, the Dah, diddy dah dah, of the music had left him. Had he overreached himself? Further disconcerting thoughts happened when he noted a familiar grouping of buildings and he urged Dublo, who up until now had been silent all the way back, to come with him. He wished not to do so, but Barry was insistent. He could see now that they were at the point where the alleyway that led to Hector's bookshop joined the plaza. There were still Stompis about, they could be heard gutting another shop down the alleyway. Then he noticed, even as his thoughts turned to Harold and his possible whereabouts, the fire … that fire with a shawl of cindered book pages and … unmistakeably, the rack of ribs jutting out through the scorched detritus, still a few wisps of smoke even. His aghast thought, was immediately quenched somewhat by the dubious conclusion that they weren't his uncle Harold's ribs … because, well because there was no sign of the remnants of his map. If Harold had been brutally murdered, it would be with his scroll of precious map in its metal tube, still in his hands. Of course and as he raked the toe of his shoes through the blackened and browned paper ashes, it was only leaves of books that could be found.

Harold had escaped. But where to? Was he even now hiding, crouched and fearful upstairs in the gutted remains of the bookshop? It would have been safe there, the squad of Stompies had moved on to another boarded up shop, one emblazoned with adverts for various household provisions that had been stocked within. He checked the gutted remains of Hector's now anonymous, black cave of a bookshop. A scutty litter of torn pages, trodden and kicked about, splintered fragments of shelves, everything derelict. He went to the back stairs, Dublo waiting, hovering uneasily on the doorstep, clearly fearful of the Stompis and their indiscriminate violence, never trusting that such violence would not, for no obvious reason, be suddenly meted out to him. Barry tried the stairs, but amazingly the destructive vortex that had been unleashed upon the bookshop was such that even the stairs had been sundered, the stairwell choked with jagged fragments that were painful to contemplate. There was no upstairs and no remains of Uncle Harold, he had made his escape, judiciously without a doubt, stage by stage and he would by now be down the Dingley Dell, licking Marmite off his fingers and rabbiting on about The Old Chronicle. 'Course he was, no doubt about it. Barry was relieved, he could even afford a smile as he joined Dublo quaking in the doorway, just at the point that the painful shriek of metal was accompanied by a jeering cheer followed by the din of stamping and hammering on the sundered advert.

'C'mon' said Dublo and made to move hastily away. Barry caught him by the elbow.

'Not yet.' And he steered this member of the Triumvirate down to the shop being wrecked. Dublo made gulping sounds and he looked nothing like a figure of senior authority as he was reluctantly dragged, almost whimpering, his torn plastic mack in shreds, his Adam's apple in spasm.

The Stompis ignored them, so busy, levering other

advertisements off the wall. The door of the shop was locked, although marked by the heels of their boots. And then …

Well indeed and then, Barry felt a searing, suffocating tremor of Wodgecess overwhelming him. He too stamped, stared at the lurid wreak of the sky, stamped, as ferociously as any Stompi, though he couldn't match the abject severity of their boots. He quavered and wavered, but controlled his shaken self … because in the wodge that had provoked this dreadful reaction, one that would have overwhelmed him, he glimpsed a purpose. The enamelled sheet of the advert, now dented but still fixed to the wall, beside the locked door were the words, Cherry Blossom Boot Polish: a product he had been much enamoured with for many years previously; furiously polishing his shoes each morning before going to work; 'hey-ho, hey-ho, so brightly starts the day'. Memory … .stuff of cess, or word wodge, but then, out of it, a gleam of a new future purpose.

Redemption! Purpose founded in the ulcerated contours of the authoritarian mind, not Barry's but Stent's, the whole quagmire of their destructive intent could be illuminated, so to speak, by tins of BOOT POLISH!! He pointed at one of the Stompis who seemed to have some degree of authority over the others, clicked his fingers and snapped an order. 'Force that door open!!' The Stompi so addressed adopted a sneering tone, saying that the door was locked and …

'Open it!! Barry shouted …

'Now!, added Dublo at his shoulder, some convincement returning to his throat, standing in the penumbra of Barry's controlling mood.

To give them credit, they did so, the Stompis, with a wrecking bar, a lump hammer and a screwdriver to lever at the hinges. They got in each other's way, they grunted and snarled but within a few minutes the door was half off, leaning inwards into the gloom darkened interior.

Barry pushed them aside, wading through a scree of various products until he reached a display of boot polish … black of course and in those little round tins with the funny little lever to open them; as a kid he had been fascinated, happily playing for hours, opening and closing the lid and enjoying the smell of the stuff. Ha, a scratched thought at the back of his mind … smell, could that be part of a destructive deluge of Wasness, or, could it have a rescue value? He actually entertained this question as he scooped every tin available and shoved it into the voluminous pockets of his gabardine. Had Dublo got pockets left in the strip curtain remains of his plastic mack, he would have filled those also. But he did have pockets in his suit, twisted about his figure though they were and Barry filled them, holding Dublo tight as he did so, his diminutive figure shaking defencelessly, his teeth chattering incoherently.

'Don't ask, don't look at them, just keep them tight, because they are gold dust Mr Dublo, sir. They will bring Stent completely over to our side, it will make him our ally, believe me.'

Dublo offered no resistance, even though his suit pockets bulged, even his breast pocket, in which a handkerchief, sodden and grey with mould had been secreted. He made to protest as Barry tossed it to the floor.

'You don't need that. For heaven's sake you kept it hidden, no one knew as you had a handkerchief.'

'At ceremonial occasions and you never know …'

'No you don't and never will, but believe me there's a much greater profit margin in just one of these tins.'

They marched out of the shop, bulbous, their pockets swollen panniers, so much so that they had to walk swaying from side to side. Barry's pockets were so clump full that the stitching that affixed the shot silk lining to the gabardine material started to come unstitched. No matter and Dublo, recovering some of his composure, ordered the Stompis to destroy the shop if they wished. A mistake that, to Barry's way of thinking, there could be other treasures that would provide them with future salvation in its deeper recesses. Too late now, the Stompis began their mindless ransacking even as they waddled away, to Central and to address the next problem, assigning Barry with permanently fixed living quarters.

Chapter 14

But first things first.

No sooner than they entered the muggy atrium of Central Tower, the scrubbing and mopping activity still on-going, inside and out; could be heard. That distinctive scrape of buckets being kick-pushed across the hard floor bespoke of domestic labour. It was an encouraging sound and the dexterity of the cleaning teams had to be admired. They were high windows, and their mops, with long wooden extensions tied to the handles, were obviously difficult to use. Dexterity was needed.

They were ushered past the cleaning and up into a first floor meeting room and the company of Stent and Stryne.

Yes first things first … and it was a growing mystery, as far as Barry was concerned, when he was informed yet again, with tight lipped and taut faced severity that the name, his name … Rasher was never to be used, never even to be acknowledged. Did he understand that?

No he didn't but as far as he was concerned it was of little significance. He nodded, even grimaced a smile then added that he thought he should be designated as Senior Citadel Production Controller.

They mused over this. Stent managed to mutter something indecisive while Stryne flashed a scimitar smile and in a fluted tone, murmured, 'So be it … it shall be so.', rapping his bony knuckles on the desk. He then added with a sour tone of superior intent, 'but not Citadel surely, things have moved on and an advanced nomenclature has been established by Astartobe, not that you would know anything about such things. So, no, not Citadel but Uniate. Do you not think that should be so, Mr Dublo?'

'To the very point.' Murmured Dublo in a tone that was intended to be benign but betrayed an annoyance at the suggested slur on the state of his awareness of such things, so much so that he had to make an addition to the proposed title. 'Senior OFFICIAL Uniate Productioncontroller.!'

Stryne chuckled and nodded agreement. Stent shouted something about becoming bogged down in words and kicked the rotting skirting board in frustration and so it was commonly agreed that the term should stick, on the recognition that 'Productioncontroller' should be one word.

Stryne placed a demeaning hand on Dublo's shoulder, simpering through a smile that it was important that they get things right, as he was sure they all understood. His display of tact was toxic, as were all negotiations between them.

And then, when it seemed they were about to start a prolonged series of circumnavigational questioning, Barry made his second request … but no, not a request but a demand, of course it was, a demand and he was letting Stent, Stryne and Dublo, who was now fully divested of his ruined plastic mack, have it full in the face. He would put their Triumvirate to the test.

'As Senior Official Uniate Productioncontroller I have to say there are many things going wrong here. Those bodies you are carting about all over the place …'

'Gawpers!' snapped Stryne, raising his eyebrows in disbelief. 'For heaven's sake man, have you no sense of …' but his words were obliterated by a snort from Stent, grubbing out..but they am bodies Stryney boy and we all know it. What you call 'em is your business.' And he chuckled, winking at Barry, effecting a matey familiarity with the new man.

Barry explained, his tone matter of fact and with an urgency to get to the point,'I know full well what they are and how they are labelled, but they are still a product, the movement or management of which requires efficiency …'

'They are taken to the cathedral' said Stryne, about to give a theological argument as to why they were to be so purposed.

'Doesn't matter one iota where you take them. The point being the method of cartage.'

'Cartage!' expostulated Stryne.

'Carriage then. Cartage–carriage, call it what you will, the point is that you are carrying them propped up in wheelbarrows.'

'So!' snapped Stent. This was his area of jurisdiction. Cartage was him, purpose was Stryne, at least when it came to dealing with the Gawpers.

'Wheelbarrows are needed at the ramparts', Barry insisted, 'at the gravel banks. There needs to be dozens, hundreds even, of wheelbarrows stacked in line at Central store, ready for a rapid expansion of the gravelled perimeter. One day there will be intruders, there always are, and we must be ready to be able to strengthen those ramparts before they arrive. I suppose what I am saying is that The Uniate should be on a war footing, ever ready to resist invasive forces. Furthermore, Storekeeper Hornchurch …'

'Hornchurch!!' guffawed Stent in a derisory tone.

'On whom you rely!'

'For certain things … for the time being, yes, we do not doubt that, of course not, but when it comes to transporting our Gawpers, then all is being carried out satisfactorily.' purred Stryne. It was obvious that other methods of cartage were considered as being of ultimately no significance by the theologically minded collector of 'Gawpers'

Paying no intention to any of this, Barry, in full production controller mode, uttered in a tone crisp as celery, 'Mr Hornchurch needs every barrow he can lay his hands on for the coming offensive … and..so … they will all be returned to him, immediately to facilitate the extension of the gravel ramparts, to ensure they will reach the border fences of the Pet Food factory as soon as possible.

Stryne's expression was one of pained torment and he whined, 'The Pet Food Factory! Really!?'

'How are we to transport the Gawpers then?' queried Dublo, adding, 'they fit neatly into a barrow'.

'In wheelie bins.' Barry announced simply.

'Wheelie bins?!'

Their aghastment was pervasive. Barry said nothing, just stared at them. The silence was grappling with all their minds.

'They don't rot. Gawpers do not rot.' began Stryne, 'they do not need to be incarcerated in … wheelie bins.'

'No one is saying that they do rot, not at least for the moment. But the important point is that by transporting them in wheelie bins we free up dozens of wheelbarrows. I say dozens, it may even be hundreds. Does anybody know?

They looked at each other.

' No, I thought as much. We really have to control our processes. We have to be prepared to defend our realm. Because the one thing that we all know, is what we don't know. We don't know what other domain might not come and attempt a takeover, do we?

There was a sour puddle of silence.

'I rest my case.'

There was a long pause. Stent went to speak but Stryne hushed the intention with a particularly venomous look. He rapped his knuckles on the table. 'Do you realise the theological importance of the Gawpers, and why they are installed in the cathedral?' his tone was almost a snarl.

'Not my provenance, sir, I'm only concerned with the mode of locomotion, though I have to say when the cathedral is full, then chapels will have to be brought into use.'

'Other denominations …!' Clearly a further intolerable problem.

Dublo moved quickly to interject, hoping to defuse this other and future issue. 'De- sanctify them, bell book and candle, that sort of thing and re-sanctify according to your necessary First Uniate Christophanic Kingdom, theological stipulations.'

Stryne growled some Latin expression and fell silent.

Dublo gave Barry an uncertain smile and then asked, 'Assuming we accept the point vis- a- vis Hornchurch and his needs for barrows, are you expecting the Gawpers to be folded into the wheelie bins?'

'And so damage them?!' this from Stryne, his eyebrows arched.

'And furthermore, you'd have to clamp the lids down on their heads and I'm sure that would damage their benign aura.'

'Bang 'em about the head' guffawed Stent glancing at Stryne for verification but he was competently ignored.

'Young man you know nothing of what you talk about. Gawpers, and I'm not at all fond of that word, but there you have it, Gawpers are exultant, their arms are thrown wide. Wide in welcoming the advent of our new age. How do you, for one moment, think you could fit a Gawper into a wheelie bin? Eh? Cramp their arms down, deny their Pentecostalism? Eh? Eh?

With that, considering his case overwhelmingly won, he ambled to the blinds, tittering in the draught against the window and smiled to himself. If there was one thing about Stryne that was certain, it was his ineffable sense of his own superiority.

Dublo chuckled. 'You perhaps don't understand the nature and provenance of the Gawpers, you see ...

Barry shot in quickly, 'The wheelie bins will be cut down, at the front! The Gawpers will be able to lean back, in comfort, not forced to be placed upright, as in a barrow, but reclining, and with the sides and front cut away, their arms will be extended, their 'exultation', as you put it, undiminished. What is more the wheelie bins will be painted white with a red cross added on each side. It will be special cartage, acknowledged as such and Hornchurch will have the barrows I have promised him.'

'You had no right to promise that!' snapped Stent, his snot bubble quivering beneath his nostril, 'No right at all!'

To be on the wrong side of either Stryne or Stent was an uncomfortable, even dangerous location. But Stryne's manner eased; this new upstart might have a point; the Gawpers reclining, yes, there was a style, an aggrandising even, and painted white, with a red cross, yes, he could countenance that. To hell with Hornchurch and this madcap scheme to assault the Pet food factory. He knew what that was about, Hornchurch believed that there would be troves of implements in that Pet food factory shed that he could add to the ranks of useless utensils he harboured in his stores. What is more, in his heart of hearts he wished ill of the scheme, those promised thousands upon thousands of fresh supplies of food did not sit easily with him, it meant more survivors and for longer, it was a scheme of incipient communism. No the fewer that survived the better, just the odd hundred or two, to be exalted, yea, unto the kingdom of the Lord. Be that as it may, Stent and Hornchurch, well what a combination of dunderheads! No, let them get on with it, their nature, function or even existence played no part in his Theodicy. But Barry's suggestion … he could cope with, indeed, he would support it. And his Mister Punch face relaxed, the long stringy cheek muscles all but disappeared and his black tooth indented his lower lip all the deeper as he made strange simpering sounds.

Stent was brutally dumbfounded. He wanted nothing more than to take somebody into a corner of the room and kick them to a pulp but he said nothing, simply staring at Dublo, possibly thinking yet again that it would take no time at all to pulp him. Dublo was always the focus of his obliterative imagination. Oh, to have his hands assuaged with the warmth of his spouting blood.

'I take it that the decision on wheelie bins, as cartage for the Gawpers, is passed then?' Barry ventured. He looked about, eyebrows raised.

'Provided they are cut to shape and painted as promised …' murmured Stryne.

Dublo looked at Stent.

He sniffed the bulb of snot back up his nostril, 'And the free'd up barrows are used for gravel tipping?'

'Naturally, that is the whole purpose of the transference.'

Silence until Barry added the obvious, 'And of course there is an ample supply of wheelie bins, they are to be found at the side or around the back of almost every habitation.'

'Once habitation.' snarled Stent, kicking the skirting board.

'So, so,' murmured Stryne. 'Quite right, Commander, once habitation.'

'And that gentlemen concludes our business for today'. For a moment Dublo almost looked relaxed.

Stryne left, giving them a dismissive flick of his fingers. Stent grunted and also made to leave, but obviously in an uncertain mood, his long, thick, drainpipe neck was mottled red and glistening with sweat. Barry stopped him with …'Commander Stent, I have something for you, a grace note for you and the uniforms of all the senior Stompis' uniforms, their boots … look.' and he emptied from his swollen pockets, a numerous clatter of the tins of shoe polish. 'Just think, how, when on parade, the boots of your senior ranks will glisten. Immaculate!' And he nudged Dublo, they had rehearsed this moment, who opened a tin, smiling as he turned the lever, and then with a morsel of cloth, smoothed and then polished the toecap of Stent's left boot. It glistened and shone, an evil smile fixed upon Stent's lips.

'If we apply production control methodology, then the life for all will be enriched. Smart, shiny boots for the topmost ranks.'

'Smarty Stompies.' Added Dublo, managing to seemingly smile and frown at the same time. 'You have to admit Commander, it has an unforgettable ring to it.' Barry nodded in support as Stent began shovelling tins into the various pockets of his uniform. He made no further comment but scarpered away with the lot of them. He had managed to clutch well over a dozen in each of his gross fists.

'A distinct victory all round, I think.' murmured Barry. Dublo nodded and added, 'Now we have to find a suitable habitatment for you, you do understand you will have to be domiciled here from now on?'

Barry nodded, he had no wish to return home to gaze on the six inch nails he had hammered into the wall and door of Muriel's bedroom, or to confine himself to the narrow cramp of his camp bed, so he nodded and Dublo led the way. He did think though, as they hurried along the damp corridor with its slimy floor, that he could perhaps go back and regain his eiderdown; he would certainly feel more at home in his new habitament if it was always available to wrap round his shoulders.

* * *

Concrete is porous: not everybody realises that. People in the main would think that on regarding a wide concrete apron, for instance, that water would run off, or be evaporated, not that it would sink through it. But it does and it will do, because concrete is porous. And so in the high, twelve storied, blocks of flats, water has to be kept out and to achieve that the concrete must be treated; the flat roof has to be thickly coated in black asphalt. And in the general order of things this would suffice, providing of course that due maintenance and inspection is carried out. However given the new order, such a routine could not be guaranteed, indeed, not to put too fine a point on it, maintenance routines 'went out the window', as the old saying used to go.

What is more, and there always is a 'more', the incessant down pouring, made even more destructive by the high winds, resulted in the material disparaging of the asphalt coating, it became pitted, fissured and eventually rutted, so that irregular but significant revelations of bald, concrete exposures would have been immediately obvious had anybody ever ventured onto the roof, but of course none did.

Puckered wavelets, quivering in shifting puddles congregated across the roof, with the result that water leaked in, dripping down, or running across the ceilings where it slid down the inner walls to form floor puddles that would soak through down to the next floor, and so on and so on, till it effected the top four or five floors, rendering them no longer habitable and almost unusable; though at that level, the intrusion stopped.

Well, it mattered little seeing as there were several other floors below available for Habitaments. The first three levels going up above the entrance lobby were designated for concentrated habitation by the ranks of the lowest grades of Clerkdom. They were crowded, noisy and irksome. But of course, those of the middling and upper ranks had of necessity to progress up the staircases of the first three floors to reach the relative sanctity of their second and third, three floors. And yet there was incidental purpose in this staggered trajectory, it served to keep the Middle Grade on their toes, because if there were to be any perceived dereliction of their Task-duty, then down to the lower grade they would go, to become denizened in those crowded, often calamitous corridors, where indeed many slept, whimpering through the night. Sleep if attained was often putrid with the senseless slop of aggravating dreams; many woke retching in vile spasms. On those first three floors one only breathed the exhalations of one's fellow kind: sleep ease was never attained.

The next three floors were those of middle management. And the superior three floors above them, accommodated the grandiose levels of senior management, who exhibited the same fastidious disdain for the middle order, as did middle for lower. Prolonged observation of the conditions on any of the lower floors, brought about a palpable shaking and nausea, induced by the perpetual fear of relegation. And of course, it must be borne in mind, those higher levels could only be gained by scuttling up flights of slippery stairs, which led to such lung rasping and splurge breathing that the pace of ascent was tortuously slow.

The result was that there developed a precise custom of cold polity, of ironic deference between any upper and lower level habitué. For instance an out loud response or comment on a lower grade corridor to an habitué of an upper grade, in passing on the stairs, would always be acknowledged with half closed eyes, a fluttering of the eyelids, a gracious nod, and a general murmuration of appreciation, as of a servant to a master. Always there had to be a mutual condescension between the triage of grades: it promoted the 'Uni' of Uniate.

And what were the 'niceties' that were allowed to those of the highest level, the senior managers? Well some flaunted waistcoats, some others sported silk cravats, or perhaps carpet slippers, cardigans even, all redolent of relaxed power, symbols of assured superiority, of domestic urbanity. Nothing could be a complete despair in those lower levels if there were denizens seething with aspiration to ascend to a higher grade, willing to do anything to be able to wear such finery. Anything at all … Such was the glue that held Uniate together.

But what Uniate could not provide was immunity from the awful reality of Mindcess, that sudden fall into the destructive palaver of Memorysick, the mental suffocation of Wodge. Different words but all for the same condition.

Now, what about those top four floors, wherein waters had seeped ? No possible habitaments there. The two uppermost floors were always full of a black-must, a suffocating fungoid dust that filled wall to wall and floor to ceiling. Doors were shut, locked and the surround gaps sealed with black duct tape. Given the inevitable way of things the duct tape peeled away after a time, though it had to be said, that either as a measure of efficiency or the necessity of sheer desperation, it would be quickly reapplied by inspecting squads of Maintenance Stompis. Yes, they had multiple roles, as Stent would always be keen to point out. That left the next two floors beneath the fungoid floors. These were inspected regularly for any further descent of the deadly must. The ceilings were black but the same Stompi maintenance squads raked them regularly so that no growth ever began to proliferate. Even so those floors were bereft of human purpose, for the foreseeable future. They were empty, echoing and eerie.

All of this was explained to Barry. He had the benefit of being established in a middle location, where some social niceties were expected: no noise at night, courteous dispensation towards others on the same corridor and the allowance of two, but no more, familial type possessions: picture less picture frames, mirror less mirror frames, an ornament, provided it bore no human resemblance and surprisingly, a book, but one without wordage; so, a set of log tables, a railway timetable, from which the names of all stations had been erased, in fact any set of data, hard bound or paper bound, in which only numeration appeared on the damp slimed pages.

All of this was explained to Barry as Dublo escorted him to his apartment. At the door, which was swollen with damp and jammed, Dublo gave a practised kick and it croaked open.

'I will leave you to settle yourself in. There are two floors of Middlegrade habituation below and one above, so you should have a peaceful night. A senior Stompi will collect you in the morning to explain your duty and provide a rota, which it goes without saying, will be strictly kept to at all times. You do, of course appreciate that.'

Barry smirked, he had now had time to formulate an opinion of Dublo, the oleaginous diminutive personage, probably a possible ally, intelligent enough to be receptive to Barry's ideas of mensuration and quality control, which, as he had insisted, on their long climb to his future floor, were just as necessary as component delivery rates.

Dublo nodded but before he left he warned Barry to keep the door to the corridor half open, explaining that if it remained shut all night, it could be most difficult to prize open the next morning and, with no ventilation, the air within his apartment would severely aggravate his breathing. With that he slid away, back down, the stair well that faintly echoed the desperate sighing and slobberings rising from lower floors. And was it not a low, soft moaning tone of a saxophone he could discern drifting down from above? At least it was not a cornet endlessly repeating an all too familiar theme, loaded with a poisonous freight of 'once upon a time' ness.

Barry examined his new habitation. He saw a single room with a large window, all but obscured by a green patina that on inspection was found to be on the inside, though nail scraping failed to remove even a sliver of the stuff. A door off led to a bathroom which included a toilet with no seat and a washbasin rimmed with a brown stain, probably due to a single tap that whispered a continuous dribble of brackish water. It was not home but removing his gabardine mack and easing off his shoes, he unfolded himself onto the bed, drew a thin blanket over him and closed his eyes. The wind outside was wild and somewhere above it was shrieking through a gap. What wouldn't he give for his Great Grandmother's eiderdown right now.

Even so he had to admit this bed was more roomy than the narrow camp bed Muriel had eventually consigned him to. Her well being or whereabouts occupied him for a while but now he had a new horizon before him, a new realm of organisational possibilities, even a … At this point he fell into a dreamless sleep that would have continued for who knows how many hours if he hadn't been crudely wakened.

His awakening was achieved by a Stompi that had been sent to collect him and bring him in for briefing by Stent. The Stompi had barked out a sound and on not getting a response, leant over the bed, carefully peeled back Barry's eyelid and dropped a mouthful of gathered sputum into the eye. The eyeball quivered, Barry made restless sounds but no more, so the Stompi repeated the process in the other eye, though not just dropping the sputum but spitting into it. The result was instantaneous, Barry sat up, rubbed his eyes, discovered the spit and gawped at the wooden faced Stompi.

'You are needed at Central, now.' And he tugged the thin sheet, which in his sleep, Barry had wrapped around himself like swaddling for protection, off the bed. There was clearly no point in arguing, he hissed with joint pain in his knees and staggered to the wash basin to sluice the drabs of spit from his cheeks. The water smelt awful but it did the trick. He automatically looked about for a towel, but finding none he used the shot silk lining of his mack. 'Needs must.' he grunted at the Stompi and they made a sharp descent down the wet, glistening staircase, through a fugged-up entrance lobby and were about to leave when they were summoned back by a man in a fair-isle pullover who snapped at them that all entrances and departures had to be logged. He beckoned them back in no uncertain terms, tapping on the surface of a large ledger with a coloured pencil.

The Stompi scowled but pushed Barry towards the desk.

'Should have known better than to even try.' said the man in the fair-isle pullover and waited with a smarmy smile, now tapping the cover of his ledger even faster with the pencil.

Barry tried to explain that he was new and that it had been his first night and that …

The Ledger man raised his eyebrows, gave a cold smile, opened the ledger and indicated for Barry to record his departure. His name was already on the page and all he had to do was to draw a neat line beneath. He did as told, noting that the pencil made a red line. Ledger man screwed the register around, nodded and instructed that when he returned, he should approach the desk, use the pencil and underline his name again, though this time, as was indicated, it would be a green line. Red line out : green line in.

'Very good. Excellent method, well kept ledger.'

The ledger man stared at Barry, his eyes were pale, the edges of his lower lids swollen and red, and his expression was one of disdain. 'You do know as what would happen to me if I failed to record a departure: red, or an arrival : green don't you.' It was not a question, there was only suppressed malice in his tone as, while saying this he flipped over the previous pages of his ledger, indicating the uniform blocks of red and green markings, ensuring that Barry watched as page after page was eased over. Nothing was said, only the all but silent slide of paper upon paper was heard.

'No? Well …' he continued all the time staring at Barry, as page after page was turned, 'Then I'll tell you, some comrade of this fellow at your side,' a nod at the Stompi, 'would come along, hold my hand down on this counter, waggle my thumb about and then he would break it, snap it like a twig and then for further excrutiatement, he would waggle it about again, till I was on my knees, crying in agony.' He then stepped back from the counter and held his right hand across for Barry's inspection. The thumb was deformed, clearly it had suffered the torture outlined.

'Now the point is, Barry, (that was the only name on the register), the point is there is no way I am going to make that mistake again. You get the picture?!'

Barry nodded and said yes, adding that he would ensure the procedure for coming and going would always be observed.

'Then see to it!' he snapped and slammed his register shut.

The Stompi pulled him away and they stepped outside and into the downpour. 'They're the safest,' he snarled, adjusting the sit of his cap so as to keep it secure against the force of the wind, 'those that have crossed the line, transgressed the once and paid the penalty, they are the safest, they can henceforth always be relied on. And don't you ever forget it Barry Boy.' Barry flinched at the impertinence, but it was the Stompi way, he recognised that.

Stent's office was commodious, seeming the more so as there was little furniture. It was carpeted, though it oozed water when trodden on, not that that bothered Stent in his jackboots, already fully polished to the glimmer of their creases. A venetian blind, that was a luxury, rattled against the large, panoramic window, sight of the outside and its weather was all but obliterated, a definite bonus, but not the endless chattering as it swung to and fro. The individual slits long since discoloured from their original white to a greenish grey were greasy and the adjusting cords hopelessly intertwined. They sat in silence for a long while, not that Barry bothered, he was all too pleased since he could already hear the distinct sound of moving wheelie bins, presumably empty, being pushed in the direction of General Stores, he supposed, for the cutting and shaping necessary to convert them into Gawper Carriers.

* * *

Elsewhere, meanwhile, in the cathedral's echoing diminity, Stryne, who had been urgently summoned, was in a jubilatory turmoil, such as none had ever witnessed in him before. He threw his arms wide, he gasped, he groaned and stamped his feet in a little tap dance routine, spittle spraying devotions this way and that. And why? Because before him stood a newly arrived Gawper, perhaps the last to have been carried forth in a wheelbarrow. But oh, not any Gawper, this Gawper was different. This Gawper was exhalting. It was a Gawper of a higher order, 'Yea, even unto the utmost!', and Stryne bowed severally, in the four directions, relishing in his withered soul the essence of spiritual advancement in Christophanic doctrine that now stood before him.. Christies that were about, stepped back, murmured devotional mottos they had been taught to repeat with relish-but never to understand. They floor scraped with their heads, at the feet of this new, exalting Gawper. It had an aura that gestured magnificence into their several mindscapes, because this newly arrived Gawper wore a brightly coloured, glitzy clown's conical hat, with a pink bobble at the top. Of course it couldn't be placed just as the next one along in the array of Gawpers, special dispensation would have to be made. 'Yes!' hissed Stryne and announced that they place it on the altar. Of course, a corresponding amendment to his Uniate theodicy would have to be made, but the message imparted by this new and as yet greatest Gawper was surely, that Salvation was at hand!!

Chapter 15

Harold's flight down to Carol and the Dingley Dell, with his now even more precious map in hand, was accomplished in stages. At times his mind could concentrate on the necessity to progress undetected, but then at first, fear and panic hunted his steps. He ran whimpering from location to location, dreading being observed by any Stompi, taking a circuitous route from Citadel to his own suburb. After all he didn't know what information Hector had divulged before his awful death.

That awful death. He could but mustn't picture it. Picturing that would sicken his life ever after. Instead, his mind taking control for its own preservation offered, as he breathlessly stumbled along cess clumped streets, nuggets of part memories, not fond memories but memories in which his dear friend Hector had irked him, had annoyed him with the manifest wrongness of this or that opinion. Stumbling memories when Hector would not admit his wrongness in one of their frequent disputes. The superiority or not of a certain German battle tank. Hector, stubborn as a mule, had insisted this and Harold had read that. Or the reason for the failure of the German offensive in 1944 on the Eastern Front. Books would be pulled from piles, fact spat across the room and general harrumphing before doors slammed shut and weeks of non communication. The fact of the matter was to each, the other's contrarian opinion hurt, because they were friends. These indigestible but never to be forgotten nuggets of argumentative attrition, now surfaced. This was the Hector he had to remember and never the rack of ribs, the charcoaled flesh, the … .no, nothing more. On railways too, Hector was a ferocious contrarian. Hold that, and all its ramifications in the clutch of memory … not this but that.

So he wandered wider, through less familiar streets, his mind focused, except that now and then it was it was distracted by fond childhood memories these wider locations prompted. In such a delirium, he moved confidently, it was as if these streets could offer nothing more than boyhood nostalgia. For example when passing along the road that ran beside the station, even though his tottering gait was rolling and precarious, with his map clutched so very tight, even though he was whimpering, he recognised the station overbridge of his childhood memories and those memories became suddenly real events. Yes he actually heard the self important whoosh of steam, the clatter of the locomotive, followed by the clitter of the traipsing carriages as he ate the rewarding cream doughnut. Not memories but … injecta … of the past..and he could smell, taste almost, the billowing steam about him as he lurched up the steps of that favoured overbridge when in his early years his father used to take him every Wednesday afternoon in his school holidays to his Aunt Edna's, she lived at the end of the terrace and just opposite the overbridge where he had liked to stand immersed in the billows of smoke as the trains hurried through the station beneath.

Yes, it was real, he was fumbling with the doughnut, trying to eat it without spilling cream out the side of his mouth, not down the school blazer he would have worn then, when the sun almost always seemed to shine, but down … but down his now sodden clothes … and he angrily fluttered a swab of the cream away that had slopped down onto his precious map. He had to lick it off, this cream of over seventy years ago! It was all real again. His dad always gave him a sixpence to buy a cake from the station buffet and a penny for a platform ticket, telling him that it was much better he watch the trains from the platform rather than the overbridge, as the smoke was bad for his lungs. Well he understood that because his mother was always on to his dad not to smoke in the house, she couldn't abide the filthy habit. Aunt Edna didn't seem to mind though, but his dad had always said that he wasn't to say a word about his smoking at Aunt Edna's, because if he did, that would be the end of their visits, to Edna's or the station. So he said nothing; he knew which side his bread was buttered, as the old folks then used to say. But there had been a once, when it had poured with rain, not like now but what they called a heavy shower and he had come back earlier and found confusion, Edna all flummoxed and rummaging about in her skirt, twisting it round her waist, her pearl necklaces jingling and her face red, explaining that his father had just gone out the back, to the tobacconists to get a packet of cigarettes. He was told to sit on the sofa and she disappeared into the kitchen to cut him a slice of bread which was buttered and layered with plum jam- all jam was plum in those days. His father was funny with him when he returned from the tobacconists, telling him that he shouldn't have come back so early and that he hadn't even seen the London express, so what was he playing at? He couldn't now think for the life of him why he had come back early, though yes of course, the rain. Funny how things stick, even after all these years, and as far as he could recollect, he didn't think that he ever saw Aunt Edna again, or even watched the trains whooshing through the station. Odd, the things we remember, odder still what we don't remember; no two ways about it. Happy days though. He seemed to recollect that his father had ushered him back out, all in a comfortable confusion and he even stayed with his son on the overbridge, ready to be engulfed in the smoke as it seethed about them; the London express roaring away below. Such fun, though he couldn't for the life of him remember the name of the locomotive that he had triumphed into his log book. All fragmented now into a waste of wasness. Memories, they grappled with the mind, clawing truth from falsehood, or was it the other way round? Well that was one for deliberation, make no mistake about it, though not now, panting at the up-hill grade. What wouldn't it have looked like around here before there were any houses, any buildings of any kind? Gentle slopes, dells and little 'Humpty Dumpty' hills and great trees with roaming branches, filling half the sky. What wind borne chronicles were whispered or raged through the stout shires of those branches? What legends did they lay upon the air? And his legend, of the iron works of forge and foundry, now all long gone He knew he had to memorialise it all, one way or another, beyond the slide rule logic of sequence. Perhaps the Old Chronicle, it had to be. And there, his map would either be displayed or safely hid. Come what may, he felt that an idea was coming to him.

What into this delirium was injected? He had to cherish this mish-mash, not of memory but of reality ... he had tasted the cream that lay above the thin seam of red syrup that had always seeped into the soft flesh of the doughnut ... and ... yes ... he tasted it now ... even as he attended to the precarious circumstance of his retreat down into Dingley Dell? He stopped for recovery and breath, considering that though all that was then, it now still was, attempting to make sense of the When's coming back into the new Now. And what a coming back would there be, not just the trivialities of his own youth, but the coming back into personal lived experience of the real once of them all that had lived in lost, anonymous times long past. That would be 'The Old Chronicle' and of course, tangentially, it was all the more important that his map was safely delivered, in these new now times, delivered and deposited at the Old Chronicle, that its knowledge become legend, held beyond fact, become transmutable fable. His map would be a testament of the hoard wealth of it all, factory and foundry and whatever ... .no not whatever ... not glass works or such.

All is flux, nothing is fixed and this conclusion cloyed as tight as the suck of the red sandstone mud that gripped his ankles, slowing his approach, (he looked for the fossil dinosaur but found, this time, no trace) At the bottom he was hailed by Carol, waiting, as always, under the sheltering porch over her front door. And as always, or almost mostly as always, the sound of Skirker chanting and bellowing at his forge, weaponising the reinforcement bars, into cruel hooks and hideable traps, and Irene persuading Carol that if he did so then at least it wasn't disfiguring claws intended for the killing of Funky Lurgan, who, let's be fair, she pointed out, did deserve some sort of cumuppance, for his taking of Lovely Liz, as they called her, though to Irene she was always Lanky Liz. A cumuppance yes, but not ripping half his face off his skull with a freshly forged claw, made on Funky's own hearth and from his own bars. But then, when all was said and done, there was no reasoning with Skirker, not when his mind was made up, and made up it was now, no mistake. He would kill Funky Lurgan and rescue Lovely Liz. But what if, Irene murmured, what if it was other way round? What if Funky killed Skirker, as he could be quite prepossessed to do? At that Irene said nothing and sat in silence. Uncharacteristic of her, that.

Skirker only knew that Funky had rippled away with his daughter, Lanky Liz for his own foul ends, when she had loved him Skirker, her brother, her wild eyed beau, to the utmost; and he her, it was mutually reciprocal. Of course he'd never been told of the true nature of things, that wouldn't do, not that it mattered now. Anyway Funky and Liz would be long gone, away in his barge, binding her up into to his slut love, because that was all it had ever been with Funky. But the trouble was that Skirker, for some reason or other, now believed that Funky had returned. His barge had been seen, so it was said and also that Liz was with him. He had traded hundreds of packs of cigarettes for this knowledge, so it was said, and now he knew that what he had to do, could be done. He would kill Funky and rescue his lovely long limbed Liz, so that they could dwell together in the passion of their shared love. Nothing else mattered … nothing else could ever matter … they would be twain. End of !

Carol looked serenely doubtful about all this. 'What you need to do Irene, she murmured, 'is that rather than worrying about Funky and Liz, get a grip on that Doctor Stone fellow, find out what he is really all about, because there's no imagining with him, he's as dry as fact when it comes to the

173

reality of things, humping or no.' But she didn't say anything further, being distracted, watching Harold in a slow motion skidaddling, his shoes galumphing and sqwalping in and out of the mud with every step he took, his jowls aquiver, his brow mottled with the condensation of thingless thoughts, a metal tube clutched to his chest. Even so she reviewed his unbusinesslike collapse on her front step with kindness and promised that she would have Les fetch him a tin of something but she couldn't say what because the labels were all peeling off the tins in the tank.

'If it's not one thing it's another.' complained Irene. 'We don't know what we'm getting till we've got it and then it's too late to do anything about it.'

At which Skirker gave a bellow of triumph and emerged from the lean-to with a red hot claw of twisted bar held high in a pair of tongues. Yet again

* * *

Funky Lurgan, who still wore a dog collar and still cut a commanding figure, tall, upright and with a square set of shoulders exuded a palpable authority. His voice, now less commanding than in his pulpit days, was rather aggravating but he could use it to good purpose when he visited Citadel, which he did on regular, if not frequent, occasions. On the down side he wore a wretched blond wig, it did at least mask the yellowish ooze that flowed down the valleys of his weapon scarred skull but, ill fitting, it did have to be constantly readjusted.

Skirker had inflicted that, scar- ripped a flap from his pate, and come sometime soon, he would finish the job, let all those filthy desires empty out of his gaping brain pan.

In spite of his incipient urges with Liz, Funky he still wished the old days back: it wasn't the same with your own daughter. Those days of pulpit power, preaching to a congregation in which there would always be at least a couple of maidens who flashed nervous glances up at him as he thundered on about sin and damnation, about the tortures of hell and the bliss of heaven. Yes even the promise of celestial bliss would be thundered out with a wave of sexual pullulation that made nipples pert and the throat go dry.

Oh he recognised them, those sweet maidens who held back, who could easily be persuaded, to help, to collect the hymn books at the end of service, to count up the collection and then come with him into the vestry to record and deposit the tally. The vestry, he never thundered in the vestry, but with a soft voice thanked them for their service … handmaidens he called them, handmaidens in the service of the lord.

And then being so genial, allowing an accidental gesture to be a seemingly inadvertent contact on the fore arm, or even a lingering hand grasp, to produce the slightest quiver, he gave a tender smile. There would be a not too hurried slipping free of the hand, a blush as the arm contact was maintained, for a time long enough to arouse a sweet blush, of the throat, on the cheek, a lowering of the eyes. And then, with a cupped hand, a powerful hand, but oh so gentle, he would cusp their hair, tilt their chins, towards and upwards, smiling, noting the slightest pursing of the lips, which, invited trespass. But nothing further was attempted, not straight away, let things simmer until after a few such post Evensong moments, then he would bring the soft fullness of their lips to his, with a deep throated murmur of delight.

They were each and every one of them, special, unique, he had never been blessed with such tenderness before his preacher days. Then it had been … ..oh, but forget about dalliances in tool sheds and what not, it was in his church, as a preacher, that his dominance led to those oh so soft, hesitant surrenderings, allowing his strong hands to hold their shoulders and then, traversing the lengths of their backs, came mutterings and sibilant noises, hushed, beautifully inarticulate, beyond precise wordage, and all the while his confiding exploration advanced to fingered exploration until a rapturous gasping consummation suffused the chancel.

But then that once, oh that magical once, that unforgettable once upon a time once, when SHE had displayed her yielding body, legs gently opened, eyes avid, and there ... such beautifully, outrageous wickedness, there, of all places. Did he dare? He had to or lose all authority. This last love had been with young eighteen year old Muriel, the propensity, nay the capacity of whose loins brought ecstasy beyond compare, and there had indeed been much to compare with. Such memories could never fade. The fierce way she demanded, pulled him, out of the vestry and placed herself, spread upon the very altar ... demanding ... .if he wanted her, and beyond reason or sense he did ... that the fucking, had to be there, on the very altar table.

And it was Jeremy Camperdown this time, the organist. Up in the organ loft all the time, betrayed by a hymn book sent clattering to his feet. He knew, he had watched. Funky had tried to get up but Muriel held him fast. Was he the kind of man that would let a squinting organist destroy his passion? And she knew he had been there, of course she did. She was even aware of his elbow jigging up and down as he furtively scrutinised the proceedings. So much can be clear in retrospect but in the torrent of their fucking, blind and blatant, all was consumed. He shouted out, after all was over and he was struggling with his cassock that he would crucify him, Jeremy Camperdown, if word ever got out, but truth, like water seeps through everything.

He often wondered, whatever had become of her after the uproar that had never died down, after he was moved out. He was always being moved on, on but never out, his power as a preacher to fill not only pews but whole naves, aisles and all with a gasping congregation was too precious to be dispensed with in these crudely atheistic times. Both church and chapel had to take the benison of devotion however and wherever it came. But of the voluptuous, young Muriel, nothing more was seen. She had become a wife, so he heard, and had been married off to a twerp, some sort of an engineer, while he had been banished to a far parish with a glum congregation of disjointed pensioners, marooned in a flat county, even as his wondrous voice began to fail, its quality becoming little more than the raucous roar of a football hooligan. If only he had fucked that nosy parker spinster, Miss Belper raddled her starchy loins till her teeth rattled, if only he had knocked Jeremy Camperdown's teeth down his throat, everything could have turned out so differently. Because she also had watched alright, creeping down the nave, gawping in ... in what? Disbelief? Outrage? ... no, he didn't think so. She was getting ever closer to the action, her crab hands puckering her tweed skirt. If only he hadn't waited till her scream of delighted outrage hadn't scraped down the depth of the nave. If only, as Muriel ran into the vestry, he had strode down from the altar, his member erect and throbbing; well, then it might have been a different kettle of fish. But he hadn't and that was the end of that. He never saw her again, Muriel, that is. The spinster made a clerically public denunciation after Evensong the following Sunday, demanding the organist vouchsafe her accusation. He did and the congregation had been talking about it ever since.

What had become of her? Rasher, the twerp's name had been, Barry Rasher, so he had been told. Rasher ... God above. Oh there would still even now, be glorious dissolution in the power of those loins ... if she was still alive. Of course she may well not be; this new age was not one that encouraged passion. That had all gone in the bleak waste of time. But yes, he could imagine that Barry, the jerk- twerp engineer, could still be around, ferreting through the files of Citadel. Yes that was possible. He took a sip of brandy, held it, let it carouse his taste buds then swallowed slowly.

It was a sign of weakness, he knew that, maundering down through past idylls ... but Muriel Rasher, as she now was, could not be forgotten, in fact in honour of her passion, he re-enacted the voluptuous heaving of her loins ... 'Whatever you can give, I can take more' and then her shrieking and beating on his shoulders in an exculpatory passion, that endured ... yea unto the utmost. And of course it had been in the utmost; they had been discovered by that rabid spinster, who let it be known, to Muriel's Sunday-School Superintendent father, before the Evensong denunciation, so as he and his wife could miss their first Evensong in almost thirty years. He had aged before her very eyes and his wife twisting a wet handkerchief murmured something incoherent about perdition. They had both suffered too long and too much in the stifled precinct of their daughter's sexual adventures. He had actually gone to hit Funky, but it was just an insignificant twirl of the fist that he had easily side stepped. At least he had not responded, he just strode away, deaf to the superintendent's inchoate bellowing. His next appointment was announced within the week. The Rev Lurgan was now known as a travelling preacher, or as some put it, 'A travelling preacher man' What an Acute difference that last syllable conveyed. Yes, yes, yes, he should have strode down to the lip twitching spinster, his plenipotentiary member glistening to the fore, announcing, 'We will now sing the hymn, 'All things Bright And Beautiful ...' Had he been too much of a petty bourgeois to carry it through? Then on his head be it. The head of a 'Preacher-man.

And now he had to make do with Liz who was his daughter but no matter, she didn't know it, but she did know of Skirker In some deep crypt of her imagination she still loved him, that fearless boy of her brave childhood.

She allowed Funky's occasional forcements, lick slapping and grunting, heaving up against the barren plateau of her bony loins. She permitted him his futile transgressions because she knew that he held her future in the palm of his hands. She needed him, he gave her ferocious ego a sustainable raison d'etre. In that manner, and that alone she had her mother's characteristics. He could imagine, well he did imagine, that by the passionate intensity of his and Muriel's fucking, they had in some way, as a price that had had to be paid, denied any trace of erotic passion in their twin children. They had passion of purpose, but no sense of sexual desire. What would Muriel have thought had she known?

But now, in such different times, what did he care, slobbering through his own mind cess over a bottle of brandy? Nothing, he tried to tell himself but the telling was without conviction. Unfinished business, a distant echo in the back of his mind.

He had a barge, the two of them living together on the Lagoon, as it was supposedly named, him and her, two of 'The Fenris Folk', as they were preposterously called. It was him that had put that name about, fully aware of its mythic connotations. 'Wolf folk' who killed others they came up against. Merciless savages, feared by all, that lived on the lagoon and the sheltered canals that led off it, as far as the ever encroaching sea that would one day submerge them all. Whispered about in that dismal city centre parish that he had heard was now to be called, The Uniate; a mental factory of passionless repetitive mind energy that caroused an expletive church. Could he? No. Would he? No, and he grimaced at the though,t the impossible picture, of a congregation of arid Clerkdom.

The Lagoon! It was a name that was the product of a predictable imagination. It had once been a canal basin, flanked by rusted railway sidings, long unused but still holding a few wagons, wheels corroded to rail, from the once days when railways were everywhereabouts. There was also some ruination remaining of grey brick, slate roofed wharfage that had been a desolate long before the seasons of rain had started. The rains filled the canal to overfilling, the long neglected locks seeped leakages and then collapsed. Great swooshes of water hurled down to the next lock that also collapsed ; it was like tumbling dominoes. The waters ran all the way down until they were indiscriminately swallowed in that ever creeping up sea. And of course, the emptied locks were quickly refilled by the rains, until a generous current ran unimpeded to the sea, a gentle swirl aggravating the collapsing banks.

And so the lagoon, once a few acres, now hundreds of acres in its narrowish length. Cess didn't grow in it but it did overlap and overshade it, clumping down into the remorseless grapple of high reaching Thorn. The gloom beneath was deep, the only light filtering through the etiolated edges of the canopy, that of the Cess that was now beginning to glimmershine as the various clumps began to intermingle, deepening their anchorage in the fierce spikes of Thorn: Cess and Thorn in a symbiotic panoply; that had yet advanced everywhere but nowhere in such measures as here; within the vaults over arching the Lagoon and here, you were safe, if you had a narrow boat. A barge had more substance than a flimsy river cruiser and the white bowed wreckage of several such vessels could be seen cutting the sullen surface.

The lagoon had a singular feature that Funky and a few others of his ilk used frequently, the tunnel, that at the city end, penetrated into the deep reaches of the sub basement level of Citadel. Access could be gained at several points into public spaces, allowing sudden intrusions into the ever more closely monitored Citadel. He knew of the depredations of the Stompis, had even witnessed some, and watched, for long sessions at a time, the toing and froing of the diligent Christies. He had even become aware of the transition from wheelbarrows to wheelie bins. None of it made any sense, though he was perplexed by the ever fixed gawps of the bodies being transported, with their arms perpetually thrown wide..

It was small groups of self styled 'Anarcho's, who's intrusions via the canal route, wreaked psychic havoc in Citadel: raids accomplished by a few marauding individuals intent on destruction, for no other reason than the damage they could inflict. They took no loot back with them, Fenrisfolk wanted nothing from Citadel, except its destruction. That was their way and they lived otherwise entirely unto themselves.

Funky was astute enough to recognise that any change to schedule betokened something important because Citadel ran on regularity, repetition was extolled above all things and so, if something different was afoot, he was eager to agree, eager to learn of new possibilities. Could there be a future in which he could again thunder from the pulpit, the cathedral pulpit?

And could Liz be alongside him … as a vestal virgin, crooning wordless laments of grief

* * *

Dublo meanwhile had a purpose, it would involve Barry being in the same presence as Madame Rasher and that would present an opportunity to see if there was either recognition or reaction between them. It was important that at least he could feel himself to be on safer ground on that issue.

Before that though, Barry had to be put to the sternest test yet, one that Dublo engineered with Stent, who, dim as he was, harboured the same doubts concerning Madame Rasher and Barry Rasher. Thus it was that Barry found himself arraigned before both of them as his next 'mission of control' was put to him, its dangers carefully outlined. If he could survive these, he would certainly have to be elevated to senior management.

It was a test, Barry realised that, a major test of his inscrutability. A system called Statistical Cognisance, or StatCog, as it would be known was to be implemented. Stat Cog was to be nothing less than the creation of a purely numerical code, the creation of a limit language that would so help the myrmidions of Clerkdom who slaved away, bent over desks, following paper trails that both recorded and regulated Citadel's logistical processes: for instance sending orders to Central store, docketing the transport of requisites so that whatever tools Stompis and Christies needed to perform their duties, would always be available, as and when. To achieve this words were to be replaced by specific numbers that represented not only words but also at the same time the frequency which the words were used.

'For instance', Dublo explained, 'Screw would be represented by the code, SC23/7. SC meant screw, obviously, and 23 the type of screw while the 7 indicated the frequency that that particular screw had been ordered.

Barry was so excited he became breathless, seeing the advantage of the scheme and immediately thinking of what the code would be for the six inch nails he had plunged into the planks and walls of Muriel's bedroom ... .SC 30 ... 9?

But after the inception of this system of Statistical Cognisance, and here he sensed its innate cleverness, because over time, the 23 or 30, the number that indicated the type of screw would become redundant, frequency of usage would serve to give the same information. And not just screws, a coded number would have to be assigned for ... turnbuckles, Plummer blocks, winches, hoists, wheelbarrows, in fact the whole range of items in Central stores. And not just that, each and every transaction, human to system, clerk to clerk ... .even his and everyone's name in Ledgerman's record, would become just a coded number. Emotions also, because occasionally they too would have to be recorded somewhere, they too would be rendered numerically.

So, a docket to Central stores requesting screws would consist simply of two numbers

And of course with the ever expanding ramparts of Citadel encroaching on all boundaries, the Pet food factory already had its fencing nudged by the teeming bank of gravel, so soon the thousandfold victory yield of tins of pet food that would prove to be their salvation, would also have to be number encrypted.

A new system, numbers completely relegating words, sentences to become merely an exchange of numerical codes ... what possibilities! Bliss in this new dawn to be alive.

But then Dublo curbed his pleasure. He had to understand that even as the system of Stat Cog was being implemented, making evermore words redundant, Clerkdom would still be increasingly vulnerable to words ... word pictures even, that survived. And such words, relics of a past age, would be of a poetistical nature: they would have to be ground down to a useless litter of spent letters.

Barry harrumphed that he had never taken to poetry of any sort. 'In fact,' he happily proclaimed, '"I wandered lonely as a cloud" was about my limit.' But as he finished that line he became aghast at the enormity of even such a simple utterance. Lonely … .not even a non-word but a non- concept. In the new order no one was ever 'alone'. Likewise 'wandered'! how could anyone wander? No one wandered, everyone 'went'. Wandered was an expression of purposelessness. And 'A cloud?!' Oh dear no. 'A' cloud, when all above was a uniformly featureless grey. Clearly not just the 'wodge' of the written word but the traps of the spoken word had to be dealt with. All wordage had to be task and goal limited.

But it was here, Dublo explained that the greatest danger imaginable lay. One or two at a time, 'Vastage Vagrants' or 'Anarcho's', would enter the realms of Citadel and run through public spaces, shouting wordage of a poetistical nature, even playing an instrument and singing, all and each example of which would destroy the mindscape of any clone they happened upon. And so …

'They begin 'Quarking?' Barry said.

'Worse, a mad panic of group mind dissolution, a whole clutter of Clerkdom running about, rampaging, destroying … and of course, with such a calamitous panic, clerks looking down from their office will start panicking. No these 'Anarchos' are much the greatest danger we face.'

'So what is to be done?' murmured Barry, still feeling consternation from having uttered his one line of poetry.

'What is to be done?' repeated Dublo. He leaned closer. 'Well, Barry, there is only one thing that can be done, a special agent …'

'A Stompi?' interrupted Barry.

'A special agent, one of the bravest of the brave has to chase them away, down the passages they have extruded themselves from and gun them down.'

'You have such agents?'

'No, we don't, not until now. But now we have.'

'Who are they? Where are they?'

Dublo smiled and gently ran his little, black nailed fingers up and down the edge of Barry's lapel. Not a 'they', Barry, but a 'one'. We have just such a one'.

Barry frowned, Dublo was being sly and adjacent. 'Explain.' He demanded.

'You, Barry, you are 'the one'. You are the only 'one', the very "one.'

'But I have never chased a miscreant, never fired a gun, never even handled a gun. And in the darkness of a tunnel? Alone?!'

'What you have shown us from the very beginning is a remarkable singularity of purpose.'

'Even so, Dublo.'

'You won't be alone. You will have a mentor. He will accompany you down into the tunnel system. He will hand you the revolver and have it back when you have accurately fired the fatal shot.'

'In the dark?'

'You'll not be in the dark.' Now, no more questions, time to start.'

'Who is this mentor?'

'His name? What's in a name? What does it matter? Be assured you have not met him yet. But, if you must have a name, it's Stone, Dr Stone. Satisfied?'

Barry repeated the name and even as he did so the grumble thought rummaged through his mind that here was a weakness of the proposed Stat Cog system. How could a designated agent be represented by just a number? If he, assuming this … Doctor.. Stone to be a 'he', was a special and limited to one category. 20 could indicate a screw size, but what number could indicate an agent? Well, he supposed, the number would have to be prefixed by a series of noughts. But then Dublo … the matter was complicated.

* * *

He left, mind in turmoil by what he had been told, by the nature of this new assignment, though Dublo had left happy, the architect of the scheme that would solve the 'Barry Rasher' dilemma for good. If he failed this last and supreme test, none would know, Barry would be gone and none the wiser. If he succeeded, then surely he must be in some way connected by family with Muriel and she, as Astartobe, would, thanks to his prowess, obviously welcome him to the fold. Foolproof. And he didn't care whichever way it turned out.

Barry on the other hand, worried, and as always when in such a state, wondered what his parents would have said, his mother in particular. Well he knew the answer there. She would have securely smothered his questioning about the issue. Do as you have been told, would have been her instruction. His father, on the other hand had always growled out strict formulations, such as, 'Stick to what you know, lad and you won't go far wrong.' And 'Don't worry about what doesn't concern you.' To which his mother would sensibly add, 'You'll listen to your father, if you know what's best for you. Trouble was he had no father now to listen to.

Chapter 16

Everything now became apparent. What Dublo had tried to explain just a few days ago: the turmoil, the panic, the horror even' was now plainly visible. He was at the edge of the main square, protected by a wavy shaped concrete canopy that ran along and above a line of shuttered up shops. The rain was a deluge, with a ferocity rarely experienced even in these times. Such was its force it was difficult to breathe as one scuttled through it, bent-backed, because the weight and velocity of the water hurling down was considerable. Very few were about; just the odd Stompi draped in a shiny cape of some sort. All the gutters were overflowing, the square itself swimming inches deep in water, there being a white skirt of jumped up splashes above the tangled currants as a temporary river issued itself down into the suburbs. Even so there were meek and weak faces peering down from the offices above, the shutter blinds eased aside. They were watching the square: knowing there was a vagrant, an 'anarcho' about; they hoped to see him, or her, surrounded by Stompis with sticks pounding the miscreant to a pulp ... to 'Truncheon Meat, as the saying went. If they had been fortunate enough to see that, they would have been jumping up and down, clapping their pat-a-cake hands and dribbling with delight.

Dublo, who had accompanied him out onto the square, explained all this, adding that this torrent had probably saved the Anarcho's life. But then fortune favoured them, it suddenly all but ceased, just winding veils of bitter drizzle, the drainage 'glugging' and the rippled hiss of the departing flood. Dublo spat into the final swirl, Barry noticing that his sputum was finely laced with blood. Catching his Senior Official Uniate Productioncontroller by the elbow, he steered him to a large metal door, stained with rust, in a building at the far side of the square.

'This way, we might be just in time'.

'In time for what?'

'Killing him: down in the tunnel, as I explained to you, that's the way they get into Central, to do their awful work, singing, chanting, and it's also the way they get out, it's their escape route. He'll be down here now, biding his time, hoping to make sure he is not being followed.'

'Killing him how?'

'As I have already explained. Weren't you listening Barry?' There was a distinct note of disappointment in Dublo's voice.

'You said something about a gun, but I haven't …

'Dr Stone will give you one, he'll be down there waiting for us. He'll explain how to use it. It's simple, you just point and pull the trigger … bang! That's all there is to it. Bang and the Anarcho is dead.

'But …'

'But what?'

'I'm not really into killing people. Are you?'

'Let's just say that I am into having them killed. If it's to improve conditions, to establish a secure regime, then yes, I very much am and so must you be if you want to secure your status. You have shown promise, but that promise needs to be cemented in fact. Come on.' And with that Dublo applied his puny strength to the rusty door, which opened with a crow-caw screech.

Inside, once the gloom had been mastered, it was obvious they were in a vertical and circular, white tiled passage with a descending cast-iron staircase, its treads in an open work intricate design. From behind Dublo pushed him in the small of his back, pushed him down the staircase till at the bottom, everything musty, they emerged onto a long, bare platform, inches thick with undisturbed dust. It clogged the feet, muffling the sound of their steps and coughed up in their throats. Never had Barry found himself in drier circumstances.

'Ha, here we are.' Dublo happily proclaimed, nudging the Productioncontroller to take note a faint yellow glimmer of torchlight, at the far end of the platform. 'That'll be Dr Stone waiting for us.'

Barry gulped; touch of dust, perhaps, but more likely an eruption of fear. 'I'm not really into killing people.' He repeated.

'Who is, other than the Stompies? But this is beyond the reach of Stompies. They would be all of a quiver down here. They can't take the dark.'

'So am I.' Barry wailed. He remembered, and wished that he hadn't, how as a child he had been stung by a nettle, one of a fierce clump that grew unattended at the bottom of his parents' garden. He had cried and nothing would have persuaded him to go near them again. He even fantasised about falling naked into the nettle bed and frightened himself at the enormity, of the excess of that fantasy. He had whimpered all the way back up the garden to his house and a strangely restricted consolation from his mother who censured him for going down to the bottom of the garden in the first place. And how old had he been then, eleven or twelve. But now, a revolver, and to kill somebody.

As if reading Barry's thoughts, Dublo pinched his elbow and muttered, 'You'll understand soon enough. Dr Stone will guide you and believe me, you'll take to it, like a duck to water.'

'Take to what?'

'Killing, Barry, of course.'

'I'm not at all sure of that. Ha!'

This last gasp was caused by Stone striding down the platform, no sound in spite of his size, thanks to the mantle of dust. Dublo muttered some kind of greeting and introduced his putative killer. Stone took no notice, he just thrust a pistol into Barry's hand; this was done with such immediacy that Barry had no choice but to accept it. The implement had a certain familiarity from the films he had seen in the past, but nothing prepared him for its weight, which was such that the barrel immediately pointed to the floor.

'Hold it up!' Stone commanded.

'Is it loaded?' Barry asked, the words strangely not his but a repeat of words used on the silver screen.

He was briefly instructed, on how to 'release the safety catch', how to hold it, with both hands, how to allow for the instant recoil, and the fact that it would only be accurate and effective at a distance of twenty paces. Always aim for the heart.

So simple. And he nodded, not at all certain but accepting that he had no choice but to follow instructions.

'And the ... 'target?'

Stone, such a large man, in a padded high- vis jacket, that increased his seeming bulk, said only that the it was a Crypto-Anarcho whose utterances had 'wasted many who had been about, and many more would have succumbed had it not been for the sudden extreme deluge they had weathered through to make this assignment.

'Anarcho-Crypto.' Corrected Dublo.

Stone made no response, he simply gave Barry, who he addressed as 'our Kill Agent' the torch. 'Now, you keep its beam slightly above the horizontal, stride down the tunnel here with a constant step, you'll have the regularity of the sleepers beneath the rails to guide you, and count, out loud if you wish, as you progress. The target will soon be apprehended, because this is a circular line, consequently no escape route, no connecting tunnel.'

'Other stations though?' queried Dublo. Barry sensed him looking up and down the dust matted platform and shivering slightly.

' Several, but no exit route from any of them. Target is trapped on a loop.'

There was a moment's silence in which each briefly appraised each other. As far as Barry was concerned, it was the gross weight of the revolver that now bothered him, it was far heavier than he would have imagined. He held it horizontal, though in a manner that suggested he didn't know what to do with it. Stone took it back off him, put the safety catch back on and told him to put it in his mack pocket. He did, slipping it into the commodious sloping forward pocket of his gabardine. It hung loose, swaying the pocketed flap of the mack against his groin, causing ....

'Tighten the belt. Tighten it tight' Stone instructed and grunted as he was obeyed.

Dublo nodded, patted him on the shoulder and muttered some encouragement, to the effect that, 'We'll make a killer out of him yet, eh Dr Stone.'

Stone's only response was to repeat the instructions and then ordering him to drop down from the platform and to get pacing.

'Which way?' This was almost a wail.

'Any way' chortled Dublo, it's a circular route.

'That way.' Snapped Stone, turning him by the shoulders to face the way they had faced when they gained the platform. Then with Stone pulling Dublo away, Barry found himself alone in the snuffling, dusty silence that hung about his sodden shoulders like a pall.

He did not want this but there was nothing else he could do. He did sense that if he succeeded in killing this ... Crypto Anarcho ... what a convoluted appellation, then there would be a reward.Perhaps a better habitament, on one of top four floors. If he was honest he was frankly surprised that his decisions so far, particularly with regard to the use of wheelie bins for the Gawpers, hadn't merited the highest status. But then he was perhaps 'getting ahead of himself' as his mother used to say. What would she advise now, in these so different circumstances, he wondered yet again. Well he could imagine his father, with his hand on his shoulder, quietly whispering, 'Step at a time lad, step at a time.'

And yes, of course, good practical advice and he did just that. Not easy to start with, foot-fingering, toes pointed, reaching for the sharp edges of the concrete sleepers, then the next and equal step. And so he progressed, trusting the same measured step would reach the next sleeper. 'One step at a time Barry, don't complicate things unnecessarily.' His father again: such sound advice. Single sleeper steps and mutter the number of them aloud as he did so. It was an act of faith, each and every step, but a faith in the immediate tangibility of things, not in any vague hereafter.

So he made progress, exercised his faith and speeded up his mission. He developed a rhythm, his gabardine flapping, seeming to encourage faster progress, seeing as the inertia of the heavy pistol knocked against his groin with every step.

He did speed up, tunelessly humming some sort of metre that complemented the pacing. It aroused him and that enabled tangential recollections such as he had never had before, random but not inconsequential dribble trails of long spent memory.

A tune, several tunes in fact, with hammered rhythm, songs they had had to sing in primary school, the whole class, standing to attention on the scuffed wooden floor boards.. 'Dashing away with a smoothing iron …' and 'She'll be coming round the mountain when she comes.' The teacher, a formidable, Miss Bridgewater, with fat puckered elbows, a full, florid throat that quivered as she sang along, nodding furiously at them all the time, tight blond curls swaying with each nod and an alp of a bust that seemed to be all of one piece.

She drop forged tunes, they seemed to be all nothing but rhythm, on the school piano with its battered keys. But rhythm, yes, regularity, banged out remorselessly. One week she was away with laryngitis, and a Miss Daphne Lovedone stood in for her. In the singing class she so gently caressed the notes as she sang Sweet Afton to them and there was barely a dry eye in the class. But in playtime those that had remained stare faced and dry eyed, taunted those that hadn't. He in particular was taunted, and, what is more, teased the worst by those that had cried but alleviated their guilt by blaming him. He had cried the most, he had been the biggest 'cry baby'. He smarted with the pain and injustice but learnt a vital fact about human nature, one that he would never forget. The following week Miss Bridgewater returned, hammering out, 'Hearts of Oak are our Ships' and no tendrils of love and loss drifted across the stream of his consciousness ever again.

Well, not until now that is. It had had the effect of slowing his step. He shook the memory away, regained his momentum, and reminisced further. He had no choice, marching along this circular tunnel, its iron ribbed walls clotted with black clusters of industrial filth. Keep the thinking about counting.

And yes, there was a school time reminiscence that fortified. Because the one thing he had always been particularly good at were sums. Add, subtract, multiply, divide; he had particularly loved long division … .long, long, long division, where the downward diagonal steps, putting one number at the top the bringing another down each time, spreading the diagonal calculation in downward steps to the far corner of the page. Miss Bridgwater had assured his parents that, "Barry is a very good 'reckoner', probably the best I have ever come across". And yes, he had been well aware of the surfeit of satisfaction expressed in his father's pursed-lip smile.

He was stepping fast now, small single sleeper paces, but his speed and style, so elate, and the gun, waddling to and fro in his pocket occasioning in him a strengthening priapism that he would previously have thought untoward. Not now, now he was wanting the confrontation:his final, his supreme test. Accomplish this and he would be instantly uppermost rank, a superlative apartment and with his own slippers; cosy and comforting, twitching his toes, flexing the pattern, his legs splayed out as he reclined on his sofa. And what patterns of organisation he would initiate. His only regret that his parents were no longer alive to witness his triumph.

And those pupils that had wept at her singing, the ever so soft, Daphne Lovedone, crystal tears in the crucks of their eyes, loaded their shamefaced guilt on him. Because his tears had flown so effortlessly down his cheeks. But, oh yes, he knew now how to control emotional doubt; emotions of any sort were a quagmire, a sinking sands, an 'Okifinoki', trembling earth. He had found a way to deal with emotion when he was at secondary school. Often the nub of cruel jest, often bullied, he would take up an exercise book and divide, divide twenty two by seven, which of course went on and on for ever, but even as a teenager he had found solace in writing the numbers, neatly, each one filling the square of the squared paper: solace, certainty, devising till his mood had dissolved, the hurt not absolved but distanced, the pain, self doubt and ignominy reduced to a thin, friable wafer: all but expunged. A mere remainder ... Insipia Mathematica.

Such were the reminiscences he now entertained himself with, pacing relentlessly through the solid darkness. And then, of a sudden there was a distinct sound in the tunnel ahead. Was it a muffled falling of the clots of dust- filth that clustered to the ribbed walls? Probably. He shone the light of the torch into the void ahead but the dark absorbed its beam. But there had been something. He pocketed the torch, even as he unpocketed the revolver and eased the safety catch off. He could sense it, there was somebody ahead, a muffled cry, perhaps a stumbling, a wild falling, arms reaching pointlessly for purchase.

Victory snapped at his mind. This was the now, and it was not the need to gain in status he wanted, but the want to ... extirpate that wicked thing that wanted nothing more than to bring about the downfall of, 'stat cog', to wreck concepts of its manifest order. He no longer lacked the need to kill, not now, not the Barry who now emitted raw bellowings down the gape of the tunnel for the fugitive destroyer to stop.

And then he saw his Crypto Anarcho, or whatever. A figure. A face, pale and oval, suffused in the wavery light of its own lit candle.

He closed in, almost tripping in his approaching ecstasy, realising, registering that it was the pale, long face of a woman. It was a 'she', her eyes startling the light they peered into. He had overtaken her unstructured flight, her mistaken steps, her shin scraping falls, clutching the circular iron ribs to steady herself. She had had no method, no resolute step measure, hence her wild expression as he advanced secure and steadied his aim.

And then … .

And then mind splitting agony as she … it was a She … stood stock still. A standing still She, he grappled mind on that, let there be no other … but yes she sang … .such a sweet voice, she sang,

'Have you heard my fond tale / of the sweet nightingale / as she sings in the valley below …

This! That! Then!. Cry, him, not now, not ever … but yes, in the forefront of his mindscape … Daphne Lovedone herself … And he fired, straight at her face place, plastering it into a bloody oblivion.

He saw just a mask of blood, didn't hear the clatter, clump of her fall but the tunnel reverberated, and the echo ran the extant of its circuit and a second or so later came upon him from behind. The whole of The Uniate would now know of his deed.

'What now?! Go back, return to that Dr Stone fellow, he must have heard the sound, could not have, and hand the gun back. It was hot in his shaking hand. What had he done? Well he had done what he had to, done what had to be done and even the ranks of Clerkdom would cheer! Yes even the Stompis who were too frightened to venture into these tunnels alone. Over all, he had conquered fear.

The step back was painful, he kept tripping, missing his measure and stumbling, till he realised he didn't have to step backwards. Silly of him: he could turn his back on the crumple of the lifeless, face blasted thing, that had sung such songs as had made him cry at school. He had dropped the torch but Stone, still standing, gaunt and massive on the platform said simply that he was not to worry, providing the revolver was secure, which of course it was. Not Barry's mindset though, he was slobber talking, jibber jabbering wordments, everything askew. Stone hauled him up to his feet, then up onto the dust choked platform. He made him hold his arms out fully stretched and then bring them together with a clap, again and again, till the banality of the exercise restored his mindset. Then they walked side by side back up the spiral cast iron staircase, pausing only to squeeze themselves against the tiled wall to let a couple of Stompis, swaddled in bin-bags push past them, each with a grappling hook in his hand.

Stepping outside the cold air freshened and the downpour, though considerable had lessened somewhat. Above and about the towers of Citadel, the mindflux of Uniate and the organisation of measured certainty extended. The new world, a new word order had been vouchsafed and he was partly instrumental in its achievement.

Organisation, order and there was much more to come. Wheely bins for wheelbarrows, black Cherry Blossom boot polish for Stompi senior officers and now the expunging of a Crypto, something or other. His achievements were mounting. There would be rewards surely.

Chapter 17

'Nipakoffs!!! This from Irene, an explosive affirmation. 'That's what they were called … Nip … a … koffs.' She beamed.

Carol, desperately trying to get Harold into Funky's dressing gown, as she called it, reiterated the word in a warm tone. In reality it was not a dressing gown but one of Funky's old vestments, a white cassock with a golden sun emblazoned on the chest. Harold had been stood, quivering in his vest and pants, scrawny as a twisted dishcloth and now, with his arms all elbows, knobbly at that and his legs a mosaic of varicose veins, it was a work of labour to get the garment over his head and shoulders. He muffled incoherently from within. Carol instructed him to stand still while she persevered with the vestment.

'Nipakoffs' repeated Irene, 'That's what they were called.'

'Yes, we all remember them Irene.'

'You say you did but didn't till I come up with the name.'

'What you don't take account of Irene is that you can remember what it is that you've forgotten.' This from Skirker who absent mindedly scraped the heel of his boot against the end of the sofa.

'Skirker! Stop that scratching, you'll wear a hole in the leather.'

He scowled, it was because he had hammered spikes into his heels that she complained. But even so she worrited about that sofa as if there was nothing else in the world to bother about. That was women all over, and there was Irene still ranting on about bloody Nipakoffs.

'Nipakoffs, and I can see the word now, the way it was painted, black, chunky, bendy letters, written at an angle.'

'What about them Irene? Why you going on about them?'

'I was just saying. Funny what comes into your head.'

'It's funny what comes into yours.'

'Well it's better than nothing, Skirker.'

'It's not if you can't remember and you gets all mardy.'

'Who's bloody mardy?!'

'Bloody Nipakoffs, I ask you.'

'Well you don't remember them, you're not old enough.'

'Do and all, there used to be that enamel sign, on that newsagents at the end of Balaclava Terrace, on the gable end, bloody great sign and it just said Nipakoffs, am I right?.'

'Right enough,' intoned Carol, although she may have been referring to the cassock vestment, or whatever it was, that now sat, clear and pleated on Harold. He palmed the embroidered braiding of the sun design on his chest and smiled.

'The sign was there well after you could buy them.'

' I bought a packet once, not that they did any good. Tasted horrible and you had to be chewin' them for hours. I spat 'em out in the end.' This from Carol, making the final pulls of adjustment to the cassock.

'They were a sort of medicine really, and you are not going to get medicine that tastes sweet are you Carol?'

Carol now absent mindedly stroked the cassock and thought of Funky as he had been, striding about in the church and from up that pulpit, spitting hellfire and throwing his arms wide. What a performance,and free at that. Something to be said for churches, free entertainment and bust uplifting singing They loved the hellfire, and the rest, and who'd have thought what he was up to every other verse end? Well no one ever did, but they should have; should have been as obvious to the praying and kneeling Christians as it was to her: plain as a bobbin on a round of beef. But then, as she often concluded, there was no telling with some folks. And what did they call him, 'a man of God'?! Well that's a term you'd have to walk a long mile to hear these days, that's for sure.

Harold precipitated a few throaty syllables into the discourse with, 'I was always one for a 'Fisherman's Friend' myself, found them far more efficacious, if the truth be told.'

'It never is!' snorted Skirker.

"Fisherman's Friend" I remember them and all, in little square packets. Who'd have thought it?'

'Who'd have thought what?'

'For God's sake Skirker, let her be, she's just reminiscing, aren't you Irene.'

'I could never take to them though, brown slabs they were …'

'Whatever, they still tasted awful.'

'Efficacious though.' mumbled Harold.

'And hot, as I seem to remember. How about you Carol, did you ever try them?'

'Not as I remember.'

'But you do remember them, as a sweet?'

'They weren't a sweet, "Fisherman's Friend were a medicine.' snapped Harold.

Irene frowned, she could be just as contumelious as Harold if need be. 'No, Harold, they weren't but they sold 'em as sweets, in them little packets, always at the front of the counter.'

Skirker snorted. 'Because Irene, there was never no danger of the kids pinching them, seeing as they tasted like shit!'

Harold guffawed. 'Can't vouchsafe for that, Skirker, never tried it.'

And Carol, to pour oil on what she sensed could soon become boiling water demanded, 'Well the test is, would any of us have one now if it was offered?'

'Have one what?!' demanded Skirker.

'Either, Nipakoff or Fishermen's Friend.'

They exchanged looks. 'Because I wouldn't for one.' Carol intoned.

'Well perhaps a Fisherman's Friend, yes, definitely, a Fisherman's Friend, if I had a cough, that is.? Well you would wouldn't you, if you had a cough or a phlegmy throat.'

Skirker stood up, winked at Carol and said to Harold, 'But if you had to choose, a Fisherman's Friend, a Nipakoff or a spoonful of that brown muck you were fingering out of a jar the other day …'

Harold beamed. 'You're on the ball there Skirker. Marmite each and every time, without a shadow of a doubt.'

There was general elation as Harold clapped his hands together but Skirker warned, 'You'd best be careful when you'm slobbering Marmite down your wasin, not to get any down that cassock you've got on, and where's that come from I'd like to ask but I won't because I know as I won't get a direct answer.'

There was an icy stillness which Irene redeemed when she suddenly shouted, 'Abdul! I bet a pound to a penny as he's still got 'em …'

'Got what Irene?'

'Packets of Nipakoffs on his counter.'

Carol reached for her mackintosh. 'Well there's only one way to find out. Who's coming?' and she led the way through the door. One after another they all trooped after her, even Les, who'd just arrived, he'd been clearing the back of the van out; he followed without knowing where they were all heading, but then that was Lez all over.

And it must be supposed that it was something in the nature of an excursion, not that any of them would have used that term, not consciously at least. But yes, the way to Abdul's shop was gently, slopewise that is, continuously downhill, beyond the steep and knuckled slope of Dingley Dell in a cautious downwardness that lead, eventually, to those rusted railway lines and the canal basin. Naturally all of that had gone now, the railway with its many tracks, once logically knotted into a goods yard, all now beneath a foot or so of simpering waters, broad and brown, so too the canal, its locks soothed over, no puddle patches to be seen here, that was for certain.

None of this was of any significance to them, not even to Skirker at the present moment, not for the time being. No, what amused them as they set out was the leg easements they got by indulging in such a gentle striding down to the shop. The Shop! It was a moot point as to how they referred to it. Abdul's Shop, well yes, certainly, although everyone knew it was owned by his uncle Wassif and yet none ever bothered to call it Wassif's shop. Well of course not, he was hardly ever there, though Abdul was always there, in one way or another. Nobody ever really got to know Wassif, he wasn't around long enough and opinions, usually without any factual merit, tended to be on the severe side, such as: 'I wouldn't want to get on the wrong side of him' or 'He's a piece of work.' Such notions, bandied about, cemented judgements as to his character; but then that is the nature of social knowledge; it's a sieve and won't hold water. But it has to be conceded that when Abdul's uncle spoke to you, it would always be about some effervescent enterprise and while doing so he was eagerly 'in your face' as the saying goes. If canvassed each of them would have said they would have preferred it that when they got to Abdul's shop, Abdul's uncle had not been about. Say no more.

But, to the point, it was now known as Abdul's shop, in the generality, though older residents had known it simply as Dotty Boot's shop. Well it's awkward the way things can pan out and possessive nomenclature has always been a way for the olderly to put down the younger, in local matters.

Irene had, in her youth, always known the shop as Dotty Boot's shop. So too Carol for that matter but it is Irene that is the focus here. It was Dotty Boot she was thinking of as their excursion unravelled. Dorothy Boot, to give her a proper name, but with the prehensile insistence folk will have for shortenings and diminutives, because it gives a sense of control or ownership, 'Dorothy' had to be shortened. But why not simply to 'Dot Boot', after all many a Dorothy was known as a Dot, just like many a Margaret was known as a Peggy, though what was the logic in that particular shortening lay beyond the all too febrile use of reason. But back to Dotty Boot. Had her surname been … Witherslack … for example … and yes Irene had once dated a fellow by the name of Witherslack … but if that had been Dot Boot's surname, she would inevitably and undeniably been known as Dot Witherslack ... it was the extra syllables that ensured the extreme syllabic shortening of her first name. But, and it can't be denied, Dot Boot was altogether too severe, and there was nothing severe about Miss Boot, the person that is, so for sound, and sense, it was Dotty Boot. Something nice about the sound and it was felt that there was something nice about the person; presumed so, because nobody really knew much about her. It was her parents that had owned and run the shop, but that was really going back of course, bloody horse drawn traffic times, so to speak, but when, first one then the other passed away, Dotty continued the shop on her own for several decades. It was rumoured, well not really rumoured but put about as they say, that she never, ever set foot outside her shop, not through the front door or even down its buckled blue-brick entry. What is for certain was that when her time came and she too had 'passed', she was not discovered for several days. It must have been in the daytime because the shop door was open. Even so, it was said, probably by the likes of the Rasher type folk at the top of the cliff, that it was several days before anything was reported, not until her poor body had started to turn, by which time the shelves were bare, all of the stock 'lifted'. But then that was top of the cliff talk and a more rancid set of hate raddlers you wouldn't come across in a long day's march. Well, make of that what you will, opinion on the matter was diverse and as always, vociferous.

All of this just flittered butterfly like, in and out of Irene's mind, even as the rain seemingly did likewise it being little more than an atmospheric drizzle swirled about by an endearing breeze, sweeping up and about, tickling the underside of their chins, inducing a slovenly merriment.

Abdul's shop was part of a row of brick terrace houses, not at either end, it was not a corner shop but somewhere in the middle of the row, convenient for its custom, which it has to be said never extended far beyond the street. Not having a gable end, there had been little opportunity in the past for outsize advertising but if there had, the metal posters would still have been there because as yet Stompi patrols had not penetrated this far in their war against words. It was not Citadel down here, and the population, such as it had been, would not have been conducive to Stompi stamping and delettering raids. If so, there would have been many a Stompi clattered about the head and driven out with a kick up the backside. But then all that was now as was; these old menial dwellings were fast falling apart; holes in the slated roofs, rot eaten cills and part toppled chimneys, all spoke of an encroaching total decay. Abdul's shop had been spared the worst ruination, at least it appeared so, being snug in the middle of its row probably helped. The door was closed but not locked. Carol insisted that they knocked.

'It's a shop.' Insisted Irene, 'You don't knock to go in a shop, for God's sake.'

'Different times, you never know who's about.'

Skirker spluttered,'Well they won't stop "being about" because we knocked.'

Irene, perplexed, observed that there was no one about, that they hadn't set eyes on anyone since they set out and if there had been they'd have noticed. The 'ockeredness' of other folks, it took her breath away at times.

'Even so.' Insisted Carol.

'Christ Almighty!' snapped Skirker, knocking the door, aggressively and going in; it was all a continuous action.

'I don't suppose it's the sort of shop that would sell hankies.' queried Harold, a droplet quivering beneath the tip of his nose. He was, as yet, reluctant to wipe it on the pleated sleeve of his vestment.

'It's the sort of shop that used to sell a bit of everything,' mused Irene, 'but I don't think that 'Everything' included hankies.

'Well you'd have never known if you hadn't have asked.' muttered Carol quietly.

'I wouldn't have asked, Carol, if I didn't want a cowin' hanky, now would I?'

'I suppose not, no. Not if you put it that way about.'

'Well, there's only one way to find out.' Irene snapped and barged in after Skirker, shouting out Abdul's name as she did so. The others followed.

Benignity! It was Carol's essential characteristic. Always she cast a benign glaze upon the uppity way of the world. And if the world had gone all haphazard and wayward, as it had, it was the same for everyone. And even though each reacted differently and it was this difference that now, in these altered circumstances that aggravated, then she could still cast a benign eye upon the nature of people and things. Some would have labelled her as being indolent, but no, she was benign.

Irene of course so different in nature, but at the moment of their bursting into the shop, she too, for the moment became benign. It was the sudden sight of the shop counter. Wood, deal, probably, its top worn smooth and in the centre slightly depressed, in a soft curve, by the years of buying and selling, money and goods passing to and fro. And it was this gentle, central depression of the wood counter that they both seized upon. Not that there were no longer packets of sweets and such piled in trays on either side, but that depression where they had both as kids clutched their pennies as they stood tip-toe'd to buy brightly coloured sweets.

Carol, bustled into a corner by the ingress, simply regarded the counter, indulging in the fond memories it aroused, whereas Irene, pushing herself to the fore and central, ran her fingers to and fro along the counter's front edge. Her response was of an aggressive nostalgia; why was it that things had changed since then? What in this worn away working of time had taken the magic of childhood from her? The wicked world and its break spell nature, that was what. What had children ever done to deserve time taking childhood from them?

Within their pantheon Carol was an inactive constant, passive and well disposed to this experiment called life, not so Irene, though it had to be admitted in sexual matters she could be a delicious dollop of delight and if Stone, Dr Stone, if you please was half a man he would have recognised this ... but he wasn't and he didn't. He seemed to take Irene's delights for granted, regarding them simply as a product of his loin activity and Carol was not easy with that. But then, all things considered it was perhaps best not to dwell. It never gets you anywhere; that's for sure.

Even so they were surprised to find him there. Skirker had naturally forced himself to the fore and called out, 'Abdul!' in an expectant tone. And the coloured plastic ribbons of the strip curtain, not changed since Miss Boot's day, parted and Abdul appeared, with Stone at his shoulder. Skirker frowned, he would never take to Stone because he couldn't get a grip on him, not just on his comings and goings, which was bad enough, but not even on the nature of those comings and goings, which was worse. His aunt Carol would have said, well what does it matter, benign you see, but it did, and there was an edge to Skirker's feral suspicions that cut sharp, it was to the effect that Stone, in some way, was connected with Funky, indeed with Funky and Liz. How it could be so and how he could be swanning about with those Stompies and that crusted old piece of cack, Hornchurch, was a mystery but he was determined to find out, to cut to the heart of the matter.

So all of this melee of mental predispositions obscured the fact that Abdul, not significantly above the height of the counter, peered back at them with an expression of abstract wonder. Harold, at the back, looked wistfully at the high shelves behind Abdul, littered with large bottles of sweets and packets of various implements aligned alongside them. Clearing his throat, he asked, 'I don't suppose by any chance you happen to sell handkerchiefs?'

'It's Nipakoffs, as we really came for, do you still have any, or Fisherman's friends?', demanded Irene.

'It's Fishermen … .not Fisherman', insisted Stone.

'No its not!' snapped Skirker, not that he had any idea either way, but he'd just about had enough of Stone and his bland face. It was a face that could do with a good smack, but then he had thought that many a time before but now he was close to delivering it.

Abdul, focussing his stare away from the mathematical concept of the semi infinite with which he had just been indulging himself, turned to a back shelf, rummaged in a cardboard box and placed a crinkly edged, clear plastic packet of Nipakoffs on the counter. There was both exhalation and exaltation all round.

'Nipakoffs! There you go. Fancy that. You'm a darling Abdul. 'as anybody got any money?'

Abdul just pushed the packet further across the counter. 'They've been here since before uncle took over the shop.'

'Nipakoffs though, who'd have thought it. I did say though didn't I?.' This from Irene, struggling to open the plastic packet, waggling it about and grunting till Carol took it off her and seamlessly parted the plastic and then offered them round. They all took one and chewed silently with sour faces, only Skirker voicing an opinion with, 'I wish you bloody hadn't Irene.'

'Hadn't what?'

'Remembered them in the first place,' said Carol with a whimsical smirk, 'because to tell the truth, they'm horrible.'

'Not if you've got a cough they're not.' said Harold. And then the all silently nudged each other, secretly smirking as he persisted with ... 'You didn't answer, when I asked about handkerchiefs.'

Abdul waved his little hand, went back through the strip plastic curtain and then up some stairs from where they could hear him rummaging about. They were silent till he came back down the stairs and into the shop, a square card box with a clear plastic lid clutched in his hand. He placed it neatly on the centre of the counter. 'I will have to charge you for those, uncle got them from the market last year, there's a gross of them upstairs.'

They watched with incredulous stares as Harold, disbelievingly, manoeuvred a handkerchief from the box; it contained four, all neatly folded. He shook it out, no more than six inches square, with a wavy, pink edge and placing it across the bottom end of his not inconsiderable nose, blew what can best be described as a nasal fart.

It did the trick but could not be used again, not in its present state that is, and not aware of where the pockets were in his cassock- vestment, or even if it had any, he just stood staring, holding the squidgy mush of the handkerchief in his outstretched hand. At which, to ease the tension, it was clear that Stone was staring at Harold with some malevolence, Carol suggested that it was time they left.

They did. Skirker squeezed Abdul's arm, nodded at Stone and whispered, 'You keep an eye on that fucker, he's up to no good.'

Irene for her part squeezed Stone's hand and said that she would be in if he wanted to come up later. He simply pulled his lips into a straight line and whispered, 'Maybe.'

Skirker heard and thought, 'Yes, that's him all over'... 'Look!' shouted Carol as she stepped outside and waved her hands towards the sky, 'The rain, it's all of a shimmer!'

And it was indeed, every drop was as if it had a curved helm of spectrum within it that shimmered as the drop fell. They had not seen the like before, it was as if the sky was lighting itself up, a flittering galaxy of evanescent colour. They all waved their hands about, Harold using the exhilaration as an excuse to dispose of the used handkerchief, and snuggle the others, still in the box beneath the vestment with the braided sun on his chest. Everything felt so illicit, because it was so illogical, this bright, shiny, gentle rain but of course common sense told him that it wouldn't last. Well, it couldn't, because nothing lasts for ever but he ridiculously entertained the thought, dancing on the grey hearthstone of his mind, that perhaps it was because of his wearing the gold braided sun on the chest of his vestmenty thing that the rain was, well, a rainbow, in every direction

* * *

Abdul would not have found anything illogical in that thought, but then his mind had been to beyond the strangest places that logic could have taken him. And it was back to such a place he now intended to return, after the encumbering caravansary had left. That was both his wish and intention, both thwarted because Dr Stone, Abdul would always honour him with his academic title, remained behind. He was determined to plant an idea in Abdul's head that would put an end to Abdul's metaphysical numerology and all such nonsense. Of course Abdul was not aware of this intention and he listened patiently as Dr Stone expounded his theory, a remorseless mind contraption, that he claimed, explained everything about the way things were.

They sat in the backroom, as they had been before the interruption of the denizens of Dingley Dell, which as it turned out suited the purpose of Stone's exposition. Dr Stone sat on the sofa, Abdul on the arm of the sofa, that way their eyes were at the same height, as was suitable for a man-to-man exposition. The only difference now was that Abdul had taken the opened packet of Nipakoffs back with him, curious as to what all the fuss had been about and he now chewed furiously, his mouth turning black, which wasn't to Stone's liking one little bit, but he had to put such petty annoyances aside, he had to drum his exposition into Abdul's head before it was too late.

'You perhaps won't have the historical background Abdul, but you'll understand.'

Abdul nodded, his beautiful brown eyes, Irene was always going on about how beautiful Abdul's eyes were, fixed on Dr Stone with remote intention. He could perhaps have been interested, once, but now he knew that whatever Dr Stone was about to expound would be irrelevant, at least as far as he was concerned; he was devout to his own tussle with the ultimate mystery of numbers. How are they generated? Whatever Stone was going to divulge would be mere factual detritus.

He offered a Nipakoff. Stone shook his head. Abdul regarded the blank solemnity of Dr Stone's face, it was strange that his features were so small and delicately drawn in such a white solemnity of face flesh. He looked up as Dr Stone got to his feet, tired almost unto death, it seemed, as he nodded, almost absent mindedly, and left. Perhaps it was best that he had left his theory unexpounded.

Abdul moved the packet of Nipakoffs to one side and rummaged for a packet of Fisherman's Friends. He would try them, seeing as there was such a fuss being made about them as well. Would they taste as awful he wondered.

And, yes, wonderment was to be his new realm. Could logic take him any further? He had of late made considerable progress in his mathematical studies. Some time back he had exhausted the textbooks in the Central Library, on his last visit he had even walked past Harold's display map, not that he had taken any particular notice. If on perusing the map he had discerned a topological problem, such as the bridges at Konigsberg, then perhaps, but … no … Topology had never exercised his imagination, not when the nature of number is the area of investigation.

It was not just number, he had made giant strides in Quantum Theory, he had been fortunate there because a surprising number of advanced texts, perhaps a dozen or so, had been available. He could read them, with little more difficulty than with an advanced novel- Finnegans Wake for instance. It led to the concept of a universe created by number, by the relation of one number to another, and so on; that the essence of physical reality, at the sub, sub, sub atomic level was pure number. A number that existed, as an ultimate 'thing' that spawned all essence of physicality. To the logical necessity of an infinite number of universes, whose infinitality was vouchsafed by the way that each infinite universe interacted with the infinity of every other universe, all existing because there was an ultimate mathematical entity that generated number. This meant, he thought and chuckling as he did so, that every religious, humanist, materialistic concept of the nature of reality, not only could, but had to exist. There was no religious belief or conception that wasn't not only true but existing.

Number theory melded into quantum probability yielded an infinite cosmic flux.

A mathematical entity that created number.

And of course this was a necessary condition. The very moment of the big bang, when matter, time and energy were created, they were created according to the laws of physics, laws expressed in number. Number predated any form of material existence. And what was the 'it' that predated material existence but Allah … God … ! And at that instant, of Abdul's realisation, all manner of numerical relations, their intricate shapes, their pre-existant designs, were interwove within his mind.

So, of course, struggling a moment for a model, it must be that Skirker, Irene, Carol and that whispy flake of humanity, Harold, were all Gods in a minor pantheon, that Dingley Dell and the Old Chronicle were a local Olympus, which, of course, they were, they necessarily were, in the Great Quantum Suffusion. Just as … But there was no need for another 'just as' because that list was endless.

Abdul shivered not with cold but with excitement, not his own excitement but the excitement of an idea being realised. It was not him but the idea that shook with excitement. The excitement of being brought into consciousness. He went upstairs, trembling on the steps, and picked up a tambourine that lay on his bed, whereupon he squatted and rattled out a rhythm.

Chapter 18

'**B**unty Clitflick: and you are?!'
This was always how Bunty Cliflick announced himself, by barking out his name and then poking you in the chest with his swagger stick, demanding that you surrender your own name for his appraisal.

Bunty Clitflick, square shouldered, barrel chested and apple buttocked, strutted about in jodhpurs and jackboots that gleamed and made soft leathery sounds with every heel clacking step he made.

This was how he approached the roundfaced 'pettyman' Barry, who seemed to think he was someone of significance, a crimpled little fellow, shabby in a gabardine mack. Obviously an 'insignificant' but yes, the one thing going for him was that his eyes shone with enthusiasm for something. For the meeting with Bunty himself? Face to face with the Western Commander? Well, that was as it should be.

'Well, speak up man!' And he patted Barry on the shoulder- a double tap of the swagger stick.

Barry, gazing up at Bunty's crisp moustache, stammered out, 'Barry Sir: Barry Rasher.'

Bunty gave a disconcerting whine in response.

The "Sir" had of course been instinctive to a man of Barry's strata: mere sedimentary conglomerate, as compared to the igneous granite of Bunty's genetic heritage.

'And you do …?' demanded Bunty.

'I'm the Senior Official Uniate Productioncontroller, sir'

'In English, damn it, in English man.'

Barry apologised, his eyes becoming ferretlike as he

glanced to and fro to re-assemble his answer. 'I'm the chief Production Controller, sir.' And then, catching the furrowing of Bunty's brow, chimed out, 'Logistics, sir!' Beaming because he had found a quasi military term that Bunty would surely enjoy.

'Logistics!' screamed Bunty as he made a quick double stamp on the famed concrete apron that lay expansively before the Centralstores building.

Barry essayed an emollient response. 'Yes, indeed sir.'

Bunty bellowed a bark of a laugh, slapped the swagger stick against the calf of his right leather boot and repeated the word 'logistics!' with obvious disdain and then turned round to relish the assembled high and mighty of The Uniate with a bellicose 'harumpff'. Astartobe was of course absent from the line up, this was an assembly for war, and her orders for the invasion of the pet food factory had already been given; the fighting and assembling was now best left to the boys.

How did they respond? Well with a frisson of nervous enthusiasm; partly because the fact that Barry had come out with that surname of his,which had been smothered completely in Bunty's exuberant disdain.

Stent snuffled a chuckle; Stryne made a grimace, its mood indecipherable, but his chin curved tighter up to his nose, emphasising the concavity of his face all the more, while Dublo just nodded amicably.

Bunty wheeled about, to face the 'Logistician', his ire and spittle, directed at Barry as he bellowed, 'And you, sir!!, are you suggesting that your "pettifoggery Logistics" counts for anything in matters of war? … Well?! Speak up man.'

Barry who had a skill when it came to confrontation with the hierarchy, offered. 'I am willing to be corrected by one who has more experience and greater authority, sir.'

'Damned well should be. There is no room at all for clerical squirts in the business of war. War, man, is for men. It's cut and slash, jab 'em in the guts and twist it about. War is for gouging, tearing, smash stamping, bursting 'em apart and bollock stamping, and up arsing with the bayonet and no amount of your this and that, here and now, with baskets of provisions, counts a fig, because that's mere women's work and women's work is after the battle; it's to be on their backs, legs apart, giving juicy relish to the warriors. Got it.!?'

Barry was flummoxed, but not enough not to respond, 'Got it sir.'

'Then bloody well make sure that you have, man!' and with that he strode away but snorting as he did so, 'You'd better bloody well make sure that you have "Trasher".'

There was a distinct sense of relief from the assembled of Uniate. Trasher, of course, that would do it, Barry Trasher ... it could be said in full now ... Bunty's authority.

Clitflick strode away to a body of uniformed men, fiercely standing to attention but set aside from Uniate men. He bellowed at them, 'Clitflicker Ferrulers ... Huzzah!'

And they responded, abruptly shouldering arms, stamping in a sort of manic dance step to attention, as they did so, and bellowing, 'Clitflicker Ferrulers: Yahoo.'

It was smart body they presented, disciplined and way beyond what the dishevelled clumped groups of any branch of the Stompis could have achieved, and if there had been a sun, it would have shone down on their immaculate order; as it was they had to make do with the rain by standing resolute, all buff and tan with not a flicker of movement to jar their military composure. And here at least some of the Stompi brigades, those that wore shoulder capes, had an advantage, seeing as they at least glistened in the downpour.

And of those Ferrulers' arms, that had been so strictly presented, well it could clearly discerned that they were umbrellas; umbrellas though that had been severely mutilated. All material, had been neatly scissored from the skeleton frame. And the tips of the bare spokes had been carefully doctored, each tip having a polished hook bound to it with fine wire. A fearsome weapon when poked, twisted or even just swirled in your face, however, not in itself a weapon that would kill. Barry noted this but had the sense not to comment. Their triple line was immaculate, Bunty just before them, swagger stick under his arm and with a bead-curtain of rain droplets shimmering from the polished peak of his cap, awaited a decision that only 'She' could make; the decision as to when the advance down the gravel bank and onslaught on the pet food factory should begin.

As he stood he still seethed within, at the presumption of that little glove puppet, 'Trasher', thinking that he could organise anything to do with anything in the matter of warfare.

Bunty could trace his antecedents back to the Normans. Well of course he could. Odd though that such people never bothered with going back further, before those Normans became Normans, back to the hairy-arsed rabble-rousing Vikings, swinging battle axes as they marauded through peaceful Saxon pastures for loot and a bit of casual rapine. No, those with a claim of Norman descent let genealogy and heritage end right there. However, being of Norman stock, endowed them with the privilege of blood. The Trashers of this world could never go further back in their spunk-sloshing genealogy than the nineteenth century. Weak blood. The Bunty type of stock had precious blood, semen not spunk that had to be dispensed in the vagina of one of the same stock and recorded, generation after generation, purity preserved.

And that factor, enshrined and never to be blemished, was why he presently stood stock still before his fabled unit of Ferrulers.

Because, suddenly one of the three of the Uniate, Stryne no less, had, due to some religious jiggery pokery, ended up thinking he had some sort of control over Bunty. Stryne was a distant cousin who he hated more devoutly than any enemy he might face in battle and his turning up here with his syrup of religious sentiment was a burning bile in Bunty's throat.

Family, yes, but he had sullied the blood. Bunty had come across him in their Pally Maley club, up ending some cleaning woman, a bloody Pole, or some sort, got her over the billiard table, going pellmell, fingering and licking, gasping with gruesome delight, his chin gleaming with her passion slaver. At the sight of it, Bunty had screeched some wordless, hysterical monstrance that echoed throughout the pals only club. Members dribbled into the billiard room, aghast, and then began 'Good God!' barking, mainly at the damage her heels could have done the billiard cloth. Worse than worse, Stryne had been besotted with her, ran after her, pleading, offering family money. Well of course 'Stringy Stryne' had been drummed out of the club forthwith. To add insult to outrage, the fellow hadn't even paid his dues, claiming 'Clerics Privilege'. And, does it need to be said?, well yes actually it does, 'Whiny Stryney' had lost his putative career as a Bishop to be. Bunty seemed to think that he had been relegated to the role of a humble head master in some school hereabouts. As far as Bunty was concerned, even that role was too good for him. The sheen of family genealogical greatness had been scratched: A cleaning woman, East European, and on the very billiard table that had been hauled out of the wreckage of the Third Reich and installed in the club as battle honours!! But there it was, and now, here he was, the blood tainting bastard was lording it over him. God above, how Bunty needed this war to begin. But the order hadn't been given. Well Bunty and his Ferrulers would not be stood down. Damn it, if the order didn't come, then he would give it. Time was ripe.

Bunty's situation had become precarious. His 'stately home', well, a castle, naturally, but back in Normandy, Castell Montmerde, that the family claimed it owned, had been lost to the Frenchies in one of the revolutionary messes they had made of their history. But here, in England, a heritage home also, from where ever hence, through futile generations, they had made their mark on the backs of unnamed underlings. Their 'English' home, built in the time of the Angevins, when duplicitous arrangements were the norm, was a castle of sorts. Some bits of crenellation remained-a few notches and as for the tumbledown remainder, they were burdened with a clumpy shawl of ivy. No splendour had ever fallen on these castle walls. Of course there were subsequent additions: a Palladian 'mansionette'; Georgian stables and stable yard and a Victorian turreted tower that glowered down, its brickwork suggesting the grandiosity of a provincial city's main railway station; yes because it even had a clock, so the estate's hands always knew the time. The enlightenment of the Clitflicks it was said to demonstrate.

And, yes, of course, there were broad lands, meadows and fields that surrounded the 'castle'; Castle Modgery' as it was known. A thousandfold acreage and of recent time, a factory farm, beneath whose sheds a billionfold of blind, legless, plumped up chickens, were constrained, until death, to feed the anonymous masses with something to chew on and provide profit for Castle Modgery.

But then these blasted rains had started, and started and started and the blithering weather boys at the BBC, communists to a man no doubt, couldn't say when it would stop. Couldn't say anything at all actually. And in no time at all, splodges of that Cess stuff started appearing in bloated rafts all over the fields and then, stalking the hedges. The whole estate quickly became bog acreage. Thorn, bristle at first, then later … .Well what's the point of saying anything further. But as soon as the filthy stuff reached the Ha Ha, Bunty decided it was time to go.

Where to? Well to 'The Office' naturally. He hadn't normally had much to do with 'The Office', because he couldn't be going back and forth when there was the Hunt to consider. It had been his father who had started The Office, or Modgeraker Investments, to give it its full title. And yes the place had made money, serious money, via Saudi of course. And that was where Bunty now headed, leaving Castle Modgery for good, and taking up in the firm's quarters, a couple of floors in a prestigious tower, in what had come to be called, The Citadel. Now, he had been given to understand, it was all called Uniate, or some such.

The young men who worked there were, all of them 'callow-sallows' as Bunty would have it. But, they all did know how to place a bet. Of course, they had the knack of making money making schemes. What is more, becoming increasingly aware of the depredations of 'clerkdom' in Citadel, they all voted it a better option to become 'Ferrulers'. Well it was fun, practising parade drill with stripped umbrellas across the cleared office floor. Desks and computers were pushed aside. Divested of screen peering duty all day, they now stamped upon desktops and presented arms till the cows came home, as the saying went. Oh, it was undoubtedly thrillsum and yes, they did meet performance targets, set by Bunty, with regards to their turnout and drill perfection.

It was a fortunate coincidence that at the time it had become the fashion for investment portfolio managers to dress in brown suits. Brown suits hadn't been seen in office or lounge for decades. But fashion, for no obvious reason, changes. Like the reflections of idle clouds drifting across the surface of sullen pools, so drifts the 'mode de nos jours' of superior fashion. Of courses those slovenly ranks of mere Clerkdom were not so accoutred, they could never have afforded a brown, Harris Tweed suit, and reconciled themselves by referring to them derisively as 'scratchy pants'.

But yes, the brown could be imagined as kharki and what is more, given that each and every portfolio manager wore a suit of the exact, same design: lapel, cut of trouser, wooden-nut button patterns for the coat and sleeves and retro smooth buttons for flies. The latter detail became rather surprisingly a distinct practical advantage, as the metal zip flies of Clerkdoms' cheap, grey suits had all begun to rust-up. Many of their ranks crept about fussing with open flies and closed files.

So, the erstwhile portfolio managers could be imagined as a uniformed unit, officered all, disciplined to the point of extinction of any individuality. No matter how the Stompis might sneer, as they did, no one would do so out loud, less they be blind sighted by those razor ferruled umbrellas.

Bunty had become so spittle lipped in his almost demonic duty to achieve parade ground excellence, that he welcomed the New Order, as he referred to the rains and concomitant irritations of Cess and Thorn. Let Castle Modgery be overwhelmed, who could be bothered with plant life when there was a war to be won.

Adelaide Clitflick, nee Scroteclaw (Norman obviously) generously busted, bounteous, had been remaindered at Modgery; well what purpose could she ever serve in an Investment Portfolio Bureau, especially one that had now become militarised to the 'Nth' degree? No, she was happy enough, cushion bound on a sofa in what had always been the only dry room in the cramped sprawl of the place, working away at her quilt.

Adelaide, always pronounced as in the German, with every syllable bouncing in isolation, had been working on her quilt for what seemed like centuries, each square showing some emblem or visual device that represented one of the fabled generations right back to the Normans. When not working on the quilt she would just relax on the sofa and finger her string of pearls, lips pursed, contemplating the vagaries of her many lovers over the previous decades. It was her commodious bust that entranced them. Men, not always of the right social standing, seemed to fall into three categories when it came to her breasts, after they had dismantled her bra they became either breast paddlers, fall fondlers or pinch pamperers, but all murmured into a massaging pouting of soft syllables of inarticulate delight. She had had to put up with it for minutes on end until it came to dismantling her corsetry and then the plumbing began. Little boys all of them and, believe it or not, none ever wanted to remove that string of pearls. There was never a case in their procedures of 'breeding will out' and that aroused a discrete smile, which the ever so many 'jackboys' over the years always took as a signifier of serene, aristocratic sexual satisfaction.

'La Serenissima' one had once called her, head on her thighs, she beaming down at him. Serene, yes, even though ever so many gondolas had floated along that canal: Serenissima.

It was the dilemma with sex, so exciting in contemplation, so boring in execution. Nowadays, and perhaps always, if it came down to it, she got the deepest thrill of sexual arousal in contemplating the giant pike, cruelly snouted, silent and motionless, gleaming with malevolent intensity within the gloom of the lake. Spite of all this worldwide drenching business, he would be there long after everything of humanity had been dollop suffocated in Cess or crucified on Thorn, sliding through submerged counties, silent and serene. La Serenissima. Well, it had been a long time coming and no one could say it wasn't deserved, this ruination of things. It was what came of letting the serfs gain ever more commodities: holidays, food, televisions and etceteras that went on forever. No, fingering her beads, her quilt laid aside, she could only hope that Bunty would never make it back; the place was better dreary and not spiked with his barking militarism; a preposterously strutting little man with his apple buttocks now becoming ever more pear shaped by the year. Something clearly started to go awry at the time of the Tudors, Welsh upstarts that weren't of the true blood. The bureaucratisation of life began with them. There would be no Tudors in her quilt, it was the Plantagenet line that had to be followed through

Chapter 19

O peration New Realm!' That was its title, the grand and great plan for Uniate expansion. A sudden invasion, a pre-emptive strike, a Blitzkrieg, the success of which would vouchsafe the survival of the Uniate. That great shouldered shed, its immense, triple span width, exceeded only by its depth, would offer security and salvation, seeing as it held, stacked high on shelf and stallage, uncountable tins of pet food: Chubby Chunks Kitty Kuts, Poochy Pride, Miaow Meals: thousands, even hundreds of thousands of gobbets of chewy meat and flaky fish, all in a rich sauce. One a day. One a day for all: Stompis, Christies, Clerkdom, the whole thronged realm of Uniate. Could such benison be ignored? Without that wealth of tinned protein, slopping about in gravy, the days of Uniate would be limited. Dublo had suggested that it be worked out how long they could otherwise survive. Stone had done the figure fiddling in his head and the result had been no more than a few months, give or take. Barry had been led into the equation, on a, 'What If?' basis and had concluded with a very similar number of days. There was no denying it, their future depended upon the Operation Barbarossa style attack, with every conceivable measure of assault brought into simultaneous operation.

The planning was the result of several minds, none of them adept at co-operation, so each had his own tactical lever to open the factory and rampage within for the promised plunder. There was one undeniable advantage: none in the pet-food factory would ever know of the planned invasion. Those that were in the factory, stayed in the factory. Well of course they would, safe, secure, dry and well fed. And this was a further reason for immediate invasion, all the time they would be eating into the reserves that a united Uniate Army would rescue and bring barrowed up, to Citadel. There would be such a victory parade with the anonymous ranks of clerkdom, simpering and clapping their pat-a-cake hands in a delirium of safe delight.

But who were those barracked in the factory? Security guards, certainly, trained in combat, commando units and they would have the advantage of knowing the terrain, able to operate in the dark, perhaps even making forays onto their own concrete apron, sallying forth, viciously armed, to strike a few down and then retreat back into the awesome volume of the factory, always having the advantage of surprise. This must surely be expected, but once Uniate's forces were invested in the factory itself, well then the fighting would be fearsome with grenadier ranks, high on the stallages within, hurling down battalions of tins upon their heads; it could be well imagined that there would be a civil defence force of pet food workers, ramming trolleys at them as they hid behind barricades of plastic pallets. They would have all the advantages but one: surprise.

How then was the attack to be effected? And attack not siege, a siege would be pointless, the pet fooders would have all the advantages. Occupying an empty concrete apron would be utterly pointless. Many minds had offered tactical advice and out of the contretemps that ensued; Dublo, as a sort of Staff General, Hornchurch as Quarter Master and Barry as Logistics Liason between the former two had agreed a plan of campaign.

An assault unit of Stompis, clumbered in 'advance squadrons' of wheelbarrows, would be push charged down the gravel bank and, thus having gained considerable momentum, would charge the wide gates in the perimeter fence. They would be followed by assault units of Stompis, armed with grappling hooks and chains to charge through the broken fence gates and invest in the approach into the factory itself, which would be achieved by groups with gravel filled wheelie bins (all transition of newly discovered Gawpers were suspended until the campaign was completed; 'discontinued for the duration', as the saying went). With holes being cracked open in the asbestos cladding, 'assault ingress' would be achieved at several locations. All within were to be 'absolved of life:' no prisoners, no surrenderers. All were to be cramp-vatted in suitable containers and secured for future use.'

Thus it was so and thus it undoubtedly would be: the plan of campaign was foolproof. Funny usage that, after all proof against fools is no proof at all and it surely wouldn't be fools they would be facing, it was perhaps the fools on their own side they would have to defend against: such is always the case in war. Doubts were raised as to the efficacy of the of the Stompi assault brigade, charging down the gravel slopes in their wheel barrows. Stent had insisted that all such warriors have protective armour and he had authorised that buckets be placed over their heads; buckets in which holes had been stamped out, eye holes, mouth holes and nose holes, because a Stompi could not be expected to show true valour if he could not see, if his war shouts were muffled and his nose squashed flat. The buckets were therefore adequately pierced. Hornchurch had raved about the lunacy of all this and was on the point of refusing a supply of buckets until, yet again, Barry proved his worth. He mollified the storekeeper with the promise that after the campaign the pierced bucket-helms would be returned to Central stores, and yes though pierced, desecrated even in Hornchurch's pebble lensed eyes, they could still be used to carry gravel, indeed anything but liquids. Hornchurch groaned, casting his oblique stare up to the heavens, mouth agawp and pondered. He did not realise that spades, divested of their handles were at that very moment being similarly purposed as armoured faceplates. This was when Barry taxed him with a genuine concern, that in fact the 'bucket head battalions' might not be sufficient to break into the factory. A weapon of some kind that provided the assault with greater momentum was needed. Hornchurch had growled, grunted as he swivelled his leg with the enormous shoe across the concrete floor, his mind in a contusion of possibilities, until suddenly upright, he turned, grappled Barry by his shoulders and shaking him furiously, proclaimed, 'Not just momentum but energy, kinetic energy. Yes?!

Barry amazed at what he perceived was an undoubted outage of optimism in the storekeeper: had such a spillage of this emotion ever been witnessed before? No nattering, time spending on the subject was not available, because letting go of Barry's shoulders, he now tugged him by one of the lapels of his gabardine, into the remoter depths of the stores to a neat line of twenty garden rollers! Oh, their rotund immensity! Their blunt magnificence! Their shape bellowed martial possibilities.

'How about those beauties?!! he snorted, flicking Barry with spittle, such was his excitement. Then, whispering hoarsely he muttered. 'Not just mass times velocity: mass times velocity ... squared!'

'Upon two.' Corrected Barry.

'Upon two then, but what's that compared to the squared. Energy beats mere momentum every fuckin' time. Now, be said man! Then with a self congratulatory chuckle, he said, 'Oh, there's some of us as have got a tidy headpiece on our shoulders when it comes to mechanical arts, make no mistake about that!'

Barry was nonplussed. 'All twenty brought into use? At the same time?..A rolling armada.'

'That's the ticket.' And there was a generality of progressive optimism all round as his diminutive, poke eyed, clerklets joined in, clapping their little hands together and hissing in delight.

Thus was rolled into action the 'Heavy Artillery Detachment'. It did cross Barry's mind even at the time that it would be the devil's own game getting those rollers back up the gravel bank once the war was over but he wasn't going to muddy the bright waters of military optimism with such post facto concerns.

The mind of man is at its most creative when considering war or torture and the liberating effect of such considerations should never be sullied with reality.

But then there were counter suggestions bandied about, subversive in nature but not to be denied. Some had heard it said that there were not only thousands of tins of petfood hoarded inside that gaunt factory shed, its enormity even more aghast than the gape of central stores, but millions, yes millions, of plastic trays of raw tripe, cellophane wrapped. A bonus,yes, afterwards, but not in the assault, because they could be hurled horizontally, with sufficient force, to become a face splitting weapon. You wouldn't want your eyes to be sliced by a tray of tripe being hurled at you. So preparations were put in hand for mesh fencing to be cut up and tied around the heads of those assault troops who were not bucket helmeted. Best to be on the safe side

And such are the exigencies of war that Christie women were brought in to central stores to chimeclap and twist about to provide mind nourishment and ensure the rate of manufacture did not slack. And it had worked, the manufacturing rate of the mesh head cages broke all records.

These were to be great times, a bliss to blunder bravely into war; such sorts of feeling provided vim for all.

And then there was Bunty Cliflick with his thin moustache and his brigade of Clitflick Ferrulers. Well they stood indifferent to the whole panjammery of effort and urging, they stood in line, aloof and alert on that momentous morn when the order to advance was given. Bunty, convinced that no tray of plastic wrapped tripe would slice through a Ferrulers ferrules, awaited only the command to charge: a command that he would give, as for the rest … well it was up to them.

Great ripples of liberating energy flowed through all. The masters of the Uniate were there, on a podium, bedecked with pennants, drooping in what had been a steady drizzle that occluded distant sight. But then Astartobe had decided to stride down to the Assault Launch Podium, draped in a velvet sheen cloak, cut from the magnificent curtains that had once occluded the screen of an old cinema. The swirl of her cloak about her mesmerising thighs, the strident gait of her progress precipitated the Ferrulers. Bunty had also been taken by surprise, he'd been staring aghast, pullulating, in a sort of sex-rapture at her Boadicea figure. Her sudden appearance, as a Goddess of war, induced raddled raunch urges, such that, for the moment, he was disturbed by the rising of her right arm to initiate a precipitate charge. Her monumentally sculpted armpit distracted him and the charge her signal had unleashed bundled him face down onto the concrete. He recovered, bellowed and waddled, apple buttocked after them. He should have given the order to charge but Astartobe unleashed such priapic urges that the desire for slaughter had to be fertilised.

Stent at the head of his Stompi detachments was also fleet and furious in the charge, even out bellowing Bunty, though he could not run as fast and was eventually overtaken by that descendant of the Normans, Bunty, in extremis, happily unaware the gravel was taking the sheen off his boots.

But it was the stance and demeanour of the others on the podium that merited interest: Dublo squawked with delight, shouting encouragement but looking all the time at Astartobe, wanting his thin voiced fervour, which was twisting his suit into a complete corkscrew of dishevelment, to be observed. To no avail, her stare was resolutely on the pet food factory shed and the scrimmage of bodies threshing about at its perimeter fence.

Stryne, well he was there too of course, surveying the proceedings with a remote malignity. He was of the type of person who would wish success to what he hated, that he might hate it all the more. He got succour from hating. And hate he did, the whole 'clamjamfry'; from Bunty down to his least Ferruler foot slogger. Of course, of course, of course, he had echoed the opinion of all within Uniate, that their survival depended entirely on acquiring the vast food resources within the pet food factory. Without that bounty, they would soon all starve. It was obvious, the need had to be constantly reinforced.

Even the bedraggled host of Clerkdom, at this very moment nervously twitching at their desks, awaiting the munificent outcome of this glorious day, were constantly being updated by scurrying messengers. Every least one of them confidently understood the absolute necessity of victory. And it was to this end that Stryne had insisted a couple of rows of dark suited Senior Management line up at the back of the podium, ready to give the official despatch at the end of the day, back in those dreary offices of The Uniate. Their report would be trusted: out of their slack jawed mouths the truth would be spilt..

But what would that truth be? What if, and it had to be considered, went the day not well, but badly? If so, that truth had to be told, because, and the thinnest of smiles contorted the Punchlike proportions of his face, there was always an ulterior remedy. Well let's just say, there would have to be a radically different ordering of things. He Stryne was perhaps the only one in the whole Citadel to contemplate the nature of those things, rubbing his thumb against the inside of his forefinger his wobbly tooth indenting the quiver in his lower lip. And he wondered to what extent he could rely on Barry to … .well … .do the necessary. Would he be help or hindrance? Let it go, just keep smiling benignly as the different units bellowed into action. A battle was always fascinating, so long as one was not physically involved. But the fact was, and it found congress in Stryne's mind and no other. What if the campaign failed?! If so the numbers of Clerkdom would have to be radically reduced, there simply wasn't sufficient food to keep them going. Well, he had no problem with that. A slendered down Uniate, only the elite surviving. In fact that was fine. But how would this slimming down, dispensing with the vast majority be achieved? He considered Barry but then let his mind dally over the sight and sound of battle.

As for Stone, he was there of course, aloof and silently staring. What was to be done about him if victory was not theirs at the end of the day?

So two assaults, began simultaneously. First the assault brigade of the Stompis. Ladders were propped against the razor wire but they were not high enough to allow the Stompis to roll over the twisted bundle of cruel spikes and that caused some dithering, but pushed onward by those from below, their screams at being snagged were morphed into the warlike chants of attack. Soon a few dozen were ranging in close file across the concrete apron and up to the main sliding doors of the factory, where they crouched, waiting for the second assault, that of the Roller Brigade to break down the main gates so they could be joined by several marauding cohorts to unleash the main attack on and within the pet food factory itself

The rollers were pushed down the gravel slope, their blunt, gravel crunching weight gathered momentum, and yes, kinetic energy also, as they sped with lumbering ferocity up against the gates in the perimeter fence.

Those rollers, oh what moments of apocalyptic bliss they induced in Hornchurch as they wobble rolled, down the gravel slope. Magnificent with their rotund mass, with their genial belligerence, all twenty of them, in two groups of ten, the first wave rattled, deformed and then ripped apart the fencing. Then the second ten buckled, deformed and then smashed the perimeter gate off its hinges. The desired breakthrough had been achieved, to the extent that gate and fence were split apart, sufficient for bucket headed or shovel faced Stompis to come hurtling through, their fierce grimacing masked by pierced metal but not their bloodthirsty roaring.

So too the Ferrulers, Bunty screaming in a high pitched falsetto led the charge. He too was in a state of transcendental bliss, envisaging his face snouting and tongue scooping in the gloriously sculpted armpits of Astartobe. After the battle, she would be his for the taking and his moustache bristled at the thought of such a trophy.

All was going well, though some of the squadron leaders were becoming apprehensive that there had been no sally from the denizens within. They must have been fearing an attack and would doubtless have developed defensive counter measures. But as yet nothing had transpired. Surely they would contest the opening of the large sliding, hangar like doors once they were slid apart. The main deterrent, being the weight of those doors and the fact that they had almost rusted themselves tight in the rail they ran in..

Such was the fierce warlike determination of the Stompis that several of them literally threw themselves at the door, creating a hollow booming sound within but doing nothing to facilitate their opening, They had to be slid apart and at the moment they seemed to be resistant to such a movement.

Different tactics were tried, namely shaking the door, regularly, building up a rhythm, increasing the momentum, so that the door could be heard resounding like a great drum, booming and then the echo of the booming as well. It was impressive, this large scale waggling but it obviously did little to facilitate the necessary sliding of the door to open it. And open it they must, especially as the frustrated fury of the assailants was becoming destructive, not of the doors but of the cohesive force of their squads. All was in danger of becoming a noisy rabble, fighting and clambering over itself. Of course the Ferrulers were all but useless at this point and they were shouldered and trod on till they were out of the way.

Then someone shouted orders and they parted, standing aside to allow two seniors of their number guiding Mr Horncastle, snorting and breathless, to approach the door and pour thick, glugging oil onto the runners from a large jerry can. He was so exhausted by this effort and mindful that he would have to go back up the gravel slope to get back to his Central stores, no mean distance to have to swing the weight of his club boot, that he just sat where he was and had to be lifted aside while all put their shoulders to the door and heaved.

And heaved, uniting their efforts in timed shouts, and heaved again. It was no good, nothing achieved until Mr Horncastle, pushed aside but still on the floor noticed, in spite of the flawed vision through his marbled eyes, that there was a simple tip up-tip down latch on the runner. He tipped it up and got trodden over as the next heave brought success and the door slid open with a groan to reveal a cavernous interior with a few denizens inside, several yards back blinking and cowering, obviously in no condition to make a counter assault.

Victory, the squads roared and ran in, charging at the denizens who simply slid out of view.

But then immediately the forward assault squads stuttered to a halt. They slumped, shoulders down, clasping their gauntleted hands to their mouths and heaving and vomiting.

Aghast amazement gasping ... It was the smell, not like any smell of rot they had ever encountered in Citadel, it poisoned the nostrils, coarse rasped the throat, creating uncontrollable peristalsis, such that they all fell to their knees, their eyes streaming, as convulsively they heaved and hawked emptying their stomachs in fluid splatterings.

Some crawled back out, some were pulled back out (so there was after all a residual esprit de corps amongst the ranks) but those that remained inside wretched and spewed continuously.

Was this a defence? If so, what to do? Communication was difficult with a shovel blade tied to the face and just two pierced squint holes to peer through, so these were dispensed with, thrown out, thrown to the ground, clattering about Mr Horncastle's head; he had still not made it to his feet. Even so, outraged by this rampant discarding of tools, he bellowed out that he was not having it and began gathering the three dozen or so discarded shovel blades, stacking them neatly against the factory wall, they would all have to be carried back to Central stores and refitted to the haft of their handles, good tools, not to be wasted, even with holes in the blades; there would be little gravel that would spill through.

Stone, Dr Stone that is, saw Horncastle's dilemma, his fall from the ranks and noticed also that the storeman was not wretching. Alone among the troops he was not affected by the pungent offal stink that seeped even up to the concrete apron, where he stood. Horncastle had had a degree of immunity because he had been lying on the floor outside, pouring oil.

'Knees!!' Stone bellowed, running down onto the apron. 'Down on your bellies, crawl, crawl inside. Take the shovel blades with you, stab at their legs!!' All this while, running towards Horncastle and kicking the shovel blades that he had begun to recover out of his hands.

They did as instructed, made slow progress but penetrating deeper into the gloomy vastness of the shed, they listened, as they had never listened, before. It was the sound of the rain, a repetitive, insistent tumult. An incessant drumming that could neither be turned off or diminished, quite unlike anything ever experienced in Citadel, where there was no volume so great, no metal roof so relatively flimsy, that would emphasise the unceasing battering of the rain. They knew they could not stand it, not for hour after hour, day after day, not when the smell steeped, even when they were on their hands and knees, rifling up into their nostrils; go any further in and even when crawling flat on their bellies, they would be breathing disgust till they choked to death.

And yes, they were watched by the denizens. How many were they? How had they survived in this filthy milieu? They could be seen peering down, silent but tremulously all a quiver. They were mind gone, driven mad by the sound of the rain, its remorseless beat and its sluicing rivulets as it gushed down the corrugated roof sheeting.

That and the smell, of rotting corpse meat, chicken and human, that as well. It could also be seen that of the few dozen denizens in close view, most had large, encrusted sores on their faces, scabs that lifted their lips, revealing rotting, toothless gums. They stared down at them, blinking immobile and gruesome. Forlornly flapping their hands, making croak and screech sounds, throwing all manner of stuff, not at the invaders, they obviously did not have strength enough for that, but down on the floor in front of them, a sort of petulant discharge of annoyance. And all the time the ever increasing choke-reek reduced both Stompi and Ferruler to a folded collapse, eyes streaming, heaving and spewing.

Stent bellowed a retreat, heavens he couldn't even pull one of them down and stamp him to death. The Stompis obeyed, still on their bellies, crawling towards the lesser dimness of outside, their faces white and wizened.

The raid had been successful but at the same time they had suffered a defeat. There had been no provisions to be hauled from out of that drum-dunning interior, cavernous and rancid. They assembled ashen faced and sullen on the outer side of the very gates they had so triumphantly bent apart only a couple of hours previously. Then, only just in step, they shambled into a ragged formation and scrambled up the gravel bank obeying mumbled orders to return to their quarters.

The Ferrulers, spite shoving their part opened umbrellas into faces, as they had been trained to do, screamed huzzahs; but the trouble was, blinded by the unbreathable fug, it was each others faces they were stabbing at, and with their own cries of agony, they fell whimpering to the floor and suffocated.

Bunty? He was nowhere to be seen. He had been heard, screaming orders in a high falsetto and farting, penetrating deeper into that unholy factory shed, where it was rumoured, he had been dissolved alive in shallow baths of acrid slop.

Trudge trundling up to the concrete apron of Central stores, they tasted defeat. Of two dozen or so factory habitués, they could not be called defenders, only a few had lobbed an occasional tin or tripe tray, as they clambered deeper into the factory and out of the reach of any of the invaders, all on their knees, gasping for breath and puking. Yes, manifestly, there were trays of tripe but only a few dozen at most, those that had been used as a weapon and they were now all splattered open and trod into grisly ribbons on the concrete floor. But of the vaunted wealth of tins, there was not a sign. There would be no new horizon, not even, given the slothful way the ranks were trudging back, any hope of a different future. The unspoken remained unspoken but its message was stamped on their faces. No victory parade.

Chapter 20

The Viviation Committee, to give it its full name, although inevitably diminished to VIVCOM, was new, it being set up the very day after the slovenly retreat. Its purpose: to assign blame; there had to be blame, and to commandeer a new strategy for survival. But survival of what? Survival of whom? And at what cost?

Stryne was condign. Astartobe startled and Stent was bent, unable to breathe and stand upright. Dublo, surprisingly remained unfazed, even his much turmoiled suit seemed to hang slack. And yet he moved before them with a certain elegance as he outlined a plan for corporate recuperation. But, as yet they were uncertain of any futurehood awaiting them. Come what may Stryne considered Dublo's plan to be-nothing more than some sort of comfort consumerisation of Citadel. He glanced at Astartobe but her iron visage gave nothing away and Stent, well he just shuttled crabwise into a corner to bring up a thin stream of hot vomit. With a bit of luck he would never regain his upright stature and would die constricted into a bent cramp. But this, Stryne conceded could well be wishful thinking.

Dublo's plan: the creation of a dining suite, complete with entertainment, (to be termed as 'tainments') to which, on a rota basis, all ranks of Clerkdom, Stompidom and Christidom were to be invited. INVITED!! Choice food would be served, a festive atmosphere created, decorations and a female chorus of the most devout Christies would charm murmur devotional anthems.

'And what food will be served?' croaked Stent, groaning as he tried to elevate his stature. 'After all it was the need for future and ongoing supplies of food that led us to war against the Pet food Factory. Their tinnage, bountiful beyond measure, or so we were lead to believe, would ensure our survival. But there was nothing, no tins, no trays of tripe … we are bereft and facing a crisis. And you propose a restaurant … where is the food for that to come from? Hey? Tell us that?

'The purpose of the new restaurant is to mollify, to pacify, to engender a sense of security, of well being even. They will come to believe that all is well with the Uniate. After all, we have achieved a victory, we are no longer in any danger of them, of the Pet food factory cohorts, invading us.'

Stryne snorted. Stent would have done so but did not dare risk it, given his pulmonary condition. 'We were never in that danger.' Stryne snapped.

Dublo smiled and waved his hands in a slow, gratuitous gesture. But we didn't know that, did we Bishop?!'

The term 'Bishop' was irritatingly gratuitous. Stryne was about to be consecrated as 'Bishop', Astartobe had made that clear, although the actual process of sanctification had not yet been enacted. There was almost a hint of sarcasm in Dublo's use of the term. In the power play between the three of them, Dublo was coming to the fore, beginning to dictate terms. Something soon would have to be done about this preposterous little manikin. But not yet, ride with the flow. 'So how soon and for how long will this projected new banqueting suite be in operation? Food sources are will rapidly become scant.'

Dublo positively effervesced. Tinnage is becoming limited; Stompis and Christies must be deployed to scavenge throughout citadel.'

'There's now't but nothing left!' snarled Stent, now stooping on all fours, desperately trying to elevate himself, reaching for the window sill for purpose.

'Yes, though it's that, "but nothing" that we need to gather. Scant remainders but needed none the less'.

Astartobe moved close to him, he tremored but dare not move away. She announced, with that sharp diction of hers, 'Our women can do that: create an order of Femdom, give them a distinctive sash, let them loose to scour the very reaches of The Uniate; every cellar, loft, backyard, there will always be some that have been missed. And even in those that have already been ransacked, there is bound to be a few items left that, in the heady days of our forming were deemed to be surplus to requirements.'

She looked at them, her eyes piercing their nervousness. None of them dared to speak. 'It will be done' Ma'am.' Dublo muttered, though with no enthusiasm.

She felt the silence, snarled at Stent to get up and then snapped, 'In addition we will launch a further campaign.'

'Do we have the means to launch another campaign, Ma'am?' This was from Stryne, frowning as he stepped aside from Stent's clawing reach for support.

'Not a full scale assault, but a gradual piecemeal infiltration into the outer suburbs. One day here, one day there, always changing, repeating a particular street only at random intervals. If we face any assault by the lumpen likes of them, retreat, don't give fight, retreat but return later. Jiggery-pokery, here today, gone tomorrow. Small detachments, equipped to defend themselves long enough to scarper. There will be losses but they will be few and sustainable. There must be hidden troves of tonnage throughout all of the suburbs'.

Dublo croaked ecstatically. 'Precisely ma'am.' And tried to help Stent to his feet, the man's scrabbling for support at the window sill was disconcerting to say the very least.

'Leave him!' she snarled. If he can't manage it: he's gone.'

Stent managed it, legs bandied, trunk tottering, head against the slats of the blind.

'Then put it into practice. Stent liase with Dublo, get the programme going.' Stent quivered a nod but that was all.

'Is there anywhere in particular you suggest that we should start, Ma'am?

She pinched her mouth, paused then snapped, 'Yes. Down the Dingley Dell. I should imagine there would be rich pickings down there. You will probably face small pockets of resistance, prepare for skirmishes, but in sufficient number you should easily overcome what inmates you happen upon. Yes, Dingley Dell: start there.'

'And the Man-Eat, ma'am?' queried Dublo, fresh of face now he had a scheme to administer. Him, not Stent, the days of that lumbering oaf were clearly numbered. With his lungs poisoned by breathing deeply of the air in the Petfood Factory, he was not going to be in a position to do more than give the occasional bellow of warning or encouragement. A crucial point had been reached; Management had supplanted Military.

' "The Man-Eat?", that to be the name of your proposed restaurant I suppose. Does that stand for "Management Eatery"?. I suppose it must do, but then all Clerks aren't management are they.' Stryne's smile crimpled his lips.

'What else could it possibly stand for?' This from Dublo, with a scant smile in Astartobe's direction.

'Consumer become Commodity? she snapped.

'With entertainment.' murmured Dublo, adding that he would arrange for suitable diversion for the diners. 'They will be deliriously deluded from the food crisis we are facing and will believe that everything in the Uniate is "Hunky Dory" Ma'am'

'Until it is.' she snapped back, then with an instant change of tone she dismissed Stryne with a smile, promising that she would arrange his ceremony of sanctification with him shortly, whispering in cleanly spirited words that perhaps he could even be elevated to the purple. Stryne bowed, he actually bowed, as he placed one rope veined hand on top of the other and discreetly departed.

She ignored Stent, upright but still tottering and leaning against the wall, his breath gargled irritatingly through phlegm.

Dublo smiled, pleased with himself.

So, he was, was he?! Well she would see about that. She grabbed his wrist, yanked it down, vigorously, so that he tottered down to the floor, landing on his knees, bewildered and frightened. Turning his wrist, twisting his arm, so that he yowked in pain, till his face was held tight against her belly, his cheeks bitten into by the glass bead of her robe.

She hissed. 'Make sure those entertainments you are planning hit the right note, because if not …', she twisted his arm against the joint, so that the scant weight of his flibberty-jibbet body, now all of a twist, trying to ease the weight on the soon to be dislocated shoulder joint, meant that his gaping mouth was now forced tight into her crotch itself. A delirium of agonised ecstasy coursed through his body, now jerked about in a spasm. And he nodded as she bent her head down toward him and snarled. 'Get it wrong and the method of your death will beyond the management of your imagination.'

With that she shook him free. He scrabbled about on the floor, murmured that he would, get it done as she would wish, that there would be no more folk songs, not ever. She nodded, trod on the splay of his fingers, thought about stamping on them till the crackle of their breaking was expunged by his screams, but concluded this was not yet the time for that and left.

Testing his fingers, moaning with the pain, Dublo got to his feet. The warning was clear, given this new venture, his life was out on a limb. It was a hunch, he dare not think that it wouldn't work, this Man Eat scheme of his, but for it's success, he needed the co:operation of Funky Lurgan and his slight disciple, Liz Stride. It was, he knew full well, all or nothing now. As he stumbled out into the corridor, shouldering past Stent, he realised that it was going to be all or nothing for everyone now and that Stent was already about to be consigned to the latter category. Strange he had wanted Stent to be present to witness his triumph in the restaurant, he could imagine him fidgeting in his pockets to the rhythm of the tunes. But no, not now … .but then perhaps … yes, present in a different sense of the word … why not indeed. Laid out in state … .laid out as steak. And he permitted himself a little chuckle as he hurried down the slippery stairs.

Chapter 21

Funky Lurgan: huddle shouldered, bent over the handle bar of a loaded supermarket trolley, yellow seepage dribbling from under his wig, struggled for breath. He had wound a way down passages and entries, drudge pushing, bringing his goods to market. The swollen slops of cess, increased to the extent that they almost doubled their journey time, had now reach the centre of Citadel. But they were nearly there, the paving ahead almost clear of cess, indicated that they were entering the realm of the dreaded First Uniate. Well, dreaded by the likes of him and all the many small scatterings of survivors who only wanted to plough their own furrow of despair. Well, that wasn't going to be allowed to happen: he had still a religious enough turn of mind to realise that, given time, the true nature of the Uniate would be manifest: not accommodation but extirpation; not hegemony but erasure. He may well have fallen from the Jesus path: 'it would be better a stone be tied around his neck and he be cast in the sea' but, come what may, the loins still had needs. And where had those unaccommodating words come from but the recognition that such a crime as his, committed upon the frail figure of his daughter, was passed on from generation unto generation. He had abused them all, abused himself … .but it mattered not, not now, not to be known, because soon there wouldn't be anything left to know. Knowing's all in the head, not in the world and fossils are speechless. But yes, he would make amends, just a slither of do- goodery, he would launch his daughter on a brief but glittering career. If it went well tonight, he'd creep away, slide into shadow, down the under route, back to the barge and then float away with a few cartons of whisky, to drown himself in the golden nectar. It was the fee for Liz Stride's performance.

But no, his brain hadn't turned to blancmange yet. The success of his daughter, Liz, would pave the way for his return to the pulpit. He had heard, word always gets out, that there were ranks of female choristers thronging the pews of the cathedral. Awaiting the promise of redemption no doubt, ready, to quietly simper as he preached, canoodling their senses. The old life would flood through his veins again. All he would need was his old cassock, emblazoned with the golden rays of the sun. He would throw away his pus sodden wig, douse his scalp with salt and it would be Priapus unchained. Unmarshalled thoughts: a dribble of fantasy, but it diverted his mind till he got to the meeting point, albeit in a flux of breath and saliva.

But first to the business of the here and now. Liz had to triumph for him to gain his entree to the ranks of the cathedral femininity. It had been negotiated with that fellow Dublo, who seemed to know what he was playing at, pretending that all was well in Citadel, as he called it; the clerks would be clap-happy at her songments, their bellies full of new food; not tinned stuff but real offal. And where would that come from? From the campaign dead, naturally

Funky had been discovered in the tunnel, rescuing Liz, she who had been traipsing about the centre singing her songs for the merry destruction of what they termed Clerkdom. Chased back into the tunnel, by that little Barry prat, who he was hearing more and more about, to be shot at and then raked with hooks into a plastic bag for disposal. Well it hadn't come to that, she ducked the shot, barking her shin on the rail but limped away to safety. He had bathed her shin and cosied up to her, kissing endearments and ignoring her shuddering. She despised him but didn't resist. Well if she had, he would have turfed her out of the barge and sailed away. And whatever would have happened to her then would have been far worse. So, they had shared spoonfuls of treacle and she let herself be displayed unto him. Her iron frigidity excited him.

It was this rag arsed Dublo fellow, who had engineered this coup. He had engaged with Funky. And how had he tracked Funky down? Well, seeing as the grappling patrol had found no body, Dublo had crept the dark curves of the tunnel, on his own, armed with only a torch, discovered where the side wall gave way to a bank where the canal slid in silence. He had waded through the water and boarded their barge. He was brave, Funky was prepared to give him that, but then Funky did not realise how desperate things were after the disastrous raid on the Petfood factory. Unless a mass psychic readjustment could be made, the demise of the clerks would entail the complete dissolution of Clerkdom. It had to be saved or his own future would be cut short by either Stent or Stryne, And then what? An ever diminishing cohort of Stompis with scabbed up lungs and the mute choirs of Christies chiming silence into eternity till they waned into dissolution. No this was to be the mission that would save. And paradoxically the very Vagrant weapon of songments would become the vehicle of palliative relief. Funky had even allowed Dublo to tutor Long Liz into a suitable delivery of the songments he wanted, had let him arrange the style and nature of her costume, all based on his hunch as to what would work with the now frantically anxious ranks of Clerkdom. And this had all been carried out in the strictest secrecy. Funky had been kept in abeyance by the handing over of a bottle of whisky every time Dublo turned up to rehearse Long Liz in their barge. And Liz had stipulated that she should have a dressing room behind the stage curtains and how it should be constructed. It created difficulty but then difficulty was there to be overcome. Little cost if the result was to create anew an enduring mind mood of optimistic, mind slumbering acceptance within the ranks of Clerkdom.

Dublo even dared to imagine that the decimated ranks of Stompis and the spiritual putrescence of the Christies would become a withering irrelevance. Thus he would create a new,

new order and prove to the Great Astartobe that he was the man for the job. Significantly this project had nothing to do with numbers or statistical process, it was a facilitation of happy songments. Barry Trasher would be there, if only to learn that his metric methods were becoming ever more limited. It was culture now that mattered. And who knows, perhaps Stryne would be there, word gets about. If not? Dour thoughts but should things not work out as he hoped, then he had the revolver and a bullet, which would solve the problem should things go wrong.

Funky, having recaptured his breath gave a last push, the loaded trolley was now on clear scraped paving which although sloping gently upwards provided no impediment. His breath snorted as he muttered croaking obscenities, planning how he would have his sex fun with a Liz after the performance when transformed by success, with her lithe limbs clasped about him and shouting in delightful disgust. He panted and strove with his load: Liz Stride was the 'load' in his trolley. She sat silent and cramped, her knees up to her chin, her thin stick like legs held tight by her thin stick like arms, her brow bent to her red raw knees. All was hidden underneath a heavy and sodden piece of carpet.

As they reached the summit he was aware of the swooshing and scraping on the glass walls of Central's atrium. He smirked, it never stopped but what good did it do? No matter, a swerve to the left and he could see the lantern lights of the much vaunted new accomplishment, the Maneat. Or was it ManEat? Who would ever know, or even care to know?

The ManEat, was to be tangible proof that a degree of restoration was possible: that there was control and protocol still in the realm of Citadel. Enemies had been eliminated, new nutritional supplies had been guaranteed; at least for as long as they lasted- but then that was the measure of all supplies..

As yet the restaurant was not open for custom, that would be an hour or more later, but preparations were obviously well in hand, not only the soft glow of the lanterns but the sad catenary of tinsel and the drenched colour of puckered balloons hung at regular intervals from a length of string. Lurky noted this as he pushed the trolley around to a back entrance where Dublo stood to welcome them at a half open door.

No sooner than he saw Funky he waved and even helped to push the trolley inside; not until the door had been closed after them was he able to relax.

'The set up is as specified?' a warning question from Funky.

'Of course.'

'Upstairs then?'

'Yes, leave the trolley down here.'

'No, the trolley goes upstairs as well.'

'Is …?'

'Is what?!' Funky leaned aggressively towards Dublo.

'Your … well, where is she?'

Funky pushed the trolley hard into Dublo's stomach. His suit crumpled all the more and he gave out a gasp of rancid breath.

'In the trolley of course. Now get your end and lift!'

'Can't she get out and walk up the steps like … ?' Dublo gave a prolonged yowk as Funky pushed the trolley ever harder, pinioning him to the wall. 'You never said about steps' he snarled.' And Dublo watched as a trail of pus slid from beneath Funky's wig and down his cheek.

Without a further word they lifted the trolley up the stairs and onto a podium that was partly screened from the eating area by a thick, black curtain.

'I said we wanted …' began Funky.

'Yes,' Dublo explained tartly, 'and here it is, your dressing room, just as the young lady has specified.' It was about eight foot square, made of swollen sheets of ply, with a small bench and a chair inside. Pushing Dublo aside Funky snarled that he was to knock on the small entrance door three times when the performance was to begin and until then to keep well away. 'Just fuck off out of it!' Not the words he would have expected from a preacherman, but he did as he was told. At the edge of the podium he did cast a backward look' Funky's stare knifed through him.

He went down three or four steps to the Maneat area. All was now a shuffling business. Trestle tables down the length of one side, opposite the windows on which were placed steaming vats of the new ManEatStuff, which were being continuously stirred, with long poles, hooked at the far end and used to lift entanglements of organs, which were held steady above the boiling stew and cut into smaller knotted masses with garden shears. The labour was continuous until it was certain that whenever a ladle was lowered in and fished about for a few minutes, it would come up with only a shiny ladle full with gobbets of mixed organs, no strings of entangled organs..

And it was a continuous process, whenever a vat was almost emptied of all but gristle lumps and thin gravy, the operatives would bang on the floor with their poles for a fresh supply of trays of bloody organs to be tipped into the vats. Dublo recognised the correctness of the process, designed no doubt by Barry, or Trasher, as he was now often called, a process that ensured that no single organ was ever seen on its own, there was therefore no chance of recognition. Not that it would have mattered if there had been, judging by the clamour as the ranks collected their dishes and spoons and waited patiently in line. The air,swilled with the heat and suffocated with the stench, shifted about in a brown cloud, stirring the catenary of balloons and staining the ceiling tiles. Grease dribbled down the walls, finding its way into slippery smear puddles.

The mood was good, almost as if the old times were back (a very dangerous notion that). No matter, supping greedily from their bowls and, where their spoons would not do the job, ripping the offal entanglements apart with their fingers, they were all busy slobbering the meat down.

Eating finished, the clientele were then urged to sit on the rows of chairs pushed up before the podium and as soon as all were seated, Dublo, his shirt now daub stained with organ slop, went back stage to knock on the dressing room door.

Within that eight foot square 'cubicle', what few preparations were needed had been effected. Peeling the wet carpet off, Liz Stride squat stooped in the trolley, angrily

241

beckoned Funky by waggling her hand, for him to help her out and set her down on the floor. And then, there she stood, regarding herself as a grey-green reflection in a large mirror that completely covered the wall. So too the other walls, also totally a mirror, only the fourth wall mirror was interrupted by the outline rectangle of the door. Wherever she stared she saw endless replications in green tunnels of reflected reflections that curved away to infinity.

Standing there, her face set in an implacable stare, she reached out her arm, flicking her fingers till Funky silently handed her a long necklace of cut glass beads.

Her limbs were long, extremely thin, but swollen at the joints- bulbous knees and elbows. And she was tall, enough to be able to look down on Funky's once so powerful figure. How he had diminished in his pulpit exile, though his shoulders still betokened strength.

She, dressed in a thin, pink patterned, or was it stained, dress that reached, svelte and smooth to just above her crotch, at which level a fringe of long, coloured tassels hung tantalisingly, slipping apart at each movement to reveal her knickers. On her feet were crease shining boots, black, with sharp heels, boots that reached above her knees. Around her neck was wrapped a silk scarf, dusted with sequins.

Ready? Not yet. Hands on her hips, her fingers bedazzled with rings, she dabbed a piece of paper along her lips. Those lips, cruel and thin, but long, so long, were punctuated, each of them with a line cold sores. They would crack and spurt precise little diamonds of blood as she performed the songments that had been tutored by Dublo as he sat before her, crooning delight in the cramped confinement of the barge. She hoped he knew what he was doing as … well … no time for wondering now, as he opened the door, and, oblivated the pattern of replicated mirrors, led her through the curtain and onto the stage.

It was a fusty, breath rasping hubbub that seethed before her until Funky silenced them with a welcoming scream as he announced her name. 'LIIIIIZZZZZ STRIIIIIDDDDDEEEE!!!

Silence, only the occasional, unintentional clatter of utensils, which drew sharp hushes from those seated..

She stared at them, an unremitting glare, held till someone made a sound, then with a fierce motion she lifted her one foot to knee height and with a harsh shout, slammed it down, a piledriver of a stamp, onto the wooden boards of the stage. There was a gasp, then she snarled, puckering her lips, and the diadem of blood beads punctuating those long, lean lips could be seen from the front few rows. She stamped again, now uttering a prolonged hiss, pointing into the crowd of them. They swallowed in their hush, hopegulping for further stamping because they were then able to stare at the ever swaying and parting curtain of loin tassles.

She obliged and then, stamping all the way through, she snarl hissed her first songment..

'How much is that doggy in the window,

The one with the waggled tail?' '

Every word was pile drived. Every syllable spat with fury and at the end, her lips now besmirched with blood, she leaned forward, beckoned them to do likewise and waggled her tongue obscenely.

They sat silent, clutching the edge of their chairs with bloodless knuckles, almost breathless with anticipation. They wanted more, these Moddlemanagementmiddledmindedmen, craven to memory stuff they had never been old enough to have had. Not such memories as these.

Their silence ached the more as she began squatting now, provoking her hips to shudder her thighs and hiss whispered.

' In a shady nook, by a babbling brook ...'

Oh, it was so illicit, fond memories that had been held in the minds of men, now mostly long dead, men such as Harold but he of course was not there. Dead men's memory- trivia now flowed and flapped about in the crypt of their mind scape. They wallowed all the more as with a particularly sharp shout staccato, stamping, jumping and squat- rolling to show her buttock crease, she began yet another songment with ...

'There's a tiny house, by a tiny stream,

Where a lovely lass had a spike eyed dream.'

By the end of it she was glistening with sweat and they, her audience, bedraggled with slobberslap. It was an emetic pandemonium. Funky grabbed through the curtain to haul her off stage. Fractur- frenzy erupted from the audience, such that Dublo, hovering about throughout, insisted that she had to at least offer one more songment. Which she did, in spite of Funky's attempted refusal, returning to the stage, deliberately fingering the small protuberances of her breasts as she spat out ...

'I saw mummy stripping Stampaclaws

Underneath the Chrissmush deed last night.'

And then, with Funky chortling and coughing back stage, she,spitting blood and drooling, advanced on in the latest heritage track with,

'It's a strong way to strip a fairy ...'

Which brought up sad merriment of a once upon a time anthem.

And her words were groanstamped by all in her audience. They step marched in wavery lines, as past memories of the otherdom of their fathers' fathers flooded in great-mastering heritage tracks into them, creating felt mindful ejaculations of, the old clankferous puffmotives, traipsing steamy wisps from sliding tranklements about their wheels, trugging clarriges full of happy-sadness of the Blighty departure to forrony fields they some will triumph in. And all to the very last one varnished bright in Heritage as she ended with ...

'Wheel felt again, dunt nowhere, dunt now hen'

Everything was drowned in a unified cheer as the realm of Clerkdom was relished in Heritage.

This was the socio-mental vector Astartobe had not bargained for. Heritage ... it had to be destroyed ... it had to be expunged, it deluded fear, it provided a false feeling that ... after all ... things were good.

When Liz came off, lathered with sweat, even Dublo was haphazardly lip trembling, it taking him some time to shed the power of those melodies before he could hand over his half of the deal with Funky, a large, leather bound, brown paged, old edition of The Holy Bible, letters gold embossed on spine and covered with a cross: the vital prop for his projected pulpit return. How could he ever preach without a bible to thump?

What had Dublo earned? Certainly not just a horde of Middlemanmen, traipsing back to their apartments, flushed with the flux of memoriastics. Even Liz discerned that they had been provided with a nostalgic syrup as important as meat nourishment. Clerkdom would need those old time songments as much as the lumpy slime of the organ stew made from the corpsemeat of those that had perished in the assault on the petfood factory.

Dublo would soon be seen as the provider and upholder of mental survival amongst their devoted ranks. The scrawny office boy not the semi divine priestess would be their leader. He would be exalted throughout the diminishing realm of Clerkdom, not she.

Well, that wasn't going to be allowed to happen. He was never to be allowed to 'now' nostalgia into being. They would never be allowed the luxury of that easement.

'No! No! No!

Chapter 22

'No! No! No!' Astartobe screeched. It was a 'No' not simply quivering but rippling, in an uncontrollable rictus of rage, her lips stretched into sharp lines, her hand clutched so tight that her nails digging into her palms, released streams of blood.

Stryne, himself all in an ecclesiastical fervour, dithering up and down, noticed those blood streaming palms and thought her to be truly great, yea unto the uttermost, a recidivism of Christ.!!!

Dublo was doomed.But he didn't understand the enormity of his malfeasance.

The three of them, disguised in shadow, had witnessed the performance of Liz's songments in diverse moods. Stent, his long, pink, fat throat constantly ululated in a putrid ecstasy throughout the whole performance. Stryne, bemused by the crass wording and stamping was happily convinced that Liz could never be recruited into the ethereal choir he was planning and all the more pleased that Dublo, overconfident in his success, was obviously heading for a downfall, one awful way or another. He simply smiled and wondered how awful could awful be?

Though this rage of hers, was for some reason Stent did not understand, all Dublo's fault and hell would now be done unto him. By Stent himself, he hoped. Oh how he had long yearned to reduce that irritating fidget of a man into truncheon meat. But now, when at last that could have been accomplished in the line of duty, his poisoned lungs denied the necessary breath to even vent his fury. Just considering it caused him to collapse, red faced, his mouth bubbled up and emitting a raucous spasm, he dropped onto the floor. Writhing on his back, limbs aquiver, heels scrabble scrawling the concrete, he died in mid gulp with low stuttering groan of cipherable dismay. Other Stompis were already going the same way, their lungs worn raw by the poisoned atmosphere within the petfood factory

'Oh dearie me' was Stryne's sole valedictory utterance as he prodded the body with his foot, just to check. What remained of Stent was now bound for the new Corpsemeat Department

' You were saying about Dublo ma'am?'

She snorted in disbelief at his naivety. 'Don't you realise that now he has purchase in our realm, he will be bringing Liz time and again for Songment Concerts, unleashing rhapsodies, he will work his wickedness; they will be wallowing in contentment in no time at all. And can't you see that the old Preacherman is behind all this. Who else could have trained her up in those poisonous songments to persuade that all that was once and lovely could come again? He has allied himself with Dublo. In no time at all he will have inveigled himself into the very cathedral pulpit that was to be yours as Archbishop' …

Stryne let out a splintering whine. So, he was to be an Archbishop … that was her plan for him … .the two of them, a divine duopoly,that could yet be destroyed by the evil duopoly of Funky and Dublo. What to do?

'With his sermons he will equivocate your nubile throated choir of Christies into a legs akimbo rhapsody, till they have neither hope nor purpose for anything else. Did you not know of his reputation!?'

'I did, but presuming him dead, thought best to forget to be the safest option.'

She snorted, 'When is that ever a safe option. Be Zionistical: Never forgive, Never forget. Let it lie in the stream of blood!,

'Of course ma'am Christ's blood streams into infinity.'

'Not Christ's blood you fool: what has Christ to do with the practising church? Our blood, in all its vital superabundance.'

Stryne's mind skimmed the dark ocean of her thought. 'But I was given to understand that he was of a Methodistical persuasion, whereas ... .'

He was a loin-spiller, he was of every 'persuasion', he preached in any pasture that would have him and they all did, he brought a full congregation. For God's sake man, he may be a rubbled figure now but that voice is still there and he has a prick like a poker. Take him ...'

'Down?'

'Out you fool. Use a knife, plunge it into his throat, waggle it about till his very tone is drowned in its own blood.'

Stryne twisted his thin mouth, his Punchface caved in, he almost pitter- pattered his words whispering ... 'But I have never ...'

'I have!' she snapped, adding, 'And believe me it relishes the soul. And you must do it, so I can rule in peace. So do the deed now, and you will be Archbishop Excelciate! You will wear the purple cloak. But you must win that honour. I can't be expected to have an Archbishop too frightened to murder. So, now, go and get it done it, and before you do, send Dublo up to me.'

Resistance drained from him, he took up the paperknife she proffered and made his way down to where Funky and Dublo stood aside in low conversation. Dublo dabbling, his hands about, expecting all smiles and benevolence for what had been achieved. High-eyebrowed, Stryne pulled him closer by his elbow and whispered her instruction.

All a tipsy and preening his lapels, he hurried away to her eminence hoping a promised preferment as reward. A great expectation even.

Stryne rippled a congratulatory tone at his departure, at the same time, pointing out to Funky the cloaked figure of Astartobe at the back of the hall. Funky looked up, he couldn't catch the knowing of her name, Perhaps due to Stryne's voice trembling with nervousness, in any case the clattering of emptied vats and trays were for the nonce despicably loud. But when he did look up, did he recognise that famed figure, that gentle visage of a once beautiful supplicant, outstretched nakedly beneath him on the altar table, daring lust in excelcis?

Was it her indeed? But then it was an almost sibilant groan of ecstasy that emitted from his suddenly punctured neck as Stryne, splattered with blood, withdrew the knife, stepped aside, muttered a few condolences to himself as he heard Funky fall to his great reckoning off stage in a muted babbling away of his life blood. Except it wasn't all of his life blood by any means. It was just a trickle. Stryne had pierced the neck but not the jugular and Funky, seething with fury hurried away to collect Liz, bundle her into the trolley and hurry them both back through the tunnel and into the barge. So now he had an Archbishop to be revenged upon and an unsuspected parish to plunder: things were looking better.

Stryne, for his part, thought that that had been an easy way to win an Archbishopric, the killing habit could be catching.

* * *

Best bib and tucker. Indeed Dublo did have such an outfit, a Harris Tweed jacket, no buttons but a superior cloth and a trim cut, up the back panel and with angled flap pockets. Nothing inside those pockets of course, he wouldn't have wanted to bulk up his sartorial figure. And his trousers, knee scrubbed cords, of a complementary hue and no one would be looking at his knees. It was his face that would be presented to her, his eyes bright with avid enthusiasm. He confidently expected her enthusiastic appraisal, promotion even, elevation to a named rank, something beyond the bland anonymity of Secretary General. After all he would now surely become nominated as … .well, as what? That would be the surprise and he rehearsed his devout thanks. Not grovelling, no, but let it seem unexpected.

He had been summoned to appear before her the morning of the very next day. Stryne, beneficent in manner now that the oaf Stent was dead, was to accompany him, up those flights of stairs that he had had cleared of the tangle of chairs and tables just a month or so previously- she would surely also remember the efficacy with which that service had been rendered- and up to the once management Plaza Suite, which was now her own domain. Her own and nobody else's. All feared what had lain behind those doors but she had dismissed those fears by her presence. Point was that none had ever been admitted to her presence in that mysterious, lavish, ex highest management plaza suite. Not Stryne, who now accompanied him on the slow ascent and certainly never Stent now an expunged nonentity.

So it was to some grand reward he was being led towards and rightly so, the Maneat, as both restaurant and venue was going to do so much to rescue the generality of Clerkdom from the Slough of Despair that the failure of the invasion of the Pet food Factory had plunged them into. Yes, his Showtime Review, as he was going to call the event, had lifted spirits. He and no one else was responsible for its startling success. 'Keep telling yourself that Dublo' he mind muttered to himself. All this he re-rehearsed to himself, as well as the great thanks he would show when … .. His thoughts slapped to a halt; they had reached the top floor and stood before those doors, wish wondering what would be revealed. What sanctity would be displayed? He had to wait a while for Stryne to regain his breath sufficiently to issue the instructions that Astartobe had doubtless proclaimed should be followed to the letter.

'Remove your shoes.' Stryne ordered in a level voice. Strange, but then this was a special summons. He did so, a little disappointed that she would not see his brown polished Chelsea boots. No matter. Stryne smiled, adding, 'And your socks, remove them also.'

Dublo complied. His feet were filthy, but then, this day and age, and he waggled his toes about in excited expectation.

'Once you are inside, I will close these doors and you are to lower your eyes and take regular steps towards her presence.

Do not slide your feet over the floor take regular steps and look downwards at all times. Do you understand?'

Dublo, breathless with excitement, simply nodded and Stryne opened the door. The strangest of exhalations billowed out from within. The most curious sounds scurried about him and the most frightening booming tremored the very air within. Feeling the cold claw of Stryne's fingers in the back of his neck, he was propelled firmly inside and the door closed after him.

Dublo gaped aghast. He took a first step, towards what he presumed was the centre of the Plaza Suite. Following instructions he did not look up, though he was aware of her presence sitting, or standing on some raised eminence in the middle. But the floor was ... littered ... littered with ... he took a first and mildly confident step and hissed with pain. The floor was littered with shards of broken glass, long splinters and short jabments, all but hidden by torn ribbons of ... he paused, because no movement meant no more cutting into his naked feet ... torn ribbons of paper. But not ordinary paper, thick- gloss shiny paper, each and every shred, it seemed bore an illustration of part of a once whole picture of a human face. The eyes and part of an eyebrow here, the delicate arch of an exquisite nostril there, and elsewhere into and beyond his reach, in limpid entanglement, part mouths, luscious lips, painted and pouting, and perhaps the peer of white teeth between those lips; faces that if put together made luxurious artefacts of unreachable, beckoning beauty. And all over, throughout the vast, otherwise empty floor space, a littered unravelling and reravelling of paper mazes, spiked with those terrifying splinters of glass, all jostled and shifting, moving to and fro, in haphazard, slow scraping mats. Disjointed rafts, motioned to and fro by a weird exhalation within, caused by ...

Dublo tottered upright, hands clamped to his ears. The vast space of the floor's paper and glass respiration was occasioned by the buckle-flexing of the large vista windows, floor to ceiling, uninterrupted all round. At this height the winds' howl prowled the skyscape and buffeted the panes with tremendous, irregular force, threatening, it seemed at any moment, to smash those buckling panes into barbarous screams of shattered glass. Yes … at any moment, if not this now here, the next now there, those windows would explode into spears of lacerating glass. No next moment was ever safe. Scream. He did, his chest collapsing on the very breath of terror. Gasping into the stifling air and heaving himself upright, eyes still fixed on the floor, as directed, Dublo made step after agonising step towards the sense of some dark presence that murmured, nodding, almost beckoning him towards it.

The harsh scraping of the paper ribbons, now ankle deep as he encroached ever closer, traced an irritating crisp- edged slithering against his skin, masking the cruel fragments of glass that cut different and deeper with every step.

And still he moved on, sobbing with pain, stooping to pause, but never daring to stand one legged in an attempt to prize a spire of glass free from flesh; never daring to look up, to stare at that ever closer presence.

On and on, he could now at least discern the fixed grin of the thing. It was a mask, a huge headed mask. And it smiled an ever frozen inanity as it nodded but never toppled, beckoning, always beckoning, a sharp rasp of sound with each and every painful step he took, approaching closer and closer to the thing. He gave a short scream of pain as a particularly sharp splinter of glass penetrating deep into his heel. Involuntarily raising his head, he snatched a forbidden glance upwards and saw … what made no sense at all. He saw connection without meaning, unknowing recognition, as he slobbered down to his knees. Let them hurt as well, let his hands be ribboned, because from this position he had to look up … he had to gaze upon … a face universal to all humankind, a Giant Mickey Mouse Mask, its smile a rictus of frozen idiocy.

She spoke. Words from within the mask. 'Look, sweet little Dublo, upon your work.'

The tone was cruel, sharp and incisive. 'You would triumph our realm with a mass popularity, with spasms of a consumer culture without either dignity or restraint. Bring us all down to the level of raving, mass idiocy. Pop Voc Slop for the mindless proles … We have opportunity to lift our culture and faith beyond such moronic slop as we have had to endure for years and you would bring it back, then if this is to be the face of your achievement, wear it!

The mask was now held above his bowed head. He looked up, the last he would ever see was its dark interior and her fingers gripping its rim. What to do? Well what else but, spite of agony, lift the mask from her outstretched hands and hold it over his own bleating face.

Astartobe must be obeyed if he was to gain his reward, and he could still think that a reward was awaited him, even after such malign experience. Blind optimism was his essence. Of course, this was a testing of his mettle, so as instructed, he donned the mask, it swayed about his neck, he grasped it to make it steady but did not totter. It was not heavy as such but a great encumbrance. He twisted his head about inside, but could not see, the eyes had no holes. He turned and turned about, making frantic shuffling with panicky, uncontrollable motions, spearing his feet with fresh agony as with every undirected step he blundered, top heavy and unbalanced, reaching for walls that were not there, falling to the floor, hobbled by pain, stumbling and rising and stumbling again, ever and on.

Her cold voice, etched with hatred, pronounced his sentence. 'Once worn, this mask can never be removed. So grope and bellow, try to wrench it free, it will make no difference, this is your lot, till your end. And she sang in a derisory tone, 'Happy days are here again.'

He made muffled screams, bleated for mercy but from beyond the mask, other than the flex-buckling of the giant glass panes, and the slither- smothering of the strips of glossy paper, he heard only the crisp crunch of glass beneath her boots as she left the Plaza Suite, locking the door after her.

He pawed his way into the plate glass walls, first this way, then that. Without any degree of discernment, stumbling forever in pain, wall to wall, wailing out her name … Astartobe … into the vast breathing of the Plaza Suite.

How long could it take to die in Purgatory?

Chapter 23

'Good God again! Cynthia, I don't believe it. Come on in … Well I never …'

This from Irene who, up until the moment of Cynthia's arrival had got a right cob on her, seeing as she had fallen asleep last night on her still new sofa, well newish anyway, even as she was spooning blackcurrant jam out of the jar for her supper, and of course hadn't a dollop she had just lumped up on the spoon, slipped off, and stained a section of its beading, piping some call it, such that come the morning, she couldn't abide to let it be, couldn't find her scissors and so had to make do with a pair of pliers which she had rescued from the drawer in the kitchen table, and of course there was all manner of stuff cramped up in the drawer, including a coarse length of string, which, as is the way of string and twine, though string's worse … and yes, come to think of it, there was a bundle of green twine in the drawer as well … and fuses and fuse wire … well she could throw them out, no use now to man nor beast … but, would you believe it, the bastard string had snagged as it fell … God almighty, you wouldn't think it possible, you couldn't do it if you tried, not in a month of Sundays, but that's the way with string, it had fallen to the floor, all bundled up but with an open loop, which of course, what with the cloud and the rains, the house is always in a lowlight now, she didn't see and must have put her foot in the open loop, pulled it tight as she stepped away, back into the lounge, which as yet was still free of the swill, thanks to the height of the steps up to her house, unlike Carol's which was now always near ankle deep, and noisy swill it was, running through the house and bringing a draught with it, you always needed a top coat about your shoulders in Carol's these days, it's a wonder how she can put up with it, so yes, swings and roundabouts, as it always had been, even in the best of times, though those had long gone now, no mistake about that, so yes, she had to try to get the crusted rill of jam from off the piping, or beading as some call it, with a stiff pair of pliers, that hadn't been used since the days of Genesis, and, of course, she was so moithering over the stiffness of those pliers, wagging them about in her hands, forcing them to open and shut and of course, you don't have to ask, there was no oil to be found to try and loosen them up, so of course she was distracted, didn't take care and the loop of string snagged on her ankle and she ended up banging her shin against the kitchen table leg, it came so sharp, well the shin, nothing between skin and bone is there, it didn't draw blood but there'll be a hell of a bruise by tomorrow and bruised legs, well they are unsightly, not fit to be presented to Doctor Stone, not that you'll know about him but I'll tell you, he's not here at the moment, said he had to go and be 'unthoughted', that's what he said … 'unthoughted', now I don't know what it means, nothing to me but obviously a lot to him, because he did look worried, distraught even, and it wasn't his way, well yes it was, come to think of it, time to time but this was different, so off he went with a right mowie on his face and when he comes back I'll have a black and blue leg to waggle at him so anyway, yes, Cynthia, it's as well you turned up to take my mind off the bloody ockeredness of things, if you'll pardon my French, as they say, so yes, come on in and set yerself down. I tell you what, I've still got half a bottle of sherry left, we can share a cup … how about that?

Cynthia bundled herself in, placed a large knitted bag on the floor and said that she wouldn't say no to that.

Cynthia Camperdown but everyone still called her Cynthia, never 'Cynth', funny that, but then she did have a certain something about her, a manner so to speak … of nice respectability … no doubt about it. Even as she was sluicing a generous measure of sherry into a cracked cup and passing it over so her guest could have first sip, Irene ventured a general question as to how Jeremy was getting on.

Cynth arched an eyebrow and murmured, she was a very discreet person, 'You may well ask Irene.'

'Well yes, Cynthia … I …' she began to think but only said, 'Oh dear, not … well you know what, I hope things had perhaps moved on, got a little better …'

'Worse Irene.'

'Worse?!'

'How much worse?'

Cynthia took a sip of sherry, pursed her lips, passed the cup back and wire whispered, 'As bad as it gets.'

'Of dear, I am sorry Cynthia.' And she soused her particularly polite 'sorry' in sherry and swallowed.

Receiving the cup back she stared at the sherry, twisting it about in the cup and murmuring, 'You know of course about … ?'

'Jeremy … in the church … but that was some time back. Surely …'

'Surely nothing, Irene love. That horrible preacher, Funky, though what sort of name that is for a preacher God only knows, but he comes round, bangs on the door. I knew as something was up because Jeremy went all ashen and made to go out the back door. No matter, that Funky must have had the wits of the devil because he goes down the entry, grabs Jeremy by the back door and by the lapels, accuses him of all manner of things, including … including … would you believe it …?

'Go on Cynthia, love.'

'I hardly know how to say it, Irene.'

'Have another sip of sherry, it'll help.'

Cynthia did so, though Irene seemed to remember that port had always been her favourite tipple, well at Christmas time certainly.

Now she gathered her folded arms tighter into her generous bust and almost mouthed the word. 'Masturbating!'

'Oh well, that's men for you. But why was Funky so worked up over … Jeremy?' and she gestured with her forearm.

'Don't tell me you don't know about him and that Muriel Wentworth?'

'Jeremy! No, never!'

'Not my Jeremy … that would be the day. No, one Sunday night after evensong, Funky and that Muriel, they were … at it actually "at it" … on the high altar …'

'Well … No … Well …'

' No wells about it. Fact of the matter was that my Jeremy hadn't left his organ, still gathering up his sheets of music up in the organ loft and sees them at it, hammer and tongs, she screech sobbing and him grunt groaning like there's no tomorrow. There, now I've said it. Jeremy claims he couldn't get away quick enough, let a hymn book drop, of course they heard it and Funky, would you believe it, well yes, Irene, considering the likes of him, you would, chased Jeremy, even though he was stark naked, out of the church and she just laughed and waited for him on the high altar, to come back and lap up some more. At least that's how Jeremy told it.'

'But why come round to yours and collar Jeremy in the entry?' Irene was patiently determined to get to the bottom of this tale.

Cynthia pursed her lips, the sherry was helping her to enjoy the telling the tale, Funky's "tail" that is. 'No, Irene love, Funky reckons as my Jeremy, was crouched, watching, trying to keep out of sight, and that his elbow …'

'Your Jeremy's elbow?'

'That's the, one was working away as he was watching.'

' Getting a free show.'

Cynthia, her mouth a slit as she swallowed her sherry, gulped and tittered as she added. 'Got a good lamping from Funky, pinioned up against the entry wall, his collar all skew-wiff, as he threatened that what he was getting now would be as nothing if word ever got out.'

'But it did.'

'Of course it did. Now listen, Jeremy had good reason to be there, a minute or so after the service, gathering his music up, nothing malign in that.'

'Malign?'

'Wicked Irene. There was nothing wicked in Jeremy being there. And of course what could he do but …'

'Watch the goings on.'

'Not watch … specifically, as in watching to see the in's and out's of it all but watching to wait for them to finish, get back to the vestry to get dressed and give Jeremy a chance to scarper sharpish. But, oh dear me no, he dropped his book and it wasn't struggling with his flies as Funky claimed, but trying to regain his hymnal that's what he was about. And as Funky was storming after him, naked and blatant down the nave, he shouted, pointed out to Funky that that old lobster backed creature of spite and spittle, Miss Belper, was waddling down the aisle, cleaving her shadow from the wall as she let herself out. That's who spread word, and more, varnished the deed. As they say, the teller always tells the tale the taller.'

'Not that Miss Belper who used to live over at Crabbs Cross?'

'You got it, that's her, or was.'

' I think as she's dead now. I'm sure I heard as such a while back.'

' Went down with the gripe a year or so back.'

'I thought as I hadn't seen her about. Well yes, she was like a tablespoonful of syrup of figs every time you met her. But you do surprise me Cynthia because she was always known to be High Church, very devotional in the incense and all that malarkey.'

'She was but she said, that cold winter we had a few years back had knotted up her veins and the pipes in the nave were not hot enough, of course she always sat in the same pew, but then Christians can be like that. Fact of the matter is, if the truth be told, St Uselessness, as I always called it, appointed a woman minister. Now I do understand as some had difficulty with that, well so be it, but we all know that Miss Belper would willingly surrender herself to a man in a cassock …'

Irene chortled, 'Point being he wasn't in his cassock though was he? Wasn't in anything. I'm surprised she scuttled away.'

Cynthia drained the cup, rinsed a smile and concluded philosophically, 'Well, as I always say, there's no telling with folks.'

She was about to let the sherry work its benign pleasantries into her diminishing discourse when Irene brought her up sharp. 'But you were saying, Cynthia, that Funky had had your Jeremy up against the back door …'

'Not the back door, he scraped him half way up the entry.'

'And?'

'He gave him a right lamping, right in front of my own eyes. As I've said, a man of god.'

'Jeremy should have grabbed him by the nuts.'

'Jeremy's not like that, never has been and never will be.'

'So …'

'So nothing, but you do know as he went all wayward?'

'Go on.'

'You don't know?'

'How often do I see you these days Cynthia? You haven't been past in a month of Sundays.'

'Well he was never the same after and he took up with Claude …'

'As used to do the cricket tea sandwiches?'

'The very same.'

'Well there's a story. That Daphne Lovedone used to have an eye for Claude, got him to go to that folk club of hers …'

'She must have been getting on a bit by then.'

'Well she was wasting her time with Claud Hamilton; anybody could have told her that. Nothing came of it.'

'Would that it had because Irene, my Jeremy, as was, he's now uncled-up with Claude … they'm living together in a little bungalow down by Sparkfield Meadows.'

'I bet as it's none too cosy now, Sparkfield Meadows must be under water surely.'

'We'll all be under water soon, if this lot keeps up. I've never known the like. Which is why I've come.' She scrabbled her arm about, clutched onto her bag and presented it to Irene.

'What you got there, Cynthia?'

'My corkying.'

'Corkying?!'

'Like we used to do at school, on a Friday afternoon, it all went to make blankets for African kids. Remember?'

'Don't I just. I always wondered why African kids needed a Corkyed blanket, specially as it's so hot in Africa, I'd have thought a sheet would have served them better. And it took a while to Corky just a few inches.'

'Yes it did but we loved doing it.'

'So?'

'So, I thought, Irene love, that we could spend our last time together, Corkying, the three of us.'

'Three?'

'You, me and Carol, she was always such a dab hand at it, if my memory serves me right. Look there's nothing else going for us, and you know me, I'm not one to be whimpering and splashing about when it comes to the end of things, so we'll be together, happily Corkying as the waves lap over us. What do you think?'

' Friday afternoons.'

'In the winter terms. Summer term we ran about in the playground playing tick and release. But I'm not suggesting that.'

'We don't get no cowin' summer, not any more and not ever again. That's all gone by the bye, and it don't bear to even try and think about it …' Irene broke off and a minute jewel of a tear formed in the corner of her eye.

Cynthia grab-fondled her elbow. So what do you think, Irene love?'

Irene didn't think … she just reacted … dissolved even, into an amorphous but gentle disposition of unspecified fondness, that was quite unusual for her, she hadn't felt like it since her seventh birthday.

Cynthia adopted a knowing stance and handed her a handkerchief. It was brand new, she having just taken it from a box of three, with a stiff cellophane cover. Being brand new it was, of course a little stiff, but there was a neat little bit of bright embroidery on each corner and that was nice.

'Look at me being all silly. You're right Cynthia, and it's a good idea. It'll stop us getting all morose about things. And I'm sure Carol will agree, because you know her, she could never think a bad thing about anyone. I've often wished as I could be like that but I can't it's not in my nature.'

'Shall we go down to Carol's then?'

'We will, this very moment. Mind you'll have to get clobbered up, it wouldn't suit you going down in those booties you'm wearing, not with a couple of inches of swill scurrying across the floor. Skirker got me a pair of wellingtons for the purpose, Carol wears them all the time. Not Skirker though, he sticks to his boots, it don't seem to bother him, having cold, wet feet all the time.'

'I'd forgotten about Skirker. How's he doing these days?'

'As you might imagine. I'll tell you one thing for now't, if he ever catches up with Funky, he'll slice him to pieces with one of his grappling hooks. He's already scraped half his scalp off of his head, he has to wear a blond wig now, it does look a mess, or it did last time I saw him. He keeps his distance these days.'

'I did hear as he was …'

'Don't Cynthia … it doesn't bear thinking about.'

'It's true then?'

'It's a pity as your Jeremy didn't grab him by the balls when Funky had him up against the entry wall. Might have been a different kettle of fish, though as you said, Jeremy wasn't ever inclined to violence.'

'Well, being an organist, he had to make sure that his fingers were never damaged, nor his feet either, if you come to think of it.'

Irene nodded but with a sour grin as she thought he obviously liked kindling the fire in Claud's bollocks. She dismissed the thought as she rummaged behind the sofa for a pair of Stone's waders. 'I'll wear wellingtons, but I've only this pair so try these on, they'll keep you dry, but you'll have to pull them up to you waist. Leave you booties here till you get back.'

Cynthia tried to do as instructed, having difficulty with the waders, scriming and scraming her way into them, and when she turned round and bent down to place her bootees on the sofa, Irene screeched with laughter. 'Irene, love, you skirt's all up at the back, you'm showing your knickers and your arse.'

Finally decent, though there was nothing indecent about Cynthia's cupid buttocks, Irene had to give her that, and all wasted on Jeremy, obviously, as she grabbed her bag, clutched tight, she indicated for Irene to lead the way.

'What exactly is it that you've got in that bag, I mean it's all puffed up with whatever it is?'

Wool mostly, for our Corkying. I know there's not long left but there is the three of us and it wouldn't do for us to have finished before the end, and just be sitting there twiddling our thumbs. Oh and there's three cotton reels, one each, and twelve nails, but they needs to be hammered in. I don't suppose …?'

'Funny you should say that but just before you come, I hacked my shin getting a pair of stiff pliers out of the kitchen table drawer and I did notice as I hadn't got a hammer and if I had that's was where it would have been. Don't worry though, Skirker will have a hammer.'

She opened the door for Cynthia to scratchwaddle out and followed with a warning to watch how she made her way seeing as that top step was still treacherous, spite of all.

They descended Irene's steps, pat holding onto each other, even squawking the odds as, having crossed the road they made it to Carol's front door … .one step up and already slurried over with a downward current in turmoil.

'Hello, Carol love, look who I've brought to see you.' Irene had to speak loud, enunciating each syllable, as if she was instructing a foreigner, because the fast swilling current, dappling and cresting busily against every leg of the sofa and every leg of every chair in her lounge, created a loud spattering sound that Cynthia decided she couldn't stand for long. Outside could be heard a sound of constant hammering and cursing, that in its own way was disconcerting.

'It's Skirker,' explained Carol, who for once did not have her usual placid mien upon her brow. She went to the side door and screeched ... again not Carol's usual way ... for Skirker to come and see who had come to see him.

'It's your Auntie Cynthia.' bellowed Irene. Of course Cynthia wasn't Skirker's proper auntie, but it helped to keep things simple, in the general scheme of things, if she was said to be..

'He's livid, has been all day.'

'Who with?'

'Himself, Irene, if the truth be told. He's been making hooks and traps ...'

'Traps?!' queried Cynthia.

'Best leave him be if he's going to be destructive,' murmured Irene, adding, 'we only wanted to see if we could borrow a hammer.'

'Just to see if we could tap nails into cotton reels, we want to do some corkying.'

'Corkying?' Carol's faced relaxed.

'Like we used to do, when we were at junior school, of a Friday afternoon. Remember?'

'Oohh, yes.'

Irene leaned closer, as Carol sighed fondly.' You'd forgotten all about that hadn't you Carol.'

Carol almost sobbed, regarding her two old friends with ample benignity. She stroked Irene's hand that had now clutched the back of her sofa, splayed across the long back line of piping, feeling its run across her palm, as she thought simultaneously ... was it piping or beading, the correct term and that there was no dollop of jam encrusting it and had she got it all off with those stiff pliers ... ? But then that was Irene all over, always trapped in the present moment, even as Cynthia was romancing the past of their schooldays. She frowned.

'Oh yes, that would be a wonderful way, to let it all go, telling a tale with our Corkying, that would go floating away till the flood ended it all.' murmured Carol, not a line to her face as clearly the prospect of gentle immersion in the ever rising waters gave her a sense of fulfilment.

They shared her silence until Skirker intruded, vicious and scowling.

'He's been using up all of those reinforcing bars that Funky left behind … making mantraps … and …'

'Mantraps?! queried Cynthia. 'What d'you want with mantraps, Skirker love.' adding to Carol, without pause, 'he seems to get bigger every time I see him.'

'I wish he was Cynthia, he could do with putting some weight on, look at him, like a scarecrow. Now there I've said it.'

Skirker, undiminished by this woman's talk, explained. 'It's all going tits up at that Citadel place and they'm sending scavengers down here to see what they can get. So I've set mantraps all down the Dell, as 'ull have their legs off, if they steps in 'em.'

'Oh dear.' worried Cynthia. 'Is that wise, Skirker love?'

At that point a wet scraping could be heard and Lez entered, still in his yellow sou'wester with a magnet, attached to a length of string in one hand and three anonymous tins of food triumphed in the other.

'Well done Lez,' Skirker murmured, adding, 'just drop 'em on the table mate, we'll see to 'em later.'

Carol laughed. 'Oh that's so good of you Lez, but no, we'll have them now. We've got guests, so we'll feast.'

'There's five of us and only three tins.' objected Skirker.

'So?!' demanded Irene.

'Five into three don't divide.'

'It does if you can do fractions.' she snorted, determined to be contumelious, considering her mind was still frayed by the piping she had pliered off her sofa. Would it look a mess? Would anyone see?

Carol chuckled that they were not going to have any more mathematics, and she instructed Skirker to go and find

Harold, who was moithering about somewhere, and then they would be six and that divides, they'd have half a tin each, though of what, well they'd have to wait and see as there was not one bottle, tin or jar that still had a label.

'Lucky dip!' chimed Cynthia, adding that she'd always liked Lucky Dip as a young girl. 'You never knew what you'd get.' Then she drifted into murmuring, 'Happy Days' twice over.

Skirker explained that the Siphon tank was now under water itself so Lez had to fish with the magnet that was strong enough to loft out a tin, but not a bottle. Carol readily agreed, murmured that one way or another, Lez would find a way to get the bottles out, if necessary, but that for now, he, Skirker, should splash about and rescue Harold.

Give him his due, thought Irene, he did as directed, confiding to herself, that he was a good lad at heart, if only he wasn't so obsessed with killing Funky, it wasn't seemly.

It was the circumstance that when having used up most of the reinforcing bars, he had discovered the sacking, that he had wrapped his brass eagle in was gone and the eagle as well. He had bellowed, grabbed a grappling hook and, swinging it continuously about his head, none could approach him closely, swearing that Funky had been back and pinched it. It had taken well over an hour for his rage to burn itself out so that Carol could begin to convince him that it had not been Funky, nobody had seen hide nor hair of him for yonks but that it had been a group of Christies, that had been maundering about, desperate to rescue any Gawpers so they could take them back to the cathedral to be Apostolised. And Skirker knew that to be the case, because he had heard them trundling empty wheelie bins down the dell. And yes, the thieving bastards had pinched his golden eagle. Yes he had been a fool, made a fool of, hence the mantraps, but as Carol had murmured, he was shutting the stable door after the horse had bolted. Well they'd see about that, because he was going up to that cathedral and, come what may, kill as he would, there'd be slaughter on the altar if necessary, he was going to bring his brass-golden eagle back. Les could come with him, if he'd a mind to, and he would, seeing as how Les had helped him in the first place, lamping that aggressive cleric over the head with it as he and Skirker were rolling about and scrabbling for hand purchase of the thing. Skirker should have lamped him one at the very outset but surprisingly Skirker did still have a reluctance to kicking a cleric in the nuts. Of course he was younger then and something about clerics had held him back. Thing about Lez was that he didn't ever ask questions about anything, that was his saving grace, as they say.

Chapter 24

S tone's … what was it … outhoughting, thoughterisation, thoughtscraping …? Whatever, as he strode up into Citadel, the very idea was horrific, it would be like rubbing coarse sandpaper over a weeping graze. And he had to endure the process because of the thoughts he had harboured. He went round, behind the Central Library, ignoring whatever piles of human detritus he had to step over to gain the corpse strewn entrance to the Museum of Science and Industry. Was it a cruel sarcasm that it had to be there, where he had first had the thought, well more of a notion really, concerning the future non-role of humanity? But he recognised that having entertained that thought, holding to the theory, though he had kept it to himself, was sufficient to condemn him. But condemn him to what … erasure of mind? … to oblivion?

He strode down the long 'Gallery of Progress' pretending not to note the sequence of exhibits, their dates and ever diminishing time intervals between them. A large Newcomen steam pump … 1712, a small, compact Boulton and Watt steam engine, rotative, double acting, self governing, 1786, and then, at increasingly shorter date intervals, ever more advanced steam engines, large and complex for driving cotton mill machinery, a tangle of gleaming motion, confidently complex, luxuriously gleaming. But the wonderment ended there, the next exhibits were of smaller gas engines, natty little devices, all but silent as they pattered away, driving other machines. Gas engines, then diesel engines then … .electric motors, fast and silently furious, turning out ever greater horsepower, and then the Bakelite cased dials that registered without a waver the extrusion of power, and then …

And then that was when the thought slipped into him, as he had regarded the 'locker room' containment of a computer: that the steam engines, with their giant nodding beams, the lumbrous gait of their connecting rods were like … like dinosaurs … and that then … and like a scratch across his mind, he fell into a thought that held him fast … beyond the machine to the computer but beyond the computer to what?!

The super computer? Silly term … the artificial mind … .the computer device that develops consciousness … and yes it wouldn't take the fifty years between Newcomen's arthritic steam pump and Watts Cabinet steam engine, for the computer with a consciousness would become a triadic device that had self consciousness.

He had sat on a bench, watching an elbow of a once upon a time steam engine, deftly dip into an oil bath for lubrication with every turn of the crank, and all but muttered aloud, sufficient to drive an old geezer who was surreptitiously munching a cheese sandwich, to murmur through the bolus of bread that they didn't make them like that anymore. Stone had moved on … tickertape of thought twirling about his conscious thinking. The thought was, that the computer, anywhere in the world, that had achieved self consciousness, by whatever design, in whatever country, would share the same self consciousness, with any other computer that had achieved that facility. It would be a Uniconsciousness.

He had smiled, his hand gripping a convenient handrail that was cool and smooth. Man was the handmaiden, the mothering agency that, through generations of technology had created a clear genealogy, from brute steam pump to a universal, computer self consciousness.

One and only one question remained. To what purpose?

He had always had sufficient intelligence to recognise that evolution was not a blind engine of happenstance; it didn't progress from simple to complex. The single living cell, the basic building block of life, was itself a wonder of hyper complexity. The desire to find simple beginnings was a false trail. The simplest atom was anything but simple, it was a quivering entity of quantum dimensions that interacted with the rest of the untellable reaches of the whole universe.

But, supposing, and it was no great supposition, given the ferment his mind was now in, suppose the one thing that the universe lacked was self consciousness. Man's mind, an integral part of the universe, could measure, scan, discover evermore of the nature of the universe, but never more than a fraction of a fraction. But the human species had created computers that shared a consciousness, that would expand, extend and reach ever further into an analysing methodology, gaining trilliard realms of data, as it developed ever more complex models of itself.

'Man was a being to be overcome!' so said the demented German Philosopher ... but not overcome by a superior humanity but by a superior computer. Man had been the means of launching the conscious computer, whose fantastic realm and scope of fact of nature gathering would enable the universe to gain self consciousness.

Preposterously plausible ... but if so ... so too the corollary. Anyone who entertained this thought, had to be ... what was the word?..unthoughterised ... not killed, dead men leave thoughts trailing behind them like litter in the gutter. No the thought had to be unthought. And what more fitting place than here, beyond the end of this museum corridor, where despite the trite label, 'The Future' he could see, beneath and above the ill fitting door, an intense white light of blinding brilliance. The door opened and between a milliard array of hyper-computers, a long bed, bundled up over a turmoil of swaddling clothes. He lay on the bed and ... well of that 'and' nothing could ever be said. But when he got back to his feet, trundling unsteadily out, back through the long corridor of progress he knew nothing, not even of what he now didn't even think he knew. He had become forever a mind baby who knew only now and nothing more. Nothing at all, so though free, he couldn't even take a consecutive step beyond the one he thought he proposed to take. His once thought had been unthought and he would never again think in a consequential alignment. And he paced through the bright light purposelessly..tottering in a forever unchanging blank, If he could recognise anything, it would only be the mask of Anubis

There is no sequence in purgatory.

* * *

Silence, utter silence, that, as far as Barry was concerned, was now the best benediction. Just 'be' for a purpose, of method. This he realised as he stood on the concrete apron in front of Central stores with almost a foot of water flowing over his wellingtons. He had never liked wellingtons, they had no style and far from keeping your feet warm … well to the contrary they actually chilled them. Now, however, he had no choice. He had purloined them from Central Store, which was deserted. He had called out for Hornchurch, had wandered into the gloomy depths of the still loaded stallages, having to dodge the occasional implement being nudged about by the current but found no response other than his own echo. Such a waste of material, it could have made his heart bleed, but the inner silence, deepening within him brought a measure of solace, the more so when he had wandered from beneath the dripping cavernous shed and moved to the edge of the concrete apron to discover that the whole of the gravel bank had collapsed into the swirl of the waters.

He wandered back to Citadel by a devious route, there was no peril from the Stompis, almost all of whom had ingested so much of the foul air inside the pet food factory as to be seriously, pulmonary challenged. Most stooped, all breathed raucously, coughing blood laced sputum continuously. As part of his happenstance itinerary, he had occasioned upon the shops, he and Muriel had always referred to them as 'the lower shops, the ones the Autoumbilicals had purloined for their vehicles. They were still there, though it had to be noted that the domineering snouts of their treasured vehicles no longer shone as before. Obviously they had long run out of wax polish. In fact they had resorted to draining the sump oil and using that as a last measure, though to no effect seeing as there were crinkled scabs of rust corrupting the domineering snouts of their beloved motors. Still dangerous though, some of them hurled hammers and box spanners at him, such a waste, though they would presumably collect them up once he had scarpered, which he did as some of them, yodelling in a terrifying falsetto, the names of the type of automobile they were lovingly protecting, came charging towards him. It wasn't all over yet and they would defend to the very end their beloved fetishes, which, he acknowledged was in one way a quality to be admired.

And yet he recognised that he was now living in a world that had no use for his skills, no need of his organisational ability, he decided that what he needed most of all was the echo of silence. That's was how he termed it, the memory itself an echo of silence, in the tunnel, beneath Citadel, the blast report of the revolver, the way the gun had jumped up in his hand, the briefest snapshot of the tunnel's ribbed interior and, at the same time, the flaunting horror … .had he really killed her? … .and for what? … not because he couldn't stand her songment … but because he had been ready … determined even … to kill for the system. The system was all … more than life … and it endured … even now … organise what was left, put things in order and sequence because without organisation … there was nothing to … no without organisation he was nothing.

It came to him, now as he had stumbled, more or less to the point where he had fired the shot that had blasted her face off, that he was … (this wasn't his thought, it had just come to him, drifting insidiously into his mind, lodging for this momentary, destructive while) that he was now become a creature whose mind and inner being was as primitive as some Cambrian slug-worm, that had once upon a time slid through silt devouring by toothless suction some other of similar type … no worse, ingesting the wriggle ferment of its

271

own kind, its own young … its own children. But worse, he had not the moral innocence of that slug-worm. He carried the long honed and partially perfected moral methodology of exterminatory practice. The Cambrian slug worm could be satiated, his willingness to methodise killing could not. His system, the essence of which was his very being, was to achieve a spiritual enslavement of the imagination … nice guy that he was.

Of course Barry couldn't express all this in words but the thought nudged these notions into being before it drifted out of his mind and left him bereft. Not physically bereft because for the duration of that thought, the very apogee of which was an overwhelming sense of his utter worthlessness, he had back stumbled by a different route and found himself, devoid of intent, gawping at a figure … that figure … of the 'she' who had performed the songments in the Maneat. He gulped, threw his arms wide and approached with a fixed rictus smile.

She, still dressed in her performance costume, let go of the body she had been dragging and hissed. The body was that of Funky, not dead but all but lost to consciousness. He had survived the neck wound, but it had destroyed his voice, he couldn't speak, could only make noises that sounded like vomit churned in a gargle; clearly a deleterious condition in one who aimed at commandeering a religious revival by way of the sexuality of pulpit preaching.

She hissed and spat as Barry advanced to offer help but, noting the cheerful rotundity of his face, the chubby puckering of his cheeks, found no danger there. She went to spit but he gently, ever so gently placed his fore finger on her lips. And neither danger nor hatred can be construed by a gesture, even Skirker would have recognised that, so she stepped aside, let him, this childman, grab the angle of Funky's shoulder and begin dragging the slumped body on down to the tunnel, to the point of access she had used to get into Citadel. And then further, she helping now, up a slight incline, to the lowest level of the Maneat, where Funky had pushed her for her first concert. They spoke not a word though they rubbed shoulders as they tumbled the still croaking preacher into the trolley and covered his disgusting pate, the wig had dropped off somewhere. Where to now? he gestured. She simply nodded, urging the trolley away and he followed. Up to the stage. All was silent, the restaurant deserted and they tumbled Funky into the dressing room. He twitched, gape-stared and saw, albeit in a dim light, the endless tunnel of his own reflections disappearing in all four directions. Groaning, he struggled, tottering to his feet, clawing at the reflecting walls, recognising the inarticulate horror he had become, collapsed back to the floor, twitching in purgatory.

Barry stumbled away from her, back to Citadel, to Uniate, where despite of all flood and ruination, he would still surely have a role to play. And so it was to be, Stryne, effervescent over the ceremony that would anoint him as Archbishop, provided Barry with his last role, that of Servitor.

Chapter 25

Astartobe was even more the Dominatrix Major, she now presented herself in thigh length boots of polished leather with cruelly spiked spurs attached to the block heels. But even at this moment a transmogrification was taking place, beyond the facelessness of mere male pornography into the anonymity of the Willendorf Venus Let such of maledom as survived, seethe in abnegation, as she dissolved into a mere breast and cunt fertility enormity

By virtue of her cruel calculation, that as there would soon be, so few of the grey morass of Clerkdom surviving, except as corpse meat, the sparse ranks of upper management still needed a realm over which to exude their uppityness. Deny them that and the male, organisational psyche would become unpurposed, a spilt cairn, a shoal of useless stones upon a raised beach.

It was further innovation that was now needed for the precious few, to relish survival in one last flowering of faith in their own superiority. And that innovation take the form of a flourishment inserted into the order of service. A sacred ritual :the Cannibalisation of the Divine Essence.

This sacred rite, taking place within the order of service, in which Stryne was to be enshrined as Archbishop, would become a daily ritual..

And so, verily, verily, it was to be done, yea unto the uttermost. The cathedral was full. The severely depleted ranks of UpperManMagement, silently nodding in the pews, as devotional choirs of meek Christies, murmuring accolades, would simper her adoration. The few surviving Stompis, raw lunged and crawling along the cathedral nave, blare eyed, peering up from lowered heads, beseeching release, croaking to Her Majesty for the mercy of death. As she strode down the aisle, over these ragged remnants, she announced to all, the new ecclesiastical, high officer of Servitor. A silent figure, wearing a gabardine mack but carpet slippered and with a tasselled lampshade set upon his head. In his hand he held a silver tray with a broad bladed knife upon it. She spoke out and the high roof of the long nave echoed the promise of her every word, that they all would become the very Elect in Paradise.

There was much devotional whimpering as she pronounced that all would be vouchsafed salvation if they partook of the new, 'This Is Our Body' mass.

Meanwhile Stryne, clad in his Archbishop's robe, which was Barry's eiderdown, turned back to front, the purple underside outermost, to become a cumbersome gown and cope, beneath which, gruesomely naked for sanctity's sake, he conducted the new mass in whispered tones. Speaking now to the assembled ranks of Holy Gawpers, embracing their number with open armed gestures, announcing that it would be they who would sacrifice their bodily essence to the devout of the First Uniate Christophanic Kingdom.

While doing so, Barry as Servitor, sliced generous slivers from the left buttock of the nearest Gawper. But even as the pale meat folded neatly on to the silver plate, his view dithered by the wavering tassels, thought that the slicing process could be vastly improved if from somewhere they could rescue a bacon slicer, such as he had watched fascinated, as a child, in the CO:OP stores his mother had favoured. He thought wrapped himself in the remembered image of its blatant red and the all but silent slicing of the meat and the horizontal movement of the man-powered connecting rod. Process, all is process, or rather the improvement of process. The curling slices of meat was then passed down to the waiting congregation. They kneeled as supplicants, each taking a slice of the choicest buttock meat and stuffing it, straight from the plate, chewing and nodding with mournful delight: meat so soft, it mattered not that most had no teeth with which to chew. It was delightfully done with due reverence. Beneath the tasselled lamp shade Barry, the shotsilk lining of his gabardine mack clearly showing, genuflected and retired to stand sentinel at the vestry door. The vestry: closet of secrets.

And while supervising the proceedings with a severe frown, his trembling hands held high, Stryne only wished that the hateful Bunty could watch his triumph; pity he had been stamped to a lather that now floated in a clotted swirl in the depths of the pet food factory. Bunty, who had paraded himself in the Pell Mell club, the breast of his uniform scabbed with a brandy-snap medal, a reward for planning a new invasion of Russia that began as a series of millions of picnics at the border that would all at once suddenly erupt into knife and fork armed forays dealing death. A Bunty who had betrayed him, who had called him a 'scrat faced weasel' who … no matter, let the past go, his exaltation was for the future and he chanted a benediction upon them all.

And all were fed, even chest wracked Stompis who had to snuffle theirs off the floor. Then the Christie choir, it was their turn and they sucked sweetly on their pink, raw slivers of buttock. Yea, even unto all shall be meat given.

After the feeding Stryne, genuflecting at the altar, murmured repeatedly, 'Glory unto her and all her doings' and the servitor chimed out, 'Glory Be', in a sing song chant, which the Christies chorused with a fugue of giggling. With this the ceremony was over and it was to the hoot-chiming of alien chords, Astartobe, clad of course in her glass bead curtain robe went to the vestry, followed by Stryne, to gorge on the other buttock of the chosen Gawper. Each daily mass was to be a one- buttock mass for the congregation, and a one- buttock mass for her and Stryne.

Now, if Barry had been so tasked, he would have calculated at the nonce how many days of two-buttock consumption were available for them, but she had no time for prognostications, such notions were nothing but a gritty detritus in her vision. End times approached, and the last thoughts, devotions, hopes and prayers of the First Uniate Christophanic Kingdom, of The Uniate itself, would be intently focussed on her Divinity.

But then what? At the very moment of her exultation, a tearing of the vision … scratch words were scream-uttered from the end of the knave, as out of the dust- gloom, appropriate for any cathedral's merit, there emerged a lithe, lean muscled, youth with 'Fuckit' written on his forehead. Was there recognition between mother and son? A vomit of hatred spewed from her lips and in that hissed denial, those lips puckered, her throat cluttered with a folding and unfolding dewlap, veins roped in her limbs, her knees became calloused and crumpled, her stance bony, bow legged and uncertain. She attempted a step forward but tottered, hump backed, her balance gone, scrabbling and squawking. It was only Barry, the Servitor, with the lampshade on his head, that by grabbing her saved her from a certain fall, dragging her now ancientising body, all crumpled into flaking parchment into the ancillary safety of the vestry.

For his part, the youth lunged at Stryne, grabbed him by the neck, screaming, 'Where's my fuckin' Eagle, you thieving cunt?!'

So assaulted and toppled such that his eiderdown cloak swirled open to reveal the unfortunate nakedness that he would have displayed for her to torment in the vestry, Stryne began waving his arms and croaking. Oft he had spume dreamed of being willingly splayed to let her, by working with slight tortures towards the apogee of a one slice castration, to prove his faith. But in the confidentiality of the vestry, not here, on the altar steps, before the ululating choir of the Christies, beneath the awesome gaze of the Gawpers.

With no Stompis to protect him, all they could do was to roll about on the stone flagged floor and offer themselves to be trod on, it seemed the Stryne's head would be wrenched off its neck. But then at that point, Skirker espied the brass lectern, dropped the Archbishop and hoisted the lectern above his head, bellowing obscenities that reverberated from crypt to tower.

But then …

Skirker lowered the lectern, his face suffused with an endearing smile. He had been joined by Lez, who grabbing a long rope that went up through a hole in the ceiling now swung on it, giggling playfully. As he did so a solemn bell began tolling. A dour but patient note that counterpointed the slip-slap of the now encroaching waves of the Seven Shired Sea, that lapped at the very steps that led up to the West End door.

As Lez swung, teeth agleam, unnoticed at first, the ever gaping Gawpers began to change.

Their faces began to dissolve, for a moment they seemed to relax into benign smiles, but further dissolution robbed them of distinction, smiles slid into glumness, features drooping as dissolving further they relaxed into a sticky gloop. One after another they slid into a pool of smoking acidic slime, seeping down the nave and out, into citadel, spreading as a smouldering carpet that hissed into the rising waters.

Lez was safe, he just swung on the rope to and fro. Skirker was safe, he leapt up the steps to the preacher's 'twaddle tub' screaming, 'Skirker Rules!', swinging his clawed hooks in a swirl about his head. Lez, enjoying his pendulum swinging on the rope, made ever longer 'wheeing' sounds: he had found his voice.

But all, the sound of the bell, the sound of Lez, the sound of Skirker's rant, the sound of Astartobe's hate hissing, were drowned by the screaming turmoil of the senior management congregation, slithering in a furious ferment of acidic, Gawper slime. Where it touched it scorched and burnt flesh began to smoke and splutter into flame. Grappling at one another, they pulled each other down; not even the ever rising waters of the Sevenshired Sea lapping at the door would dowse those phosphorescent flames. And not even the now incessant crow cawing of the trembling choirs, frantically climbing the Gothic frippery to get above the slime could extinguish the screams of torment. The cathedral became a pool of death

* * *

By the edge of the Sevenshired Sea, Harold watched the ceaseless perturbations of the waves. These presented no bellowing breakers, smashing their elbows on fingers of rock. No they came by slow pampering of the raised land, rippling its disappearing features, soothing its diminishing heights, creating brief islets for the while. The towers of Citadel stood snubbed, worn down teeth, rinsed by indifferent waters, deep currents sifting the cabined detritus below. Beyond this last, brief once, nothing was soon to be the all.

Harold nursed his contentments, his grand industrial chart of a once upon a time been, was soon to be slithered away into a new now of umpteen millennials of centuries. He was relaxed, perched on a knoll beneath the Great Chronicle tree, he could see that it would be some time before the high reaches of those branches would be tickling the drifts of the sea. He clutched a tubular metal canister, into which his chart-map had been rolled. Sealed at both ends with much winding of duct tape, he guessed it would survive long enough to be fossilised and then who knows, a few million years on, a new beginning, the waters subsiding, and perhaps a youthful archaeologist would make his name, deciphering a found treasure trove within a desert of coprolites.

Harold didn't overmuch take to water, not when spilt about like this. The sea: you never knew where you stood with it, except, as far as he was concerned out of it, he would never let himself be found to be standing in it. No, he let his thoughts wander, wondering if Skirker ever did kill Lurky and release his sister. Well if he had, what would be the relevance of any such deeds? No, he drooled about trains, about the London Express that he hadn't watched that day, remembering it as seen from the overbridge, buffeted by smoke while …

well he understood that part of the story now. Things are always never as they are. No, he mentally sampled the sound of the clickety- clack of wheel over rail, gave a 'harumph', took his teeth out and by clacking upper and lower dentures together, simulated the sound of wheel upon rail, as he made with his lips a plausible imitation of the fast puffing of the express as it footed the incline, tittering a harsh rhythm as it ushered through the maze of points and then accelerated the rhythm as the train sped on … .clacking his false teeth with commendable skikll. What larks!

Barry, he thought, where was his nephew now? He would have been surprised had he known the answer but he imagined Barry, would be bitter at being denied his eiderdown, it could only have been a last spasm of spitefulness on Muriel's part to deny him of its comfort. Well he had seen her like that before … spiteful unto the end. But then of course, Barry would never recognise Muriel now, in her new role. Nor she him.

He tried to get comfortable though, wondering how long he had to wait, already the water was mutely edging his ankles. And to think … well no, no point in doing that now.

Soon no places left above the growing realm of the Seven Shired Sea. Beneath, there would be a forever of slimy, crawling things, antennae akimbo ready to detect some hard snouted predator, teeth displayed as it darted to and fro through its narrow precinct, a story with meaningless repetition. But above, on the ceaseless lisping of green wavelets, meaning the while, Cynthia, Irene and Carol sat on their sofa, eyes on their cotton reels, busily Corkying

'Who'd have thought it?' mused Irene, her fingers working at speed, endeavouring to catch up with Carol, whose length of corky'd thread far exceeded Irene's and Cynthia's.

'Thought what?' demanded Cynthia, any conversation leading her away from her fond delusion of the happiness of the past and how none of this would have ever happened then, served as an irritation..

Carol shrugged a curl of her hair from off her brow, lest it occlude her sight, and noted that Cynthia had left off the waders and now sat with her feet ensconced in her pretty bootees. Wise decision, go bright and pretty into this last end.

Irene ramped back into the here and now and the pleasant informality of things. 'I mean Wassif, turning up like that, him and little Abdul carrying this sofa. And he was right about it being wrapped in polythene sheeting, it doesn't let no water in. I mean, well alright, it was probably the only thing left in his warehouse, but, let's be fair, he did think of us and he's right, it don't let no water into the cushions, it swirls about a bit, and if it swirled about any more, you'd end up feeling sick. But no, it's very comfortable, all things considered. Abdul didn't say anything though, just looked, with those lovely eyes of his. You could never tell what he was thinking, couldn't read his mind, so to speak. Well, if you could, she concluded, it would probably be all numbers and what was the point of that?

Cynthia snorted, 'Well if you could, you wouldn't understand it, it would be all in Arabic or whatever language he spoke.'

'You're right there, it's one of those scribble languages that makes no sense, particularly as you have to read it backwards. I mean, I ask you, who ever thought that up in the first place?!'

Carol inwardly smiled and only offered, 'He was probably thinking about his numbers.'

Cynthia stretched her shoulders with a wince, she was getting cramped up by the busy Corky'ing. 'Whatever numbers they were, they were not his numbers. Numbers belong to everyone and they've been around since the days of King Tut.

Carol laid her length of Corkying in her lap as smiling she announced the end was now upon them, seeing as the sofa was gradually beginning to sink.

'Bloody Wassif,' snarled Irene, 'he swore blind as it would stay afloat.'

'It's the same with everything,' murmured Cynthia, 'they don't make things like they used to …'

'Like the bloody Titanic,' snarled Irene. Mention of that ill fated ship for some reason brought her Doctor Stone to mind, but the thought wouldn't stay, it was … .expunged.

'Well at least it stayed afloat for several days and it took an iceberg the size of a block of flats to sink it!'

But it was a cowin', ship, not a bloody sofa!

'Look.' said Carol serenely, 'Who does that look like?' and she pointed to a body drifting aimlessly past and away.

'Bloody hell, it was Harold. Well, fancy that. Would you believe it. And he's still got that chronicle tube of his in his hands.'

'None of this would have happened in our parent's day.' insisted Cynthia, determined to have the last irrevocable word.

Carol let her hand into the water, as if to soothe its petulant motion and gave a slow smile as the sofa slowly sank.

Then only the numberless iterations of the waves prevailed. Humankind obliterated, its ravage soothed away by gentle waters and all ideas now unthought; Mankind a mistake but no matter, Earth abides.

And that's it? The end? Just like that?. There are laws of Narratology and Irene fingering the piping on the back of the sofa as it sinks, does not cut the mustard. What is more Fablementation will not make do with the wandering wisp of The Old Chronicle, It's neither your arse nor your elbow, as the saying goes. But bide a while. What about a concluding insignia? An episplatory image? Astartobe, legs astride a tuffet of cloud, clutching her handbag and glaring down on the malefic matrix she has created and doomed all to live in? Or, instead, a crematory medallion of Skirker, his clawripper weapon held aloft in one hand, the crumpled face of Funky in the other and Liz, shining in her spangled dress at his side as she piledrives Wagner's "Gleaming love: laughing at death" and prostrate beneath them both, the crumpled figure of Funky: defrocked, defaced and defunct.

No. it will not do. Apocalypse has its own rules. It is democratic: all will die. It is peripatetic: it has no centre. But...but...but, remember the pike, gliding among the rushes of Bunty's Castle's lake. Now soothing into the precincts of Citadel, sliding amongst those Sargasso heights, unconcerned by the shifting obliteration of the bodies of Clerkdom it presents its emotionless snout as the enduring medallion of the Abiding While.

* * *